PRAISE FOR KATHLEEN NANCE!

MORE THAN MAGIC

"*More Than Magic* is an undeniable treasure trove of pleasure, bursting with magnetic characters and a bewitching plot that's sure to capture the imagination of fantasy and romance readers alike."

—*Rendezvous*

"Nance follows up her previous tale of magic and fantasy with another winner. Ms. Nance has a very special touch!"

—*Romantic Times*

"An astonishingly original story in a world which contains far too few paranormal romances, *More Than Magic* is more than satisfying."

—*Affaire de Coeur*

THE TIES THAT BIND

For a gentle kiss, for a touch only at the lips, it was thorough. The throbbing, the pulsing filled her, and a curl of excitement, like the curl of smoke from a fire, rose from deep inside her belly to set her aflame throughout. She pulled once on the confining ropes, then gave in to the magic.

"By all the gods, I've missed you, Joy." The kiss deepened, eliciting small moans of pleasure.

He shouldn't feel so good, smell so good, taste so good.

Only his groan of desire and the scrape of his chair as he shifted pulled her back from the simmering need.

"Let me go, Mark," she whispered, then repeated more strongly. "Let me go."

Slowly he lifted, and his hand dropped from the ropes. "You're free. Any time you want."

To Joy's surprise, when she tested the knots, the rope undid itself and fell to her feet.

Magic. He was magic. Quicksilver and shadows.

Other Love Spell books by Kathleen Nance:

MORE THAN MAGIC
WISHES COME TRUE

THE
TRICKSTER

KATHLEEN NANCE

LOVE SPELL BOOKS NEW YORK CITY

*The romance community is one of support and
encouragement. For three ladies who have given most
generously to me, both counsel and friendship:
Rexanne Becnel, Metsy Hingle, and Nancy Wagner.*

A LOVE SPELL BOOK®

June 2000

Published by

Dorchester Publishing Co., Inc.
276 Fifth Avenue
New York, NY 10001

ISBN 0-505-52382-5

The name "Love Spell" and its logo are trademarks of Dorchester
Publishing Co., Inc.

Printed in the United States of America.

ACKNOWLEDGMENTS

With many thanks to:

Don McCall of Alternative Agri-2000 and Reed and Terry at Pacesetter Farms for showing me their farms and birds and telling me all about ostriches, breeding, feathers, and eggs.

Denmon Britt, executive chef of Cafe Degas for answering my many questions about being a chef.

Dave Irvin for answering my questions about parachuting.

Michael Shannon and Jerry at Aero Resources for showing me what it means to sky dive, and for getting me up in the plane, and down, safely.

And a special thanks to Christine Schwaiger, who took a day from her busy schedule to introduce me to the beautiful land and people of Folsom.

Any liberties taken, or mistakes made, are mine alone.

THE TRICKSTER

PREFACE

The Myth of Io

The maiden Io, beautiful and sweet, inflamed the lust of mighty Zeus. With gentle words he wooed her and became her lover. Fearing the wrath of Hera when he lay with Io, he covered the earth with an impenetrable fog, but Hera, wise to her husband's ways, sought him out. To protect his lover, he gave Io the visage and voice of a snowy heifer and claimed she had sprung, newly formed, from the earth.

Hera did not believe him. She asked for the heifer as a gift, and cowardly Zeus, unable to think of a believable excuse why he should not, gave his lover to his wife. Hera set the hundred-eyed Argus to watch the heifer, separating the sad maiden from her grieving family and preventing Zeus from restoring Io. Zeus sent Hermes, the messenger, to free her. Hermes, glib of tongue and full of tricks, played a lilting tune on his pipes and told an enchanting story, lulling Argus to sleep. Then he cut off the head of Argus, freeing Io.

Still vengeful, Hera sent a gadfly to chase and torment Io. At long last the unfortunate maiden came to Egypt, the country of the long river, where Zeus was allowed to return Io to her female form, with the promise that he would never turn his attention to her again.

Thus, the legend of Io concluded.

The story, however, does not.

Prologue

Zeus sat in his presidential suite at Jupiter Fireworks, tossing lightning bolts at a sooty bull's-eye target and feeling bored and guilty.

The boredom was familiar; living three thousand years meant a lot of boring days. He'd brought on his worst troubles, and created his warmest memories, with schemes concocted because he was bored.

Guilt, however, was new.

"Comes from getting old," he grumbled aloud. "Makes you take stock and want to set things right." He tossed another tiny bolt at the target. It hit with a sharp boom followed by a puff of smoke.

Zeus squinted. He'd missed the center. His eye just wasn't what it used to be. "Old," he muttered again. He figured he had just three—maybe four—hundred years left.

He swiveled in his leather chair. Reflected in the glass

wall of his penthouse office, Zeus—or Zeke Jupiter as he was now known—could see his image: a trim salt-and-pepper moustache, receding hairline, some wrinkles, body still strong, but slowing. Behind the image spread the distant Rocky Mountains.

He'd always had a fondness for mountains; they reminded him of the craggy peaks and volcano-warmed springs of his home world. That was why he'd chosen to settle on Mount Olympus when he and his followers were exiled to Earth so many centuries ago.

They'd done all right here, more than all right. Ancient Greece had been a bounty, fertile and ripe and generous. And such freedom they'd had. Of course, being considered a god had conferred certain advantages.

The Titanic Oracle, the ruling council of his world, hadn't expected *that* twist. Zeus chuckled to himself. The Titans always had underestimated him and his followers. Like Hermes. The glib trickster had smuggled bits of their technology with them, and thus they had become the gods of myth.

For a while, their desires and whims had reigned supreme. Eventually, though, men stopped worshiping the gods and usurped the Olympian mystique with their own technology. His followers grew restless, and one by one the gods had slipped away. Some were allowed to return home, some preferred lives outside the rarified atmosphere of Olympus, some had died.

Even his wife, Hera, had left him, not that he blamed her.

Eventually, he had abandoned Olympus to live a hundred lifetimes among the humans, amassing a fortune and, in the process, gaining a little wisdom and a little guilt.

During his glory, he had enjoyed many women. A fond

smile stole across his face as he remembered the gentleness of Io, the nurturing of Leda, the composure of Callisto. Yet, his actions had left an unexpected legacy in their lines. Love, the deep and long-abiding kind, eluded his lovers' female descendants. They fell in love with the wrong man, or chose unwisely, or listened to the drum of practicality instead of the flute of desire. They did not trust in the magic that was love.

He'd once shared a love like that with Hera, until he'd destroyed it. That his early actions were born of his anger at the exile and a false sense of omnipotence made no excuse.

So, what to do? Zeus rubbed the gold, lightning-bolt-shaped ring on his forefinger and aimed at the target. Lightning crackled from his fingertips. He nodded in satisfaction. Dead center, this time.

Before his time on earth ended, he would do two things, he decided. First, he would break the legacy of misfortune by helping a woman of each bloodline find that special love. Second, he would find Hera. Hades, but he missed that woman.

He'd start with the matchmaking. He had a hunch it would be infinitely easier than regaining Hera's trust.

Zeus punched the intercom button on his desk.

"Yes, Mr. Jupiter?" replied his secretary.

"I've decided to take a vacation, Mrs. Hunsacker. Starting now. I'm turning off the cell phone."

"How can I contact you?"

"You can't. Not until Monday, when I let you know where I'll be." He'd take the weekend to figure out a plan and get settled. August was a slow season for fireworks. Fourth of July was past and the New Year's celebrations were still some months off.

"What if something important—"

"It will have to wait."

He heard Mrs. Hunsacker's teeth click together in annoyance. His secretary guarded his privacy with the tenacity of Cerberus—the dog who stood sentry at the gates of Hades—but she always wanted to know his whereabouts.

This, however, was something he needed to do in private.

"Have a nice weekend, Mrs. Hunsacker." Zeus disconnected the intercom. He strode across the plushly appointed office to a paneled wall. One push of the concealed button and the wall opened to his private elevator. It had only two stops: this office and his highly private domain on the undesignated thirteenth floor.

Once there, he turned on his computer. He'd installed all the hardware and software of the fastest, most advanced systems available, plus a few modifications and features unknown to humans. With those, he identified the descendents of the gods.

He'd start with Io. She had been so sweet, so unassuming, so in love with him, and so wronged. He'd made her look and sound like a heifer to protect her from Hera, but Hera had demanded the gentle animal. And he'd given Io to her. Zeus cringed in memory.

Yes, he owed reparation to a daughter of Io.

He focused on the view screen, choosing options to narrow his search. An unmarried female in her twenties, of direct lineage to Io. Names sped across his screen, and he chose one, a woman in southern Louisiana named Joy Taylor. Her town would celebrate its annual Mushroom Festival in a month; the upcoming need for fireworks would provide him cover for being there.

The Trickster

He printed out the name on a clean paper, then placed it in a hollowed stone on a table opposite his computer. There were still some powers of the gods that human technology could not match. He sprinkled white crystals into the stone. Touching his finger to the paper, Zeus rubbed his ring. An arc of lightning set fire to the paper. Smoke rose through the crystals, creating a faint image of Joy Taylor as she was today.

She stood on the porch of a house, her home he assumed. It appeared to be a pleasant place, peaceful and still. A battered truck jostled down the country lane toward her.

Joy was of medium height with light hair. Red, maybe? He sighed in pleasure. She had Io's beautiful wide eyes. Were they also blue?

Beside her stood a handsome, fair-haired man, who looked at her with fondness, then leaned over and kissed her cheek. Joy gave him a faint smile, but Zeus noticed she did not kiss him back. The man got in a Cadillac and drove down the drive.

"Good, a suitable male awaits her." Zeus rubbed his hands together. This reparation business was going to be easier than he'd thought.

The image wavered with the fading smoke as the truck passed the Cadillac, then pulled up to the porch in a plume of dust. The driver emerged and headed toward the porch. He was a dark-haired man with tight, faded jeans, well-used boots, and a walk bolder than Hermes' when he'd stolen Apollo's cattle.

The man turned slightly. Zeus caught a glimpse of the face, and his complacency dissipated like the smoke.

Hermes! Not the actual Hermes, but one of his seed,

many generations removed. The features, and walk, were distinctive.

Hermes, the charmer, the trickster.

Zeus swore. If this matchmaking was going to work, then he was going to have to keep this descendent of Hermes away from Joy, for a son of Olympus meant only trouble for a woman of Earth.

Chapter One

Matthew Mark Hennessy had returned, just as he'd promised he would. Too bad he was six years too late.

His truck jostled down the country lane toward her, a plume of dust marking its unerring course. Joy Taylor had no doubt who drove it; the wings-and-hand logo on the side was unique.

She remembered another truck of Mark's, his first, also black, even more battered. It was the first place he had kissed her, the first place he'd— Joy dragged in a deep breath and tried to quell the expectant fluttering in her belly.

This time would be different. Mark's sweet words wouldn't tease out her wayward notions, his smile wouldn't turn her softer than a downy feather, and his loose-hipped walk wouldn't set a fire that destroyed all her good sense.

19

"—think about it."

Joy, wiping a drop of sweat out of her eye, turned to the blond man towering at her side. "What?"

Seth Beaumont gave her a grin as big as the rest of him. Joy did not consider herself petite—not at five-eight with twelve extra pounds she couldn't shed—but Seth made her feel tiny. Overwhelmed, almost.

"I'll take it as a good sign," Seth said, "that my marriage proposal left you speechless."

Seeing the truck turn into her long driveway from the corner of her eye, Joy was tempted to answer "Yes" right then. Seth was everything she wanted in a man to marry: pleasant, unfailingly honest, utterly trustworthy.

The word died in her throat. She'd be using Seth to put the barrier of a fiancé between her and Matthew Mark Hennessy, and Seth didn't deserve to be used that way. Marrying a man out of need was her mother's oft-repeated mistake, not hers.

"It's just—" she stammered, "well, the women of my family have a bad history in picking men. I want to be sure, Seth."

"I wouldn't run out on you."

"I know." Sweat stuck her hair to her neck, and she lifted the auburn strands in a vain attempt to cool off. August in southern Louisiana, even early in the day, felt like the inside of her oven. "Just give me a little time?"

"We'd be good together." Seth dropped a kiss to her cheek, and his face, perpetually sunburned during summer, turned even redder. "I gotta get to the office. Real estate doesn't sell itself." As he was stepping into his Cadillac, he nodded toward the truck. "Maybe you got an answer to your ad. You want me to stay, interview him for you?"

"No!" The answer came out more sharply than she'd intended. "Thanks, no," she repeated, softer. "I can handle it."

A shadow of irritation, quickly gone, crossed his face. "Then I'll see you later." He started the car and drove off.

Joy's attention turned immediately to the black truck. Swallowed by a flurry of dust from the exiting Caddy, it traveled the final yards toward her house.

"I can handle this," she repeated softly.

It had been seven years since the night she'd last seen Mark Hennessy, six years since the night she'd waited for his return. The night he graduated from high school, he had left her, promising to return in one year, when she graduated. After her high school graduation she'd waited all night—until the sunrise filtered through the pines and the realization he wasn't coming stole across her as inexorably as the muggy morn.

Things were different now; her walk on the wild side was over. The ostrich farm had turned a profit last year. She'd landed a culinary apprenticeship. She'd just gotten a bona fide proposal of marriage. When she walked down the main street in town, people knew her and stopped to chat. "Settled" described her life these days, and she'd worked hard to achieve that.

She could handle this.

The truck ground to a halt, but the dust hung in the humid air. Mark slid out and strode toward her.

The seven years showed on him. Not in wrinkles or a thickening belly but in a confidence, a strength, a dangerous aura only hinted at before in the youth of eighteen.

His hair was thick and dark as chicory coffee, but cut short now. Apparently he no longer needed the defiant ponytail. He had a strong jaw, a tiny cleft in his chin, and his nose looked like it had been broken since she'd last seen him. He still walked sexier in a pair of jeans than anyone she'd ever seen.

She could handle this.

He neither smiled, nor frowned, giving her no clue as to his purpose, and his eyes, those shadowy windows to his soul, were concealed by mirrored aviator sunglasses.

"Joy," he drawled softly. "Mornin'."

His honey-thick voice slid across her ears and coated her throat until accusations and questions stuck fast. Joy gripped the front porch newel, managing only, "Mornin', Mark."

Slowly, Mark lifted the sunglasses from his eyes and hung them by one bow in the neck of his functional white T-shirt. His chambray shirt—unbuttoned, rolled up at the sleeves, and layered over the T—ruffled with a single breeze, then settled. Uninvited, he strolled up the steps until he was level with her.

"You're looking good," he said gently. "I've missed you, Joy."

It was foolishness to hope it was the truth. "You had enough time to do something about it. If you'd wanted." She grabbed her baseball cap, which she'd left hanging on the rocking chair back, and pulled it on, shoving her hair into it. "What do you want?"

He tucked a strand of her hair that she'd missed into her cap. "All these years, I couldn't forget the color of your hair. I wanted to tell myself I just imagined its fire, but I knew I'd be lying." His voice was low, contemplative.

When he withdrew his hand, he snapped his fingers and a tiny, fragrant violet appeared, delicate against the strength of his hand. "For you." He tucked the flower under the edge of her cap.

Joy stepped away, trying to quell the traitorous excitement his gentle touch aroused.

She could handle this? About as easily as she could carve a goose with a spoon.

In defense, she picked up a pair of dusty boots sitting outside the door and tugged them on. "Good-bye, Mark."

Mark leaned one shoulder against the newel. "C'mon, Joy, don't be mad. We were both too young. You know it."

"Yeah, young. You were eighteen; I was seventeen. The whole world ahead of us." She stomped, settling the boots on her feet. "I'm not mad, not anymore. Just don't act like you care, okay? You don't."

His jaw tightened. "You so sure about that?" The drawl was wound tight.

She looked at him squarely. "I'd be foolish to think anything else. Say your piece and leave. I've got work to do. The birds need water." When he didn't answer, she swept past him down the steps. "Hell's bells, how could I forget how hard it is to get a straight answer out of you?"

Mark followed her as she crossed the lawn, heading behind the brick house. "Things aren't that simple, darlin'."

"Don't call me that. I'm not your darling."

"I call everyone that. Only with you, it means something."

"And I'm supposed to know the difference?"

Joy halted and faced him, arms crossed defensively across her chest. The sunglasses were back on his face, in deference to the bright Louisiana sun. August heat beat down on her head through the cloth of the cap, although the bill shaded her face. Both of them wore armor.

"Why'd you come here, Mark?"

"A job," he said briefly. Then he added, "You."

Quickly she doused the flare of hope. Did he think she was that naive? That she'd believe he'd come back because of her?

"The job? You saw my advertisement for someone to help during breeding season? You want to work on my ostrich farm?"

He shoved his hands in his jeans pockets. "Well, I—"

"Tell me another one," she rushed on. "You're Marcus, Master Illusionist. I saw you on television." Once, she'd even driven to New Orleans, two hours to the south, to watch his stage performance. She'd sat in the back of the theater, in the dark, so he wouldn't see her. "You're good, Mark, and you're going places. You don't need to work here."

"I say I do," he drawled. "You see—"

"You wasted the trip. The job's . . . unavailable." She spun on one booted foot and headed out toward the back pens.

"Word about town is you can't find anyone. Too temperamental, they said, though I wasn't rightly sure if they were talking about the birds or you."

"The birds are not temperamental!"

His lips twitched, and Joy realized she'd just called herself temperamental. Nothing could be further from the truth, except in the case of Matthew Mark Hennessy.

"I need someone reliable." She quickened her pace.

"Steadfast and steady. That's me." He drew even, not touching her, but invading that invisible band of personal space that surrounds a body. Not enough for her to complain, just enough to imply an intimacy beyond strangers. "So how about it?"

Her heart thumped against her chest, and the sweat on

24

her palms and nape had little to do with the hot morning. She could feel his magic working on her, weakening her.

"It wouldn't work." Resolutely, she walked faster. "Why, Mark?"

"Why what?"

"Take your pick. Why this job? Why me? Why now, after all these years? Do you really want the job, or are you manipulating me for some reason you're not sharing?" Once, she would have known the answer. Or thought she did.

"Darlin', your suspicions wound me."

"See, Mark, you're doing it again. Avoiding answers, changing the subject, always staying one step out of reach. Why do I keep listening?" she muttered, turning away.

"Truth is, I've been asked to perform at the Mushroom Festival."

"What!" Joy spun back to him. "I'm in charge of the budget. I don't know anything about this. Who hired you?"

"Earl Flynn."

"*Earl.*" She should have guessed. Joy's teeth clicked together, and her heels dug deep into the lawn as she resumed her walk. The ex-jockey chaired the committee by virtue of sheer flamboyance. No one had the energy to challenge him. She'd been added to the committee in an effort to rein in some of Earl's exuberance and remind him there was something known as a budget.

"That man! I'm supposed to know about all expenditures. We can't afford your fee." Even as she protested, Joy had to admit that a performance by Marcus would be a stunning addition to the festival.

"I've got a contract," Mark said mildly. "Legal and binding."

"If you're here for the festival, why did you pretend you wanted this job on the ostrich farm?"

"You mentioned it first, and didn't give me a chance to explain otherwise. I've decided to accept the offer. It's perfect."

"I didn't offer—" She bit off the useless denial. "Why is it perfect?"

"The ad said it came with room and board."

Hell's bells, she'd forgotten about that part. "Ah, that part's not inc—"

"That part's nonnegotiable," he said with a hint of steel.

She'd forgotten that side of him. On stage he was spell-binding, a compelling, masterful illusionist, but offstage he affected a good-old-boy drawl and easygoing manner. Underneath both personas, though, he was rock-hard determination. And smart.

"I need a place to stay," he explained, "incognito, while I polish some new effects for the act. Who'd think of look-ing for me as a laborer on an ostrich farm?"

Who, indeed. Marcus was captivating, accomplished, dangerous, definitely not farm material. His last perform-ance had been in San Francisco one month, two weeks, and five days ago, she knew. He might be readying a new show. She peered closer. His face looked thinner, as though he'd stopped caring about eating or was working too hard.

Maybe she was one sorry fool, but she believed him. Almost. Joy had an itchy feeling something wasn't quite right about all this.

They emerged from the tree-covered grass that sur-rounded the house, which she shared with her mother and sister, into an open field. Beyond the field lay the barren, compacted sand the ostriches favored. A trickle of sweat seeped into the neck of her T-shirt, and Joy pulled the base-ball cap more firmly on her head. "You know anything about ostriches?"

"Nope, but I'm a real fast learner."

She didn't want Mark Hennessy lingering anywhere near her, yet when she stopped at a toolshed for a metal bucket and pliers, she found herself saying, "Make yourself useful. Bring out a bale of wire."

"Sure thing, darlin'." He hefted the wire with little effort. As they walked out to the ostrich pens, he asked, "When did you start farming ostriches?"

"My mother's sixth—no, seventh—husband bought them." With her mother married again and her sister having a settled home, Joy had thought finally she could turn over the family mantle of responsibility to someone else and live some of her private dreams.

Hadn't worked out quite that way.

"How'd you end up in charge?"

"He took off about two years ago, leaving Nicole alone with the farm. She asked me to help out."

Actually, Joy's mother, Nicole, following her inevitable pattern, had called her eldest daughter to "fix it." Also following long-established patterns, Joy had.

"Looks like you're making a go of it," Mark observed.

"We're holding steady."

"Aren't you allergic to meat?"

So, he remembered. "Just beef. None of us—my mother, my sister, me—can touch it. Got nothing against cows, just can't eat the meat. Cow's milk nauseates me, and the leather makes me break out in hives."

He glanced at her feet. "That's one fine pair of boots."

"Ostrich leather."

At the pens, Joy picked up a hose, turned on the water, and took a quick drink of the lukewarm liquid before filling the water buckets. First, she watered the pens of birds being raised until they were big enough to slaughter for meat, hide, and feathers, then she turned to the breeder pens.

The farm had nine breeder pairs of ostriches, each pair housed in roaming pens set off by stakes and chicken wire. If they'd really wanted to, the eight-foot, 300-pound birds could have done major damage to the flimsy wire, but they were too dumb to realize they could and too content to attempt escape.

A booming sound, akin to a lion's roar, vibrated through the thick air, followed by a cluck-cluck-cluck noise.

"What's that?" Mark looked around.

"It's breeding season. That's the male's call to his mate. The clucks are her answer."

Mark gave a tuneless whistle. "No slow dancing, no soft caresses or long deep kisses. No foreplay? Just a 'Come here, babe,' and they're at it. No wonder we call 'em birdbrains."

Ignoring the heat and the memories his words aroused, Joy threw him a disgusted look. His grin was completely unrepentant.

She turned off the hose, then opened one of the pens and went inside. Gretna should have an egg ready for collection.

Mark followed her in. "So, what's next, boss lady?"

"Hush," Joy hissed. "We don't want to disturb Gretna. Or Hans. And I'm not your boss."

"Gretna and Hans being those two huge creatures?" He nodded at the two birds, ignoring her last comment.

Hans came running toward her, his long legs spanning the distance in a matter of seconds. To Joy's amusement,

Mark moved to her side and watched the bird with wary caution.

Hans greeted her by snapping his beak at her toes, then her shoulder—ostrich for hello. A round beak and no teeth assured the affectionate nips didn't hurt. She rubbed her hand down his neck and wings, enjoying the feel of the soft feathers. "Hello, boy," she crooned.

Mark edged closer to her. "Is he dangerous?"

"He's got you by almost two feet and over a hundred pounds and those claws on his toes aren't for show. If he wanted, he could do serious damage. Fortunately, he's a real softie. Aren't you, Hans?" She petted the ostrich again.

Mark reached out a tentative hand to join the petting session. Hans hissed and ruffled his wings. Swiftly, Mark withdrew his hand. "A real softie, huh?"

Joy laughed. "I raised Hans from an egg. He's kind of imprinted on me, and he gets a little jealous. Plus this is his first breeding season."

"Ah, Hans, you lucky bird. A little territorial, eh? Like to keep this pretty lady all to yourself? Now, that's a sentiment I can understand, truly I can. But, you see, you've already got yourself one fine darlin' over there in Gretna. You can't have mine, too."

Mark spoke with soothing calm. Hans tilted his narrow head and focused a dark eye on the stranger. His feathers settled.

It seemed Mark's charm even worked on birds.

"I'm not yours, Mark."

He looked straight at her, the sunglasses still shielding his face. "I remember when you thought different."

"Why don't you squirt Hans with some water?" Joy suggested, summer heat weighing oppressively on her lungs.

"Squirt an eight-foot beast with water? I have a fondness for this life, darlin'."

"Hans likes the water. These are desert animals. Our heat is fine, but the humidity gets to them and they need cooling. It's either that or collect Gretna's egg."

Mark eyed the nest, and the bird near it, then picked up the hose. "Okay, Hans, time for a shower."

While Mark sprayed the water, Joy crept up on the nest.

"Who was in the Caddy?"

Intent as she was on Gretna and the egg, Joy was caught off guard by Mark's question. "Seth," she answered automatically, then could have bit her tongue. "Oh, be quiet."

Gretna, spying the treat Hans was getting, loped over to him, making it easy for Joy to collect the egg. Cradling the smooth, golden, four-pound egg, she joined Mark, who was spraying both preening birds with the water.

"You were telling me about Seth?" he persisted.

Silently, Joy breathed deep and pulled in his scent, mixed with hints of sweat and spicy aftershave. So fast he filled her mind, her senses, her very breath. Her defenses against this man were thinner than a sheet of baklava dough.

"Uh-oh, you're getting silent."

His languid voice filled her with swelling heat. Mark Hennessy was just too dangerous to keep around.

"For your information, we're engaged. Almost," her abiding respect for honesty forced her to admit.

Mark's eyes narrowed, and he dropped the hose. "Is that a fact, darlin'?" He gripped her shoulders. "Like you were engaged to me?"

He shouldn't have dropped the hose.

Hans, annoyed at losing the shower and feeling aggressive in this season, spread his tiny wings and barreled toward them. He didn't have far to go, so he couldn't get much speed up, but three hundred pounds of muscle doesn't need much speed to inflict damage.

Mark reacted first. Putting himself between the bird and her body, he shoved her out of the bird's path, then scrambled to safety. He almost made it.

Stumbling, Joy caught her foot on the hose, and her hands flew upward as she tried to maintain her balance.

The four-pound egg flew from her hands and hit Mark, a direct smash to the side of the face.

Mark fell.

Hans's two-toed, two-clawed foot came down on Mark's leg.

Joy landed facedown in the hard-packed sand.

Chapter Two

Holy Mother, his head hurt. How'd he let someone get the drop on him like that?

Eyes closed, ignoring the pounding in his head, Mark sorted through the sensations surrounding him. In the distance, another room maybe, he heard a radio DJ announce the next song. Enya, "The Memory of Trees." Pretty tune. He used lush, flowing notes like that during the more romantic portions of his performance, though George Strait was more to his personal taste.

Speaking of taste, there were good smells here, too—coffee, sautéing butter, lemon. His stomach rumbled in anticipation.

Gingerly, Mark opened one eye. He was on his back, on a sofa, but not bound. Overhead, a ceiling fan whirled. A soggy towel lay across his right calf, while the one on his head dripped cold water down his neck.

With caution, he turned his head. He was in a living room. Not a glossy, decorator-matched room—he'd seen plenty of those—nor a roach-infested, stained one—he'd seen even more of them. Clean with no dust, not even on the fan blades, but cluttered. The room was a vision of bedrock America and felt curiously foreign.

Beside the sofa sat a rocking chair, a big, old-fashioned, wooden one. UFO SPOTTED IN WHEAT FIELD, screamed the lurid headline of the tabloid on the floor beside it.

Tabloids. Someone he knew read—

Joy Taylor.

Memory returned in a humiliating flood. He'd been leveled by a bird. No, not a bird, by a damn bird's *egg*.

Mark shoved to his feet, the soggy towels plopping to the floor. The room swirled around him and a shaft of pain shot up his leg, making him drop back to the sofa with a grunt.

He'd forgotten about the clawed foot stomping his leg.

Mark swore. If this got out, he'd never hear the end of the jokes from his crew.

Joy's head popped from around the door across the room. Her face shone with sweat and tendrils of her burnished hair stuck to her cheeks and neck. "Oh, good, you're awake. How are you feeling?"

"Fine," he growled, feeling anything but.

She lifted auburn brows. "A bit testy? That's supposed to be a good sign. Bet you're hungry. I'll start the omelet." She disappeared.

Annoyed with his fuzzy thinking—being less than one hundred percent was dangerous—Mark forced himself to remember what had happened. Joy had thrown something, a burlap bag, over the bird's head, and it calmed down.

After that came the limping walk to the house, Joy supporting him, talking to him, encouraging him. The long-missed pleasure of holding her had been overshadowed by a dizzying struggle not to throw up.

Inside she'd cleaned the bloody but superficial wound on his leg, then put something on it that stung like hellfire. They'd argued about calling a doctor. She'd been afraid of concussions and broken bones. He'd guessed from experience that he had neither.

In the end they'd compromised with an aspirin, ice, and a rest on the sofa, where he'd promptly fallen asleep. He looked at his watch. Eleven A.M. He'd been out over two hours.

Anything could have happened in two hours. Anything. Mark closed his eyes. This was falling apart faster then a stripper's costume. Damn. Seven years since he'd left, yet all he had to do was come near Joy Taylor and his survival instincts climbed happily into the backseat. Even now, remembering how soft and womanly and welcoming she felt set his blood thrumming.

First things first. He needed that invitation to stay.

Mark struggled to his feet and limped the short distance toward the door where he'd last seen Joy. Dizziness receding, he leaned against the doorjamb and savored the sight before him.

Joy stood next to a gleaming stove that had more dials than a cockpit, humming and cooking, a fork and a big omelet pan in hand. She'd changed into shorts while he'd been sleeping, which was fine by him. This way he got to look at her legs—long, firm, and golden tan. Sunlight streamed through the window, turning her hair to gold and copper. The shine made his eyes fairly ache. He suddenly wished he could see her eyes. Would they be welcoming or cautious?

"That smells like a little piece of heaven, darlin'."

She jerked, then turned to him and frowned. "You move quiet for a man with a bad leg. Should you be walking on it?"

"It's better to get it moving."

She didn't look convinced, but apparently she figured arguing was useless. "I was going to bring this to you, but since you're here, just sit down." She nodded toward a wooden table set with a tray holding a single plate, silverware, and a small jar of flowers. "Omelet's almost finished."

Mark sat. The kitchen was Joy's domain, and she expected her commands to rule. Besides, that omelet did smell good.

While she finished cooking, she asked about his leg and head, his vision and any pains, told him about the Chefs' Charity Night with the Mushroom festival, and slipped in questions about why he'd picked their festival and what he'd been doing since his last performance. But Mark had a lot more skill at evasion than she did at prying, and he told her only what he wanted her to know.

Trouble was, from the spark in her eye, he suspected she also knew that.

Joy turned off the stove, then spooned something from a pot at the back onto the omelet. With practiced ease, she slid the omelet onto a platter and flipped it into a fold. After spooning more sauce over it, she brought it to the table.

Mark's eyes widened. The omelet took up the entire platter and hung over the edges. "I do like your cooking, but that would feed three of me."

"I thought you might like to get a little revenge by eating the egg that leveled you."

He laughed and cut a portion from the massive omelet onto his plate. "That's one egg?"

"Yup." Smiling, she waved at the food. "Enjoy."

Mark took one bite. Crab, there was crab in that sauce. He did have a fondness for crab. "This is good."

"Thanks."

She poured him coffee, and added, without asking, the teaspoon of sugar he liked before setting it before him.

While he ate, Joy puttered—washing dishes, wiping surfaces that already gleamed, straightening what didn't need to be straightened—and chattered. "While you were sleeping I was reading. Did you know that an archeologist in Greece discovered evidence of a race of aliens living on Mount Olympus centuries before the birth of our Lord?"

"Can't say as I've heard that."

"You ought to read the article. You use mythology as a frame for some of your illusions. Maybe it would be helpful." She wiped off the counter again.

"You give it to me, and I'll read it. Now, quit your fussing, darlin'. Come sit with me. Please?"

With unflattering reluctance, she poured herself coffee and sat. Damn, it was definitely caution in those pretty blue eyes. He gave her his most charming smile. The caution grew.

Charm never had worked with her; he had some fancy talking to do before he'd get back in her graces.

"About that job," he began. "You'd be doing me a powerful favor by letting me stay; I'd be indebted to you. I'm working on some new effects for the show, and you know magicians need to keep their secrets. That barn over by the ostriches would be a perfect site, nice and isolated."

Damn, she wasn't answering. Her silence worried him; Joy Taylor was not a silent woman. Two hours would have given her some time to think, and she was very adept at putting odd ingredients together and creating a whole new dish.

"I'd be real careful with the fire," he added, trying to get her to talk to him. The fire illusions were already figured out.

It worked.

"Fire! You can't be working with fire in a barn. There's hay there and dry wood. No fire illusions, not in my barn."

He grinned at her. "Okay, no fire, I've got others to work on. So, that means you'll let me stay?"

Joy looked at him, saying nothing. Damn! She wasn't going to give in that easily.

He was calculating another approach, when she said abruptly, "You can stay here. Let the knot on your forehead go down and your leg heal."

Mark gaped at her. She'd gone and done it again. Surprised him. The woman had a true knack for it.

"There are some stipulations. One, I do need help with the ostriches. My farmhand got lured away by the promise of work in New Orleans."

Mark thought about huge, irate birds, about clawed feet, about Joy going into those pens alone. "You got yourself a helper."

She nodded. "Two, no trying to charm me out of my jeans, at least no more than you do by nature. When I say 'no,' I mean it."

Mark braced his hands on the table and leaned forward,

catching her gaze with his. "Darlin', I *always* take 'no' to mean exactly that. I've never forced a woman in my life, and I surely don't intend to start with you." Lightly, he traced the front of her throat; her skin was soft as a butterfly. He liked to see her breath catch when he touched her. "But, I always allow a lady the right to change her mind."

She swallowed; the slight motion barely touched his fingertips, and he lifted his hand.

"Okay," she said, a trifle breathless. "I think we've got that settled."

"Yes," he murmured, "I think we do."

"Last, I want you to answer a question. Truthfully. No tricky evasions." Mark sat back in his chair, wary. Lies, evasions, illusions, and cons had been part of his life from the day of his birth. For too many years, he'd not known any other way existed.

And he had found it all too simple. For some reason, he instinctively knew what to say to people, and they always seemed to believe whatever he said. He'd been told once that he had "psychic charisma," whatever the hell that was. It wasn't a fact he was necessarily proud of, but he wasn't averse to using it to his advantage.

There were only three people he'd ever known who could see right through him. Unfortunately, one of those three was Joy, and she scared him a hell of a lot more than the other two.

If she asked the right question, and if she wasn't as innocent as he hoped, the truth could be dangerous for them both.

Joy gazed back at him, straight-on and clear-eyed. Could anyone look that honest and be part of Guy Centurion's schemes? He'd say no, except he'd been burned before—and badly.

Yet, he knew, with an instinct that had saved his hide in the past, that if he refused he'd lose all hope of gaining Joy's trust again, and having Joy's trust was something he found he craved.

"The truth. No evasions," he agreed.

"How long will you stay? Breeding season lasts through September."

Relief flooded through Mark. She hadn't asked any of the myriad questions that he couldn't answer.

Trouble was, he didn't know the answer to this one. He'd planned on staying three weeks only, through the festival. Things should be settled by then, one way or another. Afterward? He'd leave her again. A magician didn't succeed by staying in one place.

The end of September was an extra three weeks. Still, his new tour didn't start until mid-October. He looked at Joy—dusting of freckles, fiery hair, sweet-kissing lips, honest eyes—and desire stole his senses. The forgotten pleasures of her throaty laughs and warm touches and gentle caring blindsided him.

Damn—he had missed her these past years, something he'd never admitted, even to himself.

Ruthlessly, Mark forced the memories away. He had very little time and letting his libido take part in his decision making wasn't too smart.

"I can stay 'til the breeding's done," he answered. "I've no need to move on before then."

Something flickered across her face. Disappointment? Had she been asking something more?

How long will you stay?

"J-o-o-y, Joy, dear." A feminine voice from the interior of the house interrupted the uneasy thought.

"In the kitchen, Nicole," Joy called back.

A moment later, a woman breezed into the kitchen, an older version of Joy, with the same curvy figure and auburn hair, although the faint lines around the woman's identical blue eyes hinted her strands had been touched up a bit. Her designer jeans were tucked into riding boots.

The woman spied him and gave him a brilliant smile. "Why, hello. Joy said she was expecting a gentlemen this morning, but I thought she meant that nice Seth Beaumont." Pure cane syrup coated her words as she held out her hand. "I'm Nicole Valcour."

"Mark, you remember my mother," Joy added drily.

Nicole shot her an irritated look. "I thought we agreed not to keep bringing up that fact." She looked back at Mark, her smile returned. "I was just a child when I bore my Joy."

Mark kissed the back of her hand, as she obviously expected him to. "Nice to see you again, Miz Valcour."

Her eyes widened as she finally recognized him. "Matthew Mark Hennessy. I'd hardly recognize you. You've grown up," she added with a purr of feminine appreciation, as her warm glance skimmed across him. "You looked different on that TV special."

"Makeup and magic." *Marcus, the illusion most people saw.* "When I'm not performing, this is what you get." He held his hands wide.

With a flurry, Nicole settled into a chair and daintily cut a portion of the omelet from the platter. She transferred it to the plate Joy handed her. "What brings you to our corner of the world?"

"I'm performing at the Mushroom Festival."

"Marcus? Here? How exciting! Are you going to do that trick with the fire? I swear, I could not see how you possibly did that."

"He also says he'll help me with the ostriches," Joy added.

Apparently Joy still had her doubts, but Nicole took the news in stride.

"Good, I'm glad you found someone." Nicole patted her daughter's shoulder, then looked at Mark. "She's been working so hard. It's not good for her health."

"I haven't been sick in years," Joy protested.

Mark gave Joy an assessing glance. In his eyes, she radiated good health. Her hair and skin shone. Everything about her . . . glowed.

Nicole leaned forward. "I don't know what I'd have done without my Joy all these months since Mr. Valcour left. I didn't have the slightest idea how to run an ostrich farm, and she has done miracles with it."

He'd bet Joy hadn't known much about ostriches, either, but she'd learned. No shrinking violet routine for his Joy.

"You know," Nicole continued, "I really thought he was the one; he seemed so perfect and we were so in love. Of course, I have always been in love with all my husbands. We had eighteen wonderful months together. One day, he said he just needed to think about things. That we'd gotten married much too fast. He said he'd be back, so I carry on. Like the annual Valcour barbeque next week. Traditions are so important, don't you think? Oh, Joy, where is Hope?

Wasn't she supposed to come home after her sleep over? And why did Seth insist on coming by this morning? What did he say?"

By this time, Mark had lost the thread of the conversation, but apparently Joy hadn't.

"Hope stayed with Eliza. They're going to the movies." She glanced at Mark. "My sister," she reminded him.

"Twelve years old, yet she's not nearly as responsible as Joy was at that age," added Nicole. "Why, Joy could cook, keep house, take care of just about anything then. She is the rock of our family. Of course, Hope has her strengths— she's such a pretty girl, when she bothers to dress up. And bright. We're saving to make sure she goes to college. She got her brains from her father."

"Mr. Taylor?" inquired Mark politely. Before, he hadn't paid much attention to Joy's family or history; he'd focused on *her*. More fundamental things had occupied him, like the way Joy thought and hoped, tasted and smelled. Like the way she quivered when he touched her and sighed when he kissed her. Like the way she looked at him, as if she saw his soul and found it something to admire.

Mark shifted uneasily on the hard kitchen seat. Those memories, those feelings weren't why he'd come back. They were the past, and he never dwelt there.

Sometimes, he was discovering, the past had a way of rearing up and biting you in the butt, just to get your attention.

"Joy's father? Of course not!" Nicole answered. "I was married to Mr. O'Neill when Hope was born."

Joy had picked up a pad of paper and was writing on it.

"I've got some errands to run. Is there anything you need, Nicole?"

"Herbal shampoo and my face cream and a new mascara. Did the pharmacy get in that specialized eye cream I heard about?"

Joy shook her head. "They said it's part of a whole line and they can't order just one product. And, no, we can't buy the whole line," she added, forestalling her mother's question.

Nicole gave a small pout that lasted as long as her train of thought. "Oh, well, it probably wasn't nearly as good as they claimed." She leaned forward again to Mark. "I trust Joy with all our finances, you know. She is so reliable and responsible."

Mark thought he noticed Joy's faint wince before she started clearing off the remaining unwashed dishes. Most women, in his experience, didn't like their only accolades to be that they were reliable and responsible. Joy was those, yes, but he'd have picked words like intriguing, creative, and sexy as hell.

Nicole made a shooing motion. "You just leave the dishes; I'll finish them. Now, go."

"Thanks." Joy pointed a finger at Mark. "And you're coming along to get that leg and head looked at. Or no job."

If it meant private time with Joy, he'd tolerate a doctor's prodding. Mark rose. "You're the boss."

Nicole tilted her head. "Joy, you never did say why Seth Beaumont came by this morning. What was so important for him that he had to be here so early?"

"Eight isn't early. He knew I'd be up, and he wanted to get to work."

43

"That doesn't answer my question."

"It was personal." Joy picked up her purse.

"Joy," warned Nicole.

Nicole wasn't going to be put off. Mark, waiting near the doorway, could see that as plain as the codes on a marked deck of cards, and he'd bet Joy knew it, too. Inside Nicole's ditzy exterior was an indestructible feminine stubbornness.

Joy stopped and put her hands on her hips. "If you must know, he asked me to marry him."

Nicole clapped her hands together. "Marry him? Oh, Joy, how wonderful. You know, I had my suspicions that Seth had his eye on you ever since we moved here. When is the wedding? You will look beautiful in white. Lace, I think, lots of lace and seed pearls. Weddings are so thrilling; I adored every one of mine. And he's doing very well with his real estate business. Land is a prime commodity here."

The knot on Mark's head throbbed from the unexpected wave of cold coursing through him. He shoved his hands in his pockets. Hearing Nicole making plans made this Seth's offer all too real.

"I haven't said yes, Nicole, so stop," Joy protested.

"Haven't said yes? Why ever not? He's handsome, kind, will be a good provider. What more could you want?

"To be sure. I won't make a mistake."

Nicole waved a hand. "Oh, don't worry about mistakes. Those can be fixed."

The knots inside Mark tightened. A few minutes ago, it was his touch, not this Seth's, that had set Joy's pulse fluttering. Not that he was ever planning to be a bridegroom himself, but one thing he was sure of—Joy shouldn't hitch up with anyone who drove a Caddy and worked in *real estate*. Not on this blessed earth; his darlin' needed someone with life.

Joy shook her head. "Don't go planning any weddings, *mother*."

Mark stepped forward until he stood behind Joy. A lick of heat spread through him when her hair brushed across his chest. He laid a proprietary hand on her shoulder, but he spoke to the mother. "Miz Nicole, wouldn't it be best to keep this quiet for now? Seems like Joy's got some thinking to do, and she can't do that if people are pestering her about it, now can she?"

A thin line formed between Nicole's brows. "No, I guess not."

"So you won't say anything?"

"No," agreed Nicole.

Joy turned and scowled at him. "How do you do that?"

Mark shrugged. He didn't know, and it wasn't something he liked much to talk about.

Joy stepped over and gave her mother a kiss on the cheek, effectively removing herself from Mark's touch, to his regret. "When I'm ready to start planning a wedding, Nicole, I'll let you handle all the details. That time just isn't now." She straightened. "C'mon, Mark."

"We can take my truck."

"Your leg good enough to drive?"

"It's fine."

Outside, Joy settled into the passenger seat while Mark slid behind the wheel and then started out.

"Turn right at the end of the drive," she said. "You'll dead-end at a paved road. Turn right again, and then straight ahead five miles. Doesn't that air smell good?"

He glanced over to see her gazing out the open window, her red hair blowing with the breeze. A stab of memory sent the blood rushing every which way inside him. The weekend before his high school graduation, he'd taken her out in a similar truck.

Like now, she'd watched out the window then, all the time pointing out little things to him, like an antique car puttering down the right lane of the highway or a lolling-tongued dog hanging out a window or the sunshine sparkling off the pebbles in the creek.

Later she'd watched his hands and mouth on her breasts, had studied the whorls of hair and the scars on his chest with that same keen attention.

The mere memory made him grow uncomfortably hard against his zipper. He shifted in the seat. *Remember why you came—to recover the ancient book of magic stolen by Guy Centurion.*

Mark was certain the New Orleans businessman had taken the unique artifact, but he was more cunning than a magician protecting his secrets.

Guy Centurion was a broker; whatever you wanted he got. The goods were never in his hands, though, and he was careful about moving them out. For that he needed the help of his pretty, new protegee, Joy Taylor. At least, that was the opinion of Armond Marceaux, Mark's contact with the Feds, who was sure Joy was up to her apron in Centurion's schemes.

Finding out that Joy might be part of Centurion's web had shaken him more than the time the hidden ball fell out of his sleeve at his first performance. The vows he'd made to her, and broken, had crashed across him along with the protectiveness and warmth he'd struggled to forget.

"You're working with Guy Centurion on the Chefs' Charity Night?" he said casually.

She glanced over at him. "You know Guy?"

Was that wariness he heard? "I've played shows in New Orleans. Couldn't help but run into him. I heard you two are close."

She braced a foot on the seat and carefully retied a shoelace, the fall of her hair hiding her face. "You've heard rumors?"

"Some," he said cautiously.

"Do you believe them?" She finished tying the shoe with a savage tug, then glared at him. "Do you believe the only reason Guy got me the apprenticeship with his chef is because I'm having an affair with him?"

Relief flooded across him, cooling his burning guts. "Not for a single second."

"Why not?"

"Because that's not your style, darlin'." He scratched his chin. "But I figure you do have one main asset he's chasing."

She gave a snort of disbelief. "What? My blue eyes? My winning smile? My less-than-stunning figure?"

Mark took his gaze off the road to linger on those assets, long enough to bring a faint tint that blended with her sprinkling of freckles.

Redheads did blush pretty.

"Well, I must admit, in my mind that figure is a stunning one and those are mighty fine assets *I'd* be chasing after, but not Centurion. I happen to know his tastes are a bit more . . . exotic."

"Gee, thanks, nice to know I'm considered too ordinary for an affair."

He'd meant exotic tastes like hired women and imported sex toys and inflicted pain, but he figured Joy didn't need to know that. "Now there you're wrong. I'd never call you ordinary."

"So, what does Guy want?" Joy ignored his soft words. *Besides a conduit for his stolen goods?*

"Your ostriches."

Chapter Three

"My ostriches?" Joy burst out laughing. "Nice to know where I stand in the scheme of things."

She twisted in her seat and leaned against the truck door, the laughter easing some of the tension that had quivered inside her since Mark had arrived.

Mark always had been so easy to laugh with. In her efforts to ease him out of her heart by remembering only the bad, she had forgotten the good. She wasn't sure she wanted to remember, but there it was.

"So, how did you come by that conclusion?"

"W-e-e-l-l," he drawled, smiling, "I do happen to know Centurion's a health fanatic and fancies himself a mentor for new chefs. A good chef with access to low-fat ostrich meat? I figured that was an enticing combination for old Guy."

"He has been a big help to me." Joy inhaled the pine scent of the woods passing her open window. "To become a certified chef takes time, learning, and a *lot* of experience. Guy's giving me a prime opportunity, letting me apprentice with his chef. He's been a help with the farm, too, teaching me how to run a business. It was his suggestion to have the chefs feature locally raised ingredients in their dishes for the charity. A lot of them are using my ostrich meat, and I hope they'll continue to use it."

Mark hesitated, then spread his right arm across the seat back, steering with his left hand draped casually over the wheel. "Be careful with Centurion, Joy. He's got his fingers in a lot of pies, and some of them are mighty muddy."

"What? You're joking. Guy Centurion? You think he's dishonest? I admit he can be firm when it comes to business, but—"

"Firm?" Mark gave her a pitying look. "Try ruthless or dangerous."

"I don't believe it." Joy crossed her arms. The idea was too ludicrous, and she dismissed it.

After a moment's silence, he said quietly, "You're too trusting, darlin'."

You're too trusting. How many times had Mark said those words to her? Lord Almighty, she didn't want to remember, but she did.

Resting her elbow on the open window, Joy let the Garth Brooks tune playing low on the radio wash over her, bringing with it a tide of memory that rendered her silent.

She and Mark had first met when he and his father drifted into the small Mississippi town where she'd been living. She was fourteen and he was fifteen. Though they'd been so different, they'd shared the bond of being the outsiders, the wanderers, her because of her mother's multiple marriages, him because his con man father soon found any locale too hot to linger.

She'd loved Mark from the first time she'd seen him—so dark and mesmerizing, so self-assured. He had a magician's hands and talents even then.

With him, she dreamed magic dreams.

Eventually, Mark's father had drifted on, but this time Mark had stayed, determined to graduate from high school. A part of her also hoped he'd stayed because of her.

It had been rough for Mark, not that he ever said much about it, and social services hadn't cared about a seventeen-year-old troublemaker. He'd stayed in a shack so dilapidated no one cared to claim it. Even then, he was a talented magician, and he made enough money to survive, but the town had branded him a hell-raiser, so jobs were few. She helped where she could—cooking, cleaning, mending—domestic things that she'd been doing for years.

And when he graduated. . . .

He became an indelible part of her that year.

After his graduation, he'd left, saying the town held no prospects, but he'd promised to come back for her. Come back in one year, on *her* graduation night. Together, he'd promised, they'd take the world by storm, he with his magic, she with her cooking.

Enough wallowing, Joy admonished herself. He hadn't come back, though she'd waited all graduation night, waited until she had no more tears to shed, until her eyes and throat were so dry they ached. He'd never sent a word, not in all the time he was gone, not even a note of explanation, and she'd be damned if she'd ask for one now.

Yet she couldn't deny that from the first, he had set her

sizzling, and dammit, he still set her sizzling. Worse, he tugged out deep fears and deeper hopes, none of which she wanted to entertain.

You're too trusting. It had taken a while, but she'd finally heeded his words.

"Too trusting?" she said at last in response. "Not anymore. But Guy Centurion's been good to me and to this community. It'll take more than veiled accusations to make me think ill of him."

"You always were stubborn." There was a moment's silence while they turned onto the winding road leading to town. Then Mark said casually, "I noticed you've taken back your maiden name."

Joy threw him a startled look. "I wanted a fresh start. You knew I was married?"

"I heard. How long have you been divorced?"

"Since a few months after the ceremony. It lasted barely long enough for me to change the bed sheets before he took off."

"What happened?"

"The marriage was a mistake; we were wrong for each other. I married out of need, thinking he'd take care of me, Nicole, and Hope. But I can't say as I'm sorry. Finding myself divorced at nineteen, I realized I was repeating the same mistakes as Nicole and grandma. It woke me up."

It had been a painful, wrenching time, but one she vowed not to forget. She'd married on the rebound from Mark and for all the wrong reasons.

Still leaning on the door, Joy rested one foot on the dashboard and draped her hand across her leg. The breeze through the open window blew hot across her neck, and her hair tickled her cheeks, but she liked this caress of summer.

"I decided then and there I'd just keep taking care of myself, make my own home, and take care of Nicole and Hope, too, not that I was fixing to spend my life sharing living quarters with them. I started planning in earnest to be a chef. Figured I'd never marry again out of neediness."

"Why would you marry again?"

"I don't know; my family's not real good about picking men. It's like a curse." She tapped a finger on her knee, thinking. "I guess, if I wanted someone bad enough to want him settled in my home. And if he wanted to be settled. I'd have to know he was as committed to me as I was to him."

"Is this Seth like that?" His gaze stayed straight ahead.

"He's solid, reliable. He wants a family. He won't run out. I like him a lot and respect him. Maybe that's enough."

"What about love?"

"After my mother's example"—*after losing big chunks of my heart to you*—"I'm not sure I trust the emotion."

"I'm not talking about Nicole's brand." Mark was silent a moment. "Shouldn't you feel something more? Some incredible excitement? Something that fills every part of you, that's so damn compelling you can't take a breath without feeling it?"

His words wove a web of magic inside her.

Her ex, the few other men who'd kissed her, none of them compared to the way Mark's touch assaulted her senses and his kisses filled every tiny part of her.

They had exchanged exploratory touches and kisses at first, but young, exploding hormones hadn't been satisfied with chaste groping. She was hesitant; he was confident.

53

The weekend before his graduation, he'd taken her out, a special day he'd saved for for weeks. They went tubing, a first for Joy. The creek was still cold from spring waters, but that hadn't stopped them from splashing and dunking each other. Kissing had warmed them up nicely. Afterward, they'd driven to a nearby catfish house for dinner, then stopped at a secluded spot near the river and watched the stars appear.

He'd kissed her, touched her, thrilled her. Such wild feelings, she hadn't known that she'd missed them or that she needed them. He'd undressed her in the truck, then carried her to a blanket he'd laid out for them by the whispering water.

He'd taken her virginity that night—no, she'd given it to him—in a moonlit site as romantic as a girl could dream of, although the reality had been too quick. She'd told him she loved him, and he'd proposed, with an offhand suggestion they run off and get married.

But they hadn't.

Joy shrugged off the spell of memory and Mark's bewitching words and stared resolutely at the landscape racing past. She'd thought what they'd shared was love; he'd been a part of her every breath. She knew now he hadn't felt the same, hadn't meant that proposal.

So why had he brought it up a couple of hours ago back in the ostrich pens?

"By the way, you've got no call bringing up that old proposal," she said, voicing her thoughts. "That was a long time ago, and you didn't mean it."

"Didn't mean it? I'm not the one who married someone else four months after she graduated."

How dare he claim the years dividing them were her

fault? Joy's temper ignited. She'd been trying to be civilized about this, trying to avoid a scene, but the man always did rile her, whether with anger, excitement, or passion.

"You're the one who didn't come back! Excitement? I tried your excitement once. It didn't work."

Without warning, Mark pulled to the side of the road and stopped the truck. The brakes screeched a protest. Dust motes in the hot sunlight settled about the windows, and the breeze from the open windows died. The sudden quiet was split only by the mellow tones of Hal Ketchum on the radio.

Joy eyed Mark with a sideways glance and saw his knuckles turn white with his grip on the steering wheel. Hell's bells, maybe she shouldn't have made that crack about the excitement.

"You want to marry Seth?" Mark asked roughly, unsnapping his seat belt with a jerk.

"Yes. Maybe." Joy backed up. "I don't know."

"Answer me one thing. Do you feel like this when he touches you?"

He didn't pull her to him. Instead, balancing on one knee, he leaned over and captured her against the door.

"Your leg," she protested. "It'll start bleeding."

"I don't give a rat's ass about my leg. I've got another pain that needs healing."

His lips brushed across hers, once, twice, waited for her protest, but she had no intention of arguing. Hellfire, but she'd missed this.

His mouth came home to feast. Joy clutched his arms, which were braced on either side of her. The muscles were tight, harder than her steel alloy fry pan. Despite the tension radiating from him, his kiss was silkier than custard cream.

Her insides fluttered like a feather spiraling high in the rising wind. Soft, she grew soft everywhere under the pleasure of his lips. Joy ran her hands along the top of his arms, stroking solid muscle and delicate hairs, until she reached his wrists. She traced his heavy watch on one side, the veins on the other, reveling in the hard feel and crisp scent of him.

Mark's tongue traced her lips. "Let me in, darlin'. Let me taste you. So sweet and spicy, like cinnamon sugar."

The yearning, banked for so long, spread like wildfire. He was doing it again.

Be honest, don't put the blame on him. This was all in her. Letting him creep past her defenses. Giving in to the wild longing she thought she'd long ago squelched. Joy's fingers tightened around his wrists. "No, Mark, stop."

He lifted his head, and his bright eyes bored into her. "What?"

"Stop. Now. Dammit, we're in the middle of the road."

Joy squirmed awkwardly upward, pushing against the door. Unfortunately, Mark was a little slower to move, and, as she twisted away, her hand slipped and knocked the door handle.

The door opened, and Joy fell. Mark, leaning awkwardly over her, crashed against her. They slid down the side of the seat and out of the truck. Mark's arms wrapped around her waist and with an agile move, he twisted. They landed on the dusty pine needles, Mark on the bottom, Joy sprawled atop him. Her breath whooshed out of her lungs.

They lay in thunderstruck silence, until Joy felt Mark shaking beneath her.

"Are you all right?" she asked anxiously.

Mark let out a whoop. "Damnation, woman, how many pieces do you want me in?"

A loud crack cut his laughter short.

"Down," shouted Mark, rolling her over till he was on top.

Her muscles protested the double abuse. "I am down! What are you doing? Adding bruises to my bruises?" Joy looked down the road behind them, then swore when she saw the backfiring car coming toward them. The driver had a full view of Joy and the man on top of her. Joy shut her eyes. "Why?" she muttered. "In God's heaven, why Earl?" She shoved at Mark. "Get off of me."

He rose with a disgustingly easy grace. Joy ignored his outstretched hand and scrambled to her feet, wincing as scraped hands and a sore behind protested. "Look, I tore the pocket of my shorts," she grumbled as Mark brushed pine needles off her back. "How did you come through without a lick of damage?"

"Magic, I guess."

Earl Flynn putt-putted past them, his eager eyes taking in each detail.

Joy dropped her head to the side of the truck cab. Why had this happened just when she thought she'd found a place to call home, a place where she wasn't the misfit.

"What's wrong?" asked Mark.

"What's wrong? Earl Flynn is the town's biggest gossip, and he sees me cavorting at the side of the road. He's also the one who hired you for the Mushroom Festival."

"We were cavorting?"

Joy glared at him. "This juicy tidbit will be all over town in no time. Get a move on. I've got to talk to Seth before Earl does."

Mark's hand lingered as he dusted off the seat of her shorts. "Still thinking of Seth?"

"Just go," she answered clambering back into the truck.

At Joy's direction, Mark parked in a small lot midway between the medical clinic and the real estate office. After a succinct reminder that she'd meet him in the diner, Joy scrambled from the truck and turned down the street, away from him.

Mark lingered to admire the view. She had such a fine walk. Her leg muscles tightened with each step, and dammit if her hips didn't hold the cutest tiny sway.

Seven years had not dulled her impact on him. He slammed the truck door shut and leaned a hip against it, drawing in a breath to quell his lust and trying to pull his gaze away.

Neither lust, nor eyes, obeyed.

When he'd finally came back all those years ago, to find she'd wasted no time in getting married, he'd sworn never to look back and never to be that . . . vulnerable again.

Mark rubbed a finger against the bridge of his nose. So, why had he brought up that long-ago proposal? And why had her casual dismissal of it rankled so much?

I tried your excitement once. It didn't work. Hell, that excitement had been one of the few things in his life that *had* worked during those years.

Focus on the present. He had a tour to arrange, one that could catapult him into the ranks of the premiere magicians like Copperfield, Burton, and the Pendragons if all went well.

If he found that stolen book of magic.

His old man had died in prison, a penniless loser, but that wasn't going to happen to Mark Hennessy.

The way to find the book was to learn how Guy Centurion was using Joy.

It might not have been too smart telling Joy that Centurion was dirty. If she were part of his outfit, she'd go running straight to him. Hell, even if she was innocent, she might tell him. He was taking a risk; Centurion could get nasty first and ask questions later.

Yet if she had nothing to do with Centurion's dirty business—and a strong part of him shouted she didn't—then putting a little caution in her was worth the risk.

Mark gave a shrug. When Centurion recognized him, the man would be suspicious anyway and he had a plan to deal with it.

Joy turned in to the real estate office, and a small twinge of disappointment that she was lost from his view pricked Mark.

He straightened and headed for the small medical clinic.

Whether Joy was a pawn or a player, he wouldn't let a skunk like Guy Centurion touch her. He'd stick so close she couldn't take a breath without his enjoying the sight.

As soon as she entered Seth's real estate office, Joy cast a surreptitious glance around, looking for the bandy-legged Earl Flynn.

No Earl. No Seth, either. The office was empty.

The wave of relief that filled her tempted Joy to simply leave, but she ignored it. That was the coward's way. Seth would be back soon; he never left the office unattended for long.

Sure enough, he walked in a few moments later, carrying a sack from the local diner. "Joy!" Spying her, Seth enveloped her in his arms and kissed her.

The kiss was . . . pleasant. It created a contented glow, like hot soup on a cold morning. She tried to respond, tried to kindle the tiniest spark, which would spread like wildfire at Mark's slightest touch.

Only gentle regret sparked inside her—regret that it couldn't be.

For one moment, Joy could not move away. Seth was solid and kind and good to lean on. He was the settling kind. Then, out the window, she saw Mark stretch before entering the medical clinic down the street. His body moved with grace and power beneath the faded jeans and casual shirt. A very masculine motion on a very masculine man. The fizzing in her blood started up again. From Mark, not Seth.

She disentangled herself from Seth's embrace. Joy hated lies and deceptions, and she was deceiving herself, and Seth, to think she could marry him now.

Grandma Idabeth had married from the head. She chose a good provider, who was cold and distant.

Nicole married from the heart. She chose men she loved, who always left.

And for Joy? Hormones all the way.

Hell of a time for the family gene pool to run true.

But this was one family curse she was determined to break.

"I didn't expect to see you so soon," Seth said, apparently well satisfied with the kiss. He held up the bag. "If I'd known, I'd have asked *you* to bring me lunch."

"I'd bring something healthier, that's for sure." Her

fleeting smile faded. "I . . . I want to explain about something. In case you heard rumors. About me. About this morning. It wasn't what it looked like. Mark's performing at the Mushroom Festival, and he's staying with me until then, helping out and . . . practicing. We were coming to town, and we stopped. I was leaning against the car door when it accidentally opened, and I fell. Mark tried to stop me, but we both fell out. That's why we were lying on the side of the road. Because the truck door opened accidentally," she finished in a rush. Lord, but she sounded like her mother.

"Is this that nonsense Earl was talking about in the diner?"

Joy's mouth snapped shut. "Ah . . . probably."

"Aw, honey, everybody knows to listen only to half of what Earl says. Especially about you. I know you, Joy. You'd never do anything to warrant gossiping about. You don't make waves, and I like that about you."

Joy frowned, surprised it had been so easy, and perversely not sure she liked Seth's easy assumption that she was innocent because she was dull.

"Is that all?" Seth leaned against his desk. "And here I thought you came to make me a happy man and say 'yes.' "

She had to tell him the truth. If only it weren't so hard. Regretfully, Joy shook her head. "I am so, so sorry, but I . . . I can't."

"Can't what?"

"I can't marry you."

"Why?"

How could she explain when she didn't understand herself the fascination Mark Hennessy held for her? All she knew was, until she got rid of it, she couldn't accept Seth's proposal. Or lead him to expect more.

"It's just . . . not right. I'm sorry."

"Wasn't it just this morning you said you'd think about it? And you took a whole half-day?"

He sounded peeved, and Joy supposed she couldn't blame him.

"A step like marriage, I shouldn't have to think about it. If it's right, I should recognize it straightaway." Good Lord, wasn't that what Mark had said in the truck?

Seth straightened and put his hands on her shoulders. "You love this town as much as I do. Together, we'd put down roots, raise our kids."

He was offering her a dream—a place where she belonged, where she could grow old. A place where she could put pictures on the wall because she didn't have to worry about repairing the holes six months later. And her mouth couldn't form around the words to make it come true.

"I really like you, and we could have a good life, but—" A tear formed in the corner of her eye.

He patted her cheek. "See, honey, you're just a little emotional on this subject—that odd notion you've got about a family curse. Why not trust me to know what's right? For now, we'll leave things as they are. We're friends, until you decide to come around."

Joy shook her head, feeling a trifle peeved that he would dismiss her decision so casually. "I can't—"

"I can wait."

"Don't. Please, don't wait for me. It's a futile, life-stealing process. Trust me." She stood on tiptoe to kiss his cheek, then turned and walked out.

Chapter Four

Joy pulled the mail out of her post office box, the last of her errands. Bills, a recipe request for ostrich sausage, an order for feathers, the customer list from the new slaughter house, still more bills. The usual.

She opened an envelope from the chef at LaBelle, the only four-star restaurant within a twenty-mile radius. The chef wrote he'd be pleased to accept the invitation to participate in such a premiere event as the Chefs' Charity Night and informed her he'd be using nutria.

Nutria! A big rodent instead of her ostrich meat. Joy made a face. She'd hoped the charity would be an opportunity to get her meat into LaBelle.

Back outside in the bright sunshine, Joy slipped on her sunglasses and glanced at her watch. She was supposed to meet Mark twenty minutes ago at the local diner. It had taken longer than expected to finish her errands; too many people wanted to stop and talk. Normally she loved the socializing, but not when she was the most interesting tidbit in the rumor mill. At least most had the same opinion as Seth—that Earl exaggerated and she was too steady to be so wanton.

The opinion was strangely annoying.

Joy hurried to the small café, then stopped just inside and smiled. Mark was already there, a cup of coffee on the table before him. The six-year-old Davidson twins sat at the table with him, watching raptly while he pulled coins from their ears or hair and ran a steady stream of patter. Their parents, eating at the next table, seemed fascinated as well.

Mark was different, Joy noted, her heart doing a little flip. The drawl was gone, and an aura of mystery radiated from him. *This* was Marcus at work. She strolled closer to watch.

With a flourish, Mark handed a coin to each boy.

"Wow, mister, how'd you do that?"

"A magician never tells his secrets." The boys' faces were crestfallen. "Well, maybe, just this once." He leaned over and whispered, while they stared in fascination at his demonstrating hands. Their eyes widened.

"I can do that!" one exclaimed.

"Takes lots of practice," Mark warned, the stage persona slipping away. He caught sight of Joy and rose. "Now, here's my lady, so I've got to go."

The two boys gave her an annoyed look for interrupting the magic lesson, but they scrambled back to their parents' table.

"I thought magicians never gave away their secrets," she said.

"It's an old trick, been printed in a lot of books. Just palm the coin . . ." His hands twisted with a deft gesture, but instead of a quarter he handed her a flower, a daisy this time. A drop of dew glistened in the center.

No way he could have palmed that! "How'd you do that?" she demanded.

He shook his head. "That one is a secret. You want something to eat?"

The greasy burger smells made her faintly queasy. "No thanks. You finished?"

"Ready to go and face the evil Hans." He laid a bill on the table, then ushered her out with a hand at the small of her back.

The warmth from his hand spread up her spine and across her shoulders, and, for the life of her, Joy could not remove herself from that heat.

"What did the doctor say about your leg and head?" Joy asked as they walked down the main street. Aside from the taut bands of desire that were a constant between them, she had always felt so at ease with Mark. It seemed both feelings had been only dormant, not gone.

"Head's bruised, needs ice and TLC." He looked at her expectantly.

"We've got lots of ice at home."

"How 'bout the TLC?"

Joy rose on tiptoe to kiss his bandaged head, her cheek brushing against his hair. He made a small, pleasured sound that pleased her as well. "And the leg?" she asked, lowering back to her feet.

"He put stitches in the leg and injected an antibiotic into my butt," Mark grumbled. "I have to go back in two weeks."

"See, I told you! It was worse than you made out."

He tweaked her nose. "Gloating does not become you."

"I get to do it so rarely with you, I'm going to savor every moment."

"As long as the TLC goes with it."

She laughed. "You got big dreams, mister."

They were nearly back to the truck when Joy's feet dragged as they always did at the dusty window of an empty building. She peered inside, noting the fireplace was still intact and the wood floor still smooth. "Isn't it beautiful? Remember that picture I've got of the women gleaning the fields of wheat?"

"The picture you refuse to hang?"

She nodded and pointed to the mantle. "Wouldn't it look beautiful hanging there?"

"You want to live here?"

Joy shook her head. "I like the farm. This place would make a beautiful restaurant, though."

"You planning on starting one?"

"Someday, with a partner. I don't want to have the hassles of hiring and firing and scheduling, of making sure there's enough napkins and dishwasher soap. I want to be a chef, to be in charge some place where I can just plan the food and cook and serve people and watch them enjoy wonderful tastes. I don't want to *own* a restaurant; I want to be its heart."

She was silent a moment, able to taste the crisp salads and hot soups and seasonal specials; then Joy let out a breath and resumed walking. She was a long way from an executive chef spot.

"A partner like Centurion?" Mark asked, his voice holding none of the easy drawl.

"Maybe."

Mark didn't answer, saying only, after a moment, "I need to check out where my performance will be."

They had just reached the truck when Seth bustled out of his office building. A distinguished-looking man, slightly balding with a pepper-and-salt mustache, followed.

"Joy," Seth called breathlessly. "There's someone I want you to meet."

Joy paused with her foot on the truck's running board and peered at the stranger beside Seth. He looked familiar. Who did he remind her of?

Sean Connery! Omigod, it was Sean Connery. Here!

Mark came to her side and lounged against the fender.

Seth flashed a curious glance at Mark, before turning to her. "Joy, this is Zeke Jupiter."

"Anyone ever tell you you look like Sean Connery?" she blurted out to the stranger.

He gave her a white-toothed smile. "Recently, yes."

"Mr. Jupiter—" began Seth.

"Zeke," murmured the stranger.

"—Zeke is here to do the fireworks display for the Mushroom Festival," Seth explained. "I thought you should talk to him. Show him where he can set up."

Joy frowned. "I didn't know we'd arranged for fireworks."

"It must have been Earl's idea." Seth leaned over and whispered, "He's also here to see about purchasing land. I suggested the Collingswood property."

No wonder Seth was excited. That listing had been with him for months. With an asking price beyond four million, he'd had trouble finding a buyer for the whole package, but the current owners refused to sell in parcels. If Seth could sell it, it would be a definite coup for him, as well as a huge commission.

Joy held out her hand. "Nice to meet you, Zeke."

Zeke Jupiter took her hand, but instead of shaking it, he kissed the backs of her fingers. For a brief moment he lingered, then slowly backed away. "Delighted, Joy Taylor."

Mark cleared his throat, and Joy performed introductions.

"Marcus? The magician? I've heard of you." Seth gave a low whistle. "This is going to be one spectacular festival."

"I'm looking forward to it," said Mark.

Joy could see Seth calculating the best locale for the Beaumont-sponsored booth that gave away fresh-squeezed juices—along with maps, key chains, and wooden yardsticks emblazoned with the Beaumont Real Estate logo.

She also saw the moment he put it together that Mark was the same man who figured prominently in Earl's gossip.

"A magician," Zeke repeated thoughtfully. For some reason, he didn't seem surprised. He nodded at the bandage on Mark's head. "Looks like you had an accident."

"More like an egg-cident," Mark said drily. "Ready to go, Joy?"

"What? Oh, sure. We're going out to the festival site. You wanted to see it, too, Zeke? Maybe you could come along—"

"The truck only holds two," Mark reminded her, his hand at her elbow urging her away.

"That's right." She smiled at Zeke. "I'll take you out another time. Oh, and if you're still in town, you're invited to the Valcour barbeque. A week from Sunday."

"Then I shall say au revoir, Joy." Zeke Jupiter looked straight at Mark. "Do not doubt," he murmured, "we shall see each other again. Soon."

A single clap of thunder boomed, sharp and biting, so

close it sounded directly overhead, though not a single gray cloud marred the sky.

Zeus scowled at the retreating truck. He had but to be near Joy and Mark to sense the lightning crackling between them. Separating them was going to be harder than fooling Hera.

Come to think of it, he never had fooled Hera.

He glanced at his companion and was pleased to note irritation on the face of Seth Beaumont. Zeus clapped him on the back. "What about you and I going out to the festival grounds?"

"I thought you wanted to see the Collingswood property."

"I do, I do, but the other's important, too." He gave a pointed look after the disappearing truck. "Those two seemed mighty chummy."

Seth flushed, and his hands gripped his clipboard. "Joy takes her responsibilities to the festival seriously. She's loyal and dependable."

Zeus gave an inner groan. Seth Beaumont might be solid and steadfast and pleasant, in other words, just the man for a daughter of gentle Io, but the Earthling didn't have a clue when it came to women. That much was obvious.

Unlike Mark, who was a true descendent of Hermes. This close, he had seen it plain. Hermes had always been one of his favorites, Zeus admitted, but that didn't make him blind to the trickster's faults. Or his strengths.

If Joy wasn't in love with Seth Beaumont, then she would be vulnerable to Mark's charisma.

My race has always meant bad luck for Earth women. If he was to bring love to Joy, break the legacy that cursed her line, it couldn't be with a son of Olympus.

Zeus glanced at Seth and sighed. He needed better material to work with. "Shall we go?"

"Wait!" A short, bowlegged man hurried down the street toward them. Zeus and Seth paused.

The stranger pulled up beside them. He turned toward Zeus and grabbed his hand. Pumping it up and down he said, "Hello, I don't believe we've met. Earl Flynn. Chairman of the Mushroom Festival, jockey, and horse trainer. Wait, don't tell me. I know who you are! Sean Connery!"

"No, I'm not," Zeus answered, "I'm—"

"No? Well, you sure look like him," Earl said, still working the handshake. "Anyone ever tell you that?"

"Once or twice." Zeus tugged his hand free.

"This is Zeke Jupiter." Seth made the introduction. "He's here to do the fireworks."

A frown etched between Earl's brows. "Fireworks? Did I send letters about fireworks? I sent out hundreds, so I could have. Welcome. We're glad to have you here, Zeke. This is going to be a bang-up festival." He beamed at Zeus and reached again for his hand.

Zeus thrust it in his pocket.

Earl clapped Seth on the shoulder instead. "Do you know where Joy is? I have a marvelous idea. Dancing mushrooms! A veritable chorus line—onstage, throughout the festival. Can't you just see it?"

Zeus could, and the image was ludicrous.

"Dani's Dance Team will do the choreography," Earl continued without breath, "but they need funds for the costumes. I must talk to Joy."

Seth jerked his head. "She just left with Marcus."

"*That* was Marcus? The man she was sprawled beneath at the side of the road?"

Zeus lifted his brows. Now here was a story worth hearing. "Sprawled beneath?"

"She explained that," Seth said tightly. "The truck door opened accidently, and she fell out. Mark tried to stop her and fell himself."

That was weaker than the excuses he used to give Hera. Zeus didn't think any one of the three of them believed that story.

"Maybe I can catch her at the festival grounds," said Earl.

"Could I ride with you?" Zeus asked. "I'd like to scope out where I can set up the mortars and firing computers. Are you going to want music with the display?"

"Music? Why sure, we want this to be the best! You'll have to talk to Joy about budgets, but we'll want a top-notch show."

"I'm sure we can arrange an agreeable fee," Zeus murmured.

"What about the Collingswood property?" Seth protested as they began to move away.

Zeus set his jaw. "I'll see it later. Why don't you come with us?"

Seth hesitated, then looked at his real estate office and shook his head. "I have some other work to do. Have Earl drop you by when you get back."

Hopeless. Zeus shook his head. The man was hopeless. This was getting more difficult by the moment.

On the way out to the festival grounds, Zeus discovered Earl drove a car the way he probably rode a horse at the end stretch—flat-out. And he talked the entire time.

Zeus pressed a hand to the bridge of his nose. Would that he had the ability to enforce silence on Earl, but that was not one of the powers the gods could lay claim to.

Zeus touched his lightning ring, the source of his powers of legend: the abilities to move long distances, to alter the weather, to far-see, and to create false images.

Yes, he could move long distances in a blink, but tempting as it was, he didn't think it would be wise to simply disappear on Earl. Besides, he didn't like to transfer too often. The energy drain was immense, and the crystals that powered the transfer were weakening. Once they died, nothing on Earth could replace them.

Instead he used the simple human ability to tune out annoyances and returned to his original problem.

How best to intervene between Mark and Joy? Zeus stroked his mustache. Maybe *he* could attract Joy. In his day, he had had a certain amount of charm. He still remembered the sweet way Io had succumbed, what the beautiful Callisto had done . . .

No, if he was eventually going to get Hera back, he had to restrain himself, save himself for her. Women expected that.

He would concentrate on teaching Seth to charm a woman.

While he kept Mark and Joy apart.

Both would be tasks worthy of a god.

They turned and drove down a rutted road until Earl jerked the car to a halt. Ahead of them, down in a small hollow, Zeus saw Mark's black truck parked where pine trees rose and resinous needles littered the grass. Wooden filigreed bridges, stone urns carved like swans, and a small island centered in a winding brook all nestled between the tall, straight pines that dotted the area. The trees added both the fragrance of their sap and the majesty of their height to make a beautiful locale.

Mark and Joy circled a large, gazebo-like structure, the

performance stage he surmised. Looking at the two of them, even from here he could see the attraction between them.

Zeus rubbed his hands together. Nothing better than a challenge to set the blood racing.

Could a site be worse for a magician to perform?

Mark hefted himself onto the platform where he'd perform, then, ignoring the protest from his wounded leg, paced across the octagonal floor, doing mental calculations. The stage was small, outdoors, and, most problematic, open on all sides.

Size was manageable; he'd have to eliminate the more elaborate effects, but he had others that were smaller scale and equally striking. With the fire he used, wind could be a problem. Yet, if his crew hung the black drapes to cut down the views and the cross breeze, it could work.

Sweat dripped down his back, and his lungs dragged in the dense air. It would be devilish hot up here. Mark rubbed a hand across his cheek, hearing the rasp of his palm against the faint stubble. He'd forgotten how pervasive Southern humidity was.

"Will it be all right?" Joy asked, circling below on the grass. "Will you be able to give the show?"

"This is just fine, darlin'." He wasn't about to give her an excuse to send him on his way. "I was once told a good magician should be able to perform anywhere, even naked on a beach."

"And you consider yourself a good magician?"

"That I do."

She leaned against the latticawork base of the stage and grinned at him. "So have you? Performed naked on a beach?"

"Of course." On stage, he crouched down until he was almost level with her and wiggled his eyebrows in mock invitation. "Want to see what magic I can do naked?"

Joy laughed. "Mark Hennessy, you are incorrigible." She fanned herself with her baseball cap. "You about finished? It's hot out here."

"Almost."

A rattling boom of thunder jerked them apart. What the hell? Again? His head throbbing, Mark scanned the hot blue sky. Not a single cloud marred the vista. Heat lightning? But heat lightning didn't make that kind of noise.

"What do you suppose that was?" Joy asked, looking up.

"Got me." *Remember to tell the crew to plan for rain.* "Give me a couple more minutes, and then we can go."

While Joy wandered around, Mark walked through the motions of his floating orb routine. It would be very effective on the charming, old-fashioned stage, he realized. Also, this would be an ideal spot to try out the Pygmalion illusion he was perfecting, where the ivory statue of a lady was transformed into a warm, sensual woman.

Like Joy.

Mark emerged from the intense concentration he put on all things connected with his magic and looked around. Where was Joy?

He spied her, then frowned. He hadn't heard the new arrivals: Earl Flynn and Zeke Jupiter.

Something about Jupiter seemed oddly familiar, though Mark knew that they'd never met before today and that he wasn't getting him mixed-up with famous movie stars. Had he seen a picture, or a statue, of Jupiter?

Mark leaped down from the stage, and the leg again protested the abuse. Damn, but he hated injuries. With a slight limp, he strode over to the trio, wiping his damp forehead on his sleeve.

"You might be able to use that hill over there to set up your equipment," he heard Joy say as he approached.

"It looks good, but I need to know how far away it is," Zeke answered.

"Ask Seth Beaumont," chimed in Earl. "He should know."

Zeke nodded. "Tell me about this Chefs' Charity Night."

Joy's face lit with excitement. "It benefits the Chef's Foundation for Children, which fights hunger and promotes good nutrition. The chefs have responded wonderfully, thanks to our sponsor, Guy Centurion."

Hearing the name again, and the admiration from Joy, Mark felt his gut tighten and the air sit heavy in his lungs. Too trusting, she was too trusting. If she were involved with Centurion, it had to be because she was too trusting. Joy had always been unfailingly honest and so easy for him to read.

Yet she'd married when he'd expected her to stay true. He certainly hadn't read that!

As he closed the gap, his gaze lingered on her: the sweetly shaped legs, the shining hair, the expressive lips. Had he lost the ability to see her clearly? Was he being fooled by the rush of desire?

"Each chef will prepare a specialty dish featuring local ingredients," Joy continued, "and people pay to sample and enjoy the wine and music. Ticket sales have been excellent, though we always hope for more."

"Will you be cooking?" Zeke asked.

"No, I'm nowhere in the same league as the other chefs, but a lot of them are using my ostrich meat."

"She's doing herself an injustice." Mark reached their side. "The omelet she made me this morning was delicious."

Joy gave him a sunny smile. "Thanks."

Heat, not from the summer sun, but from her, rose to embrace him, carrying the delicate scent of her. Mark smoothed the ends of her wild hair and inhaled. Spices and sunshine—she always smelled like spices and sunshine.

He caught himself and shoved his telltale hands into his pockets. "I've seen all I need for now, Joy," he said abruptly.

"How about you, Zeke? Anything else you need to see?"

"I think I'm prepared," he answered.

Earl cleared his throat. "Before you leave, Joy, I need money for dancing mushroom costumes."

"*What*? Dancing mushrooms?" She grimaced. "How much?"

"They will be the biggest hit, you wait and see."

"Earl, give me figures." They negotiated, with Joy tactfully turning aside the more extravagant fancies, while giving in on enough to keep Earl content.

She had more confidence, more savvy, Mark realized, than she had seven years ago.

On the ride back to Joy's, Mark brooded, casting covert glances at her. What did he know about her now? She was no longer the girl he'd known, just as he was no longer the boy she'd claimed to love.

The days of their sweet union were over. He could no longer claim any rights to her, for he would return to his magic and Joy would keep to her small-town life.

Unfortunately, he'd discovered he missed spices and sunshine.

Chapter Five

Country roads don't have streetlights. Mark remembered that fact later that night, as he drove the isolated route back into town. Thick clouds covered the stars and alternately hid, then revealed, the waning moon.

He needed to make a phone call, one that would leave no record, and earlier today he'd spotted a pay phone at the side of the feed and seed store. Even at this hour, he expected Armond would be awake to take the call.

The wind, still hot and moisture-laden, gusted into the open window of his truck. Mark's fingers tightened around the wheel, steering the truck through loose gravel.

He lived in the night; he and the night were old friends. But his night was the night of a performance under the spotlights, the night of a town lit by neon, not this night of unlit darkness. This night reminded him too much of small, dark places.

At last he pulled into the crossroads of the silent town where everything was closed and quiet. The streetlights and the beer signs in the diner created a familiarity that relieved his annoying jitters.

The phone could not be easily seen from the road, a fact that had seemed a plus this morning. Picking his way through the shadows and damp grass, Mark admitted ruefully that perhaps he'd overrated that advantage.

He leaned one arm against the store's metal siding and dialed a number, absently fingering the bandage on his forehead. The fitful bulb in the store's night-light sputtered on its last filaments.

"Hey, you old devil, how's it going?"

"Better than most days," came the dry answer of Armond Marceaux, his contact and long-time friend. "And you?"

"Things are looking mighty fine for me. I got myself a sweet new job living on an ostrich farm. Seems the lady needed a helper."

"That was fast. Marcus's charm at work? Or do Centurion's unique games spoil her taste for anyone else?"

Mark's hand gripped the phone. "Nothing's happening between them," he said tightly. *At least, nothing sexual.* Of that he was sure. She kissed too innocently to be Centurion's playmate.

"If you say," came the passionless response. "Any trouble?"

"None." He neglected to mention the jealous bird and the damaged leg. He'd give Armond no excuse to bail out; Agent Marceaux was reluctant enough as it was.

"Why don't I believe that?" came the laconic response.

Mark chuckled. He and Armond understood each other too well.

They went back a long ways—to a rough town whose name had blurred with time, just one in a long line of cities housing a one-room apartment. Even young, Armond had had a sense of justice as strong as Mark's depth of charm. Somehow, they'd developed first a grudging respect, then a genuine friendship. They'd raised a little hell, protected each other's backs, and looked to the future. Until Mark and his father had to make a quick, midnight exit.

Their paths had crossed again six years ago, when Armond was with the New Orleans police.

Since then, Armond had moved from NOPD to some shadowy agency in D.C. When he'd discovered Mark on the trail of the stolen book, he'd agreed to let the magician continue alone only for two reasons. One, because Mark had a ready excuse for being here with the Mushroom Festival invitation and, two, because Centurion had someone in Armond's department in his pocket. Armond didn't know who was dirty and whom he could trust. Except Mark. So for now the investigation was unofficial.

Armond didn't care about the book; only another magician would recognize its worth. No, Armond cared about one thing, bringing Guy Centurion to justice.

A car whizzed by on the road, and Mark shifted deeper into the shadows.

"Remember, Mark, you're there just to look around," Armond warned.

"Of course," Mark answered soothingly, but Armond was immune to the persuasions of his voice, just like Joy.

"I mean it. You do anything to jeopardize my case, keep me from bringing down Centurion in court, and I'll flay your hide a strip at a time."

"I'd like to see you try," Mark retorted. "You play by the

rules; I don't. Besides, you don't have a case, pal. That's why you need me. I find out how the book's being moved out, and then you have a trail to follow back to him. Don't worry, the snake won't slither free this time."

The wind gusted, blowing a metal garbage can lid against the store with a sharp clang. The night-light bulb flickered out, no match for the vibrations, leaving him in darkness.

Metal clanging. Surrounded by darkness.

Without warning, the green metal siding beside him seemed to shift, to surround him, to block off the air. Sweat broke out at his nape, chilling him despite the lingering summer heat. A shiver ran down his back as ice water seeped into his lungs and tightened his chest.

Mark turned until he faced the open street instead of the wall, but the claustrophobic images of entombing metal and fetid garbage replaced the hot, sleeping, Louisiana town.

He gasped in a single breath, fighting back. The beast had almost beaten him then, but it sure as hell wouldn't now.

"Mark? You all right?" came the voice on the other end of the telephone. Concern broke Armond's normally unflappable attitude.

Again, at last, self-control won. "Yeah, I'm here. I'm okay," he answered, waiting for the dizziness to recede. "Just letting you know where I was. I won't be checking in for a while."

"I'd better hear from you within the week."

"I work alone."

"No, you don't, *mon ami*, you work with me. Centurion's moving something big, and Joy Taylor's a key part of it. I know that in my gut. I can't guarantee you the time."

"Three weeks, Armond. You owe me that."

"I'll do what I can."

Mark disconnected the phone, then leaned his back against the slick, warm siding, waiting for the dizziness to recede and his heart and breathing to return to normal.

Once he was sure he was in control, he dialed his booking agent, who was likely just starting the evening. "Clive, just wanted to tell you I'll be in Louisiana for six weeks."

He held the phone away from his ear while Clive sputtered and fumed. "Six weeks! You said three! Mark, Mark, you cannot disappear like this."

"I didn't disappear; I'm in Louisiana."

Clive gave a disparaging grunt. "What about this European tour we are setting up? We need daily contact. *Daily*."

"You can reach me here the same as in Vegas. By e-mail and phone." He rattled off the number in the caretaker's cottage Joy had assigned him.

"No, Mark, you simply must come back to civilization. I have several stages begging for you—"

"I'm working on an escape," Mark said softly. "The kind you said I had to have to make this European tour a success."

Clive stopped mid-rant. "A true escape? Chained in a bag, looks dangerous as hell?"

"Yes."

"You don't do those kind. You don't work bound."

"Didn't you say all great magicians had one?"

"Yes, but I didn't think you paid me any attention."

"I'm going after the Elements Escape."

Even over the phone lines, Mark heard Clive's inrush of breath. "That escape is only a legend. No one's ever seen it done or duplicated it."

"I will." The book that Centurion had stolen was the key.

It held the secrets the ancients used for the Elements Escape, the escape from water, earth, fire, and air. It held the secret to overcoming the claustrophobia that kept him from earning a place among the true greats of magic.

"All right. You sure you need six weeks for this?"

Mark laughed. "No, I need six weeks because I promised a lady I'd help her farm ostriches."

Still laughing, he hung up on Clive's outraged sputters.

Joy awoke with a start and bolted upright.

Where am I?

Her gaze swept the room, seeking an anchor. Her ears strained for a noise, anything familiar beyond the thumping of her heart and the sharp gasps of her breath.

Concealing shadows resolved into familiar sights and sounds. Her picture of the gleaning women was perched on the dresser top. The clothes she had removed before bed were piled on a chair. She heard the hum of air conditioning, a constant in southern Louisiana summers.

The ostrich farm. Louisiana. The country north of Lake Pontchartrain. Her bedroom.

Joy pushed her hair back, feeling the rush of adrenaline settle as orientation returned. She pulled up her knees and rested her cheek against them.

It had been some weeks since she'd woken up like this, and she'd thought the nightmare was finally banished. However, she'd thought that before—then they would move again and the nightmare returned.

Always it started with a dream she couldn't remember; she only knew she was alone and lost. Always it ended with her awake, panicky and unable to remember which house, which town, which state was her current home.

Joy rubbed a hand against her face, knowing from experience she wouldn't be able to get back to sleep right away. Instead, she rose, traded her nightgown for the discarded clothes, and headed to the kitchen to do what she always did—cook.

When Mark returned after making his phone call, he was surprised to see a light in the kitchen of the house. Who was up so late? He parked near the barn, next to the empty caretaker's cottage that Joy had allotted for his use. Instead of going inside, he walked past the ostrich pens back to the main house, stirring insects to buzzing. Hans lifted a sleepy head and gave Mark a baleful look.

"Sorry, old boy," Mark whispered. "Go back to sleep."

The bird tucked his head back under his wing, as the insect noise faded. Mark could see Joy standing at the stove, and he followed the window's slash of light to her. Something he didn't understand drew him to her. He wanted, for this small moment between days, to simply be with her.

Opening the unlocked door, he called out quietly, not wanting to startle her.

She glanced over her shoulder. "You're still up?"

"These are the hours I normally keep. Plus I'm still on Pacific time."

"Did I mention I feed the birds 'bout six? Just after sun up? As my new helper, you'll want to be there," she teased.

Mark gave a mock groan. "Six o'clock is not a decent hour for a man to have his pants on, darlin'." He turned a chair from the table and straddled it, folding his arms along the back. "So, why are you awake?"

"I woke up and couldn't get back to sleep. When that happens, I cook."

She was barefoot and dressed in wrinkled shorts and shirt. No bra, he noticed with interest. Her hair was pulled back in a ponytail and she wore no makeup. The simple attire might have reminded him of how she'd looked seven years ago. Instead, watching her sure movements, he was struck again with how she'd matured. There had still been a touch of the insecure child in her, in them both, when they'd parted. They'd both changed over the years, and he found he was looking forward to discovering this new Joy. Especially when she looked as delectable as whatever she was cooking smelled.

Yet, he wondered, how well did he really know her anymore?

"What are you cooking there, darlin'?"

"Trying out a new version of ostrich stew with some fresh carrots and basil." She sprinkled the herb into the pot, stirred it, and then spooned out a small amount to taste. He could almost see her chef's instincts cataloguing the flavors and smells. "That's good. A nice acid level." She turned off the heat, set the pot aside, and then leaned against the counter facing him. "It has to cool before I put it in the refrigerator for Hope and Nicole's dinner tomorrow—or rather, today. Meals are included in your job, so you're welcome to join them."

"Where will you be?"

"Working at a dinner Guy's giving at his home in New Orleans." She met him with a steady gaze, as if daring him to repeat his earlier accusations.

He didn't. "I've got some business in New Orleans, too. Mind if I take the night off, boss?"

"Go ahead." She picked up a bowl filled with what

84

looked like homemade potato chips, except that they were a variety of colors. "Try these. Tell me what you think."

"What are they?" he asked, biting down on a red one.

"Vegetable chips. Beets, sweet potatoes, parsnips."

He paused mid-bite. "I'm eating a beet? I hate beets."

"Nothing like those sour, mushy things they fed us in school lunches, is it?"

"Darlin', I always knew you had a talent, but if you can make a beet taste good, you're as much a magician as I am."

She grinned at him. "Good. If you like them, then maybe Hope will eat them. That child is dead set against vegetables. Would you like something to drink?"

"Just water." Mark shifted to sit beside the table, pleased that Joy seemed willing to spend these few peaceful moments together. There was something very sexy, and very satisfying, about being alone with Joy in a kitchen, late at night.

Joy poured two glasses of water and ice, squeezed in some lemon, then sat down beside him. "Where do you call home now?"

"Las Vegas. That's the mecca for magicians these days. I rent an apartment and a post office box there and spend some time at a workshop Copperfield has set up in the desert. Mostly I'm on the road, tourin', either with my own crew or as a part of another show."

"Don't you ever just want to light some place?"

He took a gulp of water and thought about it for a moment. "A magician can't be successful stayin' in one locale. We have to move around. If I get big enough, get a regular gig at a theater some place, maybe. But, to be honest, I like it on the road. It's free, exhilarating . . . open."

He stared off into space a moment, feeling the faint, rippling shudders of claustrophobia. "Open," he repeated softly, drawing his attention back to Joy.

"You always did hate being confined." She traced a random pattern through the sweat on her glass.

"Still do." He touched her on the cheek, bringing her gaze up. "Once you thought that way, too. Remember how we talked about going to Europe together? I'm going to do it. I'm negotiating a tour there, to start when I finish these dates in the States. Think of it, Joy. Europe."

For a moment, he thought—hoped—he saw the light of interest in her eyes, then it died. "It was never being on the road that appealed to me," she said.

Had she given up those dreams? He found it hard to believe. Mark exchanged a long glance with her, seeking to tease out her secrets, even as he closed her out of his.

A sharp gust of wind slammed against the window, rattling the glass with eerie ferocity. They jolted apart, the intimate mood shattered.

Mark got to his feet. "Guess I'd better get to bed if I'm going to face the evil Hans at sunrise."

Chapter Six

"No coriander!" shrieked Dagobert Pasternak, Guy Centurion's executive chef. "This salmon does not need coriander."

Joy's hand jerked up mid-sprinkle. She set down the coriander bottle with a thunk. "You told me you wanted ginger, pepper, and coriander."

Dagobert sniffed. "It takes a mere look and a single inhale of the odor of the fish to realize coriander is superfluous. Joy, you must learn, the mark that separates the great chef from the inexperienced *cook*, is that the chef knows when to stop. When the dish is perfection. Taste and see."

Joy took a tiny taste of the mixture and realized he was right, damn him. However if *she'd* suggested leaving out the coriander, he'd have relegated her to pots and pans.

Dagobert was a misogynistic bully, but he was a brilliant

chef, and he didn't tolerate less than perfection. She had learned a lot from him, even though the rare times he deigned to speak to her were to find fault. Loudly.

"And your pans are not hot enough to sear the fish." Dagobert cast a withering glance at the stove.

Now there he was wrong, letting his resentment that Guy had hired her without his input hold sway. The heat from the burners scorched her lungs as she drew in a strained breath. Sweat coated her back, and her tight braid stuck to her neck.

Nonetheless, Joy gritted her teeth and held onto her temper. In the kitchen, the chef, whether a gem to work with or a lump of coal like Dagobert, was in charge. You listened, you soaked up every bit of knowledge and technique you could, you got better. You didn't argue.

When I have my restaurant, I won't make the same mistakes.

"Come, you do this." Dagobert waved imperiously to another saucier, who gave her a sympathetic glance as he shifted operations. All of them had been a victim of Dagobert's wrath, although he saved the most scathing for Joy. "Joy will do the soup."

The soup was spinach and made with cream. *Cream.* From a cow. Joy stood over the kettle, stirring. The skin on her arms, where it was touched by the steam, prickled.

That allergy to anything bovine! It severely limited her options as a chef. Training in most restaurants was beyond her—she'd spend the time scratching hives or heaving. She was lucky that Guy Centurion had taken her on for his dinner parties. Guy refused to eat red meats, except her ostrich, and it was the only reason she was able to stay here.

Dagobert looked over her shoulder. "Does it need more nutmeg?"

Joy looked at the soup, drew in the scent of it. "No."

Dagobert lifted his brows. "You know that without tasting?"

Fist clenched around the spoon, she fought to tame a stomach starting backflips at the thought. She could cook with milk and cheese as long as she didn't eat it. "I can't taste milk—"

"And you aspire to be a chef? A chef must taste. Everything. How can you hope to develop the taste memories of a good chef if you do not taste?"

Joy gripped the handle of her wooden spoon so hard her knuckles ached. Dagobert was doing it deliberately, she knew, pointing out her shortcomings, but what he said was true.

"Here, let me," he said with disgust.

"No! I'll do it." She swallowed against the acid in her stomach, then reached for a clean spoon and tasted a drop of soup. "There's enough nutmeg."

Dagobert did his own tasting, then apparently mollified, nodded and left.

Joy made a face at his back and started ladling the soup, resisting the urge to scratch her arms. She called her aversion to anything having to do with cows an allergy, but it didn't act like a true allergy since the reaction depended upon how much she took or how long she was in contact with it.

She'd survive, but it wouldn't be a comfortable evening.

"Have you found the book?"

"Not yet. I'm working on it," Mark answered, settling

down into the French chair in Cybele Petrov's Magazine Street apartment.

Cybele, a tiny, caftan-clad, gray-haired package of straight-backed indignation, glared at Mark. "You need to find that book. It is yours. It's dangerous in the wrong hands."

"Dangerous?" Mark gave a snort of disbelief. "*The Discoverie of Legerdemain* is a sixteenth-century book that revealed the secrets of the ancient magicians in an effort to prove they weren't witches. It's legendary among magicians only because no known copies exist, thanks to James I's torching parties. That's all. It's valuable, not dangerous."

Cybele shook her head in stubborn denial. "That is the common belief; it is not the truth. The source of the secrets it contains go much deeper into the mists of time, some say to Hermes himself, the first of the great magicians."

"How do you know? You told me you could barely decipher it. You read just enough to know it contained the secret to the Elements Escape illusion, before Centurion stole it."

"Because I know these things and you do not." She gave a fatalistic shrug. "You do not believe in such things, despite all I taught you."

"You taught me magic tricks," Mark answered good-naturedly.

And intangibles like honesty and kindness and self-esteem.

Mark had met Cybele when he'd come to New Orleans after graduation. She'd rented him a room; he'd tried to con her out of the rent. Like Joy and Armond, she hadn't fallen for it, but she'd kept him on anyway. Gradually their relationship grew from one of business to one of friendship. He did work around the house and listened to her tales of Mother Russia, while she listened to him talk about Joy and encouraged his dreams.

When Centurion had set him up, Cybele had lied and given him an alibi. He owed Cybele a lot.

"You have put those tricks to good use, Mark. I saw on TV how you adapted the fire rings. It was good."

"Thank you." Her words glowed inside him. Cybele did not give praise lightly, and from her an "It was good" was precious.

Cybele poked him with a thin finger, the collection of silver bracelets on her arm clanking. "You did not need to tell everyone I originated it."

"A magician always credits his sources; it's ancient tradition. Are you sure you don't want to move to Vegas? Design my show?"

Cybele waved one arm. "Bah. I am comfortable here. I have my shop, my antiques, my magic tidbits. Why would I want to move to that place of neon? You should move here. Here is magic."

"We aren't talking about the same kind of magic."

"Only because you do not believe." She sighed. "But you will never believe, so I waste my breath. Now, what about the book?"

"Armond says—"

Cybele gave a sniff of irritation. Mark knew she didn't like police of any kind, not even Armond, which was why she'd asked for Mark's help. A remnant of her Russian heritage.

The sniff turned to coughing, the spasms doubling over her small frame. Immediately, Mark knelt by her side. "Cybele, what's wrong?" He patted her gently on the back, noticing how her bones seemed more fragile, protected only by skin, no fat or flesh. "What can I do?"

She shook her head, indicating she needed no help. Soon the coughing stopped, and she sat upright again. "It is nothing. I will be fine."

"You need to see a doctor."

She gave him an annoyed look. "I am old enough to make those decisions myself, Mark." She settled back into her chair with a sigh. "Yet, I am worried."

"About this book? Do you think Centurion will use it?" Mark didn't believe the book contained any dangerous secrets, but Cybele did, and that concern might be upsetting her health.

"He would not know how." Cybele's lip curled. "That one sees only external power, but not the true power from within. He stole the book for its material value and because he was angry that I would not sell it." Cybele gripped Mark's arm. "I know you think of it as a book of rarity. I know you go after it only because it contains the secret of the Elements Escape. But trust me, it must be in your hands. No other's."

The last of the dishes came out of the dishwasher. All of the guests and most of the staff had gone home, leaving only a skeleton crew to finish the cleanup with Dagobert and Joy. One thing she believed was that you never asked your staff to do anything you wouldn't do or didn't know how to do.

Joy put away the final crystal dessert plates and smiled. Finished. Another successful meal. Shifting her shoulders to work out the kinks, she glanced at her watch. Midnight. The witching hour.

Dagobert stood at the back door to the kitchen, his hand on the light switch. "Coming, Joy?"

"In a moment. I have to get my purse. I'll turn out the lights when I leave."

"Make sure you shut the door securely." The back door clicked shut as Dagobert left.

Then . . . silence. A silent kitchen, a kitchen with all things neat and sterile. Without food out, the only colors were stainless steel and white. A shiver ran down Joy's back as she wound her way to the door. For a place that, in use, met the most elemental of needs—hunger, thirst, the desire for community—it was strangely lifeless.

She turned out the lights, then stood, purse in hand, waiting for her eyes to adjust, the hairs on her nape standing alert. She rubbed her arms, still sensitive from the itchiness that had plagued her all evening after the milk.

The kitchen was in one wing of the U-shaped house, with the other wing holding Guy's office. Tonight, the office was lit, easy to see into from the shadows that hid her. She'd been in there a few times. His office was as neat and monochromatic as the kitchen, the only sign of color there a disturbing oil painting of red and purple slashes.

She liked red and purple, but she'd never liked that painting.

Joy saw Guy there, standing beside his desk. He held something, a book she realized when he turned the pages. The book must be old, the pages brittle, for he turned them with care. Then, closing the book, he bent down beside the desk and disappeared from view. When he stood, he was empty-handed. Guiltily realizing she was spying, she left.

As she walked down a rock-outlined path, that odd feeling of sterility, of silence followed her. The air was heavy until each breath became a tiny strain and sounds were deadened in the thick atmosphere.

The grounds were perfection, each bush precisely trimmed, each sweet-scented flower planted for optimum display. The house, too, was beautiful, but it was a beauty that defied easy comfort. Personally, she preferred clutter and crumbs to sweep up.

Footsteps crunched behind her. Joy's heart jolted against her ribs, and her achy stomach clenched. Spinning around, she called, "Dagobert? Guy?"

The following deep silence was drowned out by the thump of her blood in her ears.

"It's me," came the soft response at last. Guy Centurion emerged from the shadows. "I saw you leaving and thought I would walk you to your car."

"Thanks. You didn't need to." Her heart slowed, but refused to return to normal rhythm. Sweat dotted her neck.

"But I wanted to." The tips of his fingers touched her arm, guiding her into a path. His fingers were smooth and cold, like marble. His hands were so different from Mark's.

Though Guy was in his forties, he was strongly built and very fit. The perfect cut of his custom suit emphasized the breadth of his shoulders. Only a hint of iron showed at the temples of his dark hair.

Guy Centurion was a powerful man, in both body and influence. She should have been reassured, yet a snake of apprehension slid across her. *A powerful man.*

He's got his fingers in a lot of pies, and some of them are mighty muddy.

No, she wouldn't let Mark's innuendos color her judgments. Guy had always been her friend. "I hope you're planning on coming to our barbeque next Sunday."

"I wouldn't miss it. What would you like me to have Dagobert prepare?"

"Whatever you want. We're providing the meat, and the rest is potluck. But you're welcome, dish in hand or no."

"I'm never empty-handed for a friend. How many is Nicole inviting?"

"She keeps saying 'a few friends,' but can't remember the exact number."

Guy laughed. "Then you should prepare for half the parish. Do you have enough meat?"

"We've had a bumper crop of birds. I'm sending some to slaughter next week and another group should be ready before the Mushroom Festival, so I'll get plenty of meat back. By the way, that slaughterhouse you recommended has been a godsend. The cheapest by far, and they've given good service. Thanks."

He waved a hand. "Don't mention it."

"Now that the ostriches are more settled, I'm thinking of turning some of the business over to Nicole."

"And what will you do? Start that restaurant you've talked about? Let me talk to my banker; I've been thinking of investing in another establishment."

"Thanks, but I'm not ready for that, yet. Let me make sure Nicole can handle the ostriches first and talk to Seth about the building."

"As you wish. Just remember, I'm here if you need me."

They had reached the street. Joy tilted her head to look at him. "Why are you so nice to me?"

"Because I value your talents." He smiled at her. "And your ostriches. Now, how about the Chefs' Charity Night? Who haven't you heard back from?"

She filled him in on the details, including the chefs who had yet to respond.

"I'll make a few calls this week. They'll be there, I'm

sure. I heard we have a couple of new attractions at the Mushroom Festival, compliments of Earl."

Absently, she scratched the lingering itchiness on her neck. "For once, Earl had a good idea. A magician on Friday, fireworks on Sunday. Both men are in town, if you'd like to meet them."

"I would. Perhaps we could make a foursome for golf. I heard the magician is staying with you."

She should have known the gossip would reach Guy in no time flat. "He's using my barn to perfect a few illusions." Joy scratched again.

Guy leaned away and looked at her neck. "Are you ill?" His voice held a faint repulsion.

"What? Oh, no, not sick." Joy's hand fluttered back to her side. "My allergy. I tasted some of the soup to season it. It had cream, and I didn't take my Benadryl afterward. The drug makes me drowsy."

Guy's eyes narrowed. "Did Dagobert insist you taste the soup?"

"I did it on my own. I can't learn if I don't taste." She suspected he knew about Dagobert's antipathy to her, but if he did, it had never come from her. She grinned at him. "After that sacrifice, did you like the seasoning?"

"It was superb." Guy traced a scratch line on her neck, his fingers cold despite the heated night. "You must take better care of yourself, my dear. We would not want to lose such a talent."

Joy swallowed against the cold closing her throat. It was the first time Guy had touched her in any way that could be deemed more intimate than friendship or looked at her with more than the casual eye of a mentor.

She gave herself a mental shake. She was a sorry case,

imagining advances that didn't exist, from a man who had been nothing but kind to her.

"You have a long drive tonight," Guy continued, "and it's dangerous for a woman alone. Would you like to stay the night? My housekeeper keeps rooms ready for guests."

Mark slipped through the lush darkness of Guy Centurion's garden, noiseless and invisible. The hubbub of the dinner party and the activity of the guests had covered his actions, as he'd expected.

Unfortunately, the house was too big for a thorough search in the limited time he'd had, and he hadn't found the book.

Voices on the street, just on the other side of the wall, filtered through the dense shrubbery. Mark froze. Joy?

"We would not want to lose such a talent."

Dizziness clamped Mark's forehead, and his breath caught. That fast, Guy Centurion's voice sent him back. Back six years. Back to the smell of rotting garbage and the fetters of claustrophobic blackness.

"Would you like to stay the night?"

Centurion's loaded question broke through the panic. Fury, scalding as molten gold, swept through Mark, bringing him out of the nightmare. *Guest room*? Not bloody likely. He shook off the tightness in his chest, welcoming the anger that replaced it. Listening for Joy's answer, he slowed and deepened his shallow breathing until it returned to his control.

Say no, Joy.

Guy's offer was tempting, Joy admitted. This late, she wasn't looking forward to the two-hour drive across the lake. Yet she had a lot to do at home, and some remnant of unease made her hesitant. The wind rustled through the trees, as though in warning. She even thought she caught a faint whiff of Mark's masculine soap.

"I'll be fine. Thanks anyway."

Guy inclined his head in good-natured acceptance. "Until Sunday."

He saw her into her car, then left. As Joy drove away, she glanced in her rearview mirror, and a flash of movement at the wall caught her eye. Leafy tree limbs covered the streetlights, making the road murky, and when she looked again, she saw nothing.

Must have been the wind.

Half an hour later, the fury no longer burned along Mark's veins or deep in his gut. He drove smoothly, following Joy home along the nearly empty causeway.

Would you like to stay the night?

If Joy hadn't refused, he'd have hauled her pretty butt into his truck and peeled rubber getting her away from Centurion, and damn the consequences. That wasn't, however, how he'd planned on meeting up with Centurion again.

That was what came from getting involved, from making ties to people. It made you change plans; it cut your freedom.

Mark rolled his window all the way down, suddenly finding the closeness of the cab confining, despite the air conditioning.

The damn claustrophobia. It had plagued him since childhood, since his daddy decided hours in a closet made

98

a good punishment, but the worst episode had been six years ago.

Six years. Tonight had brought it all back. For one moment, Mark did what he had vowed never to do; he revisited the past.

He'd left Joy after graduation and come to New Orleans to establish himself, to make both name and fortune, enough to support them both. Jobs were scarce for someone with only a high school diploma, but he'd managed, especially with the income from his street performances of magic. Not enough for two, though, and occasionally he'd fallen back on some of the "life skills" his father had taught him, talents he hoped Joy never found out he had, like picking pockets and conning people. It wasn't a period of his life that gave him pride.

It had cost him Joy.

When Centurion had seen one of the street shows and offered Mark a performing job, he'd thought he was set, that maybe he'd finally have something to offer Joy.

He'd been nineteen in years, three times that in experiences, yet, still such a fool.

He soon discovered the job involved more than performing for the patrons at various Centurion-sponsored restaurants. He was expected to fulfill a variety of other, less savory roles, to cross the line Mark had sworn never to cross. In his questionable past, he'd never physically hurt anyone, never used violence in his cons, never got into the seamy crimes like extortion.

Of course, the new order hadn't come from Centurion directly, so nothing could be traced back to him. Yet Mark had known who was pulling the puppet's strings. He'd been furious, so much so that he'd confronted Centurion and hadn't bothered to refuse with his usual subtlety.

In retaliation, Centurion had planted evidence implicating Mark in an assault and robbery, and Armond had arrested him. The only thing that kept him from serving time was Cybele giving him an unshakable alibi.

She'd lied. He hadn't been with her, but he hadn't done the crime either. He'd been walking the streets, thinking.

When he was released, he'd already missed his date with Joy. Her graduation. He'd promised to be there, and he'd missed it.

Then Centurion's muscle met him at the jail exit. The muscle worked him over, worked him over good, and left him in a Dumpster. The clang of the lowering lid had been the last thing he'd heard before passing out, and the stifling, reeking darkness was the first thing he'd sensed when he awoke.

Not a good awakening for a claustrophobic.

He had no memories of how he got out, only memories of gasping for breath, inhaling the stink of garbage, panic, and utter disgust at himself.

He hadn't gone to the police. Like Cybele, his upbringing hadn't left him with a real trust in authorities. There was no proof against Centurion, either in the setup or the beating. Besides, his word wasn't exactly golden with the police, and he'd been a sorry sight when he'd emerged, trembling and hyperventilating.

Revenge had always seemed a waste of energy, and Guy Centurion had enough power that going after him would have been stupid. Mark had been called a lot of names in his life, but stupid wasn't one of them. He'd chalked it up to experience and vowed never to look back.

He'd learned one thing, though. He couldn't play in the muddy fringes of the law and expect never to get dirty. He'd been on the straight ever since.

Until tonight, that is.

Until Centurion—and Joy—had prompted him to return.

Mark's truck left the straight, twenty-six mile stretch of causeway. Entering the North Shore traffic brought him out of his unpleasant past.

Never look back, he vowed. Never get tied down.

He leaned his arm on the door. The night wind blew sticky hot through his open window, but he didn't close it.

Guy Centurion once again retrieved the book, so old its yellow pages crackled. He couldn't explain why he had broken a strict rule never to personally touch the goods he supplied. Perhaps because he had seen the book before taking it or perhaps because its age necessitated a delicacy of handling.

For this book was quite valuable, he'd discovered.

He'd put feelers out to his network of select buyers—buyers who cared nothing about how he obtained their desires, but who sought only to possess the precious and rare—and the response had been exceedingly gratifying.

No wonder the old bitch had refused to sell it to him.

That alone had piqued him enough to take it from her.

He ran a hand along the scene inset upon the tooled leather. It was one of the things that had drawn his eye to the book.

The scene was taken from one of the stories of myth. He had always enjoyed mythology, even as a very young child. Some said it was an unnatural fascination in one so young, but as a child he'd had many unnatural fascinations.

He'd thrived on the episodes of gore and violence that littered the tales.

Guy ran a finger over the cow in the scene. This story had always fascinated him for it contained bloody death.

It depicted Io, in the form of a heifer, with Hermes sitting beside her on a rock. Hermes was strumming his lute, the skill of the artist so great Guy could almost hear the tune, and lulling to sleep the heifer's guardian, Argus of the hundred eyes. Behind Hermes was hidden a sword. As soon as the last eye closed, the sword would claim Argus.

Guy had always taken the cautionary subtext to heart.

Never let himself be lulled into complacency.

Never let down his guard with anyone.

Twin mottos that served him well.

He opened the book and turned a page, but the writing in it did not interest him in the least. It was in English but in the incomprehensible words of the early tongue, and the elaborate script had no value or place in a world run by the typed words of computer screens. He closed the book and put it away.

In a matter of days, it would be sold and gone.

There were more immediate problems. The shipment of gems was his biggest deal yet, and it represented an interesting expansion from his usual acquisitions. He'd have to be extra vigilant.

Joy presented another problem. He did not want her tied up with her own restaurant. She needed a seductive alternative.

Abruptly, he punched in Dagobert Pasternak's number, uncaring whether the chef might be asleep or not.

"You created an excellent meal tonight, Dagobert," he

said, not bothering to identify himself at the chef's mumbled greeting. He didn't need to.

"Thank you, sir."

"I was particularly fond of the mandarin orange soufflé. Your skill with soufflé is unmatched," he said truthfully, fingering an onyx devil mask he kept on his desk.

"I think my bittersweet chocolate soufflé is especially effective, as well."

The preening was evident, but Guy ignored it. "Would you be interested in the executive chef position at Jade?"

This was a carrot Dagobert would be unable to resist. Jade was a restaurant, yes, but a very exclusive, very exotic one. Jade, in California, and Voisin, in New Orleans, were the two plums in his collection of restaurants.

"Jade," breathed Dagobert. "Executive chef?"

"Executive chef. You shall have free rein."

That wasn't true, of course. No one in his organization was ever free, and Dagobert would discover that soon enough.

"You will have to take over next week."

"One week? But—"

"Next week, or I find someone else."

As expected, Dagobert suddenly found himself able to transplant very quickly to California. "I have some ideas about who you could hire in my place."

"I've already selected your replacement. Joy Taylor."

Dagobert made an annoyed squeal. "Joy Taylor? Sir, I don't think—"

"You are only paid to think in the kitchen."

"Is she suitable? Rumor has it she was doing a hot and heavy number at the side of the road with some guy."

Those rumors again. Guy's finger slipped, and the sharp teeth of the mask pierced his flesh. A dark line of scarlet welled out. He let it seep in a cleansing flow.

"Her personal life is of no concern to me. Nor to you. I will tell my man in California to contact you about housing until you get settled."

Guy didn't bother to listen to Dagobert's effusive thank-yous. He simply hung up.

Carefully he blotted the blood on his finger, dabbed on antiseptic, then wrapped a bandage around the cut. He scowled at the imperfection.

His plans were proceeding apace and his vast network of informants assured him there were no leaks, no suspicions.

But he had learned never to close that last eye.

No one would interfere with his plans for Joy, not Seth Beaumont, not this magician staying with her, not even the lady herself. Joy had proved to be elusively independent. It was time to draw the bonds tighter.

When he had met her two years ago, he had considered it an omen. One woman with so many benefits to share. Joy Taylor was perfect—fresh, eager, innocent, a talented chef, an attractive woman with a business that shipped all over the country, including large crates of temperamental birds.

He reached down, stroked his groin and thought about how he would employ Joy Taylor. She had so many uses to him, and he intended to avail himself of them all.

Chapter Seven

Gretna never minded when Mark took one of her eggs, the fickle bird. Collecting the eggs had become easier than pouring goat's milk.

Joy whipped her wooden spoon through her sautéing pepper strips, then added a pinch of rosemary from her herb garden.

In the five days Mark had been here, he had the birds calmer than she'd ever seen them. During breeding that was an accomplishment . . . which irritated her even more.

Freyja, one of their two mousers, pranced into the room, tail high, then wound about Joy's legs, begging to be let out.

"In a moment, Freyja. Mark's lunch needs a few more seconds."

She'd agreed to room and board for Mark, which meant meals, but today he said he was too busy and he'd fix something later after his workout. Which meant he wouldn't eat.

"Mark works hard," Joy told Freyja. "He deserves a good meal."

Ever since that first night in the kitchen, when she'd admitted how dangerous Mark still was to her peace of mind, she'd kept the contact between them light and, when he came to the house, buffered by Nicole and Hope.

Hadn't helped one little bit.

The cat meowed and butted against Joy's legs.

"Yeah, I know. It didn't take me but one kiss to realize, despite everything, I've still got feelings for Mark Hennessy," she told the cat. "They've been there all along, ignored but quietly sitting between me and any other man."

Freyja stalked to the door.

"Now that Mark's returned, I can't go on ignoring them. I have to do something. But what?" There must be something to relieve her of this fascination, this yearning desire, this pleasure in his company that seemed an indelible part of her.

Freyja, unfortunately, didn't have any answers. Joy set the pan aside and let the cat out, wishing she could let Mark out of her heart as easily.

Hoping proximity would be an antidote to romanticized memory, she had allowed him to stay. Instead, he'd invaded her dreams and the uncensored visions that came on the edges of sleep. And erotic visions they were. Her cheeks flushed at the remembrance of a magic touch and a searing kiss, fashioned from her imagination and her past.

"Proximity," she muttered, "only made things worse." She hadn't had a good night's sleep in five days. Joy traded the spoon for a chopping knife and onions. There was nothing like dicing onions for working out frustrations.

"What did the poor onions do that was so bad?"

Startled, Joy whirled around, knife in hand.

Hope, her twelve-year-old sister, stood in the doorway. She flung her hands up. "Hey, it was a simple question."

"The poor onions are a mere substitute." Joy lowered the knife, then returned to the onions, albeit less vehemently.

"So, who're you really sore at? Not me, I hope." Hope nabbed a strip of spiced ostrich Joy had cooked earlier.

"Myself, mostly." Joy gave her a tiny slap on the wrist. "Wash your hands first."

"You sound like my mother."

"No, I don't. Nicole never told you that."

"True. I'm hungry. What are you cooking?" Hope looked over Joy's shoulder. "Yuck, vegetables."

Joy slid the peppers from the pan and replaced them with the mangled onions. "Have a chip then."

While the onions softened, Joy leaned against the counter. Hope straddled childhood and adolescence, and Joy was never sure whether she was dealing with the twelve-going-on-thirty-year-old or the twelve-reverting-to-five-year-old. Whichever, Hope was growing too fast for comfort. Today, she wore biker shorts, a "Warrior Princess" T-shirt, bright blue fingernail polish, and . . . red eye shadow?

"Brody asked me to go to the movies tomorrow," Hope said casually, poking through the bowl of chips.

"Who else is going?"

"Just Brody and me."

Joy rubbed the bridge over her nose. Twelve-going-on-thirty. Did the family curse start this early? "No, Hope. Brody's three years older than you."

"P-l-e-e-a-s-e."

"You know you're only allowed to go out in groups or with a girlfriend."

"But that's *boring*. My whole life is boring. This town is boring. There's no excitement. Nothing happens."

"How much excitement do you need at twelve?" At times like this she wished Nicole showed some sense of motherly concern. Instead discipline was left to Joy, and, though she tried, she feared it wasn't enough.

"Yeah, like you would know? *Your* life is boring. You're like this doormat."

That hurt. Joy held onto her temper by a thread. She was the adult; she wouldn't let the child get to her.

Hope nodded toward the pan. "Your onions are burning."

Joy swore and turned back to her pan. She stirred the onions, then gave them a critical look, glad for the temporary change of subject. Not too far gone, the slight scorch would go well with the peppers. She piled them together, then set the plate on her warmer. "Do you really think I'm a doormat?" she asked, smarting from Hope's assessment.

Hope gave a snort. "All you do is cook for people, take care of people. You've got no ambitions."

No ambitions. A doormat. The spoon clattered to the counter. Refusing to look at her sister, Joy began pulling out flour, salt, sugar, yeast.

"I swear, Hope, one day that mouth of yours is going to be trouble. I love to cook, yeah. What's wrong with that? I like doing things for people. Is that a crime or something?"

Stress, that was why Hope riled her so. Joy crumbled the yeast into warm water. Stress from the festival and chefs' charity, from worry about finances and family, from resurrected dreams that had no place in her life.

"What are you doing?" Hope asked tentatively, roused enough from youthful self-absorption to realize she'd said too much.

"Making bread. There's nothing like pounding on a mound of bread dough for working out stress." Joy dropped flour into the bowl, heedless of the puffs that drifted to the counter. She shook in salt, threw in sugar.

"Don't you measure?"

"Not today. You ought to try it some time. Get the soy milk and two eggs, will you?"

Hope handed them to her, then drew a finger through the spilled flour. "I'm sorry about what I said. About the doormat thing. You aren't really."

Joy supposed that was the best she'd get today. She paused in her bread making to kiss her sister on the top of the head, feeling her heart give a little squeeze at how much she loved Hope, how much she wanted a good life and a bright future for her sister. "Thanks."

"So can I go with Brody?"

Joy sighed. "No. Hope, you'll have lots of time for single dates. Don't grow up so fast. Why don't you call Eliza?"

"That is so *patronizing*." Hope flounced from the room.

The truce was over. Joy stared at the empty doorway. "Well, you handled that real well," she muttered to herself.

Joy finished mixing and kneading the bread, then set it to rise. She filled two pita pockets with the peppers, onions, and spiced ostrich meat. She added some tofu, a sprig of parsley, then packed them in a basket with apples and cookies and poured a thermos of sweetened iced tea. Carrying the lunch out to the ostrich pens, she looked for Mark.

She found him in the loft of the barn, the one she'd okayed for him to use for practice—as long as there was no fire. Pausing just inside the door, allowing her eyes to adjust to the shadows, she watched him, as she had once watched from the back of a darkened theater.

There were no props, no pretty assistants, no dramatic costume, no music, no smoke this time. Yet, the magician still held her rapt.

Mark stood before a full-length mirror, watching the sleight of hand. He wore faded jeans, slung low on his hips. His dusty T-shirt hung over the edge of the loft, and his feet were bare. Silk scarves were draped around his neck, and in each hand he held a dagger.

His movements were part dance, part battle, part illusion, all compelling.

The daggers disappeared, reappeared, changed from gold to silver, went through an arm or a scarf, yet silk and body remained intact. The sunlight coming through the smudged windows was faded, but as a dagger passed through the beams, the hilt glittered. He was man against an invisible enemy, performing a duel both deadly and beautiful.

He crooned to himself as he worked, low words she couldn't distinguish. Perhaps practicing the patter he would use or perhaps reiterating the moves he wanted to make or perhaps humming the music that would accompany him.

As she watched, Joy's breath caught in her lungs, and her skin tightened with a rush of blood. She had said no flames, but she hadn't counted on the fire burning inside her.

His back was to her; a sheen of sweat coated the tanned skin between his shoulder blades. The muscles in his back rippled with grace and power. Reflected in the mirror, she saw his bare chest with the dusting of dark hair that covered his pectorals, then tapered to a line that disappeared beneath the waistband of his jeans. It was a man's chest, not the smooth chest of the boy she'd once known so intimately, yet never really knew at all.

She also saw his face reflected there. Intent, dark, a stranger.

Only twice during the routine did she spot how he created an illusion, and apparently Mark did, too, for he stopped and repeated the action until he had it flawless. Once she noticed his injured leg broke the smooth flow. Other times, he must have seen mistakes she'd missed for he repeated what seemed to her perfect moves.

Mark was different from the boy she had once known, she acknowledged. If she hadn't accepted it before, she did now. During the past days she'd seen how hard he worked, both with the ostriches and with the magic. As a seventeen-year-old, he had had ambitions, had that same confidence, but there had been an undercurrent of entitlement. The boy thought that success would be his because he deserved it.

The man expected no gifts. Success would be his only if he earned it.

She wondered what had caused the change.

She wondered how well she truly knew him.

All she knew was, like it or not, his impact on her was as strong as ever.

Mark finished the routine, wiped himself off with a towel, and then donned his shirt and shoes.

"I brought you some lunch," she called up.

He spun around, and Joy got the impression he hadn't realized she was there. "Thanks," he answered.

In a moment he joined her. The barn was stuffy, and his shirt stuck to him. The daggers' hilts were tucked under his arm, and the silk scarves wilted about his neck.

"Magic looks like hard work," Joy commented.

"It demands a lot of control. Will you join me? At the cottage? That way I can wash up first, and I wanted to talk to you about a couple of things."

She hesitated a moment, then nodded.

On the way to the small cottage where she'd put Mark—a caretaker's cottage Nicole's husband termed it when he added it to the property—he laid a companionable hand on her shoulder. "How many of those hook-ups did you see?" he asked.

"Hook-ups?" Though the weather was as hot as a sauna, the heat and weight of his hand felt a natural part of her.

"Snags in the routine."

"Just two. Plus one from your leg. How is it feeling?"

"Leg's healing. Two? Damn, that's too many." He dropped his hand, then tilted his head to look at her. " 'Course, you always did have a good eye for details."

Inside the cottage, the air conditioning lowered the temperature a good fifteen degrees. Mark dropped the scarves and daggers on the table. "Be back faster than you can say 'give me a kiss.' " He slipped into one of the two small bedrooms, and in a moment, she heard water running in the bathroom.

To keep her fired up imagination from supplying Technicolor pictures of him in the shower, Joy wandered into the cubby with attached appliances—it hardly met her definition of a kitchen.

The phone rang, and, since Mark was still in the shower, she answered. It was Mark's agent, who, when she told him Mark was showering, said, "Clive Rooney, darling. Tell Mark we've added Paris to the tour. Three nights. His Pygmalion and Elements Escape had better be perfect. *Ciao.*"

Paris. The markets. French cooking. How could you savor all that in just three days?

Joy made a note of the call, then set out lunch. She found plates, but had to make do with paper napkins instead of cloth.

When all was ready, she sat down with a glass of tea. Curious, she picked up one of the daggers and hefted it. It was solid, heavy, and looked not only real, but ancient and deadly. Gold gilded the hilt and fiery rubies studded the grip.

Experimentally, she twirled the dagger like she'd seen Mark do. Or tried to, but the blade was weighted differently than her knives and she didn't have his skill. The blade slipped.

"Careful, the edge is as sharp as the ones in your kitchen." Mark emerged from the bedroom, dressed in clean Levis and a navy T-shirt. His feet were bare still, and his hair was damp from the shower. "And it's weighted for throwing, not chopping."

"So I see." A line of blood beaded from the cut along her palm. She rose and stuck her hand under the faucet. "I hope that wasn't one of those Italian Renaissance daggers. Didn't they coat their stilettos in poison?"

"Magic may look dangerous, but only an idiot would make it truly so. How's your hand?"

She held it for him to see. "It's a small cut; I've had worse. You don't consider magic with sharp knives dangerous?"

"Not if you know what you're doing. It's not like I aim

for the heart or the jugular." He patted her hand dry with a towel, then reached in the cupboard for a Band-Aid.

"How did you do that cutting of your hand in the routine without bleeding?"

He gave her a grin. "Magic."

Joy made a face at him. "Magicians never tell their secrets."

"That's right." He patted the bandage in place, then gave it a swift kiss. It was over before she had time to react, though the feel of his lips lingered. "I'm hungry, and that food looks mighty good."

Mark devoured the sandwich. While he ate, they discussed the length of the program she wanted, where his crew could stay, which pens of yearlings would be sent to slaughter, and how she planned to ship them out. All bits and pieces that could have been covered in five minutes. She recognized the invitation for the excuse it was, but the spell of watching him, listening to him, caused her to linger.

When he finished, Mark leaned back and gave her a grin. "That was a fine lunch. Thanks."

"You're welcome." She began to gather the remnants. "Now I've got to go—"

His hand shot out, closing around her arm. "Stay. Stay with me."

Shaking her head, she resisted the tug of his invitation. *Stay with me.* The coaxing in his voice found an answering echo inside her. How she wanted to, she admitted, but he was dangerous to her peace and her plans and Joy Taylor wasn't into danger these days.

"Please. I want your help with a couple of effects. You

saw those hook-ups in the barn. Maybe you can catch me on something."

"My help?" Joy eyed him warily. Mark at his most charming was often Mark at his most devious. "What do I have to do?"

"Why, nothing, darlin', but what I tell you to. I'm the magician; I do all the work. C'mon. I got that egg from Gretna this mornin'. You owe me one for that."

"She likes you," Joy said, settling down.

"Now, I'm pleased to hear that. Best thing in my life is to be told an eight-foot bird has the hots for me."

Joy burst out laughing. "Oh, all right. I'll help."

Mark got three mugs from the cupboard and wadded up three paper napkins into small balls. He set the mugs upside down in a line in front of her and placed a napkin atop each. "This here is called The Cups and Balls and it's just about the oldest trick in a magician's repertoire. Any conjurer worth his salt knows about two thousand variations, and I want to try out one I thought of during lunch. Now you watch closely, darlin'."

Lulled by the sound of his voice, Joy stared at the cups and the napkins, at his agile fingers and the working muscles and tendons in his hands.

"I want you to just forget all those law of physics they tried to teach us in school," he began. "Those laws don't hold when it's magic we're talkin' about. See, all I do is touch the solid cup and the ball slips through, slick as silk. Solid through solid. Touch here and here. See, the ball is gone. Gone right through the cup. When I turn it over there, it appears. Solid objects like this ball don't just disappear, now do they? No, so if I put the cup down and then lift it up, the ball's there . . . Whoops, no, it isn't, but if I set it back down, let's see it if comes back, here, or here. Now, you're looking so hard, you're burning me, darlin'. Are you going to tell me what you see?"

"I see those balls appear and disappear, though I can't figure out how."

"That's good, that's what's supposed to happen here. You're doing right well, sweetheart. So the cup is down, but the ball disappeared, right? Why don't you blow on that cup just a little, blow it a kiss, see if a magic kiss can bring back those lost balls. Blow on all three cups."

Grinning at his easy words, Joy blew on the cups. They had to be empty, he'd only turned them over a second ago and she'd watched closely the whole time.

"You know, this is a mighty tough trick, breaking all these laws of physics. I think the magician needs a little of that magic kiss, too." He tilted his head toward her in invitation.

Smiling, caught in the spell of his performance, Joy kissed him. His lips were gentle beneath hers, and the kiss a brief, sweet reward.

"I think that was just about the finest incentive a magician can have," he told her. "Now, let's see if we've found those pesky balls again."

One by one he turned over the cups, and Joy laughed and clapped. Instead of paper balls, beneath each cup was a pepper strip, one green, one yellow, one red.

"How— Never mind, I know you won't tell me."

He popped one of the peppers in his mouth. "Since you were such an able assistant, maybe you'd like to try something else."

"Sure."

He got up and a moment later came back with a thin rope. Joy looked at it askance. Mark raised his brows. "Remember, darlin', the one thing a magician's assistant needs is faith in the magician. That, and flexibility. Now sit at the edge of your seat and hold out your hands, arms about a foot apart."

Joy complied.

Mark circled the rope around her waist. As he bent over her, she could smell the clean soap scent of him, could feel the soft brush of his hair against her arm, and it set her insides quivering. Her fingers trembled. "Ah, Mark . . ."

"Hush, darlin', trust I know what I'm doing."

He wound the rope about her arms, her hands, knotting it as he went. When he sat back, her wrists and arms, though separated, were bound together and fastened to her waist. Joy gave an experimental tug. Although loose, the ropes held.

"Now what?" she asked.

"Those are real ropes, real knots, right? We want to make sure the audience is with us on this. Smile pretty for them."

"There is no audience."

"Why sure there is, sweetheart. Can't you just see them all there, envying you for doing magic. So you want to tell the audience what condition you're in?"

Joy laughed and inclined her head to the imaginary audience. "I'm tied up by a rope." She tugged again, playing to the invisible crowd. "And the knots are real."

"So you're bound securely? Ah, that's fine then." He ran his hands down her arms, sending slivers of excitement through her, then up on the ropes between her arms. "Now, what you do you say? What condition are you in?"

117

Joy gave a tug on the ropes, expecting that he'd freed her somehow, but to her surprise the knots held.

"Let's try that again." He repeated the stroke of his hands, until her blood throbbed in concert with the building pulse inside her.

When he stopped, lifting his hands only the merest inch from her skin, it took Joy a moment to realize he wanted her to free herself.

She tugged.

The rope held.

Mark frowned.

"C'mon, Mark. I'm still bound." She pulled again. "Mark!"

He gave her a curious look, his gaze sweeping from her hands to her lips. "Perhaps this will help," he said and grabbed the rope between her arms in his palm. Instead of urging her closer, or freeing her, he leaned over and kissed her.

For a gentle kiss, for a touch only at the lips, it was thorough. The throbbing, the pulsing, filled her, and a curl of excitement, like the curl of smoke from a fire, rose from deep inside her belly to set her aflame throughout. She pulled once on the confining ropes, then gave in to the magic.

"By all the gods, I've missed you, Joy." The kiss deepened, eliciting small moans of pleasure.

He shouldn't feel so good, smell so good, taste so good.

Only his groan of desire and the scrape of his chair as he shifted pulled her back from the simmering need.

"Let me go, Mark," she whispered, then repeated more strongly. "Let me go."

Slowly he lifted, and his hand dropped from the ropes. "You're free. Any time you want."

To Joy's surprise, when she tested the knots, the rope undid itself and fell to her feet.

Magic. He was magic. Quicksilver and shadows.

He aroused banked emotions, tempted her with risks she was afraid to take.

She sprang to her feet. "Dammit, Mark, don't play games with me. Don't do this to me again."

His hand lifted, then lowered without touching her as he clenched it into a fist. "I can't stop wanting you, but nothing more will happen. Not unless you ask."

"Don't be expecting it." Joy fled from the cottage into Louisiana heat and humidity.

The viscous air swallowed her, and the languid afternoon slowed her steps. Sounds—the whine of a bee, the booming cluck of the ostriches, a distant buzz saw—all so familiar, reminded her this was home. They drew her back into the lazy peace of a summer day.

Mark was different from the boy she'd loved—stronger, harder, more enigmatic, all things she could love in the man—yet some things had not changed.

He was a wanderer and always would be.

She was not.

He was excitement and passion.

She was quiet and peace.

Yet, he still made her laugh and feel and yearn for more. He made her believe anything was possible.

But the risk was just too great. For other stark, indelible, unchanging facts remained.

Once he'd left her without coming back, and he'd carved

out a large piece of her heart in the process. In a month, he'd be leaving again and never coming back. She knew that, and she had to protect the remains of her heart.

To expect something more, to hope and plan and then to have him leave again . . .

That was not a risk she was willing to take.

That rope effect *never* worked the first time.

Kissing Joy was a major mistake.

The Louisiana heat would have to shrink his brain to match that of the ostriches before he forgot those two facts again.

Yet, as Mark followed Joy outside to the ostrich pens, his gut told him neither was a fact he'd be likely to accept. A primitive need had flared inside him when Joy was caught in the ropes. He'd wanted to bind her to him with more than a magician's ties, wanted to claim her as part of him.

Seems the caveman instincts weren't so deeply buried, Mark thought, his lips lifting in rueful humor.

Trouble was, Joy was so nice to hold and to kiss. Kissing her was like coming back to the only place he'd ever called home.

He caught up to her. She glanced at him, but said nothing, only sped up her pace toward the pens. Mark swore a second time; he also hoped she'd start talking to him again.

"I'm not going to apologize for kissing you," he said.

She didn't answer.

"I enjoyed it."

She didn't answer.

"You can't deny you did, too. Not with those breathy little moans you made."

She stopped abruptly, and her hands fisted at her waist. "I do not moan."

Good. Her temper was winning out; she was talking to him. He grinned at her. "Sure you do. So do I. Prettiest music I ever heard."

With a snort of annoyance, she continued toward the pens. "Next time, lose the rope."

"Next time? It warms my heart to hear you're considering a next time, but I have to tell you darlin', kinky stuff with ropes isn't normally my style."

"What is your—?" She bit off the question. "Never mind. You're never getting me to agree to that rope trick again."

Mark laid a hand on her shoulder, stopping her. "I am sorry about that," he said without a trace of humor. "It wasn't supposed to happen like that."

"What wasn't?"

"The fact that I didn't undo the knots. For drama, I'm supposed to get it on the second pass, but it never seems to work quite that way. I didn't plan that, nor the kiss. The kiss was . . . serendipity, but I'll respect your wishes and not ask for either again."

"Trouble is, Mark, you rarely ask."

"True. It's a habit. My daddy taught me at an early age to take what you want in this world."

His daddy had taught him other hard lessons. Like asking for things just got you beat up. Like caring meant losing. Like people of his ilk weren't the settling-down kind. Like confinement—of any type—was a dark and fearful thing.

Mark's gut tightened, and his breath caught. He was suddenly glad they were outside, in the heat and brilliant sun, with no walls and nothing hemming him in.

"Your daddy wasn't much of a role model, if I recall."

"You recall that right."

Abruptly Joy stopped, and her blue gaze searched his face. "You're not your father," she said softly.

She always did see too much.

He hid gnawing anger. "Damn straight about that." His old man had never succeeded at anything. Every time a con was going sweet, every time they found a place to light, his daddy managed to sour it.

That was not going to happen to Matthew Mark Hennessy.

Annoyed with the bitter memories, Mark gave a devil-may-care laugh, knowing his attempts to hide failed miserably with Joy. "I haven't thought about the old man in years. Not a subject I plan on visitin' too often."

"Did you ever see him again? After he left?"

"Once, right before he died."

"I didn't know. I'm sorry."

"He was glad to go. Cancer was eatin' him." The old guy had died in prison, bitter and broken, but Mark didn't tell her that. Daddy's legacy was an empty, battered wallet, one change of clothes, a faded photograph of him and Mark's mother at their quickie Vegas wedding, and some very bad memories.

Mark hefted up a bag of feed. "How 'bout I stack these, then I'll help you move the eggs from the incubator to the hatcher."

"Sounds like a plan."

Both agreed on the work, yet neither one moved.

He could see the pulse fluttering in her throat and he wanted to reach out, to touch her and feel the heat stealing across his fingers, but he didn't. New promises made, and old promises long broken, kept him still. He'd leave it to her to make the next move. If any.

Joy cleared her throat, her gaze still tangled with his. She took a step forward and . . .

A whirlwind of sand blasted from the ostrich pens. It swirled around him, the grains a stinging veil.

Coughing, choking, eyes watering from the grit, Mark stumbled backward, away from Joy. Another whoosh of wind and the sand followed him.

Was he cursed? It seemed every time he was alone with Joy something separated them.

"Hello, Joy." A man's voice called.

Mark gritted his teeth. Jupiter! Again!

He turned to see Zeke Jupiter striding out of the house, with Seth Beaumont at his side.

Jupiter was peskier than a horsefly. When it wasn't a natural disaster separating Mark and Joy during these rare moments of peace and privacy, it was Zeke Jupiter.

Even a skeptic had to start wondering about curses.

Always Jupiter had some excuse. He wanted lessons in how to make a roux; he wanted to discuss the fireworks display. But Mark wasn't buying the bull the man was selling.

Jupiter had reached their side. "Oh, hello, Mark. Didn't see you there. A bit gritty aren't you?" He brushed sand off Mark's shoulder, then nudged Seth.

Seth cleared his throat. "Joy, could you spare some mint from your herb garden?"

"Sure. What do you need it for?"

"Seth is making my recipe for ambrosia," Jupiter answered. "It's quite unique."

"*Seth*? *Cooking*? Seth, you never cook." The skepticism on Joy's face was plain to see.

"Perhaps we can entice you to join us for the afternoon," urged Jupiter. "All of us in the kitchen."

Mark's teeth ground, scraping across the sand that had blown into his mouth. He wanted to step in, to refuse for her, to keep her by *his* side, but he had absolutely no right, and Joy would flay him alive for even thinking about it.

"Oh, thanks, but I'm swamped with work," she answered, to Mark's relief. She looked back at Seth. "You're *cooking*?"

Seth gave an annoyed huff. "No. Zeke had this crazy notion that because you loved cooking so much, I should learn to do it. Why should I, when you'd do it all when we marry? He said you couldn't resist this ambrosia thing." He scowled at Jupiter. "I've listened to your ill-conceived and impractical advice on women all week, but no more. I told you this was a bad idea."

"It was a good idea," muttered Jupiter. "Just bad material."

Seth shoved his hands into his pockets. "Joy, when you're ready to marry me and let me take care of you, you know where to find me." He turned to Jupiter. "I've shown you every property for sale in the area. Twice. When you're ready to do business, you also know where to find me." He pivoted and stalked back to the house.

Stunned, Mark, Joy, and Jupiter stared at his retreating back as he got in the Cadillac and left.

"I already told him 'no,' " Joy said at last.

She'd refused Seth? Mark stared at her. Damn, but the woman was confusing.

"Must be the heat," said Jupiter. "He's a good man. I believe I'll make an offer on the Collingswood property for my new factory, but it looks like I'll need a ride back. If I could trouble you, my dear?"

"I'll take you," Mark offered, dropping the bag of feed.

"I need you to move the eggs, Mark." Joy dusted her

hands on her shorts. "I'll take Zeke, then run a few errands. Do you still want the mint, Zeke?"

"Yes, I think I do."

Jupiter guided Joy away with a hand at the small of her back, as Mark watched in impotent frustration. Seth Beaumont might be out of the picture, but Zeke Jupiter was still a pest.

The interloper glanced back just once, to give Mark a faint, "Got you, sucker" smile.

The sand whirled, and Mark slitted his eyes against the irritating flurry. When it died, Joy and her companion had disappeared into the house. Hans loped to the fence and nipped him with a toothless beak.

Mark petted the long feathered neck. "You know, Hans, old buddy, I thought I could come here, get that book, erase some old debts to Armond and Cybele, and walk away without looking back. Life has a way of hooking-up the best illusions, doesn't it?"

Hans merely butted the bag of feed.

Mark laughed aloud. Joy must have melted his brain. Hell, now she had him talking to a damn ostrich.

Cursed, definitely cursed.

Chapter Eight

Suppressing a pang of guilt, Mark sat in Joy's desk chair and paged through her shipment files. While she was out with Jupiter, he'd decided to search her office.

The extent of her operation surprised him. She shipped birds to slaughter and hides to the tannery. She sent meat all over the country and even to some overseas ports. Her feathers were used in industries that varied from computers to carnival costumes. She had an advertising budget, and he'd seen how she promoted the meat by developing a variety of recipes.

He didn't think all this had been in place when she'd taken over, yet Joy didn't have that much business training. Just how much had Guy Centurion helped her?

Mark glanced over her financial records. She was in the black, but there were no rainy day funds. She must have been operating close to the line the past two years. And this from a woman who claimed to hate risks?

As he paged through her correspondence, one letter caught his interest. He already knew about the crop of yearlings being sent to slaughter tomorrow. Nothing unusual in that, but what he hadn't known was that she'd switched to a different slaughterhouse/shipping company this year. Why the switch?

The company was located in southern California. According to Armond's theories, Centurion sent a lot of his stolen goods through California, for sale there or export.

Unable to rid himself of the niggling sense that something was rotten here, Mark looked through the records and discovered the reason for the switch. The shipping charges were considerably less and the slaughterhouse kept a lower percentage of her meat as payment. The difference in price between this slaughterhouse and the one she'd been using was such that she'd have been a fool not to switch.

Make him an offer he can't refuse. The line was suddenly no longer simply a movie cliche, but all too real and ominous.

A cold knot in his gut, Mark leaned back and steepled his fingers, thinking. He'd ask Armond to verify possible connections between Centurion and the slaughterhouse. Yet despite Armond's suspicions, he couldn't picture Joy in the role of willing accomplice. This interlude with her had shown some changes in her, true, changes he liked, but most things were the same. She was a caretaker, not a taker. Beyond a well-stocked kitchen, her needs were basically simple, and she was willing to work hard for what she wanted. Most of all, her eyes still held that innocent, soul-deep honesty.

An honesty that revealed, try as she would to fight it, the bonds that still existed between them.

He had been a fool to think he could walk in, then walk out like he had done before. Joy had always tangled up his plans, his feelings. That was one of the reasons—the ultimate reason when he took away all the excuses—he'd delayed returning.

Mark rubbed a hand against his chest. Stick to the problem at hand. How was Centurion using her? That shipment of birds tomorrow was the obvious answer. He should tell Armond, let the Feds intercept it. Yet if her shipment was found to hold contraband, Joy would be implicated, not Centurion.

She'd be ruined, Hope and Nicole with her, and Centurion would go free.

The way to get Centurion, and the book, would be with Joy's cooperation.

If she were innocent.

If he could convince her of Centurion's guilt.

She was innocent, he'd bet his life on that, but convincing her to doubt a friend would be difficult. Joy was too trusting. It took something big, like promising to come back and never showing up, to raise her doubts.

He'd wait to bring in Armond. Tomorrow, he'd search the shipment, see what he could find, and hope that Centurion wasn't moving the book.

"Oh, Mark, there you are." Nicole flowed into the room. She wore her usual designer jeans and silky blouse. He'd never figured out how she always looked so cool and chic in the Southern heat. A paper fluttered in her hand.

Mark braced his hands on the desk, hurriedly readying excuses for his presence.

Apparently Nicole saw nothing amiss. "We're having a few friends over Sunday for a barbeque. I hope you're planning to come."

"I wouldn't miss it, Miz Valcour."

"Good. Do you know where Joy is?"

"Zeke Jupiter needed a ride into town."

"Zeke Jupiter, such a nice man. We've seen a lot of him these days. I really do find him attractive. Of course, he's not my Mr. Valcour. So responsible, he even made sure we could keep the farm running before he left. Just like Joy would do."

The paper fluttered from her hand as Nicole picked up a picture from the desk. The colored photograph showed her with a barrel-chested man about ten years her senior. She pointed to the man. "That's my Henry. He gave me . . . power of attorney, Joy called it, before he left. Wasn't that thoughtful? Although it was rather naughty of him to run off like that. Almost two years! But I know he'll be back. He's not like the others. After all, I'm still in love with him. Unlike my other husbands. They got so tiresome." She sighed and set the picture down, then picked up the paper. "I do hope Joy gets home soon and tells me whether I should sign this."

Mark had long given up trying to follow Nicole's ramblings. Instead, he focused on the points that were of most interest. "Power of attorney? You and Joy don't own the farm?"

Nicole shook her head and gave a tinkling laugh. "Oh, heavens, no. All of this—the house, the land, the ostriches—it's Valcour property. I own half, but Henry still owns the other half. He gave me that power of attorney thing for two years, and I let Joy take care of the details. Joy tells me what I need to sign. That's why I know he'll be back, even though Joy says he's left us."

"What happens after two years?"

Nicole wrinkled her nose. "Well, I get all the farm, but I'd rather have Henry. Joy, however, never believed he's coming back; she says it's a family curse."

"When is the two years over?"

"Two weeks." Distress pulled down the corners of Nicole's mouth for a moment; then she rebounded. "But I know Henry will be back. Now, can you tell me if I should sign this?" She thrust the paper at him.

It was a routine authorization for the property tax assessment to be added to the monthly mortgage payments. He gave a silent whistle. It looked like Valcour had left a powerful debt. No wonder Joy was in such a tight financial position.

"It's probably something you could sign," Mark answered, "but you've got time to wait and ask Joy. It's nothing urgent."

"That's what I'll do, then." She left the paper on the desk.

Mark pushed to his feet. "If you'll excuse me, I have to move the eggs to the hatcher."

"Would you like me to help?"

"It's kind of dusty." He ran a critical eye over her perfect makeup and immaculate clothes.

"Oh, pish, this will wash. Joy says I need to learn more about running the farm, that I'll have to do it when she starts her restaurant. So, if I go with you, you can tell me about eggs."

In spite of her flighty ways and rambling conversations,

he genuinely liked Nicole Valcour. She was also a wealth of information, given freely with guileless abandon.

"Sure, come on."

As Mark walked to the incubators, he considered Nicole's revelations.

One of the reasons he'd dismissed the notion of Joy as part of Centurion's schemes was that he couldn't see a good motive. Not for Joy. He'd assumed the property, the ostriches, belonged to her, or to her and Nicole. They didn't. They belonged, partially, to a man who had decided to walk out two years ago.

Joy had struggled to provide security for her family, but she must be keenly aware that she might lose everything if Valcour returned. Might she be creating a nest egg for her and her family?

No, that wasn't Joy. For one thing, she firmly believed Henry Valcour wasn't coming back.

He knew she must have struggled to overcome the debt Valcour had saddled her with and to create the home she'd longed for. If Centurion hid his true purposes, offered her some easy money simply for shutting her eyes, offered her a way out of the hole, might she not grab it with both hands?

That still didn't sound like Joy.

Most likely? She didn't have any idea what Centurion was up to. She'd take the obvious—business advice from a friend, a lower bid from a shipping company—and never see the dangerous strings attached.

Herding ostriches into a truck was worse than putting rabbits into a hat, Mark decided the next day. The truck was backed into the yard so the yearlings couldn't escape, but they simply wouldn't go into, or stay in, the truck.

A bird pecked at Mark's shoelace, while another pulled on the sleeve of his shirt. He shook them off, only to have others take their place.

"They think you might be tasty," Joy said with a laugh.

"These animals will eat anything."

"Just about."

Joy and Nicole were gathering a flock together, while Mark and Hope edged their bevy of birds toward the metal ramp that would funnel them into the truck. All they had to do was get one to go up. Where one bird went, the others would follow.

Up the birds went. Down came a bird already in the truck. Mark tried to shoo it back, but he was too late. The flock of birds milled, then shifted direction, following the errant leader back down.

Hope burst out laughing. "Mark, your arms are flapping just like Hans." Her laugh startled the ones remaining on the ramp; they came to a dead stop.

Mark gave her an affectionate tousle. "And you're making faces at them. Neither seems to be working."

Nicole and Joy were having a little better luck, but not much.

The truck driver leaned against the fender, smoking a cigarette and watching with a superior smirk. He didn't offer to help.

"How did you do this before?" Mark called to Joy.

"Sent smaller loads. This is our biggest shipment of birds. Mark and Nicole, why don't you get in the truck? Mark, you stand in the doorway. Talk to them."

"Talk to them?"

"Yeah, keep them calm. Your voice seems to mesmerize them."

"Can't you see it on the marquee?" said Hope with a giggle. "Marcus, Master Illusionist. Ostrich Crooner."

"Don't even suggest it to my agent," Mark growled with mock ferocity.

Joy ignored them both. "Nicole, there are gates to divide the truck into six pens. Hope and I will herd a group up. Mark will get them back to you and keep them there while you fasten a flock into a pen."

With the new system in place, they soon had the birds ready for shipment. Mark looked around the truck once again. He'd had a chance to search it thoroughly this morning, but found nothing suspicious, no books hidden in secret cubbyholes. Noting feed bags in the corner, he called out to Joy, "Do you want me to put out food and water?"

"No feed, but water, yes. Let me get the hose."

She handed him up the hose. As Mark filled the water troughs, his eye strayed to the bags of feed. "Do they get fed at all on the trip?" he asked.

"I feed 'em along the way. Keeps 'em healthy." The driver hoisted himself into the truck and ran a practiced eye around the trailer. He checked the latches on the pens and gave an unpleasant laugh. "Wouldn't want the birdbrains getting out. Might hurt themselves." He leaned an arm against the pen, waiting for Mark to finish, then followed Mark out. He latched the back, and, in a moment, the truck was gone.

Mark gritted his teeth. Much as he hated to admit it, this was Armond's territory now.

Nicole pulled at her sweaty shirt and wrinkled her nose. "I need a shower, and Hope, so do you."

"I took a shower last night."

"Eliza's mother is picking you up soon for the birthday party." Nicole brushed at Hope's shoulder. "Last night you did not have hay in your hair and ostrich down on your clothes. March, young lady."

"Hope might as well give in," Joy commented, watching the retreating figures. "Nicole doesn't get motherly too often, but when she does, she's immovable."

Mark cleared his throat. "Joy, would you help me with something?"

Her wary glance felt like the stab of a dagger. "Magic?"

"Yes." He held up one hand, forestalling her automatic refusal. "You don't have to do anything but spot for me. Help me if I get into trouble." He gave her a grin. "I'm the one who's going to be bound this time."

Joy's heart did its automatic fillip at his coaxing. "What are you doing?"

"I'm working up the Elements Escape for the European tour." He started toward the barn, and she automatically fell in place beside him.

"Elements Escape? What's that?"

"It's an escape told of in legend. The magician is bound and enclosed in a water-filled glass casket, then buried. Above ground, a fire is set and fanned to ferocious flames. The magician escapes, defying the power of all four elements. At least, that's the way it looks to the audience."

Joy jerked to a halt. "You're nuts."

"No, that's how the illusion works—"

"I mean you're nuts to try it. I've never seen anyone do an escape like that."

"It's never been done in modern times," he agreed cheerfully. "That's why I'm going to do it."

Joy stared at him, feeling her sweat evaporate to cold.

How could he put himself in danger like that? How could she watch, wondering if each moment would be his last? "You told me magic shouldn't be dangerous. What do you define as dangerous?"

A narrow line creased between his brows. "There is a small element of risk at first, but the rest . . ." He shrugged and resumed walking. "Trust me, I'll be in no danger. That's why I have to have the initial escape down perfect. And why I want you to spot me. In case I get into trouble before I've got all the kinks worked out."

If she didn't help, would he try it alone? He wouldn't be that foolish, would he? Yet, she could tell by the stubborn set of his face, Mark was determined to do this illusion.

Joy sighed. "I'll spot you. Just tell me what to do."

They reached the barn. Inside, with his other paraphernalia, Joy saw a man-sized glass box filled with water. It was simple, unornamented, yet it awakened a dread in her that wouldn't go away.

"Don't do this, Mark."

His jaw set. "I have to."

He kicked off his shoes, then pulled off his shirt. He stripped off his shorts, and Joy discovered he was wearing swim trunks beneath. His body, nearly all exposed, fascinated her, and Joy felt her mouth go dry. He had sleek, powerful muscles that bunched and relaxed with each motion and a fluid gait that spoke of his utter control over his body.

Mark held out a stopwatch and four linked chains, each with a cuff at one end.

"Once I get in the tank, I want you to fasten me with these chains. I'll go under the water, and that's when you start the stopwatch. Latch the top, so it doesn't come off

135

with a single push, but don't put on the padlock. That will come later. Cover it with the cloth to simulate the earth. Give me five minutes. If I'm not out in that time, take off the cloth and unlatch the lid."

"Five minutes? You can't hold your breath that long."

"Five minutes." He got in the tank, then lifted up his hands.

Joy hesitated, the ache of dread so strong her fingers shook. This wasn't right. He shouldn't be doing this with only her for safety.

Mark held his hands in her line of vision. "Fasten me, Joy."

Joy snapped the metal cuffs on his wrists, her stomach twisting with each metallic click. He lifted his ankles, and Joy attached the chains to them. He sat there a moment, in a V, drawing in deep breaths, oxygenating his blood, then slowly he lay back in the water.

Joy's icy fingers jerked on the stopwatch, starting the deadly count. She lowered the glass lid and latched it. Through it, she could see Mark.

She was watching him drown himself.

He didn't look at her. His attention was all turned inward, toward escaping the trap of death. He didn't move that she could see at first, there was no room for movement, then she noticed his muscles squeezing, tiny movements that seemed ineffective, yet his hand was moving in the cuff.

Unable to watch any longer, she did as he'd asked and put the black cloth over him.

Then, she sat beside it, held her breath, stared at the stopwatch, and felt her insides freeze with foreboding.

After one minute, fifteen seconds, her lungs burned and

her vision blurred. Joy gasped, pulling in desperately needed oxygen.

One minute, fifteen seconds. Mark had already been in there three minutes.

Wait five minutes? No way in hell.

Something was wrong. She felt it in her bones.

His claustrophobia!

Joy flung off the concealing cloth. Mark was under the water. He'd freed just one hand and it pushed against the unyielding glass top. Bubbles streamed from his half-open mouth.

Trembling, Joy hurriedly undid the latch, then flung open the top.

Mark did not rise.

Cursing him six ways to Sunday, she bent over and tried to lift him. But the box was narrow, the chains a hindrance, and Mark was heavy. *Dead weight*? Dear Lord, no. Could she still remember the steps in CPR? Water splashing every which way, Joy struggled to get him upright.

"Do you need help?"

Joy glanced over her shoulder to see Zeke Jupiter outlined in the doorway. "Help me get him out of here."

Zeke hurried over and the two of them pulled Mark upright in his watery niche.

Joy hovered over him. Should she start CPR? Did he have a pulse? Was he breathing? Her fingers sought the pulse point on his neck.

Mark started coughing and swearing. Clearly frustrated, he shoved a hand through the water, splashing it over the sides.

"Guess you're breathing," she muttered, smoothing a hand across his hair.

Zeke watched her with a curious look. "What happened?"

"He was trying an escape. It didn't work."

"I have gotten out of the cuffs," Mark said tightly. "I have gotten out of the cuffs underwater. It's the damned darkness." He reached down and with a quick twist freed himself from the chains. Water streaming down his body, he got out of the glass tomb and slapped a frustrated hand against the glass. "Dammit, Joy, I told you five minutes."

"Well, excuse me from saving you from drowning."

"I hadn't drowned yet."

She planted her hands at her hips and stuck her face in his. "You weren't escaping. Next time I *will* let you drown."

Mark glared at her, then his face and posture relaxed. He ran a hand through his hair. "Sorry. You did the right thing. I wasn't getting out of there. Not today. It's just . . . I *should* be able to do it. I will, once I know the key."

His hand cupped her cheek, the touch cool on her over-heated skin. "Thank you, Joy."

For a moment, she thought he might kiss her, until he must have remembered his promise not to. His hand dropped, the cool fingers leaving a fiery brand in their wake.

Zeke cleared his throat, breaking the mood. "Mark, are you all right?"

"Yeah, I'm fine."

"Then, Joy, might I trouble you for the name and address of the tannery you use?"

"I'll get it for you." She turned to Mark. "You sure you're okay? Do you want me to stay?"

He shook his head. "No."

Joy hesitated a moment, then took him at his word. She turned to Zeke. "Why do you need the tannery address?"

"I want to get myself a pair of ostrich leather boots."

"You'll love them." As they left, Joy glanced back at Mark. He was standing in shadow, alone, watching them leave. Then he turned around and, fists clenched, stared down at the watery tank.

The next day, Armond called. "Mixed results, *mon ami*. The slaughterhouse belongs to a shell company of Centurion, but there was nothing on the truck."

"Nothing? How about the feed bags?"

"Just empty burlap."

So nothing hidden in there. "Did Centurion know you searched the truck?"

"I doubt it. We'll keep an eye on the meat coming out, but for now it's a dead end."

"If we brought Joy in—"

"Absolutely not, Mark. If she's part of it, and you do that, you could blow my case. Your girlfriend's already in trouble. Don't make it worse by letting her warn Centurion."

Chapter Nine

Four days later, Zeus stretched out on the hotel's poolside lounger and let the sun bake into him. His scheme to separate Mark and Joy was not going well, he had to admit. Those two—something crackled between them, powerful as lightning, strong as Hercules. Seth Beaumont was no antidote to *that*.

I'll have to think a bit, come up with another plan.

Sweat trickled through the graying hairs on his chest. Behind his sunglasses, Zeus eyed the nearby young lovelies. Perhaps one would massage some lotion into him. Hera once used the most sensuous balm of almonds and honey on him. He closed his eyes. Ah, but he still missed the hot springs of his native world. Before their banishment, he and Hera had often enjoyed a variety of pleasures in one.

Hera. Like many of the human females he'd seduced,

140

the young lovelies by the pool were mere shadows of what he really wanted. Ultimately, always, still, it was Hera who stirred his blood.

Where had she disappeared to when she'd left Olympus?

It was a question that had nagged him for centuries.

The ring of his cell phone interrupted his drifting thoughts. Zeus looked at the number and sighed. He supposed he should answer it.

"Mr. Jupiter, it's about time you answered my calls." Mrs. Hunsacker's teeth clicked together. "You must return. There are papers you need to sign. I have delayed them as long as possible."

Mrs. Hunsacker liked to think she ran Jupiter Fireworks; in truth she did mostly, and it annoyed her no end when there was something that could only be handled by her eccentric boss.

Zeus tilted his chin to catch more sun. "It's lovely down here. Would you like to join me?"

"Don't be ridiculous. When will you be back?"

"I'm not sure. Is there something interesting that might entice me back?"

He could almost hear the gears of Mrs. Hunsacker's mind trying to settle on something that would intrigue him. He really shouldn't tease her so. Mrs. Hunsacker never jested.

"A dog is terrorizing your fireworks factory."

Zeus sat upright. "A what?"

"A dog, sir. Huge. Black. The guard claims it has red eyes. It growls and snaps at anyone who comes near. Once the dog got into the factory and tore into some shells before he could be chased out."

"Have the animal control people remove it."

"They did. Shot him with tranquilizers and took him to the pound. The next morning, he was back at the factory. Nobody knows how. Do you want me to authorize setting out poison?"

"No!" Zeus sat back. Black dog, red eyes. Escapes any leash? Cerberus? Why would the dog of the gods, guardian of the gates of Hades, be terrorizing his factory? "Does this dog have three heads?"

"Don't joke, Mr. Jupiter. What do you want them to do about the dog?"

"I'll come back and take a look."

Mrs. Hunsacker hung up. Absently, Zeus rubbed his lightning ring, unmindful of the resultant clap of thunder. Cerberus had always liked Hera. If the dog were Cerberus, could Hera be close at hand?

Zeus smiled. Hera. At last.

The barbeque was held on the huge lawn at the front of the Valcour home. Massive oak trees provided shade against the afternoon heat as well as limbs for swings. Tables outlined the entire area, and to one side was the huge brick grill, where Mark flipped the last of the ostrich burgers onto the tray Joy held.

"I thought you said a few friends." He'd lost count of how many cars and trucks lined the driveway.

"Valcour barbeques are a favorite. Nicole upholds the tradition, even though the last of the Valcours is conspicuously missing."

He turned off the gas to the grill, then followed her to the table to load up a plate for himself. Corn bread, jambalaya, salad, spicy potatoes, baked beans, fried okra, Cajun crawtater chips—the neighbors had outdone themselves with the potluck. Everything looked and smelled so good, he was hard put to choose.

Seth Beaumont joined them. "Joy, Earl wants to organize a sack race. Do you have some old feed bags?"

"Plenty. Let me get them."

"I'll help." With a proprietary air, Beaumont placed a hand at her elbow, needlessly guiding her across the lawn.

Despite Joy's statement that she'd turned Beaumont down, the scene was altogether too cozy for Mark's peace of mind. He stepped forward.

"They make a cute couple," murmured a smooth voice.

Jupiter again. He lounged beside Mark, looking polished and cool, a plate of food in his hand.

Mark returned the insincere smile. "He's a bit bland."

"Something you or I could never be accused of, no? Would you like to join me?" He lifted his plate of food.

"Of course," Mark lied, seeing Earl Flynn stop Joy and Beaumont.

Jupiter eyed the trio. "Joy has settled well in this town, hasn't she? She's valued, very much a part of things." He gave Mark a bright smile. "So, where do you perform next?"

"Houston." Mark looked away from Joy. He couldn't envision that she would be content to have her world as narrow as Seth Beaumont would make it.

Mark and Jupiter sat at a small table on the fringes, angled so they each could watch the goings-on and keep a wary eye on each other. So far, all the info Armond had turned up said Jupiter was squeaky-clean, but in Mark's mind no one got the kind of money Jupiter seemed to have by being honest.

"How are your preparations for the magic show going?" Jupiter asked.

"Fine." His assistant and technician were coming with the equipment for the Pygmalion illusion on Tuesday. "And your fireworks?"

Jupiter fingered his ring, a hint of a smile on his lips. "I find I need to leave town for a few days. Some . . . problems need my attention."

"Nothing major?"

Jupiter waved his hand dismissively. "Trifles," he answered, then attacked an ostrich burger.

A Jaguar sedan pulling in between two large-boled oaks caught Mark's eye, and he let out a low whistle.

"That is one fine car," Jupiter agreed.

The car door opened and a man got out.

Centurion. Mark had known he'd meet Centurion here and had thought he was prepared, but the steel wings of anger that beat against his throat, trying to take away his breath, surprised him.

Joy, arms loaded with feed sacks, greeted Centurion, while Seth gave him a hearty handshake. As Mark watched, Centurion's arm snaked around Joy's waist, and he kissed her. Two kisses, one on each cheek, both lingering a trifle too long to be called neighborly.

Mark's fists tightened, then relaxed, and he drew in a slow breath. He juggled daggers and made magic with fire. Those didn't happen by losing your focus. His anger became icy calm.

It helped when Joy moved away from the kiss.

A hand fell onto Mark's shoulder, "You okay, son?" It was Jupiter's voice. Concern this time instead of warning.

"Fine."

Centurion had aged little. His hair held only a hint of gray; his body was a testament to good health and vigorous exercise. He was considered a fine-looking man by most. Would Centurion have any memory of that evening, or was it just one in a blurred line of violent nights?

Time to find out. "Excuse me." Mark set out toward Centurion and Joy. To his surprise, Zeke Jupiter followed.

"Hey, darlin'," Mark said to Joy when he reached her side, "how about runnin' that three-legged race with me?" He bent to drop a kiss on her soft, bright hair, then, mindful of his promise, stopped.

"Only in your dreams," she answered.

"Joy doesn't like to do things like that," Seth added.

"No? I distinctly remember—"

"Mark, Zeke, this is Guy Centurion," Joy interrupted. "He's one of the sponsors and guiding influences of the Chefs' Charity Night and Mushroom Festival. Guy, this is Zeke Jupiter, who's doing the fireworks, and Mark Hennessy, known on stage as Marcus. He's a magician."

"Welcome, gentlemen," Centurion murmured, his voice arid as a Sahara night. He held out his hand and touched palms, first with Jupiter, then with Mark. His hand was cold and dry; the man never broke out in a sweat. "I understand you're staying here on the farm, Mark."

"Helping the lady with the ostriches for a time."

Centurion lifted one brow. "An unusual pastime for a magician."

"I'm always up for new . . . experiences."

"He's using my barn to practice. Now, if you'll excuse me," Joy said, "I've got some watermelon to set out."

"I'll get the fire started for marshmallows." Seth trailed after her.

The three men watched them leave, then Centurion turned his gaze back to Mark. His eyes were dark, the pupils and irises seamless. "I never forget a face. We've met, haven't we?"

"Six years ago." The SOB didn't even remember him. Yet.

"You returned just for our little festival?"

"I'm a magician. I do shows. The Mushroom Festival booked me. No more, no less." He added as much persuasion as he could to his voice.

Guy blinked, then nodded. "I'm giving a dinner party on Thursday. I'd like you both to come."

"Love to," Mark answered, as did Zeke.

"Good. I think it's time I joined the party." Without further comment, Guy left.

"I don't like that man," Zeke Jupiter said.

"Neither do I."

The barbeque was a success.

Joy sat on a white, wrought-iron bench situated beside one of the oak trees a short distance from the guests. She laid her head against the rough bark, taking advantage of a lull in the activity. The setting sun was a red ball on the horizon, and soon the remaining guests would be winding their way home.

She smiled in satisfaction. Then her smile faltered as she caught a whiff of musky men's cologne.

Guy Centurion sat beside her on the bench. He tapped a thin cigar from a silver case and lit it. For a moment, she smelled the acrid scent of a struck match, then it dissipated, replaced by the unpleasant odor of tobacco.

"You know I wish you wouldn't smoke, Guy. It destroys your taste buds."

He smiled at her. "Which is why I only allow myself one, in the evening after dinner." He inhaled, then let out a thin stream of smoke. "I've spoken to the chef at Voisin. He's anxious to feature your ostrich meat in the restaurant."

Voisin was very exclusive and featured rare dishes that created whole new markets and ensured demand for the ingredients.

Joy gave a low whistle. "Tell me you're not kidding."

"I never *kid* about business."

"Thank you. He won't be disappointed with it."

"That's what I told him."

One drop of vinegar curdled the cream for her. Guy held a lot of power; a request from him was tantamount to a command. Could the chef have refused if he'd wanted? What would have happened if he had? She laced her fingers to keep from revealing how they trembled. Damn Mark for putting doubts in her.

Guy leaned back and stretched his arm across the bench top. "Dagobert is taking over Jade next week, and I'm giving a dinner party next Thursday. About twenty guests." He looked over at her. "Would you be my chef for it?"

Joy sucked in a breath, hearing the implications. If Dagobert left, Guy's executive chef position would be open. This dinner party was her audition for the part.

It was an incomparable opportunity. Her heart thumped against her chest. To have charge of a kitchen, a place of her own, it was what she'd always wanted. Guy entertained widely—she'd have so many varied circumstances to cook for, and sometimes he employed guest chefs, which would give her a singular opportunity to learn.

It was perfect.

If the audition went well, and she got the job.

If she got the job, it would mean delaying her own restaurant.

"Well?" asked Guy.

She didn't have the funding put together for her restaurant; she couldn't borrow against the ostrich farm until Nicole owned it outright. This could give her the cushion she needed, plus some good experience.

He's got his fingers in a lot of pies, and some of them are mighty muddy.

Joy thrust the thought away. She'd find out exactly what Mark meant. If he didn't have an adequate explanation . . .

"Yes, of course I'll do it. I'm thrilled. Do you have in mind what you'd like to serve?"

"You choose a menu, then run it by me. Something elegant."

"All right."

A chorus of children's laughter caught her attention, and she looked across the thinning crowd. Three children sat on the ground next to Mark, laughing with delight.

Mark held one of the barn cats in his lap, stroking the cat with easy motions. To her surprise, it was Thor he held, the one who considered being petted beneath his dignity as head mouser. In Mark's other hand, he held a string. He let Thor bat it with a paw, then suddenly the string disappeared, although Mark's hand remained open. Thor meowed and batted at Mark's fingers. The string reappeared. Over and over they played the game while the children laughed at the cat's antics and the disappearing string.

Mark being sexy she could handle. Gentle and kind was a new side of him that tugged out dangerous thoughts.

Guy ground out the remains of the cigar, then flicked the butt away. "I must be going."

"Would you like to take some ostrich steaks? I've got some in the freezer."

"I would, thank you."

"I'll get them for you."

To her mild surprise, Guy followed her into the house. While Joy rummaged in the freezer he said, "Mark's a stranger. Do you know much about him? Are you sure it's wise to let him stay with you?" Friendly concern laced his voice.

Wise? Probably not. "He's staying at the caretaker's cottage, and I know enough about him. Don't worry." She found the package of meat and held it out to him.

"But I do," he murmured. Instead of taking the meat, he leaned forward, put one hand at the back of her neck and one hand on her shoulder, trapping her, and kissed her. Not a kiss on the cheek as he usually did. On the mouth. With the tongue. A kiss with too much pressure and too many demands.

His lips were dry, and he tasted like smoke. Her stomach roiled, and Joy pressed against his grip. Guy's fingers dug into her flesh, and a streak of pain shot down her spine.

She dropped the frozen meat on his foot.

Guy cursed and released her. "A simple 'no' would suffice."

"You were hurting me."

"I'm sorry. Unlike you, that was not my intention." When she didn't answer, he added, "Surely, we've been friends long enough that you'll allow me the benefit of the doubt?"

He looked full of contrition. Did she just imagine the fleeting glimpse of something darker? Confusion swirled inside her. She wasn't imagining the sting on her lips and the ache in her neck, yet Guy had never shown her anything but kindness.

"Is this what you expect if I work for you?" she asked.

"Of course not," he answered, sounding genuinely indignant. "We've spent a lot of time together. Is it so surprising I've discovered an affection for you? You're a charming woman, Joy Taylor, and a talented one." He bent down again and brushed his lips across hers, too swiftly for her to protest, though her nerves recoiled.

The kitchen door banged open. Mark strolled in, then leaned one shoulder against the doorjamb and crossed his feet at the ankles. His eyes swept from them to the package of frozen meat.

"Your guests were leavin' and wanted to say good-bye, Joy," he drawled, the Southern accent in his voice especially thick.

"Thanks. I'll see to them."

"I must be going, as well," Guy added.

"Wait! Your meat." Joy picked up the frozen package.

Guy's smooth mask slipped. "Keep it!" He stalked out.

"It, ah, landed on his foot," Joy offered when Mark gave her a questioning look.

"My, darlin', you do have some interesting choices of weapons. Ostrich eggs, frozen meat. Remind me to keep on your good side."

His humor replaced some of her uneasiness. Joy returned the meat to the freezer, then brushed past Mark who was still lounging in the door. She looked up at him. The stance might be casual, but the jaw was set. The man hid it well, but he was angry.

So what? She hadn't done anything wrong. She didn't owe him any explanations.

Nonetheless, she had to admit, she'd been glad to see him.

For the first time, she wondered if her instincts about Guy were as unreliable as her instincts about Mark had been seven years ago.

Chapter Ten

The house was quiet. Hope was asleep. Mark and Nicole had helped with the cleanup, bringing things in from outside and tidying up the grounds, but she'd shooed them away when it came to the kitchen. Nicole went to watch television and Mark left, saying he had to make some phone calls.

Joy dried her hands on the dishtowel, then hung it up. Hands on hips, she gave a satisfied glance around the pristine kitchen. Unlike Guy's kitchen, hers, while quiet and clean, still felt like home. Perhaps it was the shamrock suncatcher in the window, or the row of well-thumbed cookbooks, or the wildflowers Mark had brought her this morning.

Much as she liked cooking and being hostess, this time afterward was very special, Joy decided. When all was still except for the softly humming dishwasher, when things had been cleaned up and put away, that was when you had a chance to reflect and enjoy.

Her stomach rumbled.

And it was a chance for the cook to eat.

She sliced off two thick chunks of French bread and made a *pan y tomate*. She rubbed the bread with garlic cloves, added a sliced tomato, drizzled olive oil over all, then sprinkled it with sea salt. She poured a glass of Beaujolais, then, carrying the bread in a cloth napkin, flipped off the kitchen light and went outside. Sipping the wine, she strolled across the lawn.

The Valcour farm had no near neighbors. Although the lights of civilization glowed against the night sky, here it was as dark and warm as hot fudge.

A rustle of cloth stirred the silence, and a faint tingle danced up her spine. Mark appeared from the darkness. He moved with singular grace, a magician's entrance that captivated her as none on the stage ever could. Her heart thumped against her ribs.

"I thought you'd be tired," he said.

"I am, yes, but in a pleasant way. I'm both too keyed up and too content for sleep. Get your phone calls made?"

He nodded, then laughed. "My agent is convinced something dire will happen to me this far from 'civilization,' and he sees his commission for this European tour evaporating. He wants to talk to me, just to make sure I'm still here. I also made some local motel reservations. My assistant, Dia, and a technical whiz kid named Jax will be coming into town the day after next. We need to put some finishing touches on the show."

"Why not let them stay here? It would be easier to work,

I'd imagine. There's a second bedroom in the cottage for Jax, and Dia can stay in the house. We've got lots of room."

"It would make our time more productive. Thanks. Where were you heading?"

"To the creek. Want to join me?"

"Sure." He followed her to the small creek that meandered through the property. They sprawled in the green grass edging the banks, and Joy took off her shoes and stuck her toes in the water. It held a touch of coolness in the sultry eve, and she gave a sigh of relaxation. The creek was shallow and slow, not sufficient even to be termed babbling, but somehow just being near it was always soothing.

She offered Mark the bread; he tore off a small chunk, then returned it. When she held out her wine glass, he took a sip.

"Isn't there a poem about a loaf of bread, a jug of wine, and thou?" he asked.

She wished she could see his eyes, but the darkness hid all nuances of his features. She could only smell the faint fresh scent of his soap, hear the rise and fall of his breathing, and feel the traitorous, sparkling pleasure inside her. " 'The Rubaiyat of Omar Khayyam,' " she answered. "Bread and wine have been the essence of hospitality for centuries."

Joy looked up at the stars, finding calm in the vista. "Do you suppose there's life out there?"

"If there is, I'd like to see it."

"I read once that a secret government agency plans to send six men and six women to Mars to establish a new Eden. They kidnap people, do tests to determine their fitness for the project, then release them, with their memory of the tests wiped out. That's what's behind all those alien abduction stories."

Mark gave a snort of amusement. "Remember how you pestered me when I made up stories about why I hadn't turned in my homework? That honest, and yet you still believe the rags?"

"Mostly I read cookbooks and culinary magazines, but I figure there's got to be a grain of truth in there somewhere."

"Are you planning on volunteering for that mission?"

"Nope. This is home. But, if I ever say I was abducted, you'll know what really happened."

"I'll keep it in mind." He fell silent. She sensed him shift, felt the warmth when his body brushed against her for a too-brief moment before he moved away.

That promise of his, that he wouldn't touch her unless she asked. It hadn't helped, Joy realized. Hadn't done a thing to keep her from handing him little pieces of her heart. They'd been friends before they'd been lovers, before time and circumstances separated them, and with every day more of that friendship returned.

She tore off a chunk of bread and nibbled it, savoring the blend of flavors. "This was a good tomato Joe brought from his garden."

"You've got a nice group of neighbors."

"I like it here, Mark. I finally feel like I'm part of a place. It's home," she added simply, looking up at him.

Her eyes had grown accustomed to the night and to the stars. The dark no longer shielded him from her, simply muted his form, though his eyes still remained hidden.

Mark looked away and sipped the wine, his shallow breathing harsh in the stillness of night. "What're the old expressions? Home is where the heart is? Bloom where you are planted? These are the ties that bind?"

"Old expressions are sometimes overrated." She knew where Mark's heart was—onstage, with his magic, with his freedom. Joy swished her feet through the cool water. "So, tell me about Dia and Jax."

"They've been with me since I started playing larger venues."

"Is she the typical 'beautiful, anonymous assistant'?"

"Typical? No way, darlin'." Mark laughed. "Dia Trelawny is beautiful, but she's never content to be anonymous. This next tour, she's getting second billing and performing some of her own magic. She's a determined lady, bound to make it to the top."

There was obvious admiration in his words. Marcus and Dia. They sounded like a perfect team. Joy didn't like the way her insides flash-froze at the thought. She knew Mark was leaving; she had his promise to stay through breeding season, but she could hold him no longer.

He soared; she nested.

"And Jax?"

"Ajax Lapinksi. A nineteen-year-old genius with computers and electronics and a sometimes thorough pain in the butt. He designs the special effects for the show, so he's coming to see the staging while Dia and I practice."

"I'm surprised you wanted to stay here. I'd think it would have been easier for you to check out the lay of the land—or stage—then return to Vegas."

"I wanted to stay," he said simply.

"Why? There are lots of better places you could practice." Always her questions came back to that. Why had he returned? She shifted restlessly, the hard ground beginning to tell on her, then pressed a hand to the small of her back.

"Back sore?"

"A little stiff. And my arms are tired." Despite the fact he hadn't answered her questions, Joy took a plunge away from safety and caution. "Do you remember that time we climbed up the rope to sneak in the theater? And I couldn't enjoy the movie because my arms hurt?"

"You complained so much, I thought they'd hear and kick us out. I also know you went back later and paid the admissions."

She leaned toward him. "Remember what you did?"

"I've never forgotten." His voice turned low and husky, intimate.

He'd rubbed her arms, massaged her shoulders, then drawn her into a kiss. Not their first, but the first that led to more intimate caresses. She had no memory of what happened on screen, but her memory of each kiss and each hesitant, exploratory touch they'd shared that evening remained too clear. Her belly started fluttering in expectation, in remembrance, just as it had in those first days. Joy held out one arm.

Mark didn't take it. "Do you want me to do that again?"

He was going to make her say it. "Yes," she answered, wanting both the touch and the kiss. Her insides were quivering like molded Jell-O. "Touch me, Mark."

He shifted so he was behind her. Slowly his hands moved up her arms to her shoulders. He kneaded them, then worked his way down her spine to her lower back. His dexterous hands worked their magic on her muscles, on the accumulated aches. Briefly, the tips of his fingers slipped beneath the waistband of her shorts, though they didn't linger. When he shifted back to her arms, he brushed lightly against the side of her breast, a touch as delicate as the silk scarves he used. Her molded Jell-O insides melted to a sweet flow.

"I stayed here because I was curious," he said in a low, melodic voice, finally answering her question.

"About what?"

Clouds gathered in the sky, blotting out the stars one by one. One thick mass scudded across the moon, casting a deeper darkness across them. A chill pervaded the sultry night. Joy shivered and slipped on her shoes, while Mark urged her back, closer to the heat of him.

"About what happened to us. Why did you marry so fast, Joy? Four months! Why didn't you wait for me?"

The past still flavored their present. It was senseless to pretend it didn't and to ignore the questions that had eaten at her for so long. "Why didn't you come back when you promised?"

There was a moment of thick silence and his strokes halted. His fingers tightened about her arms. "I was in jail."

Joy shot him a startled glance. Of all the excuses, all the reasons she'd contemplated, she'd never come up with that one.

"Why were you in jail?"

He resumed his massage with a more intense pressure, meeting the need inside her. "B and E—breaking and entering—robbery, and assault."

Joy drew in a sharp breath against the pain shooting through her chest. Cold prickled her skin, which had been so deliciously warm.

"I didn't do it," Mark added. "It was a setup. I've skirted

the law a few times in my life, don't be thinkin' otherwise, darlin', but never that kind of stuff. It took a couple days for me to get out, then, some people took a dislike to my release, and I wasn't lookin' too pretty for a while."

She shifted to face him and laid a hand on his cheek. His skin was cool, almost as icy as the air had become. "Mark, they hurt you?"

"Nothing major. I heal fast. I was in the hospital less than a week."

She traced the line of his cheek, though she could see little of it, assuring herself he was still here and safe.

She added up the weeks in her head. Her hand dropped and she frowned. "I understand why you didn't come on my graduation night—you were in jail, then the hospital—but that was only a couple of weeks! Why didn't you come afterward? You didn't even send a note. Not the whole time you were gone!"

"I'm not much of one for writing."

"Not even a single phone call?"

Mark ran a hand through his hair. "I didn't have anything to offer you. We were so young."

"You were scared."

"Yeah, I was scared. I told myself, when I missed the one date I'd promised, you'd be mad and wouldn't want to see me. Truth was, I felt like a noose was tightening around my throat. So, I delayed. It's not a fact I'm proud of; I should have treated you better. Took me four months to get the courage to go to you."

"And you found me married."

"Yeah."

The cloud cover thickened. Here, in the concealing darkness, with only the nearby ostriches as witness, was

159

freedom enough for honesty. "I was scared, too. I thought he'd help me take care of Nicole and Hope." Joy took a shaky breath. "It hurt so bad when you didn't show up that night, and not days or even a month later. Not even a word. I was so angry at you and I felt so . . . unattractive. He was flattering. Stupid reasons for a wedding, but then that never stopped any of the women in my family."

"Darlin', you were never, ever unattractive. Not to me. I always had trouble keeping my roving hands to myself."

"We both made mistakes," Joy said, with a hint of humor.

It was strange to find the defenses she'd built against him, the resentments, dissolving faster than sugar in boiling water. Strange, and unsettling, for clearing the past didn't mean the differences of today were any less difficult. A sharp breeze wrapped chilly air around them.

Mark looked upward. "Looks like it's about to rain."

"Yeah," Joy agreed. The dark had become almost palpable, and cold raised the fine hairs on her arms. She rose. "This cold is strange. We'd better be getting back."

He followed her, then stopped at the caretaker's cottage. "After we finish with the ostriches tomorrow, I need to go to New Orleans. Why don't you come with me? Take the day off."

"I've got too much—"

"Ignore it. For one day. Everyone needs a day of rest. I know, let's make a little bargain. You agree to whatever I plan, and I'll eat wherever you choose. Take a chance, darlin'."

Intrigued by what he might choose, Joy took in a deep breath. "All right."

"Good." Mark cupped his hands over her jaw, then leaned over and kissed her.

It was a kiss as sweet as the first he'd given her, yet there was so much more in it. More knowledge, more regret, more sureness. Their bodies touched, not leaning against one another, but two adults meeting, her breasts to his chest, his groin to her belly. Everywhere she felt, he was solid and strong and fiery.

A chilly gust blew around them. It set her shivering, and she could not move from that warmth.

The back door of the main house banged open, startling them apart.

"Joy," Nicole shouted. "Guy Centurion's on the phone. Something about your new job."

Mark stepped away, and a mask slid over his features. "Joy, stay away from him. Don't get any more entangled than you already are."

Joy lifted her chin, shivering as the first rain prickled her skin. "You got something besides innuendo that says why I shouldn't?"

His remote, shuttered gaze swept across her. "I'm not sure you'd believe me. I'll see you tomorrow." Without a second glance, he pivoted and walked away.

Joy stared in disbelief at his back, anger rising.

"Joy, the phone," called Nicole.

"Tell him I'll call him right back." She caught up to Mark and grabbed him by the arm, spinning him to face her. "What is it with you? First kisses then snubs? Make up your mind which it's to be, and let me know what you decide. Then *I'll* let *you* know if I agree." She thrust her hands on her hips.

The sarcasm got his attention. With one step, he closed the distance between them. Wind howled with chilling annoyance, but they ignored it. He wrapped an arm around her waist, then pulled her against him. There was no politeness in his touch, no inches between them. Again, he kissed her, hard this time, with passion and magic, and she responded.

"Kisses," he said, lifting his head, "and it seems like you agree." He let her go.

"Damn you, Mark Hennessy," she hissed, "I wish I knew what you were thinking."

He laughed. "If I told you, darlin', those thoughts will make you blush prettier than a glass of rosé. If it's any consolation, I'm often wonderin' what's going on in your clever mind."

"You always say I'm too transparent."

"I'm revisin' my opinion. Don't you know? You know me better than anyone, and that scares me worse than appearing on stage before five hundred payin' customers."

The odd wind blew again, carrying rain that froze their skin, sending Joy toward the house, Mark toward the cottage.

"So, what have you got against Guy?" she called.

Mark paused on the front stoop. "Remember I said I was set up, then beat up?"

"Yeah."

"He's the one who ordered it."

Those two acted as though Eros had hit them with a whole quiver of arrows. Young love was damned annoying.

Zeus waved his hand, dissipating the far-see smoke that

allowed him to watch Mark and Joy. Hades, he'd begun to wonder if they were *ever* going to notice the cold.

Too bad the far-see smoke didn't allow eavesdropping. He would have liked to hear what they were saying.

For a moment, he debated the wisdom of leaving them together while he returned to his factory.

No, he had to go. He couldn't let this chance to find Hera slip away. Zeus picked up his suitcase.

After all, what could happen? He'd be gone two days, three tops.

Mark sat on the steps to his cottage, a deck of cards in hand. Idly he practiced the shuffles that were a magician's stock-in-trade, keeping his fingers limber.

The anticipated storm had blown over, leaving the remaining night sultry and slow. Behind him, a low light in the cottage kept darkness at bay, but the lights were out in the main house now, the inhabitants presumably asleep. Nicole had turned off the TV when Joy finished whatever it was she'd worked on in the kitchen after she left him.

Waiting up until everyone settled, turning out the lights and saying good night to loved ones. Small domestic actions that he'd never had and never missed. Never even wondered about before now.

So why did the scene fascinate him tonight?

Fear crouched at the perimeter of his thoughts, ready to pounce as it always did whenever the idea of being trapped with one person or in one place tried to lodge in his mind.

That was one of the reasons he'd not gone back to Joy right after he got out of the hospital, had not sent her so much as a note. He'd wanted her—he'd ached to hold her and be inside her—but as he'd told her tonight, she'd scared him. Her clear-eyed gaze saw right through his masks. She wanted home and family, while he'd barely been able to breathe thinking about it. Until he'd first met Joy, home to him meant a man with a ready fist or strap and the key to a dark closet when beating didn't work.

Tonight, though, the fear was held at bay by the soft rustle of the cards and the spicy taste and sunny warmth of Joy that lingered on his skin and lips.

He'd enjoyed the past week at the ostrich farm, he realized, now that he took a moment to think about it. Being outside, watching over the eggs, seeing the chicks grow, feeding and watering the ostriches—there were some elemental pleasures there. Something about all that persuaded you to slow down and take stock. His life was fast-paced and hectic, the way he liked it, but for a brief interlude it felt good not to worry about packing up to go to the next town.

He hadn't really reviewed his goals since he'd left Joy.

Eating meals with Joy, listening to Nicole's monologues, meeting the neighbors, all gave him a new perspective on home.

The cards were a blur in his hands.

None of that was for him.

He'd have to bring Joy into his world.

The cards stopped moving. He arranged them in a neat, ordered stack, stuck the deck in his pocket, then headed inside.

Chapter Eleven

Joy knelt on the floor of the Cessna 182, the vibrations from the hard metal reaching through her legs into her throat. While her body perched between the pilot and the loosened hatch, her stomach hung somewhere in the vicinity of her toes. "I can't do this," she muttered, her words lost in the engine growl of the small plane.

"What?" shouted Mark above the noise, as he settled in close behind her.

She twisted to yell back, "How did I let you talk me into this?"

"You've got a sense of adventure."

"I think you've got me mixed-up with someone else."

"Trust me. You'll love it."

"Do you realize, the only times in my life I've gotten in trouble were when I've done things that started with you saying 'Trust me'?"

Mark laughed, then kissed her, a sweet kiss, right on the back of the neck.

They'd made a deal. If she did whatever Mark decided for the afternoon, he'd eat wherever she picked out tonight. She'd stupidly agreed, thinking he had in mind a round of golf, or canoeing at City Park, or, maybe parasailing on Lake Pontchartrain.

She should have known better.

"Scoot back a little. Flush against me," Mark commanded against her ear.

She shifted until her back rested against his chest and she sat on his strong thighs. The contact reassured her, as she felt, rather than heard, Mark fasten the four clips on her harness to his, joining the two of them at shoulder and hip. For the tandem jump, they would be fastened together—her back to his front—the entire time. She would pull the rip cord when he told her and could steer the parachute, but always Mark would be there, ready to take over if she faltered.

Mark leaned to the right, looking out the window, then gestured to the pilot to adjust their flight trajectory. Joy, attached to him, moved as he did, an action that was strangely reassuring. She peered out the window at the patchwork of green below.

The Mississippi River was easily identifiable as were the airport hangar, houses, and the golf course. Nothing looked 10,000 feet away, but she knew, to those on the ground, the plane would be a mere speck of black against the fluffy clouds. She took a deep breath to still her shrieking nerves.

"How many times have you done this?" she called back to Mark. He'd told her, but, staring at the dizzying space, Joy wanted reassurance there weren't two neophytes up here.

"Over two thousand. Darlin', I'm a licensed tandem instructor. I know what I'm doing." His hand brushed lightly against her hair. "If you don't want to do this, it's all right. Just tell me now, we'll go back down, and I'll still eat wherever you want." She could hear the humor, and the tenderness, in his voice, and knew he meant every word. "But tell me before we take that first step to the jump platform. After that, we can't get back in the plane. It's too dangerous."

The plane banked and they were a few seconds from the drop zone. A quote she'd heard once from noted chef Joyce Goldstein inexplicably came to mind. *The best chefs are sensualists who are given to wretched excess.*

At the time she'd read that, it had struck a chord in her. She'd wondered if she had it in her—the varied experiences, the vast knowledge, the sheer sensuality—to be a best chef. Joy looked out again at the green below her.

Somehow, she didn't think skydiving was what Chef Goldstein had in mind.

"Relax. Take a deep breath." Mark's voice resonated inside her. She could feel his solid warmth behind her. Dutifully, Joy took a breath and settled her goggles. "Door!" he shouted in warning, and opened the hatch.

Lord Almighty! Cold wind passed her with a roar, whipping the few loose strands of her hair. Her adrenaline level shot up as high as the plane, and her heart pounded against her temples. Two inches to her right and 10,000 feet down was the ground. The only thing between her and it, once she stepped out, was the parachute strapped to Mark's back.

"Are we going?" Mark shouted in her ear.

Point of no return.

Take a chance, Joy. Live a little.

"Yeah," she shouted back. "We're going!"

"Good girl. Now put your right foot out on the platform, right beside mine."

A metal platform, about a foot wide and a yard long and fastened to the underbelly of the plane, stretched out below the open hatch. Joy planted her foot next to Mark's and eased out of the plane, grabbing the metal strut attached to the wing above her. She crouched on the metal platform, hanging above the ground, breathing heavily. A shiver ran through her, from the rush of adrenaline and the cold of the air. Her hands clutched the strut in a grip of steel.

"Let go of the strut. Cross your arms in front of you."

She could barely hear Mark's voice above the shriek of wind.

We can't get back in the plane. Only one place to go.

Wretched excess, Joy.

Joy let go of the strut and crossed her arms over her chest. Mark's strong hands came around over hers; his arms surrounded her in a cocoon of safety.

"One," he said, rocking back slightly.

"Two." Rock forward.

"Three!" Together they tumbled off the back of the plane.

Sky. Ground. One flip.

Sky. Plane going away. Ground. Two flips.

Oh, Lord.

From behind her, Mark stretched her arms to the sides, the signal to get into the arched back, spread eagle, freefall stance they'd practiced on the ground.

It worked! Heart pounding, mouth dry as flour, Joy

stared at the ground below her, knowing Mark flew with her, atop her.

Wind, thundering by her ears with Superman speed, was her only sensation. Even the cold faded behind the rush of exhilaration. She wasn't falling; there was no roller coaster nausea.

Only freedom.

"Yee-ha!" crowed Mark. He bent her left arm and they turned left. Her right arm and they turned right.

She was flying! She knew what it was to fly.

Forty-five seconds of free fall. One hundred and twenty miles an hour. She'd memorized the statistics, but they held no meaning up here in the sky.

Mark's finger appeared right in front of her eyes. The signal to open the chute. Joy fumbled for the knob to the rip cord. Mark would get it, she knew, if she failed, but she was determined to do this herself. There, she had it!

Joy tugged the cord, and the rainbow-colored chute opened above them. There wasn't a massive jerk, as she'd expected from seeing it in movies, only a jolt, as they shifted from horizontal to vertical and their descent slowed.

Under the canopy it was quiet, she was surprised to find. They glided. Mark's hands above hers helped her shift direction, while their feet dangled above the ground.

"How you doing? Stomach okay?" he asked.

"I'm fine." Nestled against him, floating in a silent world, it was the utter truth.

Too soon, it was time to land. At Mark's command, Joy turned them toward the drop zone in front of the hangar and angled the chute down. Her feet skimmed along the grass, as her weight settled back onto her in an easy landing. At the last moment, her body passed ahead of her feet and she tumbled into the grass, Mark on top of her, the chute billowing around them, for a soft, if ungainly, finish.

Mark unhooked them. Breathless, lightheaded, exuberant, Joy scrambled to her feet while Mark extended a hand to help. She rushed into his arms and, laughing, he swung her around. Her heart pounded in beat with the wild dance. When he set her on her feet, he kissed her soundly.

"Ready to do it again?" he asked with a grin, brushing back her untamed hair.

Mark always had challenged her to do more, to be more. She hadn't realized how much of that she'd given up when she'd given up loving him.

Joy gave a jubilant laugh and an enthusiastic thumbs-up.

Mark should have known she'd get revenge for the skydiving.

For dinner, Joy chose a vegetarian restaurant called Greenwood.

"Sprout food?" Mark asked, looking askance at the brick-fronted building near the Magazine Street farmer's market. The window decorations were . . . unique. A poster of a grinning cow with the caption, THE LIFE YOU SAVE TODAY IS MINE, a plastic heart covered with glitter, and a toy stuffed bear with a sign around its neck that read ALL CREATURES GREAT AND SMALL. "I'm not going to be able to get a steak here, am I? Not even an ostrich one."

Joy grinned. "Nope. Callie Gabriel has strong opinions about animal rights, but the food is great. She's built quite a name for herself. When I came to New Orleans after my divorce, Callie gave me a job here." She tugged his hand, urging him inside. "I come here whenever I'm in town."

A rich scent, like well-seasoned spaghetti sauce, greeted him. The interior was welcoming, Mark decided, with rough brick walls, red-and-white-checked cloths, colorful candles.

And a slew of tacky souvenirs.

Still holding Joy's hand—he enjoyed the feel of it, smaller than his, but strong and warm—Mark wandered over to the bulletin board filled with postcards and read aloud some of them. "The Shoe Museum, Toronto. Wall Drug, South Dakota. Fossil Butte, Montana. Toothpaste Capital of the World. Has she *visited* all of these?"

"None, actually. When they travel, Callie's regular customers always send her a picture postcard of some local oddity and bring back a cheap souvenir."

"That explains the hula dancer made of shells and the straw baskets with Nassau written in thread. Where does the vegetable power poster come from?"

"From Callie's abiding philosophy of food. Eat low on the food chain."

Just then, a waiter spotted Joy, and he raced over to give her a big hug. "Joy, how good to see you. It has been too long. Are you coming back to us?"

Joy laughed. "Sorry, Charles. I'm happy over on the North Shore."

Charles gave a snort of derision. "A cultural wasteland."

"Charles, you're a snob. To you anything outside of Orleans Parish is suspect, and you're not even too sure about the West Bank." She stepped back. "Charles, this is my friend, Mark. Mark, Charles has been here since Callie opened."

My friend. Trailing behind while Charles ushered her to a prime table by the window, Mark suddenly wanted to be introduced as someone more important in Joy's life than *my friend*. That was how she described Centurion.

It was a startling thought, an uneasy one. Especially when guilt warned him he hadn't told her the full truth about why he'd come back.

Neither unease nor guilt, however, blunted the edge of desire that had pricked him from the moment Joy gave him the thumbs-up after the sky-dive. Every look, every glancing touch, every breath from her deepened it. She was vibrant, natural, warm. Only his promise to follow her lead at dinner, and her obvious pleasure at being here, kept him from springing to his feet and suggesting that dinner be chocolates in bed.

Charles handed them menus, and Joy asked, "Is Callie in?"

"Of course, although she has someone else as chef tonight. I'll tell her you're here."

When Charles left, Joy didn't immediately pick up her menu. "That was the job I was aiming at," she said with a wisp of nostalgia. "Sous-chef, second in command. I really liked it here."

Lightly, Mark traced her hand with one finger, needing this contact with her. "Your allergy wasn't a problem here, was it? Why didn't you stay?"

Her hand turned to lace with his. "Nicole needed help with the farm. Family comes first."

The farm. The ties to a small town and to a family. Always there was that with Joy.

The room grew stuffy, and Mark ran a finger around his collar. "I like the decor," he commented, avoiding differences he could do nothing about. At least, not tonight, not now. Tonight, none of those differences mattered.

"The food's even better than the decor."

"But what if I want things that aren't on any restaurant menu? Sweet kisses. A spicy touch. The salt of need and want. The taste of sunshine in my mouth."

Joy's bright eyes mirrored the need in him. "I'd suggest you leave room for dessert."

His hand tightened around hers, and his groin flared to life at the unspoken invitation. Mark drew in an unsteady breath, to calm heart and hormones. "Dessert it is." He leaned back, not bothering with the menu. "In the meantime, what do you suggest?"

Joy loosened their hands, then glanced over the day's specials, the blush in her cheeks fading. "The New Orleans tofu salad is good since she gets feta cheese from The Cheese Man. So are the stuffed poblano chiles, but, I warn you, they're *hot*. I know what I want—sauteed brown rice and summer vegetables with cashew-ginger sauce."

"Tofu salad? Poblano?" Pleasurable, lust-studded images faded as Mark's attention was drawn in horror to a menu filled with ingredients like bulghar wheat, lentils, and tahini. "Is there something on this that I would recognize?"

"You know, you're not very adventuresome when it comes to food, Mark."

"Didn't I eat all that macaroni and cheese you brought me when we were in high school?"

"That was from a *box*. I only made it because you liked it, and even then I had to dress it up."

"Well, it was good." He looked back at the menu. Did they have macaroni and cheese?

A woman with shoulder-length brown hair hurried from the back to their table. Like Charles, she enveloped Joy in a hug. Guessing this must be the previously mentioned Callie, Mark studied her with interest. She seemed to be the same age as Joy, and there was a friendly openness about her, an honesty that he also saw in Joy.

Maybe there was something about being a chef, about working with such elemental pleasures as taste and smell, about meeting basic needs and drawing from the fresh earth that precluded pretensions.

Or, likely, it was just Joy, and the friends she chose.

Callie turned to him, and Mark realized Joy had performed introductions. "You're a magician? It looks so glamorous. Working with beautiful women, creating illusions of wonder."

"About as glamorous, and as much practice and work, as I imagine preparing a night of meals at a restaurant would be."

She laughed, a throaty, earthy sound, that Mark found enjoyable. "Which means not at all." She turned back to Joy. "I can't stay; you know how things are in back. Before you leave, come and chat a few minutes, though."

"I will."

Callie rose and dusted her hands on her blue jeans. "We've got ratatouille, though it's not on the menu. Charles will take good care of you," she added as she left.

"If she's got ratatouille, I'd suggest trying that." Joy sniffed. "Smell it simmering?"

If that was ratatouille, it did smell good. Still . . .

Joy laid a hand on his arm. When he looked up from the menu, she grinned at him. "Trust me."

Mark gave a bark of laughter. "I guess I deserved that. Ratatouille it is."

"How was the ratatouille?" Joy asked when they finished.

"Delicious, but you forgot to mention that ratatouille meant eggplant."

"Because you wouldn't have tried it."

Mark grinned at her. "You're probably right. Perhaps my food choices are a little narrow." He ran a hand along hers, resting on the table. "You're good for me, you know that, Joy? We're good for each other, I think."

His magic hands, his soft words, spread wildfire through her. Joy fought the traitorous desire to read more into simple words and gestures. If anything happened, if things went any further, as it seemed they might, then she'd go into this with her eyes wide open, knowing it as temporary, not expecting more, not dreaming dreams like before.

She laced her fingers through his, and he picked up her hand to kiss it. A light touch, one on each knuckle, and Joy knew in that instant that tonight they would make love. All these years, she'd been missing it. Tonight she would either make a new memory to sustain her, one unhindered by virginal awkwardness and teenage worry, or she would finally exorcize the spell he wove around her.

But first, she had to talk to Callie.

As Mark sipped his cup of coffee, Joy said, "I'd like to visit with Callie a few minutes. You want to come?"

Mark shook his head. "I'll sit here with my coffee."

Joy found her friend in the tiny kitchen, chopping vegetables. "It looked like a good night."

"It was," Callie agreed. "Grab yourself a knife. I'm making stock."

Joy hefted one of the chef's knives and starting chopping mushrooms, falling into an easy rhythm with Callie.

"I like your Mark."

"He's not mine. We're friends."

Callie gave a snort of disbelief. "Not the way he was looking at you."

"How was he looking at me?" Mark so rarely showed his true emotions, she was hungry for any tidbit of insight. And Callie had an uncanny sense of who was trustworthy. It was one of the reasons Joy wanted to talk to her.

"Like you were white chocolate bread pudding and he had a powerful sweet tooth. Like he wanted to eat you up."

Joy gave a wry grin. "Only a chef would think that was an appealing metaphor."

"Are you two serious?"

"It's temporary. He's here only another five weeks. How intense it becomes during that time . . . well, it'll probably be a lot more than is wise."

"Does it have to be temporary?" Callie scraped her garlic into the soup pot.

Joy's mushrooms followed. "Yeah, it does."

"Your call."

"Now that we've dissected mine, how's your love life?" Joy added celery to her chopping block.

"I spend too many hours in here to have one." Callie whacked the end of a carrot.

"You need to live a little, Callie. Take some time off. See the world."

"Says Miss Give-me-roots-while-I'm-trying-to-do-ten-things-for-other-people."

Joy laughed. "Touché."

"So, how are the ostriches?"

"Good. Finally turning a profit. Nicole takes possession in a couple of weeks."

"Does that mean you're going to be coming back to the restaurant biz?"

"I'd like to, but—" Joy rested her knife on the chopping block. "Guy Centurion asked me to cook for his next dinner party. If it goes well, I think he's going to offer me the position as his personal chef."

"It sounds perfect for you," Callie said. "Your allergy wouldn't be as much of a problem, since he doesn't like red meat."

"And I could use alternatives to cow's milk."

Callie turned away, chopping her carrots with swift, practiced strokes. "It's a good opportunity."

"That's what I thought." An uneasy twisting crept into Joy's belly. There was a holding back in Callie's voice, something that created a frisson of unease. "Have you heard anything . . . bad about him?"

Callie hesitated, then said, "Nothing specific. I know this cop, former cop actually. A . . . friend. He rarely talks about his work, but one time, when I had a cash crunch and was looking for some investors, I thought about approaching Guy. My cop friend told me to steer clear, at all costs."

"Is your cop credible?"

"He can be a pain, but he's honest and dedicated. I decided to follow his advice." She added the last of the vegetables to the pot, then turned up the heat. "I wouldn't worry about it. Armond's pretty by-the-book. Your situation's different. It's a job, not an investment; you could always quit if things didn't work out."

"True." They dropped the matter and went on to other topics, but the warning stayed, buried at the back of her thoughts, along with Mark's.

Joy didn't realize how much time had passed until she looked at her watch. "I didn't realize I'd left Mark so long." She gave Callie a hug. "It was good talking to you."

"Don't be such a stranger."

Entering the dining area, Joy realized she needn't have

worried about Mark. He was sitting with Charles and a couple of other waiters, in deep discussion about the Saints' chances for the football season.

The man was never bored; he found friends wherever he went.

She leaned a hip against Mark's chair and laid a hand on his head. His hair was soft and thick as plush velvet. "Are you ready to go?"

"With you, darlin'? Always."

There was no mistaking the fire deep in his eyes. It was instant desire, pure and unshielded. An answering flame started in her belly, replacing all warnings, all doubts, with thoughts of only him and the night to come.

They paused outside the restaurant.

"We should be driving back." Mark rested his arms on her shoulders. His fingers teased a strand of her hair, and the resultant tug of need reached clear to her toes. "Or we could spend the night in town."

Heart thumping against her ribs, Joy traced the faint lines at his eyes. Tonight no sunglasses shielded these windows to his soul. "Stay the night," she answered. "If you want."

His arms tightened. "Darlin', I've been wanting you since before you bashed me on the head with the egg."

"It's just tonight, you know."

He didn't answer that. "Follow me, darlin'."

It was a short walk, a few blocks down Magazine Street in the opposite direction from Callie's. The sultry night, the fluid feel of him pressed against her, the memories of seven years ago and of the past days, all wove around her in a spell of magic stronger than any illusion Mark created on stage.

CYBELE'S read the sign on the shop where he stopped.

"Who's Cybele?" asked Joy.

"Cybele Petrov. I stayed with her when I first came to New Orleans. I'd like you to meet her sometime; I think you'd like each other."

"Is she at home?"

Mark shook his head. "She's out of town, tracking down a Goddess and Reptile cabinet."

Joy blinked. "A what?"

"It's used in an illusion, darlin'."

Mark unlocked a side gate, then led her down a narrow aisle between the buildings and into a mustard-seed-sized patio. Joy barely had time to take in the tinkling fountain and the statuary hidden amidst the profusion of bushes, before Mark led her up stairs at the back and into a second-floor apartment.

Joy looked around. The room was clean, but crowded with a mishmash of antiques, magic equipment, and old-fashioned furniture. An ancient fortune-telling machine rested in one corner, the turbaned figure staring with silent impassivity, while a ventriloquist's dummy sat on a horse-hair love seat.

"Is this Cybele's apartment?"

"Not exactly. She stays in the rooms out front. She used to rent this half, but lately has been using it for storage."

"This was where you stayed?"

Mark nodded, watching her closely.

"We don't have to sleep where they can watch, do we?" She gestured to the dummy and fortune-teller.

"The bedroom's over there," Mark said with a laugh.

"Good." Joy moved closer. This was Mark, the friend of her youth, the lover she always wanted. Her body brushed against his, scattering the tingle of desire throughout each cell. Then, he'd held the promise of power. Now, he was muscular, lean and hard. A powerful man, both solid and strong. And always the man who was a part of her dreams.

Tonight, she wanted to dream. Not be the practical one, the reliable one. Tomorrow there would be time enough for reality.

Tonight, she would be the dreamer, the adventurer she feared to be.

She ran her hands through his silky hair, her fingertips sensitive to the heat of him. He moved his head, inviting her further touch.

Joy cupped the back of his head, then stood on tiptoe to kiss him.

"Show me your magic, Mark."

Chapter Twelve

"This is no illusion, darlin'."

Mark swept Joy into the bedroom before she could change her mind. The heavy curtains were drawn, so he switched on the bedside lamp. When they made love, he wanted to see Joy, the tint of her skin and the sunshine of her hair.

Through fears and mistakes, those pleasures had been denied him for too long.

The narrow yellow beam of light cast shadows in the corners and created only a small circle of illumination where they stood.

Joy gave a gasp of surprise. "No illusions, maybe, but that's a fairy tale bed."

The bed was an enormous four-poster that took a two-step footstool to reach the mattress. White eyelet fabric covered it, from the canopy atop to the drapes along the sides, to the coverlet and pillows.

Mark gave a rueful laugh. "I always figured that damn bed was Cybele's way of keeping me pure. No way I was going to let a woman see that I slept in a prissy thing like that."

"Did it work?"

"Then," he said shortly, "not now."

He picked her up and tossed her onto the soft cushion of the mattress, then followed her.

"Shoes," Joy reminded him, still laughing as she bounced. "Not on white eyelet."

It took Mark only seconds to remove his shoes and shirt, and only seconds longer to add hers to the pile. Then, he was lying alongside her, holding her close, her breasts rubbing against the hair on his chest. With each breath she took, he grew harder than a magician's wand.

Cupping her head between his hands, he tunneled his fingers through the fiery strands of her hair, holding her still for an urgent kiss.

She tasted like spices, like cinnamon and ginger.

Spices and sunshine.

"I'm glad I saved room for dessert," he muttered against her lips.

Joy sank into the wonder of his kiss, even as his weight bore her deeper into the luxurious mattress. There had been no one else with him in this idyllic spot. Only she shared this adventure, this joyous excitement.

He spun kisses across her cheeks, along her neck, nipped at her ear, burned her with each tiny contact. Joy ran her hands across the muscles in his back, feeling them shift beneath her touch. He moaned and buried his head against her neck. It was a heady feeling to know she had that power over him.

Then he shifted and his fingers played a delicate pattern across her breasts. Her breath caught as a shivering fire rolled across her.

She had always known his hands held power.

Mark ran the tip of his tongue across her lips, even as his hand massaged her belly with little circles. "Ah, darlin', open for me," he coaxed. "Let me kiss you on all the places I've dreamed about."

She could no more resist the power of his voice than she could resist the magic of his touch.

He kissed her then, and she kissed him back, deep like they both craved, hard like she needed.

He was hot to her touch, sleek in her arms. Joy unfastened the zipper of his jeans and reached below. He was hard, ready, and sprang to her touch. For a moment, Mark went utterly still, while she caressed him.

Then he shifted, just out of her reach. "You do that much longer, and this is going to be over a lot sooner than I intended."

"I'm ready."

He shook his head. "No, you're not, darlin'. Not quite yet. You're not burnin' deep enough."

"Not burning? I feel like I've swallowed a cup of cayenne pepper." She didn't remember ever being this hot, not even with him.

"Let me show you," he said gently.

With a deft motion, he divested himself of his remaining clothes. He bent down and cupped her breast in his hand. For one long moment, he trailed a finger across her sensitive flesh until a flush spread, then he took her breast into his mouth. He suckled and tugged at the nipple, playing it with his tongue and teeth and lips until she knew in resounding detail what he'd meant by burning deeper.

"How much more magic do you know?" she breathed.

"Two shows a night, sixty minutes a show."

Joy burst out laughing, amazed that he could bring as much pleasure to her mind as to her body.

"You doubt me?" he growled with mock fierceness.

Then he attended to her other breast. When he lifted, cayenne had become Cajun pepper sauce.

And she was totally naked.

Damn, but he had a clever touch. "Is that what's called sleight of hand?" she asked.

"A variation only for you." Then, for the longest moment, he just stared at her.

Joy ducked her head, suddenly shy, suddenly remembering the extra pounds she always intended to shed.

Mark tilted her head up, as usual reading her too well. "No, Joy, don't be embarrassed. I was just admiring the view. It's such a pretty one, and I've been hungering to see it again for a very long time."

She ran her fingers across his chest, trailed them through the dark hair along his abdomen and lower. "It's not as pretty as this view."

"Well, now, darlin', there I'd have to differ with you." He picked up her arm and kissed the faint scar left from a burn she'd gotten when she brushed against a sauté pan. He traced the white lines left when she'd cut herself first learning to chop with a sharp knife. "Beauty isn't about perfection, you see. It's about other things. Important things. You have sunshine in your hair and smiles in your

184

voice and kindness in your heart. You're beautiful; you always will be."

He tugged her upright until she sat cross-legged on the bed. "Let me show you. Wait here." Magnificently naked, he padded into the other room, but returned almost at once. He sat opposite her, then rubbed his palms together.

His hands looked empty; he had no pockets to hide a thing. What could he be doing? Slowly, Mark spread his hands apart.

A bright light exploded between his palms, filling the space with glittering stars. A faint aroma, a mix of morning dew and flame, wafted to her. "This is how you are to me," he said simply, then he closed his fingers and the stars winked out.

He leaned over, tilted up her chin, and gave her a tender kiss.

The love she had for Mark had never gone away, Joy knew, and she doubted it ever would. She closed her eyes and drew in a long ragged breath in response to the ache deep in her heart.

As if sensing her tumultuous emotions, Mark drew nearer to her. He covered her with his body and with an onslaught of sensation that buried all other thought. His solid legs pressed against hers. His feathery touch caressed everywhere. His sex throbbed against her. His scent and his taste were part of her.

"Let me show you another adventure, sweetheart." He trailed kisses from her neck, to her breast, where he paused to tease and lift. Then, he moved lower, across her belly to the apex of her thighs. All the time, he whispered crooning words, raunchy words, magic words of what they would share, words that cast away all doubts and questions.

His tongue touched her, most intimately, most privately, moving in a mimicry of penetration. His hands performed their own wizardry.

No illusion this. Dear heavens, she *was* burning! Before, the urgency of youth had precluded the time needed for this sweet torment.

She was bewitched and bewildered. Joy clutched Mark's shoulders, kneading the sweat-slick skin. Before she combusted, she wanted his lips on hers, wanted him inside her.

Yet, she couldn't wait. She went up in flames, a deep burning that did not quit.

He waited while she returned to earth, then slid up her, to settle between her legs.

Joy held his head between her hands and moved to meet his lips. "Not alone this time. I want you with me."

"This time together," he agreed and flexed his hips.

With one stroke, he was inside her, seated to the hilt. She stretched to fit his size, to take him as part of her. Her muscles contracted with exquisite reaction.

Mark gave a sigh of pleasure and his hands laced with hers. He held her gently, yet with tighter bonds than his magician's ropes ever could. He began to stroke, first slow and teasing, then faster until their joining was as far from his control as hers.

This time, the fire did not burn alone.

She was with her love.

And it was magic.

Mark awoke in the deep night. For a moment, the soft heat and warm pressure beside him were disorienting. They were fragments of a recurrent dream. His lungs tightened, and his eyes flew open. The light was still burning at the bedside, fortunately, for he hated darkness. Then he remembered reality.

Joy. Snuggled against him, close enough to steal his breath. Her soft skin fused against his body in an enveloping caress. His nose was buried in her wild, unbound hair.

His breath caught, not in the throes of claustrophobia, but in the sweet awakening of night desire.

He'd never had a chance to make love to her a second time in one night, nor a third time. He'd never had a chance to try all the variations and intimacies he'd imagined.

He'd never held her through the night.

An odd thought, for he'd never slept through the night at the side of any woman. Always he left, before the night shadows got too deep.

Tonight, all those dreams were possible.

Tonight, he had no desire to leave, only desire for Joy.

For a moment, he admired the curve of her shoulder. His hand cupped her breasts, first one, then the other, enjoying the way they filled his palm. She had such pretty breasts, to see and touch and taste.

His fingers danced down her front until he reached her sex. There, he played expertly with her, bringing the dampness of arousal, even before she slowly awoke to him.

Joy rolled to her back and gave him a sleepy grin.

Mark took that as an invitation and slid inside.

She wrapped her arms and legs about him.

He was home.

Joy slipped out of the bed, careful not to wake Mark. It had been a night of much loving and little sleep for them both, but she was too accustomed to getting up early to sleep late.

Mark, however, was still on magician's time.

She donned her panties and T-shirt, then wandered into the next room.

Joy explored a few minutes, marveling at the oddities Cybele had collected. She saw several things that she assumed were from the collections of past magicians, like the poster promoting a Houdini performance and a huge iron cage. *Wonder what illusion that is.*

Cybele must have fed Mark's love of magic, Joy realized, almost like the mother he'd never known. The old woman was important, in more ways than Mark probably admitted.

A framed newspaper photo caught her eye. It was of Mark and was dated last year. He was dressed all in black—short-sleeved T and tight denims—one of his stage costumes that belied the notion his illusions were created by something hidden up his sleeve or in a pocket. The caption said he was receiving the Brotherhood of Magicians' Gold Medal, one of the few performers to be honored so young.

She traced the line of his face, suddenly, painfully, aware of just how well he was doing. His hard work paid off in the perfection of his performances. He was clever and creative, with a winning stage presence.

"You're doing good, Mark. I'm proud of you," she whispered.

Yet, his success, as well as her needs, would keep them separate, two planets in different orbits.

Joy turned away from the photo. She had known that was the way of it; she had her heart protected. Last night was fulfillment, not risk, and she would be content with it.

She glanced over at the settee. In the quiet, sunny rooms, the dummy's smiling face seemed to mock her. *Too late*, it seemed to say. She picked it up and hid it out of sight, then laughed at her foolishness.

For a moment, she debated going out for some breakfast, then decided to wait. She supposed she could do a little work. Joy pulled a notebook from her purse. If she settled on the menu for Guy's dinner party, she could pick up some of the ingredients before they left New Orleans.

"Joy?" Mark's sleepy voice called from the bedroom.

Joy looked from her notebook to the bedroom door. Work could wait. She tossed the notebook aside and went back to Mark.

Hades! Couldn't he leave those two alone for a single day?

From his home, Zeus peered with annoyance into the far-see smoke at the sleeping man entangled in the sheets and at the woman tenderly kissing him, then silently letting herself out of the house. It was all too obvious what they'd been doing.

Bloody hormones!

How was he supposed to bring her love, when Joy persisted in the lamentable bad judgment of her line by falling for Mark Hennessy? Io had never been that stubborn.

"It seems Joy is not her ancestress," he told the large, black dog at his side, scratching Cerberus behind the ears. "Much as I try to make her so."

Cerberus gave a sharp questioning bark.

"Joy is accommodating, but not biddable," Zeus explained.

It had been so much easier when women deferred to their men.

But not as much fun, he admitted.

Regardless, his plans were a mess. Even coming back

here had been a failure, for Hera was nowhere to be found. He would go back to Louisiana.

"Would you like to go to Louisiana, boy?"

Cerberus nodded in agreement.

Zeus gave him an affectionate pat. "I've missed you. I don't know why you came back, but I'm glad you did." The dog terrorizing his factory had indeed been Cerberus, although the dog wisely concealed his extra two heads. To the amazement of all, as soon as Zeus appeared, the dog trotted over and licked his hand. Apparently, Cerberus had gotten what he wanted—Zeus.

Zeus returned his attention to the sleeping Mark. It was time to take serious measures to break up those two.

Annoyed, he touched his ring to the smoke.

Joy. Strawberries. Lick and taste. The throes of an erotic dream enveloped Mark. *Two shows a night? Hah!* announced his drowsy brain with primitive satisfaction. *Try three and ready for four.*

The zap of electricity jolted him upright, ripping him out of the fabric of dreams.

"What the hell?" His heart pounding against his ribs, Mark laid a hand on his chest. "What the hell was that?" he repeated, his voice raspy.

He looked and listened. All was silent, not even the sound of Joy talking to herself. Nothing to explain the rude awakening.

Except, perhaps, the absence of Joy.

Mark felt his breath and heartbeat return to normal. He was left with only a residual tingling in his fingertips, a morning hard-on with no relief in sight, and a prodding instinct that something was missing.

The bathroom door was open and he felt the steam from it, evidence Joy had taken a shower, but she wasn't there now.

He got out of bed and, naked, padded into the other room. No Joy.

That nagging instinct drew him to the front of the house and the windows that faced the street. There, he saw Joy. She was walking away.

Leaving. Mark gripped the window jamb, the wood digging into his palms. His gut churned around the hollow pit in his stomach. He hated this ache of vulnerability, hated giving anyone power over him.

Yet, he wanted Joy, he admitted. That fact wasn't going away. Last night had proved it. Could he bring her into the circle of his life? She'd like the freedom, the excitement of life on the road.

His jaw thrust out, as she turned a corner and was lost to view. She is coming back, he told himself. She'd simply gone for fruit or a paper. Joy was too honest to sneak out. She'd be back.

He should tell her all about Centurion, about the book, about Armond.

He didn't dare.

Her honesty, that same honesty that drew him to her like a tot to a circus, kept him silent. If she knew even a fraction of what Centurion did, she wouldn't be able to keep that knowledge hidden.

She wouldn't be safe if Centurion thought she was no longer under his control. There was no telling what he would do to her. The possibilities knotted Mark's gut.

She wouldn't be safe, and he had found that keeping her safe was more important than Armond's justice, more important than the magic book, more important than any illusion.

He would do whatever he must to keep her safe.

Thursday night, at Centurion's party, he would make his first move.

In the meantime, Mark just hoped he'd told Joy enough to make her wary, to keep her from becoming further tangled in Centurion's web, but not enough that Centurion would suspect her. He hoped that when this was all over she'd understand why he'd kept silent.

Knowing Joy, she probably would be furious.

Chapter Thirteen

The smell of fresh coffee and sizzling butter greeted Joy when she returned, a white paper bag in hand. She followed her nose to the kitchen.

Mark stood at the counter, his back to her. He was dressed, but barefoot. Joy tiptoed in and laid a hand on his butt in an intimate caress. "Hey, stranger," she growled.

Mark spun around, spatula in hand. "Where've you been?" he demanded.

Joy raised her brows at his abrupt question.

He ran a hand across the back of his neck. "Sorry. I just . . . I woke up and didn't know where you'd gone. Where were you?" he asked more mildly.

She held up the paper sack. "Getting bagels. There's a place around the corner that makes them fresh. I didn't think I'd be gone that long or I'd have left a note. The bagels weren't ready, so I waited." She looked over his shoulder. "I could have stayed in. Mmmm, I love pancakes."

"Blueberry ones."

"My favorites. They smell good." Automatically, Joy reached for the spatula he held. "I'll finish up for you."

He lifted the spatula out of her reach, then pointed it at the table. "I'm cooking. You sit there and drink your orange juice. The pancakes will be done in a moment."

Joy sat, then fidgeted in her seat. She couldn't remember the last time she'd been in a kitchen and wasn't doing the cooking. She half-rose. "I can toast the bagels."

Mark pointed again with the spatula. "Sit."

She jiggled her foot up and down, gulped a swallow of the cold juice, looked for something to do.

Mark gave her an exasperated look. "Can't you just sit and let me cook?"

People didn't cook for *her*; she cooked for them.

Except for Mark.

Bemused, Joy settled back in her chair. Mark's easy motions were a pleasure to watch. He set a plate in front of her, along with butter and syrup, poured her coffee and refilled the juice, and then sat beside her with his own plate.

The pancakes were knobby-shaped, very brown on one side and pale tan on the other. Joy cut off a piece.

They were also delicious.

"We need to be leaving soon," she said, finishing off the pancakes. "Your assistant is coming today, right?"

"Right," he answered, a warm, speculative look in his eye. "But we've got enough time."

"Time for what?"

With those same easy movements, Mark lifted her from her seat and set her on the table. He settled himself between her thighs, and his hands slid along her legs, lifting her skirt. He bent to kiss her. "This."

Dia Trelawny was stunning.

As Joy watched from the garden, Mark's assistant emerged with lithe grace from the truck. She was a leggy blonde, had a smile like Julia Roberts, and not an ounce of extra weight. She wore red heels, a camisole top tucked into tight jeans, and long, glittering earrings.

Joy wiped sweat from her face with her garden gloves, then grimaced as she realized she'd probably left a streak of dirt across her cheek. Since she got home from New Orleans, she'd been working in the garden all afternoon, weeding and harvesting cucumbers to use for a summer soup, and had lost track of time.

"Great." Joy blew a strand of hair out of her eyes. "My hair's a jumbled mess. I've got on strawberry-stained shorts that are too tight. I'm grubby and sweaty and cranky from fluid depletion—"

Mark caught sight of her and waved. "Joy, come meet Jax and Dia."

"—and I've got to welcome a twentysomething Aphrodite."

A lanky youth who looked barely past the age of majority vaulted out of the truck bed, where he'd been sitting atop a couple of crates. Running a hand across his spiky brown hair, he surveyed the surroundings with a nonchalant look. Interested, but unwilling to admit it.

The brilliant but "sometimes-pain-in-the-butt" Jax, Joy

decided. He had a row of gold hoops along one ear, tattoos on one wrist, baggy jeans and huge sneakers, and the bravado swagger of youth.

Carrying her basket of cucumbers, Joy reached the arrivals. Mark rested his hand at Joy's waist with a casual intimacy he'd adopted since last night and performed the introductions. Jax stuffed his hands in his pockets and nodded, until Mark's frown prompted a haphazard high-five.

Dia gave her a friendly smile and didn't seem to mind a slightly grubby handshake. "It's nice of you to let us stay here."

"My pleasure."

Jax ran an assessing look over Joy. "Mark's been talking about you. No stress, it was all good, but he says you're a kick-ass cook."

"Kick-ass is his word, not mine," Mark murmured.

The comment didn't faze Jax. "Can you make cabbage rolls? My grandma used to make them, but no one in Vegas has the touch."

"I can try."

He shrugged. "No big deal if you can't." The cool demeanor disappeared at the sound of a loud mating boom from the ostrich pens. Jax's eyes widened. "Ostriches? You gonna make them disappear, Mark? That would be as kick-ass as the elephants last year."

"I think I'll pass for now," Mark answered. "We've got a great show already."

"Damn straight about that. Thanks to me. I told you those red Vari-Lite spots and the mines with glitter release would make the finale rival any show out there."

"We all acknowledge your genius," Dia said drily.

"C'mon, brat, let's get the equipment unloaded into the barn," Mark said.

"The barn? Marcus in a barn?" Jax gave a hoot of laughter, and it was the most infectious laugh Joy had ever heard, a definite contrast to her original impression of the boy. "I've never even been in a barn."

"City boy," retorted Mark. "You need to see a bit of life beyond wires and computer screens. Coming, Dia?"

"In a moment."

"Oh, I see plenty of life," Jax answered, sounding quite adult as he followed Mark back into the truck. "Remember last year when we were in Toronto . . ."

The remaining conversation was lost to Joy when Mark started the truck and drove down the rutted road to the barn. The only other thing she heard was when Jax cupped his hands and shouted back to them, "Hey, Dia, bring us a couple of colas."

Her answer was an earthy laugh and a rude gesture.

"A running joke," Dia explained. "Jax persists in claiming it's my function to bring drinks since I'm a woman." She shook her head. "Children can be annoying. Especially the brilliant ones. When Jax first started hanging around the show, the crew all thought of him as a troublemaking pest and laid odds on when he'd get into some bigtime trouble."

Dia pulled a tissue out of her purse and dabbed at her face. She wore little makeup that Joy could see, but even this close up, she had an eye-catching beauty. "My, it's humid here. I'm used to the desert."

"Would you like some ice tea?"

"Thanks. I also need to use your facilities."

Inside the house, Joy put the cucumbers away, then washed her hands. Faced with Dia's cool beauty, she wished she could take a full bath, then admitted a whole day at the spa wouldn't help that contrast. Joy held up two iced tea pitchers. "Sweet or unsweet?"

"Unsweet."

Joy poured the drink, then showed Dia the bathroom. Next she poured some more tea into a plastic cup and put a lid on it, then pulled a cola from the refrigerator. She put both into a basket before adding a paper plateful of cookies.

"Despite what Jax said, he doesn't expect you to wait on them," Dia said, returning.

"I don't mind. It's a cook thing, Southern hospitality and all," Joy added with a smile. "And it is hot out there."

Dia followed her out.

"If Jax was such a pest, how'd he get a position with the tour?" Joy asked.

"Mark saw something in the kid, something we missed. He gave him things to do, let him help, and it turns out Jax has a real talent for computers and special effects we need for the show. He gradually took over more and more of it."

Dia sipped her tea. "Mark does that with everybody, brings them in, makes them feel at home. He's a real pleasure to work with. His show is still small money-wise, so he doesn't pay a lot, but he never has trouble filling positions."

"Mark can be very charming."

Dia smiled. "He has a way of getting people to do things. Like Jax. The kid was begging to go on tour with us, but Mark refused to let him until he finished high school. *And* his GPA had to be at least two-point-oh if he wanted to tour that summer."

"Jax finished?"

"Better believe it. Got a four-point-oh, just to prove he could. Like I said, Jax is smart but annoying."

"So, what did they do in Toronto?"

"I have no idea." Dia laughed. "I don't want to know. I'd make a lousy mother."

"I take it you don't have any of your own."

"Kids? No way. My sister had four, two sets of twins. I get to be the globetrotting aunt who comes, spoils them, then leaves." She shuddered. "That's as close to mother-hood as I want to get."

Joy laughed, enjoying Dia's refreshing candor.

It took them only a few minutes to reach the barn. Mark and Jax were wrestling a shiny box out of its crate.

Dia swore. "Mark, this Pygmalion effect isn't going to be one of those where I have to be a contortionist is it?"

"No, all you need to do is—" He glanced up, caught sight of Joy, and stopped. "We'll go over it later."

"Magicians' secrets," Joy muttered, unable to prevent the quick stab of hurt at being excluded, even though she understood it.

"The code of the brotherhood," Dia agreed. "Thanks for the drink." She took the basket from Joy, then called out. "Let's get to work, guys."

"You're all invited to dinner," Joy told them.

"Thanks," Mark answered. "Will you close the barn door when you leave?"

Joy waved her hand in acknowledgment, then left, sparing one last glance for the three performers already hud-dling together and gesturing toward the box. None of them noticed her. She closed the door.

Outside, Joy leaned her back against the corrugated metal. Her breath dragged in the sultry air. For one moment she was back in the awkwardness of childhood. The chubby one, the shy one, the new kid. Watching, never quite fitting in, both alone and lonely.

She stared at the farm stretched out before her. It was beautiful. The oaks, the ostrich pens, the gardens, the white house, all shimmered like a fairyland under the heated sun.

Yet, in this moment, none of it seemed familiar, none of it seemed like home. It wasn't hers, not really, she admitted. She'd worked for it, sweated for it, worried about it, loved it, but it belonged to Nicole. Or, it would in two weeks, for Joy had no expectations that Henry Valcour would return, despite Nicole's solid belief to the contrary.

Men didn't return to women in her family.

Throwing off the feeling, Joy pushed away from the barn and walked steadily away. She had birds to water, a recipe for rabbit étouffée to try out, and a dinner party to plan.

Joy sniffed, then tasted, the rabbit étouffée. Good, except for a touch too much filé powder. It would serve for dinner tonight with a salad and some fresh peaches.

She put the rabbit away, then sat at the table, pencil in hand, finishing notes about Guy's party. Corn was fresh and greens were plentiful. Maybe a relish salad?

A knock on the door startled her, for the house was hushed. Nicole had taken Hope and her friend Eliza swimming. Looking over, she saw a woman standing on the back porch. Joy went to the door.

Her visitor was imposing. Tall, with elegantly coiffed brown hair, in her mid-fifties, Joy guessed, although her age was hard to determine. The woman could best be described as handsome; her features were too strong to be considered pretty, but her bone structure gave her a classic appeal. In the heat of summer, her perfectly applied makeup and tailored suit seemed oddly formal.

As she greeted the woman, Joy was all too aware that she still wore shorts stained from the garden.

"I'm sorry to interrupt, but no one answered the front doorbell," the woman said.

Joy flushed. She'd been meaning to get that fixed, but it kept slipping her mind since no one ever used it. Most people just came to the back or knocked. "No problem. Can I help you?"

"Are you Joy Taylor?"

"Yes."

The woman gave Joy an assessing, and not particularly friendly, glance. "This fall, my cosmetics company will hold its convention for our salesladies here. We have some special functions that I want supervised by a local chef."

"I don't do a lot of catering." Her allergy tended to be at odds with the clients' choices.

"But I understand you have. Let's discuss what I want, and you'll give me a quote if you're interested."

"Certainly." The job with Centurion wasn't a lock by any means, and she could use the work. Joy ushered her visitor inside. "Let's go into my office—"

The woman swept an imperious gaze around the kitchen, then settled into a kitchen chair. "I prefer to stay here."

"Oh, of course, fine. Let me get my calendar and price list."

Joy raced from the room to her office. She caught sight of herself in a hall mirror, and swore. No makeup, her hair a fright. At least she'd washed and put on a clean shirt so she didn't smell of the garden. Did she have time to put on clean shorts? No. The potential client didn't seem to be a patient woman.

In five minutes, Joy was back in the kitchen, trying to quiet her panting breath. The client was thumbing through Joy's dog-eared cookbook from the Culinary Institute of America.

"Have you been to CIA?"

"No, but I've taught myself using their text."

"I like women with initiative; that's why I prefer to work with female-owned businesses." The woman assessed Joy with a cool glance. She put the cookbook away and sat back at the table. "I expect only the best for my people."

Joy heard the unspoken command: *So show me what you can do.*

Opening her planner, she asked, "What's your company's name?"

"Peacock Cosmetics. I'm Harriet, Harriet Juneau."

They discussed a timetable, what services and foods would be needed; then Joy worked up a quote. The quote was a competitive one, but it was hard to tell by Harriet's reaction whether the order was likely to go her way. Harriet Juneau would make a good poker player.

"That price is guaranteed for fourteen days," Joy said.

"That should be plenty of time," Harriet murmured.

Joy leaned back in the chair. "How did you hear about me?"

Harriet hesitated. "An old acquaintance. Zeke Jupiter."

Joy smiled. "Zeke? He's nice, isn't he? I like him. We're working together on the Mushroom Festival. I can't wait to see what his fireworks are like."

It was the wrong thing to say.

Harriet Juneau drew back, clearly angry; then cold,

porcelain perfection slipped across her face. "Don't be too enthusiastic. I've known Zeke Jupiter longer than anyone, and loyalty is not his best feature."

Joy blinked. "Ah, well, I just met him, and . . ."

Harriet Juneau stood and held out her hand. "I'll get back to you. I'm going to be in town for a few days."

Joy shook the hand, then ushered her client to the door. When Harriet left, Joy leaned her head against the doorjamb.

"Note to self. *Never* mention Zeke Jupiter to Harriet Juneau again. And vice versa."

It was probably too late to repair the damage. Hell's bells, she'd blown it.

"I just hope Guy's dinner party goes without a hitch."

Joy called Guy and got his approval on the menu she'd planned for his dinner party. While they were talking, she mentioned her houseguests, and he invited them. She promised to pass along the invitation. She had just hung up when the phone rang beneath her hand.

"Hey, baby doll," Mark's agent greeted her. "Is Mark there? He doesn't answer the room phone."

"He's outside. It'll take a few moments to get him. Can he call you back or do you want to hold?"

"Tell him we need to talk. Pronto. It's about Rome. I'll be waiting by the phone for his call. *Ciao.*" He hung up.

Mark was still working with Dia and Jax in the barn. A boom box played a sultry tune. Mark and Dia were dancing, a sensual modern dance. They swayed together, her back to his front, her head on his shoulder, while Mark trailed a hand from her uplifted palm, down her arm and side, to find a home at her hip. His fingers spanned her hips, gave her a twist and she gracefully spun away from him.

The clutch of envy caught Joy by surprise.

Jax knelt before them scribbling notes. "Soft spots," he muttered, then glanced at his watch. "Five minutes, then the explosion."

"Slow it down, Dia," added Mark. "If you go that fast, the light's going to look jerky."

"Got it."

He reached down and set the music back a few bars. They repeated the steps, Dia's spin slower and more teasing this time. "Perfect. Now let's take it from the top."

Joy cleared her throat before they could start. "Mark. Sorry to bother you, but you had a phone call. Your agent. He said it was urgent."

"Clive thinks everything do to with money is urgent."

"If you're interested, dinner will be ready in about half an hour. Oh, Jax and Dia, Guy Centurion invited you to his dinner party day after tomorrow. I'm cooking."

Jax made a face. "Dinner party? Thanks, but no thanks. I'd rather make explosions."

"I'd love to," answered Dia.

Mark glanced at his watch, then flipped off the music and grabbed a towel to wipe the sweat from his face. "Let's call it a day. You've got the basic steps, Dia, and we'll work on the illusion tomorrow. Jax, after you see the entire illusion and the stage, you can put together the equipment you'll need."

"Right, boss," Jax answered. "Where am I staying?"

"With me." Mark strode over to Joy and gave her a kiss on the top of the head. "Can you show Dia her room?"

"Let me get my bag out of the truck," Dia called.

The four of them walked out of the barn. And straight into Zeke Jupiter.

"Hey, Zeke. You're back. With a guest." Joy eyed the enormous black dog at his side. A ferocious-looking dog, though the mere touch of Zeke's hand at his head seemed to control him.

His head? His heads? Her eyes narrowed, then she blinked. The bright sun was playing tricks. For a moment, it seemed as though she saw the shadow of two more heads on the dog.

"Yes, as you can see, I've been forced to return with this dog. Might you know a place where I can board him?" Zeke gave her an expectant look.

The dog gave a snarl of displeasure, and the bristles on his neck stood up, waving like tiny snakes. Joy stepped back.

"He doesn't like kennels," Zeke offered.

Mark crouched down until he was eye-level with the dog. Softly he crooned to it, and the hackles settled. "What's this fellow's name?"

"Sir," answered Zeke.

The dog gave a loud bark, loud enough for three throats.

"Short for Cerberus," added Zeke grudgingly.

"Named after the dog of myth?" Mark ran a hand along the dog's sleek coat. "Well, hello, there, Cerberus."

Danged if that dog didn't almost purr under Mark's petting.

Joy knew exactly how he felt.

Still scratching the dog under the chin, Mark rose to his feet. "I don't mind keeping him at the caretaker's cottage."

"He won't go after the ostriches?" Joy asked Zeke.

Zeke was looking at Mark, a strange look—half pride, half annoyance—on his face. "Not if Mark watches him, and you feed him regularly."

Mark gave the dog another pet. "I think we understand each other."

"Then I'll bring his dish and food." Zeke leaned over and gave Joy a peck on the cheek. "Thank you for keeping Cerberus," he said simply.

The far-see smoke dissipated under the breeze from the waving peacock feather.

So, Zeus was up to his old tricks. Kissing the woman. In all the centuries, he hadn't changed.

Hera gave a sigh of disappointment. Was anything else to be expected?

His paramour would pay, of course.

Pity. She liked Joy Taylor. More than that insipid Io.

One face remained in the swirling traces of smoke. It was a familiar face. Hermes. Or rather, one of his line, but the resemblance was very strong. The son of Olympus also watched with annoyance as Zeus kissed Joy.

Now there was an interesting possibility.

Chapter Fourteen

So far, so good.

Joy took a moment to peer out of the kitchen door, making sure the waiters were on their toes. She needn't have worried. They were all professionals.

The bowls of spicy peanut soup came back empty, and the diners advanced eagerly to baked goat cheese and a salad of mixed greens.

A fly buzzed by her ear. Absently she waved it away, her attention caught by Mark.

He wasn't seated by Dia, a fact that gave her more pleasure than it should. He looked handsome tonight. She'd never seen him out of the jeans and shorts that constituted his uniform on the farm.

He wore all black—slacks, shirt, tie—with an air of formality that she didn't associate with Mark. Or, at least, that *she* rarely saw. He was conversing easily with the people around him.

As if sensing her, he looked up. A smile played across his lips, a secret connection between the two of them.

Joy ducked back into the kitchen, brushing away another fly. Another one perched in her hair while a fourth buzzed her ear.

"Hey, check and see where there's an open window. We're getting a lot of flies in here."

Mark savored the warmth left by that small exchange with Joy. He had missed holding her, sleeping with her, in the two days since coming back from New Orleans. With her preparations for this party and with Jax and Dia around, they had neither time nor opportunity for anything beyond a passing touch or a brief word.

Things would be different once he convinced her to come on the road with him.

From the corner of his eye, Mark saw Centurion toying with a wineglass. His head was tilted, as though he listened to the woman beside him, but his speculative gaze was on Mark.

He'd finally connected Marcus of the present to the brash street kid from the past, Mark realized.

The past and present must be put to rest before there could be any future.

Time to act.

Mark murmured his excuses and pushed away from the table. Outside the dining room, however, he headed toward Centurion's office. He figured he had three, maybe five, minutes before Centurion came looking for him. Not enough time to find the book, unless Centurion had conveniently left it on his desk, but time enough to verify the floor plan and security measures.

Mark's practiced eye ran over the window alarms, noted a bodyguard outside. It would be difficult getting back in to search for the book, but not impossible. That was the contingency plan, however. With luck, he wouldn't need to.

The book wasn't sitting on the desk. Things were never that easy. No safe behind the ugly abstract painting on the wall, either.

Mark glanced at his watch. Time to get back. He reached the bathroom door, just as Centurion strode from the dining room.

The old timing was still good as ever.

Centurion's eyes scraped across Mark. "Ah, there you are. I thought you'd gotten lost."

"Not a bit."

"Excellent." His attention shifted toward his office, then back. "I'd like you to stay for an after-dinner brandy, Mark, when my guests leave."

Mark stuck his hands in his pockets. "Now, why do you think I'd want to do that?" he asked pleasantly. "We aren't the best of friends."

"Because you're older, and I believe a little wiser as to how the world works." He paused. "Because you want something. Otherwise you wouldn't risk coming back."

"I came with Dia." Mark offered another expected protest.

"My chauffeur can take her home."

"I'll ask Zeke Jupiter. He seems to like going to the farm." Not that he trusted, or liked, Jupiter, but he was a damn sight better than any employee of Centurion's.

"You'll stay for brandy, then?"

"I believe I will."

"Fine." Centurion gestured toward the dining room. "The entree should be served by now. Are you enjoying the talents of my chef?"

Mark gave him a satisfied grin. "Very much."

The meal was an utter disaster!

The flies were *everywhere*. In a mere twenty minutes they had multiplied until swarms filled the kitchen with their drone. Crawling on the entrées, burrowing into the vegetables, buzzing around her and her staff.

Joy bit her lip, biting back the tears at the sight of her frantic staff waving away the hordes of vermin and emptying plate after plate into the garbage.

Plates of grilled pork, roasted garlic, and balsamic vinegar sauce that should be on the table. Carefully prepared food she couldn't serve, not now.

She couldn't serve *anything* until she got rid of the flies.

"Open up the back doors. Get the fans blowing. Maybe we can blow them out."

While her staff worked at clearing the flies, Joy tore through the kitchen, looking for the source of the flies.

At last she found a piece of pork; spoiled and rank and crawling with flies, big and little, black and shiny blue and iridescent green. She wrapped up the meat, triple wrapped it, and threw it out.

Hell's bells, had one of her staff left it out? Had she missed putting it with the other meats? How had she overlooked something like that?

The sickness in the pit of her stomach had little to do with the flies invading her food and everything to do with the knowledge that she'd screwed up royally.

With a sharp crack of his palm on the kitchen door, Guy

210

entered. "Where is the entrée?" Flies swarmed around him. "What the hell? *Joy!*"

Joy opened her mouth to answer.

A fly flew into her mouth.

Oh, yuck! She was gagging and coughing, trying to spit it into a napkin, when Guy strode to her side. He clapped her on the back. She gulped. And swallowed the fly.

Joy stood rigid, trying not to throw up.

"What's going on?" Guy demanded.

Joy grabbed up a glass of wine and downed it, heedless of the flies she had to shoo off. Alcohol was an antiseptic. "There was a piece of meat," she stuttered. "Spoiled from being left out of the refrigerator. It must have attracted them." With the meat gone, the swarms of flies did seem to be clearing.

Guy stared at the food emptied into the garbage.

"I couldn't serve it after the flies walked all over it."

A shudder went through him. "Of course not. The fact remains that I have a table full of guests and they need to be served." He looked at her expectantly.

If she could pull off a miracle, she just might have a chance to save her job.

And her reputation as a chef.

Joy ran her mind over the supplies in the well-stocked pantry. Chicken. Andouille sausage. Rice. With the soup and salad, the lack of vegetable wouldn't be too noticeable. The bread had been wrapped and warming in the oven and the dessert was under plastic wrap, so both of those were okay.

"I can make an étouffée."

A remaining fly buzzed irritatingly about her head. She brushed it away, and it bit her on the hand. "Ouch." Joy scratched at the welt, one of many she'd gotten, though she seemed to be the only one of her staff so afflicted.

Guy reached up, grabbed the fly, and crushed it in his palm. He brushed it to the floor, then washed his hands at the sink.

"I suggest you get started."

Zeus was delighted to take Dia home. She looked so much like Leda, the mortal woman who had long ago borne his twins, Helen and Pollux. Ah, but he had loved Leda for a time. She was so nurturing, so dignified. He still recalled that interlude with warm fondness.

As they left Centurion's party, Dia turned the air conditioning in his rental car a notch cooler. "Do you mind? I don't think I've been cool since I got here."

"Anything for one so beautiful." Zeus felt indulgent, though in truth heat and humidity rarely bothered him. Such were the traits of his race. He picked up her hand and kissed it.

Dia leaned back in the leather seat and eyed him with a boldly teasing look. "Why, Zeke Jupiter, are you hitting on me?"

"Just a little, enchantress. You remind me of someone I once knew. Someone of whom I was quite fond. Do you mind?"

She shook her head and smiled at him. "Not in the least. You look familiar, too." She snapped her fingers. "I know, Sean Connery. I bet you hear that a lot."

"Frequently."

Her laugh, her smile. Zeus gave a sigh of pleasure, then one of faint regret. He had promised himself there could be no one until he found Hera.

"Say," said Dia in her throaty voice, "would you like to see a little magic when we get to the farm?"

Some promises were so difficult to keep.

* * *

Joy was bone tired when she finished in the kitchen. She hadn't seen Guy since the flies, and she didn't want to. All she wanted right now was to go home and figure out what to do about finding a new job.

The étouffée had been good, but not one of her best, she admitted. Most people wouldn't notice, but Guy Centurion had. He had been furious, coldly so.

No chance he'd hire her now. His parties were noted for their perfection, and she'd given him his first black mark. He wouldn't easily forget that.

She'd hidden the problems from the guests, but she had no illusions about word getting out. This was a small town. Would anyone trust her in a kitchen after this? She'd already heard the joking nickname she'd acquired among the staff—Fly Lady.

The pit of her stomach ached, reminding her of childhood days spent hoping this move, this stepfather, this town would be the last.

At least, she still had the ostriches to tide her over. Given time, she'd live this down. This town was her home; people would understand. They had to.

Joy trudged to her car. To her surprise, she saw Mark's truck still in the driveway. As much as Mark disliked Guy, what could they possibly be talking about this late?

She got in her car and drove home.

Mark swirled the brandy in the snifter, then took a small taste. He made an approving noise, which seemed to satisfy Centurion. His honest opinion, which was that he generally avoided alcohol and especially disliked brandy, would not portray the image he wanted tonight.

Mark took another sip, then set the brandy aside. Centurion lit a thin cigar and offered him one. Mark shook his head and waited.

Centurion leaned his head back and blew out a thin stream of smoke. "I know who you are, of course. But I expect you knew I would recognize you."

"I don't hide who I am."

"Oh, but you do. Your past, before you showed up in New Orleans seven years ago, is quite murky. As though Mark Hennessy didn't exist."

"I moved around a lot." Mark hid his satisfaction at the frustration he heard in Centurion's voice. His nomadic lifestyle hadn't left many official records, and, although his dad had a police record, Mark had escaped any charges, although he'd had his share of warnings and close calls.

Centurion studied him over the rim of the brandy snifter. "You're different from the annoying boy who made wild accusations against me. You've acquired some polish."

"And a knowledge of how the world works," Mark agreed.

"Are you back for revenge?"

"Revenge is a useless emotion. You want to know why I'm here?" He pretended to sip his brandy. "The Mushroom Festival. As I already told you, first and foremost, I'm a magician. A performer."

"I would have thought this event was too small for a man of your talents."

Mark gave an easy shrug. "I'm between gigs, readying a tour. It's a chance to try out some new routines. Easy money."

"I didn't think you were into 'easy money.' "

"My magic's different. I'll perform anywhere." Mark

214

made his voice soothing, convincing. "What other people do, that's their business."

"That doesn't explain why you came three weeks early."

"I'm sure you've seen the equipment in the barn. I needed a place to practice." He shared his practiced grin.

Centurion seemed to settle back, his tension receding.

Hell, maybe there was something to Cybele's claim that he had a "psychic charisma." Immediately, Mark dismissed the notion. Joy and Cybele might believe in that UFO mumbo jumbo stuff, but he didn't.

Time to get to the heart of the matter. "You do have something I'm interested in, though."

Centurion drew on the cigar, the only sign of his sudden tension. "What?"

"A book of magic. Ah, I can tell you know about it."

"I know about a great many things I have no direct hand in. What makes you think I have it?"

Mark decided to throw him a crumb of information, something Centurion would find by digging if he didn't already know. "Cybele Petrov. I owe her a favor. She gave me an alibi once."

"I see." Centurion tapped his ash into the ashtray. "Cybele is mistaken: I don't have the book. But I know who does."

The man was an excellent liar. Mark might have believed him, except in the words of the old adage: it takes one to know one. "Who?"

Centurion smiled. "I don't think it would be wise to tell you."

Mark gave him a mocking grin. "You're an upright citizen. Why not go to the police with your knowledge?"

"Because the person who has it would destroy it. Then no one would be satisfied. Why didn't *you* go to them?"

Mark rubbed a hand against his neck, for the first time allowing the illusion that he was nervous to show through. "I'd just as soon keep the law out of my affairs."

"I understand." Centurion almost concealed his smirk of satisfaction.

Good. Centurion expected the worst and lived by looking for weaknesses, the things he could exploit. Mark played directly to those expectations.

He stirred in the chair. "Can you get the book for me? I'm not particular about the price."

"I'm sure we can come to a suitable agreement." Centurion finished his cigar, then sipped his brandy. "So, it's the book you're interested in. Joy has no influence on your staying?"

Tension knotted Mark's gut. This came to the heart of it. Joy. Protecting Joy.

By meeting openly with Centurion, he had hoped to allay suspicions about his return, or at least delay Centurion's violent response.

Joy was another matter. Mark had seen Centurion with Joy; the man wanted more than ostrich meat and feathers. But there was no concealing Mark's relationship with her, and Joy, bless her honest eyes, couldn't hide her feelings.

The key was to stick around, while convincing Centurion his interest in Joy extended only to bedding her for the next few weeks.

"She's not why I came," The lie was easy, convincing. "But she's one reason I'm hanging around here for a few weeks."

"Only a few weeks?"

216

Mark gave an easy laugh. "Do you really think I'd get tied to one place longer than I have to? I've got too many places to go and audiences to woo."

"Joy has talents I enjoy. I wouldn't want her . . . enticed away."

His muscles tightened, and Mark thanked the years of stage training that kept turmoil from showing on his face. Instead, he allowed a masculine smirk to touch his lips. "I don't do long-term engagements."

The words tasted of ash, but it was important Centurion believed he wanted only casual sex from Joy and that he'd have no trouble leaving and not looking back. It was the only thing that would protect Joy.

"She doesn't mean a thing to you?"

"Just a good time. We agreed, keep it brief and casual."

"And what if I were to suggest you leave her alone?"

Mark picked up the brandy and finished it in one swallow. It burned from his mouth to his gut and left him dizzy. He rose to his feet.

"Couple of problems with that, Centurion. You see, she's being *real* nice to me, and I like that. Not too often I get home cooking and other . . . treats brought right to my door. Besides, I made a promise to the lady; I'd stay through breeding season. I don't like breaking promises to ladies."

He'd broken too many already.

He would not abandon Joy again.

Mark paused in the doorway. "Get me the book. I'll pay the price, then in a month I'll be gone for good."

He left. The performance had been one of his finest illusions.

* * *

Dia had a magic touch.

When she'd asked if he wanted to see a little magic, she had meant that quite literally. Zeus watched Dia move through her routine, smoothly and flawlessly. There was a grace to her performance that was sometimes missing in some of the more frenetic magicians he'd seen. He guessed it was partly Mark's influence and partly her own distinct style.

When she finished, she was panting and coated with sweat.

Zeus clapped with enthusiasm.

Dia flopped down beside him on a bale of straw. "Did you like it?" she asked.

"Beautiful," he said honestly.

"Do you think it would play by itself? Hold an audience?"

"In the palm of your enchanting hand." He lifted up said hand and kissed her on the palm, lingering just a moment, remembering the taste of a woman.

It had been too long.

Promises, he reminded himself. *Hera*.

Dia gave him a dazzling smile, and Zeus felt his blood roar through his body. When she leaned forward, and he caught the womanly fragrance of her, he swallowed hard.

Perhaps one kiss would not be cheating.

"Can I tell you a secret?" she whispered in that throaty, sexy voice of hers, her hand still resting in his.

"Of course."

"I have a chance to solo."

Zeus blinked, startled for a moment, until he realized *she* was talking about magic. "Your own tour?"

She shook her head. "Not a whole tour, not yet. But a

218

short series of performances out in California. My agent called me about them. It would be a chance to show my skills, prove that I can do an entire show."

"What about your tour with Mark?"

She bit her lip. "That's the problem. Mark's a gem to work with. He gave me a chance, when everyone else just wanted me to dance and look pretty."

A look of revulsion crossed her face, and Zeus got the impression some employers had wanted very private dancing.

"Would you miss his entire tour?"

"Only the Mushroom Festival and the following couple of performances."

"Surely he can spare you that long?"

"Except we're working on some new effects. The Mushroom Festival was our chance to try them out."

"How are your rehearsals going?"

"Flawlessly." She made an amused grimace. "For all his charm, Mark can be quite demanding."

"The Trickster always was so," he murmured. "Wouldn't he, of all people, understand what this means? Just talk to him."

"You're right." She gave him a bewitching smile. "Thanks for listening."

As he was talking to Dia, Zeus's sensitive ears picked up the sound of Joy's returning car followed by the slam of her car door. She had a habit of wandering through the farm at night before retiring, making sure all was well. Would she check out the light in the barn?

More than likely.

An enticing scheme took hold of him.

Zeus inched closer to Dia and stroked his lightning ring

down her cheek. Her eyes widened at the sparkle of electricity that danced from his hand to her. She sucked in air. He traced her throat with the ring, drawing her to him with the powers of the gods.

"Would you let me kiss you?" he asked. "Just a kiss. In memory of the lady I once knew."

"Of course," she breathed.

Zeus embraced her and sank into a luscious kiss. Such pleasure. Surely this was not breaking his vow, not when it was done with such a pure purpose.

To drive a final wedge between Mark and Joy.

Eyes closed, Dia lifted her hands to cradle his head and to lean deeper into the kiss.

Zeus twisted the ring on his finger.

And changed his visage to that of Mark Hennessy.

Joy stood planted in the barn door. First heat, then cold, then blessed numbness swept through her. Her hand clenched the barn until the wood gouged into her fingers, but she paid the pain no mind. It was tiny compared to the final rending of a bruised heart.

Only a single light illuminated the barn interior, but it was sufficient. Though the deep, wavering shadows created uncertain shapes and eerie images, the couple was as recognizable as in daylight. There could be no doubting the evidence before her eyes, though she didn't understand how Mark had gotten home first.

Mark and Dia were kissing.

No little peck on the cheek such as Mark sometimes bestowed upon women acquaintances. No grateful hug and friendly smooch for a job well completed. No kiss of comfort. This was a kiss of passion. His hands were . . .

God, the two of them were practically fused.

She had thought . . . She had hoped . . .

How could it be Mark? How could he *do* this after the night they'd shared? How could he even *be* here?

He seemed fuzzy, indistinct. Surely she was seeing wrong. Joy wiped a hand across her eyes, clearing their vision. Her hand came back damp with tears she hadn't even realized she was shedding.

Almost as though some cosmic jokester read her mind, the man lifted, glanced in her direction though she didn't think he saw her, then settled back into the kiss, stroking Dia's cheek and neck.

It *was* Mark.

His hand passed through a beam of starlight and gold flashed from his finger.

Joy shrank back into the night and pressed her hand against her mouth. Incoherent sounds battered her clogged throat. She battled them down, unwilling to draw the lovers' attention, and stumbled out into the darkness.

Chapter Fifteen

"Have I ever seen you before noon?" Mark asked Dia. He poured his coffee from the pot Joy had started earlier, wondering what brought his night owl assistant around at midmorning.

"I doubt it. Mornings are the invention of a sick mind." She grabbed a mug from the cupboard and held it out in silent entreaty.

Mark poured her a cup, then added warm milk to his espresso. He passed the milk to Dia, but she shook her head, instead taking a sip of her black brew. She closed her eyes against the jolt of caffeine.

"So, why are you up?"

Dia took another sip. "I have something to tell you, and I wanted to get it over with."

Mark set down his coffee and crossed his arms. "This sounds serious."

Swiftly Dia told him about the California performances, concluding with, "I have to leave today, so that means I'll miss the Mushroom Festival and the start of the tour." She gulped down more coffee. "I hope you aren't angry. I know it will leave you in a bind, but . . . Mark, I just couldn't give this up."

He, of all people, understood the need to grab an opportunity. He grinned at her. "I wouldn't expect you to. You are good, Dia, so I will expect you to knock them out of their seats."

She flung herself at him in a ferocious hug, her coffee sloshing perilously near the rim. "I'll be back before you reach Atlanta."

"You'd better be," he growled with mock ferocity, "because you aren't getting away that easy. The show needs you. I need you."

As the last of his words faded, Joy walked into the kitchen. Her silent glance took in the embrace, and her color paled in the fresh sunlight. "There are muffins in the breadbox," she said flatly. "I'll be feeding the birds." She stalked out the door.

Dia glanced at him. "What's wrong with her? She doesn't think you and I . . . ?"

Mark shook his head. "She knows we're only friends." After the night he and Joy had spent together, she had no basis for jealousy, he thought with some smugness. "Things didn't go well for her last night."

Dia's brow furrowed. "What? I didn't notice anything."

Mark lifted one shoulder. "I'm not sure." Between the newspaper and Nicole this morning, he'd heard some strange rumors.

"Well, I hope it's nothing too bad. I like Joy, and I had a good time last night."

"Speaking of last night, I assume there was no trouble with Jupiter getting you home."

To Mark's astonishment, Dia colored.

"Okay, what gives?" he demanded.

"Zeke kissed me, that's all."

"That's all? And it made *you* blush?"

"Well, he is a good kisser. There may be gray ash on top, but there's a definite fire down below."

"Dia!"

"Knock it off, Mark," she answered with a smile. "You're not my father or my big brother. It was only a kiss . . . for old time's sake."

"But you only just met."

"Don't try to understand." She reached on tiptoe to give him a peck on the cheek. "Who do you want me to call to come out here and take my place?"

Mark shook his head. "Don't worry about it. I'll handle it."

"You're the boss. Bye, Mark. See you in Atlanta."

After Dia left in a cab, Mark finished the last of his coffee in a couple of gulps, then pulled out a cranberry muffin. He ate on his way out to help Joy, thinking.

Dia's absence did put him in a bind, although he didn't begrudge her leaving. This was a chance she couldn't pass up, but he disliked the idea of training a new assistant for so few shows. His other staff members already had their assigned jobs.

The sight of Joy caught his eye. She was with the yearlings, spreading feed while the birds followed the wave of her hand. She and the birds, their movements were almost a dance. He knew she didn't consider herself graceful, but

Thrill to the most sensual, adventure-filled Romances on the market today...

FROM  LOVE SPELL BOOK

As a home subscriber to the Love Spe Romance Book Club, you'll enjoy the best i today's BRAND-NEW Time Travel, Futuristic Legendary Lovers, Perfect Heroes and othe genre romance fiction. For five years, Lov Spell has brought you the award-winning high-quality authors you know and love t read. Each Love Spell romance will swee you away to a world of high adventure...an intimate romance. Discover for yourself a the passion and excitement millions of read ers thrill to each and every month.

Save $5.00 Each Time You Buy!

Every other month, the Love Spell Romance Book Club brings you four brand-new titles from Love Spell Books. EACH PACKAGE WILL SAVE YOU AT LEAST $5.00 FROM THE BOOK-STORE PRICE! And you'll never miss a new title with our convenient home delivery service.

Here's how we do it: Each package will carry a FREE 10-DAY EXAMINATION privilege. At the end of that time, if you decide to keep your books, simply pay the low invoice price of $17.96, no shipping or handling charges added. HOME DELIVERY IS ALWAYS FREE. With today's top romance novels selling for $5.99 and higher, our price SAVES YOU AT LEAST $5.00 with each shipment.

AND YOUR FIRST TWO-BOOK SHIP-MENT IS TOTALLY FREE!

ITS A BARGAIN YOU CAN'T BEAT! A SUPER $11.48 Value

Love Spell  A Division of Dorchester Publishing Co., Inc.

Get Two Books Totally
FREE —
An $11.48 Value!

▼ Tear Here and Mail Your FREE Book Card Today! ▼

PLEASE RUSH
MY TWO FREE
BOOKS TO ME
RIGHT AWAY!

Love Spell Romance Book Club
P.O. Box 6613
Edison, NJ 08818-6613

AFFIX
STAMP
HERE

hers was an easy, earthy motion that was as tempting as the dance of Salome.

Blood surged through him, making him tight against his zipper. In the morning heat, sweat broke out and a shiver ran down his spine. He had missed her these past couple of days.

He wanted Joy. He wanted her with him. The thought of being tied to one person didn't steal his breath when that person was Joy.

Bring her into his world. He'd entertained the idea before; now it took solid form.

If she gave it a chance, she could be happy with his nomadic, touring lifestyle, he knew. Deep down, she craved adventure; they had shared that from the first.

She could be part of the show, an assistant maybe, for Dia would be going out on her own soon. Or Joy could use her chef skills as caterer for the staff.

It was ideal.

He could give this to her, give her what she wanted—cooking, adventure, love.

She just had to be enticed to give it a chance, and he knew the perfect way.

First, though, he had to figure out what was upsetting her. He filled the troughs with water, starting with the pen filled with birds hatched at the start of the season. The flock surrounded him, anticipating their shower. "Your dinner last night was good."

She grunted an answer.

A raw edge of worry slashed in his gut. "Do you want me to feed the babies?"

"I'll do it." She left the pen.

Birds jostled against him, pecking at his shoes and nibbling the hose. He took a step to follow her, but the birds tangled around his feet. "Joy, ah, when does the next batch come out of the incubator?"

"Two days." She didn't even look back.

Mark stumbled toward the gate, through the mass of birds. At last, he turned on the hose and sprayed, sending the birds loping toward their treat. Mark hastily made his exit, giving the birds one last spray, then followed Joy to the pen of youngest birds.

"These little fellas are cute. Seems a shame they have to grow up just to be slaughtered."

"The realities of farm life. Ostriches are no longer a breeders' market but a product market—meat, feathers, hide."

It was the longest sentence he'd gotten from her all morning. Absently Mark scratched the healing stitches on his leg. Talking with Joy was not usually this hard.

That raw pain in his gut grew. Something was wrong with Joy. She'd barely spoken to him, rarely looked at him. Something was bothering her, something big.

Was it last night's dinner? He'd thought the rumors of flesh-eating flies a bit far-fetched, but *something* had happened. Did she know he'd talked to Centurion last night? Mark gave a mental curse. What if she'd overheard their conversation? Heard what he'd implied about casual sex? Hellfire, no wonder she was angry.

Except an angry Joy was rarely silent.

Without a word, she walked to the pens to start collecting the day's eggs. Mark followed her, finishing the feeding and watering in a working rhythm they'd established days ago. He cleared his throat. When she didn't respond he said simply, "Joy."

Joy looked at him.

No, she didn't. That was the problem.

He was used to her clear-eyed, unflinching gaze. She probed and searched inside him. She took in details about him with caring eyes. She *saw him.*

Not this morning. She didn't *look* at him. Instead, the interest in her eyes was no more than that she had for a casual acquaintance. Less, actually, for Joy greeted everyone, even a stranger, with warmth.

She tilted her head, as though he were no more than a curiosity, and pushed back the brim of her cap.

Always he noticed details about her, but today they weren't reassuring. Her skin was pale, the smattering of freckles standing out in the sunshine. She looked tired, with smudges of purple beneath her eyes. Only the red of her hair shone this morning.

Worry and fear flamed in his gut. Had Centurion brought this on? Threatened her somehow?

If he had, he was a dead man.

Mark tried to think of something to say that would bring a smile or jolt her out of this self-contained misery, but for once his agile tongue and nimble brain failed him. This wasn't a time for wit or charm. Only honesty.

"What happened last night?" he asked gently, searching for what had upset her so.

"When?" Her glance was sharp, cutting.

"I heard there were problems with the dinner."

She gave a curt laugh. "If you call an invasion of flies a problem."

"Were they flesh-eating?"

"What!"

"Rumor has it, the flies were flesh-eating."

"Hell's bells, small town gossip does fancy up a story. No, they weren't flesh-eating. Except for a few bites I got." She lifted her arm. For a brief moment, the familiar spark flared out at him. He stepped closer.

Quickly the flare died. She stepped back and dropped her arm.

She wouldn't even let him touch her, not the slightest contact. Mark halted. A shaky sense that he was losing something very important washed across him.

She turned away, back to the infernal birds.

Mark stepped in front of her, not letting her retreat, determined to find out the problem. Magicians solved problems all the time, getting the illusion to work. This was no illusion, but it was something he would solve. "Was Centurion angry?"

"Yes." She walked around him and started collecting eggs.

Mark trailed her. "Did he threaten you? What is he demanding?"

"Of course he didn't threaten me."

"Then you've got the job as his chef."

"Probably not."

"Why? The flies weren't your fault."

"Everything in the kitchen is the chef's fault."

Mark paused, then said, "Centurion asked me to stay after."

"I saw your truck."

"Did you hear any of our conversation?"

"No."

That was a relief. At least he wouldn't have to explain

that away. He waited for her to ask what they had talked about, but she didn't.

"Dammit, Joy, what's gotten into you this morning?" Mark halted and put his fists on his hips. Dia's suggestion came to mind. "Is it because Dia kissed me? She has a chance to go on her own for a couple of shows, and she was just saying good-bye. You can't be mad about that?"

Joy sucked in a hiss of air, and two bright spots appeared on her cheeks. "So, now you think you'll come back to me?" She stomped out of the ostrich pens, her arms loaded with eggs, and Mark followed.

What the hell was she talking about? "Come back to you? I never—"

She rounded on him. "Why are you here, Mark? What do you want?"

"To keep you safe," he exploded.

"Safe? From what? Guy? What do you have against him?"

Mark's temper burst at hearing her eternal defense of Centurion. Ancient instincts took over. "He's a thief and a whole lot more. You don't believe me? Let me take you to meet Cybele. Ask her about the book of magic he tried to buy. Ask her about what happened when she refused, how her place was trashed and the book stolen."

The red in Joy's cheeks deepened and her blue eyes burned in concert with her hair. She swayed slightly. "So that's why you came back? To get some magic book? What has it got in it that's so important?" Her eyes widened, and she sucked in a deep breath. "The *Elements Escape*," she breathed.

Mark groaned, remembering why a magician *never* lost his cool. Expressions of temper led to stupid mistakes. He had intended to tell Joy, but not like this, and definitely not now. "That's not the only reason I came back. It was because of you—"

"Don't. Don't, Mark. No more lies."

"But, it's not—"

"You say Dia kissed you? Last night, I saw *you* kissing *her*. And there was sure a lot more about it than a simple farewell. So do not try to tell me you came back because of me."

"Joy—"

She thrust the eggs at him. Mark, busy juggling the slick, heavy burden, almost missed her words.

"Don't bother with another lie. I don't believe you, and I don't care anymore."

I don't care anymore.

"There's only one more batch of yearlings to go out," she continued in a blaze, "and I've got no jobs in the offing, so I can handle the rest of the farm just fine. You're free."

"I'm not leaving."

Her jaw worked. "The Mushroom Festival's next weekend. I expect you to leave right after." She spun on one boot heel and stalked away.

Mark stared at her retreating back. *I expect you to leave right after.*

He struggled to catch his breath in the oppressive heat and heard his heartbeat echo in his empty chest. He closed his eyes against the tumult, then opened them again, unwilling to miss this last glimpse of Joy.

He didn't know what had gone wrong and he didn't know how to make it right. This was real, and the magician had no tricks to play.

Kissing Dia last night? Mark dropped the eggs and sped

off after her. He would damn well find out what the hell she was talking about.

Sitting poolside, one of the few braving the late-morning heat, Zeus leaned back in his lounger, full of lazy satisfaction. He glanced briefly at a woman occupying a nearby lounger, her face buried in a newspaper.

Nice toes.

He rubbed his chest. Last night had gone so well. Even Mark, the glib trickster, couldn't talk himself out of what Joy had *seen.* And Zeus had made sure she had a clear view.

As an added bonus, he had gotten a very lovely kiss. He sighed. The look on Joy's face pained him, but, in the long run, she would be better for it. She would turn to that nice, if bland, Seth Beaumont and be blissfully content. Well, content at least.

Zeus snapped open the local newspaper. When he visited a place, he loved to keep abreast of the local events and concerns. In his time in Greece, it had been through the oracles and the storytellers. Today it was newspapers and e-mail.

A headline on the second page caught his eye. LOCAL PARTY INVADED BY FLIES. Swiftly, he scanned the article. Last night at Guy Centurion's party. Stinging, crawling, persistent flies. The chef attributed it to spoiled meat.

The chef. *Joy.*

Flies. *Gadflies.*

The newspaper crumpled beneath his grip. "*Hera!*"

"You roared?" The woman at the lounger lowered her newspaper.

Chapter Sixteen

Anger drove out the numbness, and Joy didn't welcome the change. She didn't want to feel anything for Mark Hennessy.

Anger was too easily transformed into something gentler in her, and loving him hurt too damn much. She didn't want to understand or to care. Numbness was safer.

The worst thing was seeing the innocent, surprised look on his face when she'd confronted him about Dia and discovering *she wanted to believe him.*

Her hand cracked against the back door, and the door flung open. She stomped into the kitchen.

Hope, eating a bowl of cereal, glanced up, startled.

"Men!" Joy told her sister. "Stay away from them. And sugared cereal is not good for you."

"Then why do you buy it?" Hope wisely stayed away from the first comment.

"Because I'm a doormat. Remember?" She pulled out a pot. "I'll make you some oatmeal."

"I hate oatmeal," Hope said mildly.

She slapped the pot back. "Then whole wheat toast. With honey. Or a zucchini frittata." Joy leaned against the counter and pointed to her eyes. "Do these look like I can't see? I see herb pots on the windowsill. I see your fingernails are painted purple. The eyes work. You know, he didn't even come back because of me, like he said. I *knew* I shouldn't believe him."

"Sis, you're babbling."

"So what?"

"You sound like Nicole."

"I do?" Joy stared at her sister a moment, then her shoulders slumped and the anger slid out of her, draining her. Only a bleak hollowness remained. "I do."

Her mother. The family curse. Trusting a man who was all wrong.

How could Mark be wrong, when everything about him felt so absolutely right?

As if her thoughts had the power to conjure him up, Mark entered the kitchen with the same resounding crack to the door.

Hope took one look from him to Joy, then, grabbing her cereal bowl, beat a fast retreat.

Joy watched Mark approach. She'd seen him in passion, in pleasure, in concentration. She'd seen anger and charm, mystery and kindness. Only once had she seen him like this, with all facades and illusions ripped away. When he had woken her in the middle of the night to make love to her.

Then it was raw passion.

Now it was raw pain.

He wasn't that much taller than she, but in the confines of the kitchen his frustration made him seem to tower over her. "What did you mean, you saw me kissing Dia last night? She left last night's dinner with Zeke Jupiter, and I didn't see her again until this morning."

Joy closed her eyes, steeling herself against the squeeze of her heart urging her to believe. Even now, when she thought she saw through all the deceits, he could fool her.

"I know what I saw. It was you and Dia; I saw you in the barn when I got home. And it was a very passionate kiss."

"I didn't kiss her."

Her eyes popped open. "*I saw you.*"

"Dia kissed Jupiter last night, not me."

The black hollow inside her throbbed. Joy gave a humorless laugh. "I know the difference between the two of you. How gullible do you think I am?"

"It wasn't me. How could it be? You said you saw my car at Centurion's. How could I have gotten here before you?"

The persuasion was thick in his voice, and she braced herself against its siren call, ignoring the resonance inside her.

No. Never again. Never again would she feel that pain. Never again would she put herself at risk, take such a terrible chance with him. She wasn't strong enough to give her heart again, only to learn it wasn't safe in his keeping, to futilely wait for his return. She couldn't do it.

Her head shook, back and forth. "Don't do this to me, Mark. Don't try to coerce me. I know what I saw."

"And I say flat out it wasn't me. Do you need proof?"

She lifted her eyes and stared at him. He had lied to her all along. He hadn't come back because of her, but because of Centurion. Because of Cybele, his career, and revenge. She was only an excuse, a convenience.

234

All her life she'd been a convenience to people, to Nicole and Hope. She wouldn't be that with Mark. She couldn't; it hurt too damn much.

Mark returned her stare, his dark eyes glittering. "You honestly think I could make love to you—and it was not sex, it was making love—then do that with another woman? What a low opinion you have of me." He gave a bitter laugh. "I'm surprised you could bring yourself to sleep with me."

"Don't you dare make this out to be my fault," she forced out. "It's about a lot more than one kiss."

He raked a hand through his hair. "I know I should have told you from the start why I was here. I'm sorry, but there were—are—good reasons. If you'll just let me explain— Joy, I'm asking you. Don't throw this away, not like we did before."

He lifted a hand in supplication. His heat flared toward her, hotter than the fires he used onstage, as incendiary as his touch. It burned at the cold knot of emptiness.

Joy clenched her hands at her sides. She would not give in to the lure of him, to the promise in his eyes and the coaxing of his lips. She would not make the mistakes the women in her family made, listening to the siren call of lust. This time, she would break the chain.

Slowly, at her continued silence, the raw openness in his face, the pure entreaty in his gaze, glazed over. Practiced charm overlaid his features, and his hand lowered.

He gave her a lazy grin. "Well, now, darlin', I see I've got my answer. You wanted an excuse, an illusion to hide behind, and you got it. You're running scared, just like you did when you got married." The drawl was deep.

Joy flinched. "And you're not?"

"Never been a secret I'm not a settlin' man. Don't worry, I'll keep out of your way." He tipped his fingers to his forehead in a final salute, then left.

Joy stood, unmoving, in the kitchen, the familiar site as foreign to her right now as a mud-brick oven. She felt as dry and insubstantial as ash.

It was the first time he had asked for something she was incapable of giving.

The image of Mark with his hand outstretched was all she could see.

His outstretched hand.

His unadorned outstretched hand.

The flash of gold in the barn. It had been from a ring!

The man kissing Dia had worn a ring. The image of it on Dia's cheek, on her breast, seared Joy's memory.

Mark never wore rings. He'd told her once it was because a ring could draw attention to his hands when he wanted that attention elsewhere.

Zeke Jupiter, however, did.

Zeus gaped at the woman he loved, the woman he had missed and hurt so badly.

Hera! After so many years!

She looked *good*. A little older, like him, but the years had given her dignity and pride.

His newspaper dropped to the concrete as he stared. She'd kept her figure, the bathing suit made that obvious, and her skin was still flawless. His arms tingled with the need to hold her and his lips longed for the nectar that was only hers, but a distance in her eyes held him still. Whatever reasons had brought her back to him, it wasn't for a tender reunion.

So many questions ran through his mind, he hardly knew where to start. "You're here," he finally managed, wary of the awkwardness between them. "Why?"

She lifted one shoulder in a delicate shrug. "Old times' sake?"

"Old times' sake would have been a millennium past."

Hera gave him a faint smile of agreement. "Maybe I'm just feeling . . . alone. There are so few of the gods still on earth."

"I saw the headline about the UFO in the wheatfield last week. Who did the Titanic Oracle come for?"

"Demeter."

"I wondered which one of us had gone home."

They were silent a moment, remembering lost comrades and an unforgiving banishment. At last Zeus asked, "How'd you know it was Demeter?"

"I kept track with the far-see smoke."

"Why couldn't I find you with it?" he grumbled.

"I've found a means of concealing myself from it."

Zeus sat forward. "Really? How?"

She laughed. "Not in this millennium will I show you. You are still up to your tricks, my husband, and I will not give you that singular advantage."

My husband. She called him husband still. Hope flared, and Zeus rubbed his ring, feeling the electricity popping inside. A waft of steam came from the nearby whirlpool.

Then the rest of her words sank in, and he rose to his feet. "What do you mean, up to my tricks?" he demanded. "I have been faithful. Of late."

"Move." She waved a hand, shooing him away. "You're in my sun."

Shooing him? The king of the gods? After all these years

237

of hiding from him, she thought she could return, then shoo him away? "I am Zeus," he thundered. "Your king. Your sun. Admit it. You came back because of me."

Hera gave a short laugh. "I came back because I thought I could stop you from making a fool of yourself over a human woman. Again. Endlessly. Why do I try to save you from your own folly?"

After he'd resisted temptation so well, she didn't appreciate his efforts. He'd even coached Seth, for Hades' sake, not that the man understood a thing about romance. The radiant aura surrounding his body expanded, beyond the constraints he kept on it.

Hera's skin turned to copper under the glow, as she rose to confront the glittering sight. Humans would be blinded, but Hera didn't even lift a hand to her eyes. "Stop that! Somebody might see you."

"I don't care." In truth, he did, however, so he muted his aura to the flat flesh humans expected. "This is no folly, but a deed of selfless good."

Hera gave a snort of disbelief.

"It's true," he protested. "Come, even the myths tell of a few good deeds I did."

"Male writers! They also called me jealous and cow-faced."

Zeus lifted her hand to bestow a kiss. Her skin was smooth and scented faintly of almond. "You were never cow-faced, my love, and you will never have cause for jealousy again." He gave a *tsk*. "Those gadflies were very naughty of you, but they tell me you still care."

" 'Twas a thoughtless reaction, nothing more."

"Shall I tell you why I am truly here?" he said enticingly. "Over lunch?"

Hera hesitated, then nodded. "I'll order room service and we can eat on my balcony. Forty-five minutes. I need to shower."

Zeus followed her back to the lobby, wishing she'd ask him up to share that shower and knowing the hope was futile. "What name are you registered under?"

"Harriet Juneau."

One hour later, as he downed the indifferent lunch provided by hotel room service, the puzzle of Hera still captivated him. Why had she sought him out? She had a purpose, of that he was sure, for she could have contacted him at any time she wished. Had she, too, felt the passage of years, the need to weave the fraying strands of life back into a whole? Did she still care about him?

No clues were to be found in her impersonal conversation and smooth features. She sat across from him on her balcony as remote as if they were mere business acquaintances.

At last, they finished lunch and settled back into their chairs, each with a glass of iced tea, a sprig of mint wilting with the melting ice. The afternoon heat drew beads of sweat to the glasses. A floor below, some children shouted as they played in the pool, but otherwise the afternoon was hot and still and waiting.

"So, what is this selfless purpose of yours?" Hera asked.

"I am trying to undo long-ago wrongs. You know what consequences remained from my indiscretions?"

"The female descendants of the women you once used now find love elusive and unlucky."

Zeus winced to hear it put so baldly. It had been more than simply "using" them. He had cared, and he had given them much pleasure in the mating. "I wouldn't have put it so crudely, but that is the essence."

"And how do you plan to break this curse?"

"Joy is from the lineage of Io—"

"I can see that."

"—and I will break the cycle by finding her a man worthy of her. I'm going to set things right in each of the lines."

He sat back and waited for her admiration.

Hera burst out laughing. "*You* are acting the matchmaker?"

Zeus set his jaw. "Who knows more about love than me?"

"Just about every one of our people. Except, perhaps, Ares. If that's your plan, I wager you are making a stew of it."

"I am not!" Zeus remembered something else about Hera that time had allowed him to forget. She had the ability to rile him faster than any woman he'd ever known. "I have found her a good-hearted man, one who will cherish her. The legacy will be broken."

"Who?"

"Seth Beaumont."

Hera gave another trill of laughter. "He is sweet, and maybe Io could have been content, but he isn't for Joy Taylor."

"How do you know?" Zeus grumbled. "You have not been here."

"But I have been watching for some time," she said softly, almost dangerously.

"Then who would you suggest?"

She didn't answer. Instead she leaned back and traced a line through the sweat on her glass with a red-tipped fingernail. "You are serious about this purpose? You do not lie?"

Zeus nodded, fascinated with the graceful motion of her hands.

"Then why did you kiss the woman from the line of Leda?"

Zeus winced. He'd hoped she hadn't seen that. "It had no meaning, but was done in the name of my higher purpose, my love."

She pierced him with a glare. "No endearments. You shall call me Hera or naught."

Zeus inclined his head in acknowledgment.

"So how did this kiss fit your 'higher purpose'?"

"There is a complication."

"Hermes, or rather one of his line. Hermes was the first of us to charm his way home."

Zeus scowled that she knew more about what had happened to the others than he did. "Joy seems fascinated by this trickster, yet he cannot be the one for her. A son of Olympus is not a wise choice for a woman of Earth."

"Since when is the heart ever wise?" Hera shook her head. "So, what did you do?"

"I cloaked myself in the visage of Mark Hennessy—"

"—And then you kissed Dia, making sure Joy saw you. All in the name of doing good."

"It worked, too. I saw them this morning in the far-see smoke. Now, all I need to do is give Seth a bit more coaching—"

"No. If she chooses Seth, the curse will be perpetuated." Hera pressed the icy glass against her neck, leaving wet drops against her smooth skin. For a moment, Zeus forgot all about Mark and Joy and higher purposes in the blinding need to lick off each drop.

Zeus wet dry lips. "Then who?"

"Ah, Zeus, you always were blind to the true needs of women. Can't you see, it must be Mark Hennessy? The curse you started can only be broken by another of our line. It's the only answer."

"The only way to repair the shattered trust—?"

"—is for her to trust her heart's choices with a son of Olympus."

Chapter Seventeen

The truck spit gravel, fitting Mark's spitting-nails mood. How could Joy have thought that was *him* in the barn with Dia? Had she just expected to see him and been misled by her own eyes? It was a technique he used often enough in his show.

Dammit, he'd thought she knew him better. It was lowering to find that Joy thought he was about as honorable as a snake.

She had tried to deny they were good together.

He'd show her otherwise.

He'd never known a woman who smelled so womanly and so desirable. She had only to look at him with those big blue eyes and he fell under her spell. Blood rushed to a lot of favorite places, and he wanted to take her straight to bed or straight away wherever they happened to be.

Joy was enveloping warmth and generous honesty, the

package all wrapped with the spice of her profession and the sunshine of her hair.

He shifted in the seat and tapped a hand on the outside of the truck in time with George Strait on the radio, trying to cool his thoughts.

Eventually, she'd let him explain about why he was here, about the reasons he'd kept quiet. He had to believe that. Joy valued harmony and fair play too much not to, and he could be mighty persistent when he wanted. Given time, she'd believe him.

Time was what he didn't have.

Mark pulled into town and parked at the pay phone. "Hey, Armond," he said when the Fed answered. "What's cooking?"

"Shouldn't I ask you that? How is the chef?"

"She's not involved. At least, not knowingly."

"You have proof?"

"I have intuition."

"You told her why you're there." The comment was flat, unquestioning.

"Just about the book. Not about you." He'd already told her more than was safe for her to know.

"You'd better be damned sure she's legit, because it will be your butt on the line when Centurion finds out you're not just there for the show."

"Centurion already made my connection to the past, and he knows about Cybele and the magic book. He and I had a nice, nobody-admits-anything conversation last night."

There was a moment of silence, then Armond broke into a string of French that had Mark glad his command of the language was limited. Calmly, Mark leaned against the

244

booth, rubbing the nearly healed wound in his leg and waiting for silence.

Finally, Armond returned to English. "I'm pulling you out of there."

"You don't have authority over me."

"I'll arrest you. For your own safety."

"No jurisdiction. Look, right now Centurion thinks he's got a chance at drawing me into his web—not realizing what a fine upstanding citizen I am and all."

Armond made a disparaging noise.

"You see, he thinks I'm still skirting the law. As long as he doesn't connect me to you, he won't make a move, at least until after I perform at the Mushroom Festival. Centurion wants to keep his standing in this town, and he won't risk my badmouthing him before then." *And I made a promise to a lady that I'm not going to break.* "What's Centurion moving out, Armond?"

There was silence at the other end.

"How can I help if I don't know what I'm looking for?"

"Gems," Armond said shortly.

Mark gave a low whistle. "He's expanding. Joy's got one last shipment of yearlings going out next week. He's got to use it for the gems."

"If you don't establish the connection to Centurion, and the gems are there, it will be Joy Taylor we bring in. You've got one week." It was Armond who hung up on him this time.

Sitting on her front porch, her feet resting on the rail while the afternoon sun baked her sunscreen-coated feet, Joy thumbed desultorily through a cookbook. Nothing looked enticing for dinner.

She leaned her head against the rocker back. "How can I deny my own eyes? It was Mark."

Yet, other, fainter evidence contradicted what she knew to be true. The ring. The fact that he couldn't have gotten to the barn before she did if he'd left Guy's home after her.

The barn had been shadowy. She'd been upset about the dinner. Had her conventional imagination created something crazy? Joy pressed the heels of her hands against her eyes. "I'm going nuts."

Who to believe? Herself? Or Mark?

Did it matter? This morning's argument had not been based on that one incident, although the kiss had precipitated it.

She'd made the right decision. Mark could not be held, not unless he wanted to be, and she'd known from the first his need for freedom was too essential. It had been part of him since she'd first met him. He was fireworks: brilliant, blazing, and fleeting. He was magic.

And she wanted . . . a home. Someone to share it with, perhaps. Stability. Her hormones, her emotions, would not rule her this time.

Joy flipped a page of the cookbook, then closed it with a clap. As dull as her ideas were, it was probably just as well she didn't have a cooking job.

Five minutes, and then she had to get back to work. She had to follow up on the distribution of the ostrich meat after slaughter and make sure the hides were sent to the tannery. She had to make sure the equipment and supplies needed for the chefs' charity were in order. She'd told Earl she'd stop by Dani's to give her a time schedule for the dancing mushrooms.

All part of the normal, settled life she'd carved out.

Settled sounded tedious. She dropped the cookbook to the floor of the porch and picked up the latest tabloid she'd gotten from the grocery, turning to an article about Fountain of Youth cures from ancient healers.

Behind her the screen door squeaked open, then banged shut.

"What are you reading?"

Nicole's question drew Joy from the paper. She pointed to the article, noticing that her mother looked every one of her years this afternoon.

Nicole gave a tiny laugh. "Eternal youth. If they knew that secret, why aren't they here today to share it with us?"

"Maybe they are, but they're hiding," Joy suggested lightly, worried by the fragile brittleness in Nicole. "Maybe someone should write an article called 'Ancients Among Us.' You missed lunch. Can I get you something to eat? Iced tea?"

"No thanks." Nicole dropped into the other rocker, animation draining from her.

Her mother was rarely silent. Joy rocked her chair with one foot and pulled hair that had escaped back into its clip. "What's wrong?"

Nicole looked off at the farm. "The two years is up on Monday."

Immediately, Joy knew the problem. What else? A man. Specifically, Henry Valcour. On Monday, if Henry Valcour hadn't returned, Nicole would acquire full ownership of the ostrich farm. Joy had known all along Valcour wouldn't return; that was why she'd worked so hard to give her mother the security she needed, but Nicole had believed he would, holding on to the dream for almost two years.

It was a painful thing to watch a dream die.

"The farm will be yours."

Nicole made a dismissive gesture. "I don't want the farm; I want Henry."

"What would you do if he came back?" Joy asked.

"Welcome him. Kiss him."

Joy made a face. "You'd just accept him back?"

"Of course!" Nicole patted Joy on the hand. "Don't worry. You'll always have a place here."

"That's not what I meant. Wouldn't you need some explanation? Have some questions?" *Like I should have had with Mark.*

Nicole's brow wrinkled in confusion, then smoothed. "But I love him."

"You said that about all your husbands."

"This time is different."

"You also said that about each one."

"But it is," Nicole insisted. "I can't explain it. Every part of me wants him back."

"What if he left again?"

"I'd wait for him to return."

And ask me to take care of you. The flare of resentment caught Joy by surprise. After all these years, she was used to her mother's helplessness. But, dammit, she hadn't asked to be the one who had to make all the decisions. She hadn't asked to care for a newborn sister when she was only a child herself.

Sometimes, she just wanted to be free of it all. To fly, if only for a short time, the way she had on the parachute jump.

With Mark.

"That's your heart speaking," Joy said roughly. "Not your head."

Nicole fiddled with the collar of her shirt. "What do you remember about your grandma?"

The odd question didn't surprise Joy. Nicole often jumped to subjects with connections no one else saw.

"Grandma Idabeth?" Her mother's mother. She'd never known her father's parents. "She always seemed kind, but . . ." The memories of her grandmother had always been faded, even when Grandma Idabeth was alive, as though the woman herself had no color. "She chose from the head, didn't she?"

Nicole nodded. "She'd grown up dirt-poor, stigmatized as an out-of-wedlock child. She wanted someone who could provide for her. We lacked nothing material, but my father was so dominant, he completely overwhelmed my mother. He was distant and cold. She had nothing to warm her."

So, instead, Nicole had followed her fancy. The family inclination had run true, though the expression was different.

After a moment's silence, Nicole gave a soft sigh and gazed off across the yard. "Henry's not coming back, is he?"

"No, he isn't."

Joy saw Mark's truck drive in from town. The plume of dust followed it, just as it had that first day when he'd returned. When he got out by the barn, he didn't even glance in her direction.

She believed him about the kiss, she discovered. No proof, but she still believed him. In so many ways, she was different from her mother and grandmother, yet, in others, they were very much alike.

Joy watched the dust settle in the still afternoon. It was time to stop dreaming about that restaurant and start taking

steps to get it. She'd used every excuse in the book—
she didn't have the money, she needed more experience,
she wanted to take on a partner first—but the truth was, she
was scared. Scared of the risk. Scared of failing. Scared of
being left on the outside, of waiting in her kitchen while no
one came.

While she was in town, she would stop by the bank, stop
by Seth's office.

It was time to start taking a few risks.

The bank wasn't going to lend her the money.

Stunned, Joy dragged herself down the sidewalk, ignoring greetings from passing friends and the stifling heat
radiating from the cement. She hadn't expected to get the
loan today. She had known she'd have to wait until Nicole
took full possession of the farm before they could borrow
against it, but she'd thought she could at least start the
paperwork. She'd passed the idea by the banker a few
weeks ago and he'd seemed enthusiastic.

That enthusiasm had decidedly cooled.

Oh, the loan officer told her to try again when the ownership of the farm was fully processed, but he'd stirred
words like "inadequate collateral" and "high risk" into the
mix. She was surprised he didn't add "flesh-eating flies."
Those opinions weren't going to change in a week.

There were other banks she would try, other avenues,
but if she couldn't get a loan from a local bank—she'd
even brought the loan officer's family meals when his wife
was hospitalized having their three children—she doubted
other places would be any more forthcoming.

She passed Seth's real estate office, then abruptly pivoted and went in.

"Joy!" Seth greeted her with pleasure, then rose from his desk to kiss her.

Joy stood quietly in the embrace.

His hands tightened briefly on her shoulder, then he lifted from the kiss and stared at her. "It's not going to happen between us, is it?" he said, the ruddiness of his cheeks fading as she pushed back.

"No," she said simply.

"You told me, but I didn't really want to hear it."

Joy squeezed his hands, the only comfort she could give, then let go. "I'm sorry. You're a good man, and I'm probably the biggest fool."

"So, if it wasn't to seduce me," Seth said with a ghost of a smile, sitting down and motioning her to a chair, "why did you come in?"

"That old house on Main Street. Do you have any idea if it will be coming on the market?"

"I doubt it. It was recently purchased from the original owners."

Surprised, Joy sat back. "I never saw a for-sale sign."

"One never went up. The buyer just made an offer, and they accepted."

"Who bought it?"

Seth fiddled with his Beaumont Real Estate pen. "The buyer wishes to keep it private."

"It's a matter of public record, Seth. I can look it up." Her eyes narrowed. "Was it Guy Centurion?"

"Yeah. You aren't working together on the deal?"

She shook her head. "What do you know about Guy, Seth?"

"What do you mean? I know that he's a good friend, and he's done a lot for this town. He's on charity boards and is always ready to help out someone down on their luck. He uses a lot of local labor."

All things she already knew and things she didn't want to hear. A knot formed in her stomach. She toyed with a button on her blouse. "Have you ever heard anything bad about him?"

"He's a businessman, a successful one. You don't get that way without making a few enemies, raising a few jealousies."

"Anything . . . illegal?"

Seth stared at her. "No, and I'd suggest you think twice before you voice that suggestion again."

"Even if it were true?"

"I doubt it is, and, besides, it doesn't affect us here. This is a small town, and there are a lot of people who wouldn't take kindly to your blackening one of the town's benefactors. Centurion's been here a lot longer than you have, Joy, and he's done a lot more for us. Whose side do you think they'd take?"

As Joy drove along the isolated roads of the Louisiana countryside, her car's air conditioning was no match for the heat beating against her closed window. Abruptly, she turned off the AC and opened the window. Hot wind blew her hair across her face and settled dust on her cheeks, but she craved the scent of the outdoors and the freedom from all demands, if only for these brief moments.

The endless green of pine and brush on either side of the road was lulling, while the challenge of driving on gravel kept her mind occupied. Joy had the uncomfortable feeling that she was being maneuvered, that someone was working to narrow her options. And what had those options narrowed down to? She could continue as she was—the ostriches, the occasional catering. She could work as a chef, though her allergy was a definite handicap in finding work. Most important, though, to do so, she'd have to leave town, leave Nicole and Hope, leave home.

Or . . . she could work for Guy Centurion.

What had once seemed a perfect opportunity now seemed like a tightening noose.

She wasn't sure when she had come to believe Mark's assertions about Guy. After all, it was just his word against all the evidence of the town. His word and her instincts.

Believe him, however, she did. Perhaps she had from the very first.

Though she often had trouble sorting through the various masks and concealing smoke that surrounded Mark, she had always believed ultimately that she saw beneath the illusions. Once she had doubted, with some reason, and then she'd ended up in a marriage that had no hope from the time the vows were said.

What had it been like for Mark to come back and find her married? The uncomfortable thought bore down on her. If a simple kiss had disturbed her so much, what must it have been like for him to find her sleeping with another man?

Shame scorched her. All the time, she'd been thinking about how Mark wasn't the man for her, when the truth was, she wasn't the woman for him.

Mark didn't need someone who wanted to set down roots and cook for people. Even if he wasn't in love with Dia, he needed someone like her. Someone who shared his love of performing, his magic, his freedom.

"I can't give him that." Joy's insides grew tight, but she had to say it aloud to make it real.

Maybe she could give him something else, though. Abruptly, she did a U-turn in the road, her tires brushing the edge of the ditch, and headed toward Guy Centurion's home.

"Hell's bells, this is madness," she said aloud.

Mark had come back for a book of magic. Maybe, she could find it for him, while finding out what Guy Centurion really wanted from her.

If she was wrong about Guy, if Mark was wrong, she'd never have another chance like what Guy was offering. If she angered him, she'd never get work in the area, not even washing dishes.

Joy drummed a finger on the steering wheel. "Ah, but what if I'm right? That Guy is involved with something shady?"

Whose side do you think they'd take? It was disconcerting to realize she didn't know the answer. She couldn't believe the town wouldn't want to know, but the tradition of shooting the messenger was an ancient one.

"So, if I succeed in unmasking Guy, I get to be the town pariah. And if I fail, my faltering career will be the least of my worries." The unpleasant thought held her chest in an unyielding grip. She shook her head, not wanting to dwell there. "Hell of a choice."

Joy was lucky. Guy's car was still in the drive at his North Shore home.

"Or, maybe make that unlucky," she muttered. Her stomach felt like someone was whipping up egg whites inside as Joy wiped her sweating hands on her shorts. "Remember the penitent and groveling approach."

Guy answered the door himself.

Her insides churned. She hated deceptions. She was never any good at them.

Joy tucked a loose strand of hair behind her ear. "I came

to apologize for the dinner and ask for another chance."

Okay, it wasn't exactly penitent and groveling, but it was direct and the truth as far as it went. That was about the best she could manage.

He opened the door. "Come in."

Joy followed him down the hall. She'd been here so many times, the place was almost as familiar to her as her own. A touch of something akin to sadness settled over her. She so wanted Mark to be wrong, to believe that people couldn't be as deceptive as Guy seemed to be, but she was too afraid Mark was right.

In Guy's office, she settled into the chair across his desk. A painting, a background of brown and black highlighted by a blood-colored slash of red across the center, caught her eye. It was even more disturbing than the purple and red one in his home in New Orleans. "That's new, isn't it?"

"Yes. The artist was grateful to sell, but I think he'll do better now that he's under my sponsorship. Do you like it?"

Joy studied it a moment, trying not to think about what Guy's sponsorship might entail. She could have very easily found herself in a parallel position. It was enough to freeze her bones.

Best to keep to the present and the truth as much as possible. "Not really. It's too harsh for my taste."

At her honesty, a certain tension seemed to leave him. "You are too much a creature of light to appreciate the finer points of darkness."

"Hey, I'm not sure I like being called a creature."

Guy laughed.

Focus on the meal, not the man; it could make a good motto for her life. "I don't know how that piece of spoiled meat got left out in your kitchen," she began, "but I accept responsibility for the fact it nearly ruined your dinner. I'd like the chance to make it up to you."

"How?"

"Let me provide the food for the buffet you're holding after Mark's performance."

"Why should I?"

"Because you're a fair man." One little lie and it tasted like sour milk. "Because I did a good job of recovering from the problems caused by that meat and because I'm a good chef."

He leaned back in his chair and gave her a fond smile. "I'll expect you to come up with something spectacular."

"I will. Thank you, Guy. You won't regret it."

"I'm counting on your gratitude," he said softly.

Joy rose to her feet, hoping she hadn't just gotten into a lot more than she realized. The idea, which had seemed very simple at first—reestablish herself in Guy's employ; find out what he wanted from her; search for the book— now seemed holier than Swiss cheese.

"Wait," he commanded.

She looked over at him. The taut skin over his cheeks held a faint redness, and the corner of his lips lifted. Whatever else he wanted, he was looking forward to telling her.

Somehow, Joy knew she wasn't going to like it.

He came around the desk, standing too close. He handed her a cassette tape. "Mark and I had a conversation the other night that I think you should know about. As your friend, I don't want you to get hurt."

Joy wanted to take that tape about as much as she wanted to handle a live snake. "Do you always tape private conversations?"

"A man in my position often finds it useful."

Joy's mind sped back, trying to recall all the conversations with him she'd had in this room.

Guy laughed. "Don't worry, your conversations are not among them." He touched a loose strand of her hair. "You are open and honest with me and I trust you will always remain so."

Joy couldn't find an honest answer inside her.

Guy watched Joy's hasty retreat with amusement. She was skittish about something; she was so bloody honest, she couldn't hide the wariness. Had the distrust Mark hid so skillfully infected her?

He ran a finger across his lips. Infections existed to be eradicated. The fact that they were sleeping together was an annoyance, but a manageable one. In the end it wouldn't matter.

It didn't matter how much Mark knew or suspected or whether he planned to do anything about it. He was a loose end, and Guy didn't intend to keep one eye open waiting for the magician to act.

Since Mark was now a public figure, the matter had to be handled carefully. He had come far from the annoying lad he once was. He had more respectability now and probably some powerful friends. But, after his show, the matter would be handled. Marcus would play his final performance.

Centurion turned back to the picture, his manicured hands sliding across the simple wood frame. The artist had not wanted to sell, to surrender to Centurion's protection, but after finding himself embroiled in an unsavory affair with stolen art and dead curators, he had been grateful for the reprieve from a prison life that would be quite unpleasant for a man of his delicate sensitivities.

Like the artist, Joy would be entangled so thoroughly after the Mushroom Festival, her honesty so completely compromised, she would have no choices.

Centurion's strong hand went down to briefly caress his groin. It might be interesting to learn what tricks the magician had taught her.

Just a good time. We agreed, keep it brief and casual.

Joy hadn't been able to resist listening to the tape, playing it in her car player as soon as she pulled away.

Mark's bored voice came through clear.

Not too often I get home cooking and other . . . treats brought right to my door.

What a jackass!

With a jab of her finger, she ejected the tape. Guy Centurion was no friend of hers. Friends didn't give friends tapes like this, a tape she suspected was edited for maximum effect. If she hadn't believed Mark about him before, she would now.

Mark was just damn lucky that she heard that odd note in his voice, the one he subconsciously added whenever he was trying to persuade someone. It was effective, she had to admit. Even knowing it, even knowing he was trying for his own reasons to persuade Guy to believe him, it hurt to hear the words.

They did sound convincing, probably because she knew how much truth was behind them. Mark had always told her that the most convincing lies were the ones that contained either the greatest amount of truth or the ones that were so farfetched that it seemed anything so unbelievable had to be true.

These lies were the former.

She didn't believe Mark cared only about sex, that he was only interested in her body—it wasn't that special a body—but she also knew that this affair between them was short-lived.

Joy threw the tape in the trash.

The woman was elusive. Joy hadn't come back to the farm all afternoon.

Mark strode into the cottage where he was staying. It was silent, for Jax had gone into New Orleans for supplies. He poured himself a glass of iced tea from the pitcher Joy kept filled in his refrigerator.

He leaned against the appliance, gulping the cool drink. A vase of wild flowers graced the windowsill, and he noticed there was a clean, lemony scent about the place. Some magazines were spread across the end table. All touches added by Joy.

His heart beat against his ribs as he took in how much like a home the place seemed now, so different from the sterility of his apartment.

Everywhere she went, Joy brought . . . comfort.

He finished the iced tea in one gulp, then went into the bedroom, shedding jeans and dusty shirt, to change into his practice clothes. He pulled on the T-shirt loaded with hidden pockets and savagely thrust on a pair of jeans.

It wasn't comfort he wanted of her. He didn't want Joy to feel she had to cook and clean for him—he'd been doing both since before he could remember and was perfectly capable of doing it in the future—but he treasured the feeling of home she created when she did.

What he wanted was a mix of that nurturing she showed

every one else and that heart-thumping, blood-boiling, mind-magic passion she showed him.

Mostly the latter.

They belonged together, free, on the road, and he had the means to show her.

If he could just find her.

He headed out to the barn to practice.

Feathers. Joy remembered the feather order when she pulled into the farm.

A significant portion of her income came from the sale of ostrich feathers used in the elaborate headdresses that formed part of the queens' and maids' costumes for the various Mardi Gras Krewes. She had an order due soon, and she needed to pluck the last of the feathers.

It didn't hurt the birds to have their feathers plucked, but it needed to be done on a regular basis to have enough feathers to make the business economically feasible.

She changed clothes, then headed out to the pens, hoping to get it done before the sun set.

Zeus and Hera glanced at one another, the far-see smoke twirling about them in a scented veil. Joy and Mark had been apart all day, stymieing their efforts to unite the pair.

Now, at last, was their chance.

Hera circled her hands around the smoke, coalescing it into a dark, swollen cloud, with only the faintest shadow of Joy in the pen and Mark in the barn.

Zeus touched the cloud with his ring.

Thunder boomed.

The cloud burst.

260

Chapter Eighteen

The rain gave no warning, beyond a thunderous crack of lightning, before a torrent so thick she could barely see her feet inundated the pens. Joy was drenched in seconds. The ostrich plumes drooped in her hands.

The urge to run was strong, but in the downpour her vision was too poor for haste, and she couldn't get any wetter. Joy picked her way across the soggy grounds. At least the sandy soil would drain the water away, and the birds would be safe in their stalls. When she turned to wait out the storm under their shelters, the rain formed an impenetrable wall of wind and water that forced her out.

She hunched over, protecting herself against the onslaught, although oddly the rain was neither particularly cold nor stinging. Just . . . insistent. A haze of yellow to the left caught her eye. The barn where Mark practiced. It was closer than the caretaker cottage or the house, and the gale winds pushed her in that direction.

When she reached it, a fierce gust blew the door open, propelling her forward. She had a brief glimpse of Mark, sweaty, dressed only in jeans, then the wind whistled around the room, knocked out the overhead light, and whooshed out the door. It slammed close.

The violent crack of the door echoed in the now-still barn. When it faded, for an ageless moment there was only silence inside, raging nature outside. Then Mark's harsh breathing broke the waiting.

"Mark?" she called.

"Over here. Do you have a light?" His voice was rougher than his breathing.

"There are some emergency flashlights in a box by the door." Joy held out her hands, shuffling her way toward them. Slowly her eyes adjusted to the darkness, until blackness became gray shapes, then gray shapes became smudged objects. The only light came from the strobe-like flashes of lightning through the row of windows at the top of the barn. Once it illuminated a metal ring about the size of a Hula-Hoop and a flowing cloth, its color an indeterminate neutral. Once it illuminated a crystal column, another prop, she guessed. Once it illuminated Mark himself, standing by the box for the Elements Escape. His face was sallow and his bare chest rose and fell in rapid succession, while his dark eyes were fixed firmly on her.

He did not like the dark, she remembered.

Joy hurried to the box, bruising her shin on a trunk, and grabbed two flashlights. She flipped them on.

Mark's sigh was audible, even above the fury of the storm.

She hastened to his side and handed him the light. Fresh sweat dotted the evening shadow on his chin. Wanting to give him something to think about other than the darkness and the dusty scent of the enclosed barn, Joy pressed her flashlight against her chin and turned it on. It would give her face an eerie glow, as though lit from inside.

"I am the ghost of Magicians Past," she intoned with fake drama. "Only the great Harry Houdini can help you escape."

Mark laughed, and the tension in him faded. "Better watch out. Houdini debunked fake mediums and seances. He was the original ghostbuster."

"I wonder what he'd say about this storm."

"That it was Louisiana in August, and it will blow over."

Joy listened to the din of the rain on the barn; it obliterated all outside sound and wrapped them in isolation. "It doesn't sound like it's going to lessen any time soon. Maybe it's decided to trap us in here."

A shiver trickled to the base of her spine at her words, but Mark just shook his head. "Supernatural thunderclouds? Not even your grocery rags have come up with that one."

Another shudder raced through her.

Mark laid down his flashlight to grip her shoulders. "You're soaked. Are you cold?"

"Cold?" The heat from his hands could have steamed the damp from her. "Not in Louisiana. Not with your touch."

His fingers tightened, and the lightning flashed in his eyes. "Joy, I didn't kiss Dia. I—"

"I believe you."

His rush of words stopped. Fists on hips, he demanded,

"You know? Then why in hellfire did you give me such a hard time?"

"My eyes saw you; I can't explain why, but they did. I'm sure of that. But I don't believe it was you, not anymore."

Mark scowled. "That doesn't make any sense."

"It's the best I can do."

"Why don't you believe it was me?"

"Because the man wore a ring, and you never do. Because you couldn't have gotten there from Guy's."

"Small facts to base trust on, but I'll take them." He plucked the soggy feathers from her grasp, set her flashlight on a bale of straw near his, then gathered her close, not seeming to mind the way her wet clothes soaked his chest and jeans.

Savoring the feel of his chest beneath her cheek, Joy leaned against him. Firm skin, a dusting of hair, pulsing heart, all were pleasing. He was hard muscle, lean strength, powerful warmth. His scent of citrus and male sweat enfolded her.

In one week he would be gone. She could deny the love in her heart or she could, for a brief time, make the lightning hers, then let it go. For she could not hold him, and she could not live waiting for him to return.

Mark laid his head on her hair. "Just when I think I know you, Joy Taylor, you surprise me."

"Me? I'm transparent as water."

"You're also wet as water." He backed up. "You need to put on something dry."

Joy pulled out her shirt, which had stuck to her chest with the embrace. Dust from the barn had settled on it. "I'm all out of fresh clothes, at least here." The thunder boomed. "And I don't think we're going anywhere soon."

"You can wear my T-shirt"—he tossed it to her—"and I think Dia left some shorts here." He crossed to a huge trunk.

"Dia left shorts with your clothes?"

"Costume trunk, darlin'."

"As though I could fit into a showgirl's costume."

"Don't let Dia hear you call her a showgirl." Mark ran a practiced, appreciative eye over her, then rummaged through the trunk. "This should fit." He tossed her a spangly garment.

Joy held up the shorts—they were definitely of the short, tight, and shiny variety—but the material was stretchy and Mark's T-shirt should cover some of the bulges revealed. She glanced around for a place to change, unexpectedly shy about simply stripping where she stood.

"I'll turn my back." Mark suited his action to his words.

Joy pulled off her sopping clothes and laid them out to dry, leaving on only her nylon underwear, which would dry soon anyway. She pulled the shorts on first; to her surprise, they did fit, though she suspected the fabric had to stretch a bit more to accommodate her than Dia. She twisted, trying to see how they looked. There was something daring about wearing glitter-coated shorts that barely covered her butt.

"Very nice, darlin'." Mark's appreciative drawl jerked her attention up to find him gazing with warm appreciation at her. "I always knew you'd look good in glitter."

"You said you'd turn your back."

"I did. I didn't say how long. I heard you rustling and fussing and just had to see the pretty sight." His eyes landed on her wet-nylon-covered breasts.

Swiftly, Joy threw on Mark's T-shirt. It almost covered the shorts, and the sleeves reached her elbows, giving her a measure of courage. She pushed up the sleeves and felt something hard in one. Intrigued, she looked inside it and discovered a small, invisible pocket. Inside were—

Mark grabbed her wrists before she delved further. He held her arms outstretched. Joy squirmed and twisted, trying to free herself, but Mark, for all his lithe grace, was strong.

"No prying into magician's secrets."

"A hidden pocket?" she asked, settling.

"You never mind about that. Wear the shirt, don't feel it."

"All right," Joy conceded with a laugh, content to let the magician's secrets remain a mystery; then the laughter slipped from her. "Mark, we have to talk. About a lot of things."

"Maybe, but not right now." Still holding her arms, he stepped against her.

While he held her open to him, she thought he might kiss her, but instead he dropped one hand. With the other still holding her, he urged her over to the crystal pedestal she'd seen earlier. He dropped her hand and began assembling magic equipment. "I need your help."

"Sure. What?"

"You agree way too readily, darlin', but for tonight I'm not going to let you take it back."

"What do I have to do?" Joy's eyes narrowed. "Is this something I'm going to regret agreeing to? Like that time you talked me into sneaking out for a midnight swim in the creek and the sheriff caught us breaking curfew? Or like that rope trick?"

"Not a thing like that, and you didn't back out then, so I'm saying no backing out now. You've helped me some with my magic, and I can tell you're curious about how things work. Now's your chance to find out exactly how I do one illusion."

"I repeat. What do I have to do?"

"Dia's gone; I think you know that. Now, I can do everything for the Mushroom Festival performance without an assistant. It's going to be hard, but I'll manage." He stopped setting up the illusion long enough to give her such a look of suffering that Joy had to bite her lip to remember she was trying to be cautious.

"Everything except one," he continued, turning back to his work. "The Pygmalion illusion. For that I need someone. A lady. And, I've got to try it out before I leave for the tour."

Joy saw at once where he was heading. She backed up. "No. No way. I am not getting on that stage as your assistant."

"You said you'd help, and you've got the shorts to prove it."

"No. No. No." Joy shook her head. "Assistants are tiny, flexible. They have to contort to fit all kinds of odd places. They're thin."

"And you're not. That's the beauty of this. That's why you're so perfect. The audience knows that, too, but it will be obvious you're not the contorting type."

"Did you just call me fat?"

Mark heard the warning note in her voice. For someone normally glib as gab, his comment hadn't said what he'd intended. He dropped the equipment and took two strides to her side, stopping her retreat with his hands on her shoulders.

He ran his hands down her arms, enjoying the soft feel of her while deftly removing the hidden coins in her sleeve pocket. He'd forgotten he'd left those in there.

"You are not even chubby, darlin', and I didn't say that. I just meant . . ." He stopped, recognizing an age-old trap for men. Joy wasn't reed thin like Dia, and he *liked* Joy's curves, the way her breasts filled his palms and her hips nestled into him, but from the look in her eye, no explanation was his best course.

A swift, hard kiss dispelled any mistaken notions she might have. At least, that was what he hoped, as he settled in to enjoy the taste and scent of her. "Does this seem like someone who doesn't adore your sweet curves, darlin'?" he murmured against her lips.

Her only answer was a satisfying sigh.

For a moment Mark forgot all plans, lost in the sheer pleasure of holding Joy and kissing her, and, better, having her kiss him back.

Then he lifted from the kiss. He rested his cheek on her forehead. This was where she belonged, in his arms, pressed against him, and it didn't matter where they were or whether they were living out of a suitcase or a closet or where the next move was.

Why didn't she realize that, too? Gently, he propelled her to the pedestal. "I'm so glad you agreed to help."

"I didn't—" Joy broke off with a sigh. "What do I do?"

This illusion was one of his best. It wasn't the glitz and flash that he sometimes liked to do. It was romantic, alluring, and full of the mystery that was the essence of magic. It was also one of his most puzzling illusions.

"For now, stand up on that pedestal." Mark helped her up, then stepped back. "The illusion starts with Pygmalion, the sculptor, the man who thought little of the virtues of womankind and vowed to remain unmarried." Mark paraphrased the voiceover he'd taped to accompany the music and the magic, his voice persuasive. "Instead, he took clay and fashioned it into a woman, a perfect woman." He moved his hands at Joy's feet. "Here I'll take a lump of clay and fashion it into a woman, a perfect statue."

"You sculpt? That quickly?"

He fastened her with a glare. "Don't interrupt. It's magic. Now, where was I?"

"A perfect statue."

"Ah, yes. The audience will know it's a statue because at one point I take the head off to situate it more perfectly and I'll knock on the hard plaster."

"I'm not going to be in there then, am I?"

"No. Now hush. He forms a perfect statue of a woman. He brings her trinkets." Here he would do routine sleight of hand, producing jewelry and adornments for the statue. "But one should never tempt the anger of the gods. The fates play a cruel trick. Pygmalion falls in love with the woman he has named Galatea. Alas, she is not a woman; she is still a statue. He is lost." Mark gave an exaggerated sigh and was rewarded with Joy's laugh. "The disconsolate suitor goes to the temple of Venus." Mark waved his hands; some of the fire illusions would go here. "When he returns, he reaches for her atop her pedestal." Mark dragged a chair over to Joy. "On stage, I levitate, but here the chair will have to do."

"You levitate? Of course. You, not me, right?"

Mark didn't answer. "Pygmalion gives his Galatea a kiss." Mark traced a hand down Joy's cheek, then bent her back, kissing her with drama and a very real passion. Kissed her until the blood thrummed for both of them, until skin was no longer alabaster and ivory but exquisitely pliant and sensitive. Until they were both breathless and Joy clung to his shoulders.

She wasn't supposed to move, yet.

He lifted from the kiss, his senses confused. For too long, he couldn't move, caught in the web of her spicy scent, her female softness captured by his arms. Her eyes gazed at him with such pure openness. Sanity returned.

Damn, he'd better watch that onstage. It wouldn't do for him to turn to the audience sporting a bulge.

Mark whispered, "Slowly, the statue comes awake. Yet, how does she? She has been standing in a spotlight, formed from a lump of clay. The crystal pedestal has not hidden her. It must be the gift of the goddess."

"How do I do that?" Joy whispered in return. Both desire and fear were in her eyes and in her voice.

He lifted her two hands. "Put your hands over your head. Graceful, like a delicately carved statue. You will look so beautiful there, Joy, dressed in white, your red hair the only color. This is how it ends, with you, dancing for me and for the audience."

Before Joy could voice the protest he knew was on her lips—that she couldn't dance before the crowd—Mark started humming the piece that would play for them and swaying his hips. Soon, she matched him, rubbing against him in a move that was both erotic and torturous. Blood settled low and deep, filling him with its heat and its pulsing need.

Mark moved Joy's hands in time to the music. "It doesn't matter what you do, just sway delicately as the hard marble of your body becomes soft, heated, warmed by the beating of your heart for your lover. Like that, yes, just like that," he crooned. "Lean against me, offer yourself to me, open to me."

She leaned against him, resting her head against his shoulder. He nipped at her vulnerable neck, then licked it with his tongue.

All thoughts of illusion vanished in a puff of magician's smoke.

His hands slid down her body, first on her breasts, then her belly, then dipping beneath the spangled shorts. He was so hard, so needy, he had to take her now, imprint her body with the feel of his, until all her reserve, all her doubts fled.

"I want you, Joy," he growled. "Now. The illusion stopped when I touched you here." He ran his tongue down her neck again, tasting the salt and rainwater flavors that lingered on her.

"Take me."

He needed no more of an invitation. He set her upright, stepped from the chair, then lifted his hands. Bracing her hands on his shoulders, she jumped off her pedestal.

Mark scooped her into his arms and held her to his chest, aching for her lips again.

Only when he had tasted and licked and drunk from her, did he lift. Her eyes were bright. Her face flushed, a mirror to the fire in him.

The rain was a merciless tempest outside. He looked around. Inside was . . . no bed. Just hay, a concrete floor, and narrow benches. Spread the capes?

No time. Urgency beat inside Mark, as relentless as the storm outside. Joy plucked at the waist of his jeans, fumbling with the button and zipper. No time.

"Ah, what the hell." He backed her up, braced her shoulders against the metal siding. "Ever done it against a wall, honey?"

"No." She lowered his zipper. With frantic hands, she pushed his jeans and boxers past his hips.

Lightning flashed. Rain drummed against the metal barn, echoing the chaos inside him.

"Now," she demanded.

Mark pulled down her shorts and with one lunge was inside her. She felt so good! Wet. Welcoming. His arms wrapped around her to steady her and brace her, while she clutched at his shoulders. Need held her taut against him, around him. He kissed her. Savage, wild, like the storm. His strokes were elemental, without finesse.

Mark plunged forward, his release strong and shattering and prolonged.

Joy's back arched. "Yes!" she shouted, climaxing.

They clung together, gasping, motionless, suspended between turbulence, passion, and reality, until Mark felt Joy sag against him.

"Yes," she whispered again, her forehead coming to rest against his.

They stood there, embracing, connected, their slowing breaths mingling, while the edge of passion lulled and heartbeats gentled.

"Let's open the door," Joy said. "I feel so wild inside, I want to share the wildness outside."

He kissed her once, then disentangled them and righted their clothing. He opened the barn door. Joy followed him, and he wrapped his arm around her shoulders. They stood there, the rain in front, the barn behind. Trees lashed under the wind, and the torrent obliterated the view.

"It's like we're the only two people in the world," she said.

Yet, for one odd moment, Mark felt as though he were being watched, as though unseen eyes peered at them through the gray barrier. "Are we?" he asked.

Joy tilted her head to look at him, then gazed back outside. "Spirits, trip away, make no stay. Meet me all by break of day."

Mark looked at her questioning.

"Shakespeare. *A Midsummer Night's Dream*." She glanced back outside. "Spirits, let us be," she whispered.

The odd feeling of being watched dissipated. With one last glance at the tempest outside, he turned back to Joy. "Come, my Galatea. Awake for me."

He led her back inside.

Chapter Nineteen

Brilliant lightning glinted off the metal edges of the costume trunk. Mark began pulling out the capes inside and spreading them over a loose mound of hay. With Joy's help they soon had an adequate bed. As they worked, as he watched Joy sway in the glittery shorts, Mark was surprised to feel himself getting hard again.

He reached for her, and she came into his arms with a sweet willingness. Together they moved to their bed of cloth and hay.

Mark stood with Joy in the center of the slippery froth of black and rainbow satin. The oversized shirt—his shirt— flowed over her curves, tantalizing rather than hiding, while the show business shorts made his palm itch to caress her. He gave in to the impulse, widening his stance and pulling her close. The press of her against his groin was almost painful in its pleasure.

Her hair had been drawn back into a clip, but the wind and rain had whipped tendrils free. He unsnapped the barrette, loosening the rest, then gripped the vibrant mass. It filled his hand with her fire. Lightning flashed, more subdued than it had been all evening, but enough to illuminate her with gold and glitter.

He had never seen her look so vivid, so wild. There was always a touch of quiet reserve about Joy that both intrigued and challenged him, but today she was . . . untamed.

The contrast tightened his gut and filled him with a riot of emotions—possessiveness, pride, satisfaction, and a savage, red desire.

Her hands cupped his neck, while her fingers kneaded the back of his head. The tiny movements sent the lightning through his body.

"I'm no statue, no Galatea. Kiss me," she commanded, her words as much growled as spoken.

His fingers tangled in her hair and tugged her head back, tilting her face for his kiss. He nipped at her lips, lifted, then slanted his head to allow greater access and deeper penetration. With a sigh of completion, he settled into the taste of her.

He loved the little moans she made, the tiny massage of her body against his. Flames burst inside him, burning away old habits and older fears.

He loved her.

All sides of her. The prim, practical Joy. The nurturing, warm Joy. He loved the woman who saw him with a clear knowledge and still cared. And he definitely loved this new side, the wild, passionate woman.

She was truly a mate, a woman who could share the rigors and uncertainties of his life, a lady with a hidden streak of daring. That she allowed only him to see and share this tumultuous side of her both thrilled and humbled him.

Mark's hands roamed beneath the T-shirt, skimming across her smooth skin, unhooking the bra with little trouble and slipping it off. He took full advantage of the skin exposed to his sensitive fingers.

Joy drew back, then laughed. "You are entirely too easy with that move."

"It's easier than ropes, and this time I've got full use of my hands."

"Show me another sleight of hand."

"Like this?" He slid to the front, still beneath the shirt, and skimmed the tight buds of her nipples, the soft curve under her breast, the delightful outsides.

"Just like that," she sighed.

"You have the smoothest skin," he told her, his fingers dancing across her.

She pressed forward, but Mark's agile hands avoided the invitation. Tempting as her sweet breasts were to cup and hold and caress, with the knife-edge of desire eased by their wild coupling, he had other inviting parts to visit first, before he settled down.

Well, settling *down* wasn't exactly what he was doing.

Joy gave a little murmur, then leaned forward to play with his neck. Her nibbling shot off sparks inside him. She followed with a cooling puff of air, apparently deciding to play, too, as her fingers danced across his chest and abdomen.

Mark's muscles tightened in anticipation, and he felt himself harden and grow longer in response to her touch, though he hadn't realized either was possible. When she found the snap and zipper on his pants and handled both speedily, it was pure relief and delight.

"See," she whispered into his ear, her breath warm and spicy against him, "I know a little sleight of hand, too." She reached beneath his boxers, "and you also have smooth skin." Her thumb stroked the length of him.

Mark drew in a sharp breath. "Damn, but you've got a wicked touch, woman." In one quick motion, he was naked, inviting more of the heart-thumping caress.

She didn't disappoint him.

Together, neither leading, both again eager, they lowered to the shimmering heap of silk and satin and velvet that was the most unusual bed Joy had ever known. Mark paused only long enough to strip off her clothes.

Once Joy might have been embarrassed to be in the barn, naked, with a man, this man, but not today. This day was for fantasies, the raw, sweaty, primal kind.

Satin at her back, dry barn air, rain drumming against the metal roof, yellow flashlight beams and gold lightning, each detail faded behind the irresistible press of hot, sleek, male flesh as Mark stretched out beside her.

His motions were never jerky, never unsure, but rather in tune with an internal rhythm that seemed as natural as the tempo of the rain.

"I love to watch you move," she told him, running a hand along the strength of his arm. "And to touch you."

He smiled at her, as though she'd given him a gift. "That's about the sweetest thing anyone's ever said to me."

His smile dazzled, too, tugging cords deep inside her, filaments that ran straight to her heart.

"Do you taste sweet?" she asked with deceptive simplicity, then gave him a string of kisses along his shoulder. "Mmmm, sweet and salt, like chocolate-covered pretzels."

"Careful there, you're making me hungry." He matched her string of kisses, ending at her breasts, where he feasted.

Wildness burst through Joy. She arched to the warm, moist tug of his lips, feeling the pull down deep. When he lifted, she gave him a tiny push on the shoulder. That lean body of Mark's was pure muscle, so if he'd wanted to resist, there wasn't much she could do about it, but he gave in easily.

"I love it when you're pushy, darlin'." Mark stacked his hands behind his head, watching and waiting, completely open to her perusal, that devilish smile teasing his lips.

Joy straddled him, feeling him pulse against her backside, then bit her lip, uncertain what she should do next.

"Now you're bein' cruel, making me wait," he teased, as always, understanding her hesitation. "Makes me wonder what you're planning. You always did have a streak of the wild. Will it be playful? Rough and sweaty and needy? If you want, I can do my part and whisper things like . . ." He did an easy situp to murmur in her ear, naughty and a little raunchy, while his fingers rolled her nipples into tight buds.

Joy thought she'd heard a lot in her life, but with a few select words, Mark had her blushing as fiercely as a nineteenth-century bride.

She hadn't thought mere words could be so . . . arousing.

Then again, she'd never heard these said by Mark.

He lay back down, but this time his hands didn't go behind his head. Instead his nimble fingers stroked her, low, where her thighs were spread across him and opened her to his invasion.

Sweet Mary, he had magic hands!

"Indulge yourself," he commanded. "Show me. Have your way with me, wicked woman."

Adjectives describing her usually involved words like helpful, dependable, and hard worker, but never wicked woman.

She liked wicked.

She bent over him.

The wildfire consumed them. Hands, lips, bodies moved in a flurry of need. No finesse, only the raw power of hot desire. Her skin craved his touch, and when he rubbed against the low, tender bud she melted faster than ice in a skillet. Fever held Joy in its restless, relentless, needy grip.

"My turn." She kissed him in a trail from shoulder to groin, her mouth circling him. Suddenly, Mark grabbed her and lifted her up.

"No. I'll be inside you when I come," he said, low and guttural.

Mark clutched her hips and guided her to his shaft. With a push, he settled inside. Joy felt the stretch clear to the tips of her toes and fingers.

Inside her, this was where she needed him to be. Mark's hips lifted, moving him deeper, then he let Joy set the pace. Instinctively, she moved to the rhythm of the rain and the thunder and the lightning, primal and wild.

Mark's hands moved restlessly over her sweat-coated skin, burrowed into the mane of fire, high and low. "Every part of you feels so damn good," he groaned.

Together, they sank deep into the satin mattress, the silk desire, and the velvet need. Through the open door, the cool, riotous night blew in, but it was no match for the coiling tumult raging between them. Joy moved faster; Mark plunged up deep and high, giving a hoarse shout of triumph as he spilled himself inside her.

The thunder exploded, outside, and inside Joy. Every muscle tensed and clenched as exhilarating waves drowned her with their pleasure.

Long seconds passed, and the tension released, though the pleasure of having Mark inside her, beside her, did not. Joy collapsed onto his chest.

"I love you," she murmured, not sure if he would hear her.

He did.

"I love you, too."

Mark knew he'd dozed, for the storm had faded to a mere pattering when he next became conscious of the world beyond Joy sprawled atop him. He was still inside her, still enveloped by her warmth, though all was softer than before. He was content to lie there, eyes closed, savoring the closeness.

Joy's muscles pulsed, setting his skin tingling, making the blood stir again.

Something tickled his cheek.

Eyes still closed, Mark unerringly found the soft spot behind her ear and toyed with it, something he'd learned could make her squirm and give a sexy exclamation.

He smiled when she did just that.

The stirring of his blood, and other organs, picked up.

That tickling, faint and soft, moved from his cheek to his shoulder, then down his side.

It was Mark's turn to squirm.

He opened one eye. Joy's head was pressed against the other side of his head. It was a pretty view, that vibrant red of her hair, but it didn't tell him what was tantalizing him.

He could feel the muscles in Joy's right arm move, but it wasn't her finger or hand touching him. *Those* he was well acquainted with.

"What you doin' there, darlin'?"

"Nothing," Joy answered with deceptive sweetness.

One long feathery touch moved from his hip to his armpit. The stroke touched each nerve in a delicate call to attention, and Mark's skin warmed under the sweet attack.

Nothing, like hell!

Now, like tiny caterpillar feet, it shifted down to his thigh to circle his knee.

"You gonna follow that with a kiss?"

"Maybe."

Muscles tightened in anticipation. Whoever knew the knee was an erogenous zone? Mark felt himself harden, though five minutes ago he would have said he was lazy and content and depleted. He craned his neck to see what she held, but her freckled shoulder blocked him.

"What you teasing me with there, darlin'?"

"Hmmm," was Joy's only answer.

Obviously, it was up to him to find out what game she played, and what she was using to play it with.

The little minx had turned into a tease. Another new side to Joy. Mark liked it. He shifted his hips slightly, seating himself more firmly inside her as his shaft swelled.

Joy drew in a satisfied breath. The feathery touch stilled a second, then it whispered along the fine hairs of his leg.

Mark began the tiny movements that started them on the path to spiraling desire. He inhaled deeply, drawing in the scent of her spice. For a moment, he debated—feed the sharp bite of desire or of curiosity?

Joy shifted slightly, sprawling more fully across him.

The tickling caress moved . . . up the inside his leg, toward his—

Debate over. With a swift, agile move, Mark rolled over, pinning Joy beneath him with his hips. He braced his arms, lifting his torso off her.

He stayed lodged inside her. He wanted it all—curiosity *and* desire satisfied.

Her blue eyes sparkled with laughter. "You lasted longer than I thought you would."

"What have you got, Joy?" Even on her back, her hands were hidden beneath her. He tugged one arm free. Her hand was empty. He freed the other arm. Hand also empty.

"Magic?" she teased.

"No illusion did this to me." Mark withdrew his shaft nearly all the way, then surged back inside her in one claiming stroke.

She sucked in a breath, apparently content to be claimed, and twined her hands around his waist. She lifted to kiss him.

"Uh-uh, darlin', not yet." Mark surrounded her with an embrace, trapping her arms, and rolled again.

He spied right away what she'd hidden beneath her— three ostrich plumes, each about a foot and a half long, one white, the others gray-brown. She'd had plumes in her hand when she'd first come into the barn, he remembered, although then they were bedraggled.

Mark sat up, cross-legged, then shifted until Joy was firmly ensconced in his lap. With one arm clamped around her hips to anchor her there, he reached over and picked up the plumes.

They had dried to feathery softness. The frothy edges ruffled when he blew on them.

Joy held out her hand. "I'll take my plumes please," she said, rather primly considering that she was stark naked with her hair a fiery nimbus, she was impaled on his shaft, and her internal muscles were starting to work him.

Mark grinned and handed her the largest plume. With the two he still held, he flicked delicately across both her nipples, gratified to see them harden to tight berries.

"Persuade me."

She grinned back at him and proceeded to show him how convincing she could be.

Of course, Mark was also noted for his persuasive talents. In the end, they both won.

Even magic must reach an end. Rosy-fingered dawn had not yet made its appearance when Joy opened her eyes, but she knew it was time to arise. The rain had ended sometime in the night. Jax, Hope, anyone could come into the barn and find them there.

Carefully so as not to awaken him, she extracted herself from Mark's embrace, his arm resting atop her breasts, one leg flung across hers. She stretched to dispell lingering stiffness in muscles not used before, then donned her now-dry clothes.

Mark opened one eye. "I hope you don't intend to make a habit of sneaking out early from my bed. Come back, and I'll show you why early morning loving is very special." His voice was sleepy and the invitation tempting.

Joy knelt beside him. "I'm . . . a little sore," she answered honestly, for there had been further times they had reached for one another in the night. Once savage and swift. Once slow and sweet.

He reached through her tangle of hair to rest a gentle

hand at her nape. "I'm sorry. You should have said something; I'd have stopped."

"I'm fine. I didn't want you to stop."

His fingers tightened. She saw him swallow and knew the time of reckoning was at hand. "Did you mean what you said last night?" he asked.

Joy ducked her head, unable to meet his probing eyes. She splayed her hand on his chest, feeling the crisp hairs and thudding heart beneath her palm. Only complete honesty. "Every word. Did you?"

"Yes."

There was a silence, taut and filled with the decisions she could not bring herself to voice.

Was there hope for something more? He said he loved her. Might he be content with her and her small-town life?

"Then you know," Mark said at last, very softly, "I want you to join the show when you get things settled here."

Startled, Joy looked at him. "Join the show?"

"Yes, finally, together, we're going to take the world by storm."

For one brief moment, Joy longed to do just that. To be the woman of last night, uncaring of the future, free to do whatever she wanted. Last night she had made love with abandon on a bed of magic satin. The need for Mark was so strong in her, she squeezed her eyes tight against the ache.

"What would I do?"

"Be my assistant. My chef. You're free to do whatever you want. I know you'll like it." His hand traced a line down her cheek. "I want you there as my lover."

His lover. The edges of her hopes crumbled.

She had always faced reality squarely. Joy opened her eyes to the dust and the gray of morning. Mark did not want ties; they were chains to him. She could not live without them, without roots.

She could not be that woman he wanted or needed.

"You want me to travel with you?" In danger of losing the final piece of her heart, she had to protect it. She had to be sure not a flicker of hope remained.

"Of course. We'll see towns, big and small, in this country and all over the world. It will be one endless adventure. You'll like the crew, and they'll love you." He tweaked her nose. "Not as much as I do, of course, but near enough."

"But, they're always changing, leaving, like Dia." Her hands rested against his chest.

"Some have been with me for a couple of years, but sure, that's the way it is. The way it has to be." A crease formed between his eyes, as though he suddenly realized that her enthusiasm left something to be desired. His thudding heart beat against her palms.

His idea of permanence was a couple of years. Joy's fingers curled. *This was too hard.* He had to understand. "I looked up your web page. You have a lot of dates scheduled. Next year you'll be home less than six weeks and those aren't even in one stretch and when you go to Europe—"

"I told you, a magician needs to perform."

"Will you be canceling any dates?"

His larger hand wrapped around hers. The agile fingers were also strong and solid. "That's my life. It's got to be if I'm going to make a success of it, and I won't be a failure."

Not like his father. Not like everyone had assumed he would be. Lord, she was so proud of what he was and what he did, and she understood the reasons why he had to do what he did. She looked straight at him, memorizing the planes of his face, the way his crisp, dark hair shaped his head, the shadow of whiskers that gave him a dangerous air.

His dark eyes narrowed, and the aura of danger grew darker.

"What's this about, Joy? Why are you making it complicated?"

"Because it is complicated. What if I said I wanted to get married?"

He took a deep breath and stood. Still gloriously naked, he paced a step away, then back to her. Joy saw shadows in his eyes, and he hesitated too long before his devilish grin chased them away. "You're asking me to marry you? Sure, if that's what you want, darlin'."

Tears gathered behind her eyes, tears she would not shed. This proposal was more reluctant than the one seven years ago. "I love you, Mark, but I can't live like that. Out of suitcases, a new town every day or two."

"Was it all a lie before?" He shoved his legs into his pants, then crouched next to her. "I thought you shared my dreams."

"You weren't listening close enough. I want to see new places and meet new people and taste new foods. But not every day. In the end, I need a home to come back to. That place where I can settle and cook and bring smiles to faces that surround me every day. I don't want to keep moving."

"Home isn't a place, Joy. Home is the person you love." He angled his head and bent down and kissed her, deep and full of raw need. When he lifted, her lips tingled with the imprint of him, and she knew she would never be able to forget. "Home has always been you. I thought you felt the same way about me. Let your home be my suitcase."

Home has always been you. The words echoed inside

her like a crazy fun house. She steeled herself against their lure, against their too-right sound, though her body ached with the fight. That was the family curse thinking. She would wither without roots.

If she tried to bind him down, he would die by tiny bits.

Or, one day the wandering man would not return.

She'd survived the waiting once. She didn't think she could a second time.

"I . . . can't. After your show, I want you to leave. I want your promise that you will leave."

Her words hit Mark with the force of a baseball bat. He pushed to his feet.

She wouldn't come with him. He was losing her. Again.

He staggered backward. "You can't mean that."

"I do. I want your promise."

"You trust me to keep it?" he sneered, the blows of her words leaving him raw and bruised.

"Yes." She looked at him. The sprinkling of freckles stood out against the whiteness of her face. Her blue eyes, her clear gaze told him it was the honest, hurting truth.

There was a reason he never liked honesty.

"Don't cut us off again, Joy."

"But . . . you're not a settlin' man," she whispered.

"I will—" He broke off the words abruptly and understanding exploded. And with understanding came an anger that stripped away the veneer of assurance to expose the swaggering, thieving kid who'd been taught to strike back quick and hard.

"You don't have faith that when I say I love you, I mean it."

"The women in my family are cursed when it comes to men. My mother, my grandmother, every one of us."

"Cursed!" Mark responded with a pithy curse of his own. "That's hogwash. Admit it, Joy, you're afraid to take a risk, so you're going to bury yourself in some hick town and cook dumplings. You're afraid to trust me, to believe me. Well, it wouldn't be much of a relationship, would it?"

Mark could not forget. Last time he'd asked her to marry him, she'd gone straight to another man's arms.

Systemically he buried the knife-edged pain beneath a practiced facade. It was an illusion worthy of the finest magician, for inside the blades were lacerating. The words grew bitter. "You going straight off to Seth, now? Going to marry a comfortable, convenient, *settlin'* man like you did the last time?"

"No!" She shook her head. "Not again. I . . . I am so sorry I did that. It was stupid, and I have regretted hurting you like that."

Mark refused to let her soothing work its magic. "Good thing, because let me tell you something, darlin'. You're not going to forget last night quite that easy. It'll be with you a long, long time. I know, because I won't forget."

She flinched and the freckles stood out in greater contrast. "I know," she whispered. "But I'm not the right woman for you. You need someone like Dia."

Hell, it was like kicking a puppy.

The anger faded, replaced by an ache in his chest that grew until it gripped his belly and grabbed his throat. He hadn't thought he could feel so naked, so shredded as he had when he'd found out she'd married, but he was wrong. This was worse.

Joy was the one person who had the power to see beneath his facades, to rip apart his painstakingly erected

288

defenses. She was a part of him, had been for many years, and always would be.

He had to figure out how to convince her she belonged with him and with the show.

Hell, it was bad enough trying to convince Joy to trust him after all the lies and disappointments, but now she'd gotten the stupid notion that she was doing the right thing by refusing him.

Joy being her most helpful was Joy at her most stubborn.

Some part of him could not give up, could not let her end it so easily.

He still had an ace.

Mark stepped away, forcing the tension out of his voice. "You want my promise to leave? I'll give it on one condition. That you work with me at the festival as my assistant on the Pygmalion illusion."

"You still want me to work with you? Why? Are you hoping to change my mind about traveling?"

"No." Joy might have trouble with lies and half truths, but Mark didn't. "I have to try that illusion on stage before a live audience before I go on tour with it. This is the place. The members of my crew all have other jobs, and you are the only one not of my crew I'll allow backstage. That's the bargain. No negotiatin'."

He held his breath, waiting for her answer. "C'mon, darlin'," he urged. "You want the festival to be a success."

"Then you'll leave?"

She didn't have to sound so eager. "Then I'll leave."

"All right."

They stood, silent, locked into their own worlds, each unsure how to break free.

"Joy! J-o-o-y." Nicole's shouts in the not-too-far distance broke the tension.

Joy's brow furrowed. "I wonder what she wants."

Abruptly, Nicole pushed open the barn door. "Joy! You must—" She stopped abruptly, taking in Joy's dishevelment, Mark's partial nudity. "Oh, sorry. Joy, you will not believe the wondrous news!"

Mark shrugged on his shirt, while Joy tried to pat her hair into a semblance of order. "What, Nicole?"

"My Henry has come home!"

Chapter Twenty

Nicole hurried out of the barn without another comment or even a motherly glance of interest or disapproval at their obvious past activities.

"Guess she's not going for the shotgun," Mark murmured, starting to put away the cloaks.

Joy chuckled, glad that the easy humor between them could still crop up. "Nicole never did do outraged motherhood."

For once, Joy was thankful for her mother's self-absorption. Explanations were beyond her. Then her smile faded.

"So, the prodigal husband has returned," she said, proud of the even tone she managed. Too much was happening. Too many conflicting emotions churned inside her to sort them out. She had never expected Henry Valcour to return, and she didn't know what to make of it.

Mark dropped the cloaks. Two strides brought him to her side.

He could always see beneath her calm facade. Why? Why him? No one else did, or even wanted to.

"His return is going to change things," Mark said.

"Will it? Maybe, maybe not. Nicole will take him back, yes, and he'll stay for a while. Then he'll leave again."

"You can't be sure of that."

"It's a common pattern, happened with husbands number two, five, and six."

He didn't answer, but she knew he saw more than she wanted him to. Looking away from his intent eyes, Joy fumbled with her hair clips, trying to rein in the wild mass of hair, but this morning nothing was fitting back into its comfortable patterns. She yanked out the clips.

Deftly, Mark took the hair clips and pulled her hair into them. He fashioned a style she'd never tried before—her hair was out of her eyes, but still loose and free.

"Thanks," she muttered, wondering how he'd acquired that skill.

"You're welcome. Cybele has arthritis and sometimes she has trouble reaching up."

How did he guess her thoughts so easily?

"Guess I'd better go and say hello to Henry."

"Do you want me to go in with you?"

The quiet question stopped her. She did, she wanted his solid support at her side, but in all her life she'd never had someone to lean on or share burdens with. No one except him, and it wouldn't do to start getting used to that again. Joy started to the door.

"Thanks, but no, I'll manage." She always did.

When she glanced back, it was to see him standing in

shadows, and one thought bit at her. Dark; he was dark and more than a little dangerous. Dark shirt, dark rough stubble on his cheeks, dark tousled hair, dark eyes that she couldn't read, dark soul with a deep light that few others saw.

He was alone with the dark.

He had never seemed more distant, and she had never loved him more.

What had she done? Lord, what had she done?

The decision was made.

"I won't be long if you want to start with the birds."

"Yes, boss."

Mark was rewarded with her faint smile; then he watched her disappear into the sunshine.

He remained in the cooler darkness, remembering the whiteness of her face, the smattering of freckles standing out in stark relief, the lashes drooping over weary blue eyes.

He let her go.

Mark tossed the remaining cloaks into the trunk, pausing once to hold one close against him, one that held the lingering scent of Joy's sweetness, that mix of spices as complex as the woman they defined.

He always knew where to find her. She wouldn't get away from him again. With Henry Valcour's return, she would be free of the responsibility of the farm and her family.

Yet, she had been so . . . resolved. She was making more plans for settling; he knew she wanted to open her restaurant. She was so sure she was making the right decision for them both.

He closed the trunk, then walked over to the Elements Escape tank. He clipped the cuffs on ankles, then wrists.

Drawing in deep breaths, he lowered himself into the cabinet. He didn't close the lid, for it was the darkness he needed to conquer.

Mark gripped the black cloth, then, pulling in one final breath, he ducked his head beneath the water and enclosed himself in the dark.

Working swiftly, automatically, with the cuffs, he forced his mind to think of something other than the narrow, lightless space pressing against him.

He pictured himself leaving after the performance, alone, and the fluttering edges of panic beat against his throat and chest. Not panic against invisible ties, but panic that he had lost Joy for good.

The fluttering gripped his gut. Extracting her promise of help with the Pygmalion illusion was taking advantage of her accommodating nature, he admitted, but desperate needs called for sneaky tactics.

The darkness bore down on him.

With each blow from his father's belt, with each minute spent in a stygian closet, with each performance, he had taught himself not to show fear and had become convinced that he no longer did fear.

It was a lie, as big as the one he'd once told himself, that Joy was out of his soul.

The panic burst outward. Mark bolted upright, lungs burning, water streaming from him. With the one hand free from the cuffs, he shoved the black cloth aside and gulped in air, then slapped the water.

Chest heaving, he rested his forehead on his fist. For the first time, doubts crept into him. Not about his love for Joy or his desire to be with her, but about his ability to persuade Joy of those two very basic facts.

You weren't listening close enough. The key was there. Maybe it was time he stopped charming and persuading and started listening.

With Valcour back—

Fear rippled over him, and the water felt cold despite the stuffiness of the barn.

Now that Valcour was back, would he take over the ostriches?

If Joy was no longer in charge of the ostriches, what would Centurion's reaction be? He wanted those ostriches for something. Would he decide he didn't need her anymore?

Zeus knocked on the door of Hera's room, wishing he were already inside, arising from a night in her bed. She opened it promptly, as though she'd been expecting him.

She probably had, he thought with a grumble. Hera had an uncanny ability to know what he was doing. Like that time with Io . . .

Best not dwell on that.

She looked both chic and cool despite the summer sun blazing through her windows. The room was oracle-neat, except for the rumpled bed. Hera was a restless sleeper, he remembered. But he had found ways to tame and enjoy that energy.

How many lovers had she had in the years of separation?

He and Hera were bonded by rituals and customs that lasted through their lives—and long lives those were by Earth standards—and those ties of mind and soul were rarely severed. Sexual loyalty, on the other hand, had never been a trait of his race. Yet, he found he'd acquired a patina of odd human customs and emotions, including ones Hera had absorbed early, like jealousy.

How many lovers?

"You look nice," he blurted out, unwilling to follow the path of his thoughts. *Glib, real glib, Zeus, my boy*. It was naught but the truth, though, and some of his honesty must have shown through, for she smiled softly.

"Thank you. So do you."

Maybe it was the eyes of love blinding her, for he wore shorts, sandals, a Hawaiian print shirt, and a Jupiter Fireworks cap.

This was the woman who had shared the worst and best of times with him, the banishment, as well as the heady elixir of godhood. The woman who had stood by him for so many years, then vanished for many more.

Could they ever return to what they were? Could they recapture the old feelings? He reached a hand out to touch the black hair skimming her shoulder, then stopped, unwilling to invite the pain of seeing her move away from his touch. His fist dropped to his side.

"I'm anxious to see the results of our matchmaking last night."

Hera leaned a shoulder against the door. "I must admit to a little curiosity myself. Far-see smoke?"

"I want to be able to hear them, share in their pleasure."

"Gloat with satisfaction?"

Yes, she knew him too well. "Shall we?" He crooked his elbow.

She linked her arm through his. "Do you want to transfer?"

"Let's be plebeian and take a car."

Even in a car, it didn't take long to reach Joy's house, and Zeus was surprised to see a number of cars in the driveway. He looked at Hera, but she just lifted one shoulder, telling him she had no more idea than he did about what was going on.

When Nicole opened the door, she was beaming. "Zeke! You must come in and meet my Henry. Oh, who is your friend?"

Zeus introduced "Harriet Juneau," and they followed Nicole into the living room. Henry Valcour sat in an overstuffed chair, the dominant force in a room populated by Nicole's fluttering friends and an avid Earl Flynn.

"Is this the man who walked out?" Hera whispered derisively to Zeus.

"Yes, now hush."

Henry was a barrel-chested man, strong and sturdy, with a face that was too rugged to be termed handsome. Gray at his temples was the only sign of aging, for it was obvious he kept himself in peak physical condition.

The man reminded him of somebody, Zeus thought suddenly.

At the introductions, Henry tilted his head to study Zeus. "You related to that movie fellow? You look like him. What was that fellow's name, Nicole, honey? The one that's got the accent you always drool about?"

"Sean Connery?"

"That's him. You related?"

"Not that I'm aware of." Frankly, the question was becoming annoying.

"You might want to check some of our genealogy logs," Hera said under her breath.

Zeus nudged her. "So, I understand you've been among the missing, Mr. Valcour?" Nicole might be a trifle ditzy, but he did feel a certain responsibility for her as one of Io's descendants.

"Call me Henry."

"Henry's been prospecting. For gold! In Alaska!" Nicole put in, snuggling against her errant husband.

"Always felt this need inside to dig deep in the earth for metals. To work them shiny and clean."

"Troll," muttered Hera, and Zeus nudged her again, although she only spoke his thoughts.

Zeus found a chair, and Hera perched gracefully beside him on the stuffed arm.

What was it that was so familiar about the man? Zeus wondered.

"Prospecting, hmmm? So, did you hit a heretofore unknown mother lode?" Zeus asked.

"I got an instinct about these things. I found some nuggets, some dust. Enough for a tidy sum. Now, I'm back. I missed my honey."

The look he gave Nicole was tender and longing. So, there was feeling there. Some of Zeus's annoyance faded as he realized the man was torn between Nicole and the inner restlessness that plagued too many men.

Hera rested one forearm on the chair back behind Zeus. "No phones, no modems, no mail service? Not a single luxury," she said drily, her under-the-breath comments audible to his ear only.

Another nudge from Zeus urged her silence. "Are you planning on going back?"

"Thinking about it."

Zeus's eyes narrowed as he saw Nicole's composure slip briefly.

"Mostly I want to give me and the little woman a chance to spend some of that nest egg I earned," Henry finished.

"*The little woman*?" Hera was incredulous.

"Can't keep the boy down on the farm," Zeus commented jovially.

"Nicole says Joy's made a success of the farm. I'm willing to let her stay on."

All sympathy disappeared. Saddling Joy with the ostriches while these two gadded about wasn't part of *his* plan for Joy. "Did you ask her?" he thundered.

The room fell silent as everyone stared at him. Hera nudged *him* this time and threw in an exasperated look for good measure.

"I, ah, just thought she might have other plans. Cooking plans." Zeus tried to repair the damage.

Henry settled into his chair, a stubborn look on his face. "We'll work it out."

That look! Zeus knew what was so familiar. He had seen that look on the face of Hephaestus, or Vulcan as the Romans had called him, god of the forge, worker of metals.

The line of the gods was very weak in this one, but it was there. He glanced at Hera, and from her narrowed eyes, he knew she recognized it, too.

Nicole with a son of Olympus? The question teased him. If Henry was a son of Olympus then, according to Hera, he could be Nicole's right choice, the one to end the curse for the family. Why had it continued to Joy?

As if his thoughts had conjured her up, Joy popped her head around the edge of the door. "Lunch is ready for anyone who wants it." She disappeared.

Zeus frowned. Joy did not look like a woman in love, glowing from a night spent in her lover's arms.

Hera rose with grace. "Excuse me, I need to talk to Joy." She strode out, moving fluidly, but with haste.

Zeus didn't bother with excuses. He simply hustled after

the two women. On his way through the kitchen, he nabbed a slice of poultry and a wedge of tomato from the trays set out, then sped through the back door.

And ran into Hera, planted in the middle of the porch. Like her, he jerked to a halt and watched Joy stride out across the grass. Mark came out from the caretaker's cottage to intercept her. Their attention focused solely on each other, they were oblivious to the two on the porch.

"Ah, the absorption of two lovers," murmured Zeus, pleased.

Mark and Joy halted a foot apart. Mark shoved his hands in his pockets. Joy crossed her arms over her chest.

Zeus frowned.

"I've got an appointment to get the stitches out of my leg," Mark said. "We can work on the illusion when I get back."

"All right. Did you finish with the birds?"

"Yes, except for turning the eggs in the incubator."

"I'll take care of it."

They stood in awkward freeze frame. Not even the thick, hot air moved. Only the buzzing of honeybees and the boom of courting ostriches broke the silence. Zeus could almost see the wall building between them, brick by brick.

Mark ran a hand across the back of his neck. "Well, I'll see you in a little bit."

"Yeah. Fine." Joy continued out to the pens.

Mark watched her retreating figure, then got into his truck and left.

All perfectly polite and passionless.

Zeus gave a huff. "By the Titans, they wasted my good deed. Humans can be so trying."

"Something went wrong," Hera said.

"Obviously. What happened to the great notion about finding Joy a son of Olympus? She doesn't look happy."

"That's still the only way."

"We'll have to think of another plan—"

"No." Hera shook her head. "We do nothing."

"What!"

Hera looked at him then. Straight on. "The heart cannot be forced, Zeus."

"They do love each other."

"For them, like us, it must be an entire, consuming love. Not just based on lust, or the assurance of comfort, or the lure of being in love. It must be all these things. We have pointed the way, but the trust and the learning and the commitment must come from within them. Otherwise, it's not deep enough or true enough to last."

Hera always was wiser, at least in the ways of women, than he. Still, there must be something he could do.

He would think on it.

He was good with schemes.

Chapter Twenty-one

You weren't listening close enough.

Mark ran through the motions of the show, his mind spinning.

Home. Wherever Joy was, that was home to him. Home was no longer a frightening, amorphous place, but a person, someone real and warm and giving.

He'd arrogantly assumed he could talk her into coming with him, that she was simply a little reluctant. Hell, when had he ever talked Joy into anything unless it was something she already wanted to do deep down? She always saw clear through him and never fell for any of his fast talking.

To Joy home meant something else.

Damn, but he'd been an ass. He hadn't been listening to what Joy wanted, hadn't wanted to recognize the stability she needed.

That was the one thing he couldn't give her.

"How long you going to stand there mooning?" Jax's question broke through his absorption, and Mark realized he'd stopped the flow of the illusions.

"Sorry. Let's see, I was . . ." He pulled himself back into the rehearsal.

"Twenty-six minutes into the show." Jax perched atop a bale of hay, a clipboard on his knee, pencil in one hand and stopwatch in the other. He shook his head. "You got it bad, Mark. I never thought I'd see the Master Illusionist brought low. And by a redheaded chef, no less."

"I didn't think it was that obvious."

"Only to someone who knows you well, and there aren't many of us around." Jax brightened. "Do you suppose that costume seamstress will turn a little interest my way now?"

"You're on your own there, pal."

"Are you ready for me?" Joy's voice came from the doorway.

"Come on in," Mark called.

"What did the doctor say about your leg?"

"Fine. I heal fast. Jax, with Joy's red hair, we may have to do less pink on the lighting for the Pygmalion illusion."

Jax looked at Mark quizzically. "Joy's red hair?"

"She's taking Dia's place in the Pygmalion illusion."

"A *civilian*?"

"There's no one I would trust more with my secrets," Mark said, low and even.

"Then let's get to work."

Being a magician was not glamorous, Joy decided two sweaty hours later. It was precise and demanding work. Her part was relatively simple; still, her muscles ached from odd positions and motionless poses. Mark repeated the sequence endlessly, so many times she lost count, choreographing each second to coincide with defined points when Jax would change the lighting or explode a smoke pot or glitter beam.

Only when Mark took her in his arms during the finale of each run-through did she have her reward. When he danced with her and brought her to life by the touch of his strong male body and the press of his lips, she felt like Galatea, opening to her lover's charms under the spell of Aphrodite.

Joy hung in his final embrace, her arms stretched above her head, her body flush against the length of him. Her skin vibrated with the contact, and her limbs trembled with fatigue. She felt like a wire, stretched taut and plucked, and was too tired to hide or still her reactions.

Carefully, Mark set her upright. He drew a hand across her neck in a loving gesture. "That's the second time I've pushed too hard, forgotten your inexperience."

"Again, I didn't mind."

Jax's low whistle broke them apart. Joy looked over to see him fanning himself. "Now I see why Mark asked you to be his Galatea. You two are *hot* up there. Every man in that audience is going to thank you, Mark."

Joy flushed at the young man's openness.

It didn't faze Mark. "I told you she'd be good."

"Is she doing the part until Dia rejoins us in Atlanta?"

Mark's arm tightened around her waist. "Nope. Just for the Mushroom Festival. Joy's staying on the farm."

"On the *farm*? But—" Jax bit off the comment, then shrugged. "You're losing a fabulous ending to the show."

The yearning that cropped up inside her—to show him,

304

the cast, the audiences, just how good she and Mark were together—surprised Joy.

"Let's call it a day here," Mark said.

"I'll get these stop points into the computer." Jax snapped his laptop shut. "But I'm going to do it in the cottage where it's cooler." He headed out.

Mark handed Joy a bottle of water. The liquid was warm, but she slugged down a huge gulp, and then handed it back. He drank with energy, head tilted back and throat working, caught in a sunbeam with dust motes dancing above his head.

When he'd finished, she said, "Let's go to my office. I have something I want to show you." She also had a few questions.

When they got outside the barn, however, a loud bark distracted Joy. Cerberus bounded past her—straight for the yearling pen, again—and Hope raced after him, calling to him.

"How did that devil dog get out?" Joy asked.

The beast leaped the flimsy wire into the pen, and raced around, his tail wagging furiously. Hope stopped at Joy's side.

"He was tied," she insisted. "We were playing and he just . . . got away. He'd be happier, Joy, if you didn't keep him tied. Besides, he always gets out."

"He's a big dog, Hope. I don't think—Cerberus! Be quiet! You two, just help me get him out of there." Cerberus never harmed the ostriches; he seemed to view them as mobile toys. Unfortunately, noise was a major stressor for the birds, and Cerberus's barks were *loud*.

Mark gave a whistle. Cerberus glanced in their direction, but the lure of the birds was too strong. Mark whistled again, then called, "Cerberus, come."

The dog stopped and directed an annoyed whoof to them.

"Cerberus," Mark warned. The dog jumped out of the pen and trotted over to them. Mark petted him. "See, he's a smart dog."

"He's a strange dog," said Joy.

"Mark, will you let me take care of him," Hope asked, "since you're busy getting ready for the show?"

"It's all right by me if it's okay with your sister."

Joy looked at the huge dog, panting, his tongue lolling, and could swear he was grinning. "A dog's a big responsibility."

"I remember to feed Freyja and Thor, don't I? Besides, I can't wait to tell Brody I'm taking care of a *huge* dog."

Brody. The twelve-year-old Hope wanted to date. "Why so eager to tell Brody?" Joy asked cautiously.

Hope giggled. "Because he's *scared* of dogs. And he said *I* was a baby."

Joy's heart sank that Hope was still trying to impress Brody. "Hope, we talked about Brody, remember?" she said gently.

"I remember," Hope responded with annoyance. "No dating. No being alone. I'm not, so spare me the lecture; I just want to take care of the dog."

"All right."

"C'mon, Cerb," called Hope. "Let's go play in the creek." Dog and girl raced off.

Once in her office, Joy pulled out two pieces of paper. "Remember the birds we sent to slaughter last week?"

"Of course. What about them?"

"I sell the birds to the slaughterhouse. They return some of the meat to me and some of it they sell elsewhere. I always ask for a listing of where they are selling the meat, so I can follow through with customers—make sure they're satisfied with the meat quality, see if there are areas to expand sales. The bigger I can get my market, the more meat the slaughterhouse sells and the more birds they buy. We're both happy."

"Sounds like a good arrangement. What's the problem?"

"This new slaughterhouse was slower to get the last listing to me and in a conversation with one of the secretaries I mentioned the problem, so she also sent me a copy. The two lists don't match. I thought it was later sales, but it wasn't, not by the dates."

"Where were these sales to?"

"Look." She showed him the pages.

"It all looks fine to me." He looked at the list, memorizing the names. Armond would be very interested in them, he suspected, although he could see no obvious misfits.

Joy leaned back in her chair. "What does Guy do, Mark? You've said he's dangerous, but you've never told me why."

"You never believed me."

"I do now."

"Why?"

"A lot of little things, things I didn't notice before. Why is he dangerous?"

What to tell her? She knew about the book. That was manageable because Centurion knew about it, too, and might expect Mark would tell her. Anything more? Joy was too transparent; it would be too dangerous for her.

"Just because of the book, darlin'," he answered easily. "It makes him a thief."

Joy's eyes narrowed. "You're lying to me, Mark Hennessy. What aren't you telling me?"

"Nothin'. Besides, you aren't working for him anymore."

Joy smiled at him. "Yes, I am."

Mark sat upright. "What?"

"I asked him to give me another chance. I'm cooking for the buffet after your performance Friday."

"Aw, dammit, Joy, why'd you go and agree to something like that?"

"I'm a cook. You going to give me a better reason why I shouldn't?"

"Don't you have enough to do that day? You're already in the performance."

"It will be tight, but my friend Callie agreed to help me out. Most of the food will be already prepared. I'll take things over in the morning. Callie will be there in the afternoon to supervise the crew and set up. I'll go over right after the performance and make sure everything runs smoothly." She lifted her brows, asking for another objection.

Mark's teeth ground. "I'm after a book of magic. He stole it. That's the truth."

"Oh, I believe you. As far as it goes." Joy pointed to the paper. "I did some digging. Those extra businesses aren't restaurants, Mark. They have nothing to do with the food industry. So why send them my meat?"

"They didn't get a lot. Maybe it's for personal use. Or a Boy Scout barbeque."

She threw him an exasperated look. "Is Guy using my ostriches somehow? I have a right to know."

"Look, I don't want you involved. I'm sorry I ever said anything and drew you into this." He thrust to his feet and paced the room.

"I was drawn into Guy's affairs long before you came,

308

wasn't I? If you hadn't opened my eyes to many things, I would have been caught. So, what am I caught in?"

He rubbed his chin, thinking, stalling. His gut twisted with the fear, wondering whether telling her or not telling her would put her in worse danger.

"You going to tell me or do I have to keep digging?" she said impatiently.

If she kept asking questions, who knew what she'd stumble onto. That settled it. "If I tell you, you have to promise to stay out of it. Cancel the job."

"Mark, I'll be safe. What can he do to me in the middle of a party?" She didn't wait for an answer. "What's he into? Drugs?"

Mark gave in with an irritated sigh and settled back into his chair. "Never got into drugs that I know. He prefers cleaner crime. Guy Centurion's a procurer of the finer things in life."

"Prostitution?"

"He may have financial interests in a successful house or two, but I meant he's a middle man. Tell him what you want, and he'll get it for you. Mostly he stays regional, with a heavy concentration in art. There are some fanatical collectors who don't care how a particular piece was obtained, as long as they can add it to their collection. The Feds think Centurion's poised to expand, but since he doesn't get his own hands dirty, it's impossible to pin anything on him."

There were still a few details he'd omitted. Like how far Centurion went to fulfill an agreement or to ensure loyalty. Joy had a good enough imagination to picture the basics, but she was innocent enough not to guess the specifics and he wanted to keep her that way.

"He's smuggling art in my ostriches?"

Mark nodded. "Gems this time."

"How?"

"We're not sure. We didn't find any in the first load."

"I've got another shipment going out in four days. We can search that."

She was bouncing in her seat with enthusiasm. Mark decided not to tell her yet that she wasn't going to be searching anything.

"So, how do you fit in?" Joy continued. "When you came looking for the book, these Feds just let you nose around?"

"The agent in charge and I go way back, and he's anxious to nail Centurion. I'm doing him a favor. I find the book and how it's being moved out, and they've got evidence."

Joy steepled her hands and studied him. Unable to meet her eyes, Mark assumed a relaxed pose, one ankle resting on his knee. "Now, darlin'—"

"You're a fraud," she interrupted.

Mark raised his brows. "Careful who you're calling a fraud, dear heart. We magicians get a little testy at that. We don't hide the fact we specialize in illusions."

"Yeah, but your illusions are better than most."

"I must admit I'm pleased with your confidence in me."

"It wasn't necessarily a compliment. It's more than the book and a favor for a friend, isn't it? You want Guy brought down every bit as much as this Fed, don't you? It goes deeper, back to revenge for what Guy did to you years ago."

"No, darlin', that's not—"

"I can understand, that kind of thing could be hard to

forget. Especially for a man. All that macho honor business, and—"

Mark shut her up by the simple method of leaning forward and putting his hand over her mouth.

"I am not bringing him down because six years ago he had the crap beat out of me."

Behind his palm, Joy blinked at the deadly calm in his voice. Mark lowered his hand.

"But you—"

"I came because of the book. I am bringing him down because this time he involved you."

Joy's mouth snapped shut.

Mark gave a satisfied nod that, at last, he had rendered her speechless. "The Feds thought you were involved. I didn't. Which leads us to our next topic."

"The book," she said eagerly. "I think I know where it is." Abruptly, she picked up the phone and punched in a number. "Hello, Guy."

What the hell was she doing?

After one stunned moment, Mark realized she was rattling off dishes, discussing a menu with Guy. A few moments later, she hung up and turned to him with bright eyes.

"I assume you had a reason for that call," Mark said drily.

"I now know he's in his house here on the North Shore. That means we can break into the New Orleans house!"

Joy expected to help Mark with the search. He expected her to wait outside.

Joy lost the argument. Mark had a lot more patience than she did. And he played dirty.

Sitting in Mark's truck, on the street before Guy's darkened New Orleans home, she flopped back in her seat and admitted defeat. The stubborn set of Mark's jaw and his refusal to get out until she capitulated were not the convincing factors, however. Instead, he had used the one fact against which she had no defense.

Her presence would put him in danger.

They both knew Mark was better at being sneaky than she was. It was not necessarily a trait to admire, but it was true. Alone, he had a better chance of getting in, and out, undetected.

"So, where is the book?" Mark asked.

She crossed her arms and explained about the night she'd worked late and spied Guy in his office with the book. "It didn't look like he twirled a lock but he pressed something," she said. "Then he bent down, and when he came up his hands were empty."

"A hidden compartment, rather than a safe?"

"Yes. Here . . ." She pressed a key in his hand. "The kitchen door key. Dagobert gave it to me once, and forgot to ask for it back. You have to punch in a security code, too. It's 052151."

Mark mulled over what she'd said, then leaned down and kissed her cheek, nuzzling her neck. "Thank you. For the information, for the key, and for staying here."

"Don't take too long."

"Be back before you have time to worry." He kissed her again, his lips warm and soft against hers for too brief a time, then slipped out of the car and, within seconds, disappeared into the vast shrubbery fence.

"Before I worry?" Joy touched her fingers to her lips.

"Then you're already late, because I started worrying about you a long time ago."

It was frightening how easily the skills came back.

Maybe it was like riding a bike, Mark thought ruefully as, for the second time, he glided noiselessly between the banana plant leaves of Centurion's garden. Once you learn, you never forget.

Except he had never learned to ride a bike. He'd been too busy learning to pick a lock and circumvent security.

His father had supplemented the family income with occasional outright thievery, but he wasn't any more successful at that than he had been at anything else. As a child, Mark determined *he* would not be stymied by inconvenient alarms or the crack of a twig underfoot, and, at a very early age, perfected skills no child should possess.

If he hadn't had his consuming love of magic, if Cybele had not taken him in, and if Joy hadn't believed in him—he would have made an excellent thief.

Now, those skills stood him in good stead as he slid through the garden. The greenery shielded him from view, though he could see no one in a darkness pierced only by moonlight and pale stars. Carefully, he avoided the motion sensors and reached the kitchen door unchallenged. He punched in the security code, then waited for the green light. The key opened the door with soundless ease.

Inside the kitchen, he stood and listened, the back of his neck prickling. Were there some cameras he'd missed? Some electronic security Armond hadn't known about? He heard nothing amiss.

Mark shrugged. If he was going to be caught, it might as well be while stealing the book rather than loitering in the kitchen.

There were a few guards in the house, but Mark was stealthier and he slipped into Centurion's office without mishap. He didn't turn on the light, but drew a pencil-thin flashlight from his pocket and flashed it briefly around.

The room was imbued with the essence of Centurion, if one took the time to notice. A heavy scent permeated the air, the odor of Centurion's aftershave. Mark wasted only a single glance at the slashing artwork on the wall and the sterile furniture, then flicked off the light.

Joy said Centurion had stood by the desk, then bent over: Mark risked the light again and ran it over the wall, but it was a smooth panel with nothing that might be a handle or a door. He stared at the blank wall in front of him, then reached low, but felt nothing. He flicked off the light. Glad for the moonlight, he ran the tips of his fingers across the wood paneling, using only sensitive touch to examine the wall.

Nothing.

Frustrated, Mark reviewed what Joy had told him. Centurion had bent down, his head disappearing from view. Bent down. Bent down. Disappearing. Maybe it wasn't the wall, but the floor.

He bent down and flicked on the light. The intricate pattern of an Oriental rug filled the small circle of light.

Mark knelt and peeled back the rug, then ran his hand across the paraquet. There, a snag, a raised spot. He pried at it, then pushed.

One segment of flooring, about a foot square, pivoted

on an invisible hinge. Mark shone his light into the concealed hole.

It was empty.

Joy looked at her watch. "Five minutes," she said, with a measure of pride. "I've gone five whole minutes without looking at the time." She had never admired heroines in books and movies who, when they were supposed to be watching, crept after the hero for the sole purpose of getting caught and creating more trouble.

She was, however, beginning to appreciate their worry and restlessness.

Leaning one arm against the open window, Joy inhaled the thick night air, redolent with sweet flowers and broken by the occasional zing of a bug zapper. She returned to her other favorite staring spot, the one where Mark had disappeared. If sheer will could bring him out, he'd pop into the seat next to her any second.

Sheer will didn't seem to be getting her much these days.

A dark shadow moved in the periphery of her vision, a hint of activity she caught in the rearview mirror. Something in the back of the truck? Had someone decided to check out the truck that had been sitting here too long?

Joy turned and peered out the back window, the muscles in her stomach knotting, but she saw only a deeper shade of black. Nothing that looked . . . human.

Visions of *The X-Files* danced in her head.

She swallowed against the acid in her throat and shifted for a better look. The truck bed was empty, except— No, there was something there, something massive and black.

The truck rocked, faint and unmistakable, as a monstrous bulk jumped from the truck back. Hell's bells, it was coming after her.

Frantically, Joy rolled up the window.

She wasn't fast enough.

A deep bark froze her. Paws landed on the window. A head peered into the car. For a moment, all she could see was pin pricks of red, like a laser pointer, three pairs set in three black masses. Abruptly the image changed. Only two red dots, less piercing, remained in the center. They became eyes and the mass became a single head, a dog's head.

The bark was repeated, followed by a friendly whoof.

Flooded with relief, Joy rolled down the window. "Cerberus, you pest. Did you get tired of chasing my ostriches and decide to stow away in Mark's truck?"

Cerberus gave another bark and licked her face.

"Eeeuw, you're sloppy." She scratched behind his ears.

For a moment, he preened, then he lowered his paws to the cement and gave another bark.

"Hush. Someone might hear you." Joy glanced around the quiet neighborhood, but so far no one was coming to investigate. She climbed out and crouched beside him. "Get back in the truck, Cerberus. Mark will be back in a moment." She gave him a nudge.

Cerberus backed up in the other direction, toward the hood, and started barking again.

"Hush!" Joy put her finger over her lips.

The dog ignored her.

"What do I need to do to get you to be quiet?"

At once the dog stopped barking and trotted a few steps down the street. He stopped, looked at her, and gave a warning bark.

"You want me to walk you?"

Bark.

Joy sighed. She didn't have a leash, but if Cerberus wanted to get away, she didn't think a leash would stop him. And, he'd had his chance to run earlier.

"Okay, boy, let's go," she said when she reached his side.

The damn dog didn't move.

"Walk, Cerberus."

He butted his collar against her hand.

"You want me to take your collar?"

Bark.

Joy crooked one finger beneath the collar. Cerberus took off. Across the street. Toward Centurion's house.

He pulled up nearer the house than where Mark had disappeared and stopped.

Joy tugged at the collar. "C'mon, boy, we shouldn't be stopping here. It's a little conspicuous."

Bark. Warning growl.

"Okay. We'll stay. You know, you're another thing to add to my 'talk with Zeke Jupiter about' list. Except the man seems to be avoiding me." Joy glanced around nervously, her finger still on the dog's collar. Her shoes scraped against the rough concrete.

Cerberus looked at her. If he'd been human, she'd have thought he was annoyed that she couldn't be quiet.

"You're a fine one to take exception," she whispered. "All that barking."

Cerberus didn't answer, although Joy was surprised to realize she almost expected him to. Instead, his ears perked forward. A few seconds later, Joy heard what he did— rustling leaves, the near silent sound of someone climbing the brick wall.

A second later, Mark vaulted over the side. He landed on his feet, like a cat. "Joy! I thought I told—Cerberus?"

"The stowaway dog wanted a walk." At Mark's incredulous look, she added, "He's kind of hard to refuse."

A sound from the other side of the wall and the light careening through the trees told of human hunters close at hand. They'd have no time to reach the truck. Mark grasped Joy's arm. "Let's walk the dog."

The three of them strolled down the sidewalk, trying to mimic a couple taking their dog for a walk.

Joy glanced back and saw the rough face of a guard appear at the top of the fence. She edged deeper into the shadow of a massive banana tree plant.

"Just some folks walking their dog," the guard called down to somebody, then, catching sight of her looking at him, he shouted, "Hey, lady. You see a prowler jump over the fence here?"

Cerberus glared at the man and started barking.

"A prowler?" Joy's voice squeaked, one reason she'd never tried out for school plays. She tried to deepen it, alter it, so he wouldn't recognize her. "Oh, my goodness! This is such a *safe* neighborhood. Shall I call the police?"

The guard gave her, then the dog, an uneasy look. "No, no police. Guess your dog would have noticed. Looks like we got spooked by shadows." The man disappeared.

Mark and Joy walked in silence, until they were certain no one was watching, then doubled back to the truck.

Mark patted Cerberus. "Good dog. You made a good cover."

Cerberus jumped into the rear and the humans took their seats.

"When did you get so good at lying?" Mark asked, starting the truck and pulling away.

"Wasn't a lie. I never answered the question. Now, where's the book?"

"Not there. I found the hidey-hole, but it was empty."

Joy gave an unladylike curse. "So, it's at the North Shore house."

"Possibly. Or else he's moving it out with the ostriches." Mark waggled a finger at her. "And don't you get ideas about snooping. We already settled that argument tonight."

"Was I arguing?"

Mark threw her a suspicious look. "Is this another of those illusionary answers?"

"No snooping." Joy held up her hand in promise.

Chapter Twenty-two

The green, manicured perfection of the par-five fourteenth hole stretched before Guy Centurion. He swung through his drive and landed his white golf ball in the center of that perfection. One stroke more, a makeable one, and he'd be on the green and looking at a birdie and the lead.

He leaned against the cart and watched his partner, Henry Valcour, drive into the early morning sun and fall short. A two-stroke lead possibly. He wasn't surprised. Guy Centurion played golf like he did everything else. To win.

"So," he asked Henry as he drove the cart to their balls, "what are you thinking of doing now?"

"I'm not sure. I've got a few things to consider."

"Like what?" No one ever knew, but Guy hated small talk. He was, however, very good at it. He'd know whether Henry Valcour would interfere with his plans before the round was over and what steps he'd need to take.

To say he'd been displeased to hear the news of favorite son Henry Valcour's return yesterday would be an understatement. The incompetent fools he'd hired to trace Valcour—to make sure there would be no unpleasant surprises like this one—had assured him the man had disappeared into the Alaskan wilderness and was dead.

Apparently Henry was more durable than anyone had expected.

Those investigators wouldn't work for him, or any one, again. He did not reward idiocy.

"I spent a lot of lonely days up there," Henry continued, "and I learned two things. One, I enjoy working with the metals. Two, I missed Nicole. I'm figuring out how to combine my pleasures."

They'd reached Valcour's ball. He lined up, wiggled to loosen up, then hit the ball. Guy frowned. The ball almost made it to the green. There went the two-stroke lead.

"Hell of a shot," he said jovially. "You don't think you'll want the ostrich farm?"

"Well, the land is Valcour property, but I bought the birds for Nicole. Joy's the one who figured out how to turn a profit from them. She can keep doing it, far as I'm concerned."

"I know a good man who's looking for work, if you could use a hired hand."

"Send him over."

Good. Henry Valcour was no impediment. One day he might even prove useful. Valcours had been part of this town from its founding, and Henry, as the last of the line, was popular.

The shipment would go out next week as planned.

Things were shaping up very nicely. He would set his

own man up to "help" with the ostriches, while Joy took her place in his kitchen and his bed and he reaped the benefits of Mark's training and influence. That menu she had come up with for the buffet was truly inspired. Truth be told, if he could have her only one place, he'd choose the kitchen. Playmates were easy to find, but Joy's allergy had forced her to learn creative alternatives in the kitchen that suited his unique palate.

He doubted, though, that he would have to make the choice.

Guy sighted down the fairway, then hit with an easy stroke. Right on the green and a foot from the cup. Maybe that two-stroke lead was his after all.

The next four days were the calm before the storm.

Well, perhaps calm wasn't the right word, Mark thought ruefully, as he wrestled and played fetch with Cerberus, distracting the dog from his favorite game—chasing the ostriches. Joy could cram more activity in one day than a hyperactive gazelle.

Each morning, she was out seeing to the ostriches with the pink of sunrise and he made sure he was right there at her side. If he was going to have only these few days with her, then he would make the most of every moment. He might not be awake while he was throwing feed to Hans and Gretna, but he was there.

After the ostriches, they worked on the Pygmalion illusion. Joy was beautiful to watch, to hold, and, his favorite part, to kiss. It was almost as though she was awakening, too, the statue illusion a mere reflection of her inner blossoming.

The illusion was going to be dynamite. Granted, being on stage would be different—performance anxiety could take many forms—but he trusted his abilities to overcome any slips in her showmanship.

The afternoons they spent in their own pursuits—Joy with her buffet and the chefs' charity, he with the rest of the show, the Elements Escape, and on the phone discussing all the myriad details of the tour. They came together for meals. Mark had tried to convince Joy she didn't need to cook for him, but she insisted she had to fix something for Hope and Nicole and that adding him and Jax was no trouble.

Mark was of the private opinion that Hope and Nicole could get their own meals. But Nicole was lost in a world that centered on "her Henry," and, when Mark spoke to Hope, she'd given him a withering look and asked if he'd ever tried to dislodge Joy from a kitchen.

So, Hope had drifted out to the barn to peer over Jax's shoulder, and Mark had drifted into the kitchen to help Joy.

Nicole had just drifted.

He'd found a certain peace in those domestic duties, a peace that he'd only known once before in his life. Joy had been the reason then, too.

When Joy pointed out the nuances of iodized, kosher, and sea salt or of sweet potatoes and yams, he thought he could discern the difference. Her nose was a lot more sensitive than his, he discovered, for he couldn't smell which was a Poblano chile and which a jalapeno, and he still didn't understand why olive oil had to be cold-pressed and virgin.

Chopping, stirring, tasting, washing, rinsing, drying—mundane chores became an adventure next to Joy. He loved the light that lit her whenever she put together some new combination or thought of some new flavor to try and it worked.

Cerberus gave a whoof and butted against Mark's leg, drawing him from his thoughts. Absently he tossed the ball, wondering how Cerberus could see it in the deep night, but the dog was unfailing in his ability to retrieve whatever he put his snout to. Sure enough, he soon trotted back, ball in mouth.

"That's enough, boy. It's time for bed."

Cerberus paused, then loped over to the main house and curled up at the foot of the steps, where Hope would find him the next morning. A light still glowed in Joy's office, Mark noticed, though the rest of the house was dark.

Mark yawned and rubbed a hand across weary eyes. He hadn't thought he'd ever meet a woman who required less sleep than he did, but Joy had energy to spare it seemed. Even she needed to sleep sometime, however.

He glanced at his watch, the dial glowing green in the country darkness. Well past midnight. A new day. The birds would go out in the morning, and the chefs' charity was in the evening. The following day was his performance, followed by the buffet.

Then he would leave, as he had promised.

And Joy would stay, as she must.

The sudden tightness in his chest made breathing difficult in the still, hot night. Mark forced himself to draw in air slow and deep, as he detoured to the house and made his way noiselessly through the silent rooms. He stood in the darkened hall outside Joy's office, keeping to the shadows while he watched her.

She sat at her desk, chewing a carrot stick and staring into space. Her hair was caught back from her face. Papers littered her desk. A cup sat beside her and the lamp provided a circle of light, like an angel's halo. Except he couldn't imagine any angel with her fire.

Just looking at her eased the tension inside of him and replaced it with the first flutterings of desire. He glided around the edge of the door, to stand at the fringes of her room, but still she was oblivious to his presence. He cleared his throat, a tiny sound. Then, when she didn't answer, he said, very low, "Joy."

Joy jerked upright, plastered against the chair back, and the carrot stick flew across the room. She spread a hand across her chest. "Hellfire, Mark, you startled me."

And she had thought she had the talent to skulk and pry in Centurion's house? Not in this lifetime. Not in any lifetime.

"What are you thinking about so hard?" He sauntered over to the desk, propped one hip on it, and then leaned over and kissed her.

Despite the brevity, it was a kiss of promises and possession. They belonged together and somehow he would see it happen. "You're sweet to taste, my darlin'," he said as he lifted. "I never can resist."

She gave him a shaky smile. "You're up late."

"Wearing out the devil dog. Why are you still working?"

"Couldn't sleep. Mark, I was thinking about that shipment of ostriches. You said you'd searched before but didn't find anything. Tell me everything that happened. I'm coming at it from a different perspective. Maybe I'll see something."

She listened, brow furrowed, while he told her what he knew. "There were bags of feed in the truck?" she asked. "How many?"

"Three. They were empty when the truck got to the slaughterhouse."

"And the driver said he would feed the birds?"

"That's right."

Joy slapped her hand on the desk. "Damn him. That's not enough bags. They must have wanted to make sure it was all gone."

"What are you saying?"

"Ostriches will eat pebbles. The driver must have fed the gems to them. You didn't find anything when you searched because the gems were in the feed, then inside my birds."

"Then, they're slaughtered. The gems are removed from the birds' intestines—"

"—And put between the slabs of flash frozen meat."

Mark could visualize the setup, and anger twisted his gut. The birds came from Joy, leaving Centurion completely clean. Since the slaughterhouse set up the sales, Joy could be kept clean as well, as long as Centurion wanted her so, but she'd be an easy setup if he needed to control her. Mark's fists tightened.

Who would suspect diamonds in a tray of frozen ostrich meat? Where better to hide the tiny, valuable pieces Centurion acquired than in a shipment of birds?

Mark gripped her shoulders. "We can't stop the shipment of gems today. The Feds are going to want to follow it all the way through. I'll call them tonight."

"I know." Joy bit her bottom lip. "It's not going to give them Centurion, though, is it? I'm the one with the connection to the birds."

Unfortunately, she was right. "It will give them something to work with. They might be able to trace the source of the feed."

She looked up at him. "It doesn't find your book of magic."

She was right about that, too. But finding the book had become secondary to keeping Joy safe, and Mark had the uneasy feeling things would come to a head this weekend.

He gave her a stern look. "Remember, Joy, you promised. No snooping."

The Chef's Charity Night drew a glittering crowd, all willing to pay handsomely for the privilege of black-tie mingling, listening to the hot music of the city, and tasting dishes from the region's best chefs.

Many of the locals were there, too, and Mark was surprised, considering the short time he'd been here, how many of them he knew. More than he knew in his Vegas apartment complex, he realized. They greeted him and asked about the show, about the dog he'd acquired, about whether his ostrich-clawed leg had healed.

It was disconcerting having so many people know so much about him.

Fresh from discussing the merits of a local winery with a neighbor, Mark sampled a mushroom tart from a chafing dish. Since the chefs were encouraged to highlight local ingredients, mushrooms featured prominently in several dishes, and he recognized Joy's ostrich meat in a number of others. He washed the tart down with a Dixie beer, then wandered around some more, passing up the nutria braised in red wine. Joy hadn't expanded his palate that much.

On the stage where he'd be performing tomorrow, a jazz quartet, Coup de Fire, played a sultry blending of sax and bass. Sipping his beer, Mark leaned against a pine tree and listened. The food, the company, the music, the sultry night, all united in an evening that was quintessential New Orleans.

The music echoed with deep chords inside him: lonely, yearning, arousing. He stood apart, alone, unconfined. As it had so often tonight, his gaze sought out Joy.

Her red hair was her only color, a flame that he used to trace her path. She was dressed in black—black heels, short black skirt, black silk blouse.

Desire scorched his gut. Mark swallowed a gulp of the beer, hoping to quench the flame of reaction that blind-sided him every time he looked at her.

It didn't work.

With his eyes, he traced the daring V-neck of her blouse to the remembered swell of her breasts and the graceful curves of her firm arms. Another swallow of beer only made him hotter, and he had the uneasy hunch this feeling would still be part of him fifty years from now.

Joy glanced his way, meeting his eyes as she had each time he had sought her. It was as though some inner sense told her whenever he needed that connection, that bond. She smiled, that smile she shared only with him, then returned to her conversation, laughing with one of her neighbors.

The gesture was so elemental and intimate, so much a part of being a couple. It was the tie he had never wanted, always feared.

Mark braced a shoulder against the tree, unsure of the support of his knees. When had he let her so deep inside him? When had she bonded to his soul? Or had she always been there?

Along with questions that had no answers, came a singular, powerful realization. With Joy's arms around him, he was as free as he could ever wish to be.

She was in her element tonight. Surrounded by excellent

food and close friends, in charge of people and events, busy directing and ordering and arranging, she worked with a smile that charmed and a determination that kept everything smooth. She looked happy, and he knew the only thing she'd like more would be if she were cooking.

This was where she belonged, not in a different hotel every night.

The thought sucked the air from his lungs. He'd never really understood what she wanted, never felt its power. Here, tonight, he knew. Hot flashed to cold and desire to fear.

This was the one thing he couldn't give her.

Mark tossed back the rest of his beer. Joy thought she wasn't the right woman for him, and she had nobly given him his freedom. Tonight proved he wasn't the right man for her, either.

He, however, was not noble.

He knew what he had to do.

Mark strode over to join her. She finished a conversation with Earl Flynn, and for one moment, almost the first of the evening, stood alone. She rubbed her hands up and down her arms, as though they ached or itched.

As he closed the gap, Mark's eyes narrowed. That bond worked both ways. Something was wrong, something more than the tiredness that might be expected as the evening slid across its apex. Her face was pale, especially in the uncertain light, and her lips were tight.

"What's wrong?" he asked, reaching her side.

Joy cast him a startled glance, then shook her head. "Nothing. I'll be all right in a moment." She pressed her fingers against her lips.

He could see her arms more clearly now. They looked blotched, discolored.

The smell of sautéing meat wafted toward him. Beef fondue.

Mark swore. "It's your allergy, isn't it?"

She nodded weakly. "I sampled all of the dishes. Some had cow's milk or beef. I must have gotten more than I realized."

He wrapped an arm around her shoulders and aimed her for the edge of the tent. "I'm getting you out of here."

"I just need to get my Benadryl from the car."

They were almost in the fresh air, when Guy Centurion intercepted them. "Joy, you aren't leaving! You're in charge of this affair."

Mark didn't bother to answer. He ushered Joy past the pest.

Joy pulled up. Of course, she'd respond to his reminder of her responsibility.

"It's her allergy," Mark growled. "Look at her arms. Look at her face. She could go into shock."

As if to give credence to his words, Joy swayed in her heels. "I'll be back in a few moments. I left my medicine in the car." Her face whitened, and her eyes widened. She clamped a hand over her mouth. " 'Scuse me," she mumbled and took off.

Centurion reared back. Obviously, being faced with a nauseated woman was not high on his list of priorities.

Not so with Mark. He raced after Joy.

She was pulling a bottle of medicine from her car. In a moment, she downed two pink capsules, then rested her head against the car frame.

"I'm calling 911." Mark flipped open his cell phone.

She shook her head and scratched the back of her neck. "I'll be okay in a minute."

"You could go into anaphylactic shock."

"It's a miserable allergy, but it's never affected me that way. The medicine will bring it under control." She took a deep breath. "It's already working."

Mark could see her color improve. "At least let me take you home."

She shook her head again. "I'll be fine."

"If this was after tasting, what would happen if you drank a whole glass of milk? Or didn't have your Benadryl handy?"

A shudder cascaded across her. "I don't know; I'd be pretty miserable, I guess. I'd prefer not to find out."

Mark prayed that she never would.

He stood with his arm around her, smoothing her hair back, until she was well enough to return to the event.

"I was told you are Joy Taylor?"

The evening was still in full swing when a woman stopped Joy with the question.

"Yes, I am." She smiled at the older woman, who was dressed unusually, but elegantly, in a silver-threaded caftan, with a line of silver bracelets on her thin arms, and rings on nearly every finger. "Can I help you?"

"I wanted to meet you." Smiling, the woman captured Joy's hand between hers. "To see who has so captivated Mark. I am Cybele Petrov."

"I'm delighted to meet you; Mark's told me about you. We were in New Orleans and stayed at your apartment, but we missed you."

"Oh, I doubt that you did," the woman murmured, but her knowing look held only approval.

Joy felt her cheeks redden, remembering exactly how she and Mark had spent that night.

Cybele patted her on the arm. "And now I have embarrassed you. That was not my intention." She tilted her head, studying Joy, and Joy got the distinct impression the woman was looking at something beyond her facial features. At last she nodded. "You're a good person, Joy Taylor, and good for my Mark. I'm pleased. Now, we need to talk." She glanced around. "Somewhere quieter."

The music and the hum of voices dimmed as Joy led her to the tiny office area set up on the grounds. They sat in the functional chairs, and here, in the bare-bulb light, Joy saw that Cybele looked sallow and upset. She rubbed her hands together.

"Are you all right?" Joy asked. "Did you get something to eat? A glass of wine?" She half-stood, ready to offer assistance.

"I am fine." Cybele waved her away. "I have been enjoying the delights from your chefs. But I am worried. Mark has told you about the book he seeks?"

"Yes. He hasn't found it yet. He wants it because it describes an ancient illusion."

Cybele sighed. "Mark believes that's all it is, but there is more. It has not just illusions, but descriptions of real power. I felt it as soon as I touched it."

"Real magic? Like genies and sorcerers?" Joy couldn't help her skepticism. Despite their short acquaintance, she liked Cybele, but this claim was a bit too outrageous even for her.

Cybele patted her hand. "You do not believe, either, but that is all right. I think you are more open to possibilities. Mark creates illusions, thus he believes all can be explained."

The back of Joy's neck began to prickle. "What do you want me to do?"

"Help him find the book."

"I am, but we've come up empty-handed."

"Please, keep trying. Guy Centurion must not sell that book. If you touch it, you will understand. You will taste its power."

Taste it? Joy didn't have the slightest idea what the woman was talking about. "I'll do my best," was the only answer she could find.

That seemed to satisfy Cybele. "The book should be in Mark's hands," she said as she left.

Joy stared at the closed door a moment, a quiver of unease rippling in her stomach; then she sighed. Cybele seemed to expect a lot more than Joy had been able to accomplish so far. She rubbed between her eyes. Guy probably didn't even have the book with him. Or Mark's cop friend would find it when the truck got to the slaughterhouse.

Still . . . they hadn't looked at the North Shore house.

She'd be there tomorrow, setting up for the buffet.

She'd promised Mark no snooping.

It wasn't snooping if you knew where to look.

Maybe, just a peek, if she got the chance?

Joy stood and left the office. Outside, she spotted a familiar figure and detoured to waylay him. Zeke Jupiter was overdue for some explanations.

She caught up with him before he could escape. "How did you do it?" she said, hands on her hips.

Zeke bit into a pastry. "Do what?" he asked innocently.

"Make it look like Dia was kissing Mark. Mark and Dia both swear it was you kissing her. I know I saw differently."

333

"Hallucinations?" he suggested. "The mind plays tricks."

"Not mine."

"So, what do you think the explanation is?"

"You did something. A hologram or post-hypnotic suggestion or something." She studied him. "You're not what you seem, are you?"

He drew himself up. "I am Zeke Jupiter, fireworks expert."

"You're more than that." She shook her head. "You're some psychic or something. And some sort of . . . power of yours made me see Mark." She dared him to deny it.

"Yes," he answered after a moment. "A holographic power."

She nodded and relaxed, glad to know there was a reasonable explanation beyond the one that she was nuts.

"Why did you do it, Zeke? I thought you were my friend."

He sighed. "I had good intentions. I wanted you to love Seth."

"Why did you care?"

Zeke lifted one shoulder and gave her an embarrassed grin. "I feel strangely fatherly toward you?"

She'd never had anyone show fatherly concern. "Seth isn't for me."

"I see that now, but I never thought Mark could make you happy. And that's all I wanted. For you to be happy."

He seemed to be telling the simple truth, and, rather than be upset at his meddling, Joy found herself strangely touched by his concern. "Mark isn't for me, either."

"Are you sure?" His glance strayed toward Earl Flynn, who was talking with Harriet Juneau. "Don't make the mistake I did. Don't let your love get away from you. You'll be sorry for too many years."

"We want different things."

"Do you? Or are you afraid to trust what you do share? Are you afraid to believe in him?"

Are you afraid to trust what you do share? Was it as simple as that? She should trust the wisdom of her heart? *Are you afraid to believe in him?* Joy tilted her head. "When did you get so wise?"

Zeke patted her on the head. "That is one virtue I don't lay claim to, not yet. I am sorry for my meddling, my dear."

"I'll forgive you." She reached on tiptoe to kiss his cheek. "Are you ever going to tell me who, or what, you are?"

"I don't think that would be wise," he said gently.

Joy decided she could live with that. A thought struck her. "Does this power of yours know how to find things?"

He glanced at Harriet again, then back at her. "I wish it did."

Later, standing alone, Zeus sipped his champagne and eyed Joy talking with Hera.

In the end, he had had no schemes, no tricks, for Joy. Only a simple truth—to trust. In herself, in her love, in her man. He hoped she would heed his advice, but the decision was hers now.

Hera smiled at something Joy said, and his heart warmed.

Would that trust ever be reestablished between him and Hera?

Or had they lost it forever?

Chapter Twenty-three

It wasn't snooping if you knew where to look. Or if you simply took advantage of an opportunity.

The next day, Joy argued with herself as she walked along the path to Guy's North Shore home, juggling a tray of artichoke tarts atop two containers of mushroom linguine. "I won't take any chances," she muttered under her breath, "but if I just happen to be in Guy's office . . ."

It wouldn't hurt to take a peek. A quick poke of the floorboard, then out of there. Joy tried to convince herself she wasn't deceiving Mark, but the uneasy feeling she was doing just that did not sit well.

Dishonesty was not a talent of hers. Her shaking fingers and pricking conscience made her clumsy. Joy stumbled on the door threshold, and, losing her balance, she staggered forward. The tart tray slipped from her grasp—

—and was caught by a blunt, strong hand. The other hand steadied her.

Clutching the linguine, Joy regained her balance, then looked up into penetrating gray eyes and a face that conveyed both polish and power. Hair of unyielding black, a trifle too precisely cut for her taste, formed a helmet for that face.

A warrior's face. The thought flashed through her, only to disappear under recognition. No warrior. This was the man who had come with Callie to help when Joy was at the festival.

"Thanks," Joy said. "That could have been a nasty tumble."

"You're welcome." He released her arm, then carried the tarts inside.

Joy followed and set down the linguine. "And thanks for saving the tarts. I wouldn't have had time to make another batch. I'm sorry, what did Callie say your name was? She kind of mumbled, and I didn't hear." Joy's brows knit. "Strange, that's not like Callie. She's usually *very* clear."

"She was preoccupied." He hesitated, then added, "I'm Armond."

"Nice to meet you, Armond. I really appreciate you and Callie helping out while I'm at the festival. Are you new? I don't remember seeing you at her restaurant."

"Quite new."

His voice was low and gravelly, full of virile timbres and with the hint of an accent she couldn't place. "Well, I'm sure you'll enjoy—"

Armond left to unload more food and equipment.

"—not being the chatty sort," Joy finished, then shrugged. She only had to work with him tonight.

Armond might not be chatty, but he was unsettling, Joy decided later. Oh, he was a hard worker, she'd grant him that. He diligently completed each assigned task. The "quite new" was an understatement, however, for he was greener than spinach. When she'd asked for a filleting knife, he'd handed her the paring knife and when she'd told him to reduce the stock by half, instead of boiling to thicken it, he'd poured half of it out.

Mostly, though, he filled the kitchen with a raw, controlled masculine energy that left Callie clumsy and Joy irritable.

Worse, every time she stopped for a breath and got the notion to peek at Guy's office and see whether it was clear, he came up with something to keep her there: a question, an accident, a suggestion.

Joy covered the last tray of asparagus and green bean spears and put it in the giant walk-in refrigerator. The kitchen was ready, needing only the last-minute preps and garnishes.

"Shouldn't you be getting to the festival?" Callie asked.

Joy looked at her watch and swore. "You're right. Are you all set?"

Callie nodded, casting a glance around. "We'll come back later for prep; then Armond will stay here and keep an eye on things. I want to see Mark's show."

"Make sure you stay for the finale; you're in for a surprise." Joy grinned at her friend, but despite Callie's pestering, she refused to say more. "Just let me take a quick glance around."

"Making sure there's no spoiled meat or fly infestation?" Callie teased.

"*Nothing* is going to ruin this buffet."

338

While Armond slowly finished folding each towel, Joy passed through the rooms. Plates, silver, and damask napkins were laid out in the dining room. The wet bar was ready to go except for ice. Hot pads and serving spoons waited at the myriad sites for setting out the food. Perfect.

Joy glanced back at the closed kitchen door, then sped toward Guy's office. Her stomach spasmed, and an icy sweat trickled down her back. Her body screamed she did not have the constitution for this, but her feet kept on their path.

Undetected, Joy closed the office door and shoved her shaking hands into the pockets of her massive apron as she sucked in air through her nose. She took one step toward the desk, then stopped. She pivoted, her eyes drawn to the étagère opposite Guy's desk. Its upper shelves held an eclectic collection of containers like an alabaster Egyptian oil jar, a woven Chinese egg basket, and an original tin of corn flakes. The lower shelves contained two rows of books, all ancient looking.

Could Guy be using the purloined letter method—hiding in plain sight?

Kneeling in front of the glass shelves, Joy ran a hand across the backs of the first row of books, scanning the titles. What was the name of the one Mark sought? Something *Legerdemain*?

Though the leather-bound books all looked old, nothing matched. The leather also made her fingers itch, but she persisted, sliding her fingers across the second shelf of books.

A metallic taste puckered the inside of her mouth. Joy ran her tongue around the odd flavor. Alum? Cream of tartar?

If you touch it, you will taste its power. Cybele's cryptic words came to mind. Was this what she'd meant?

Slowly, fingers shaking with the need for haste, Joy touched each spine. There! She could . . . taste it. She pulled the book out, surprised by the tingle of supernatural electricity that raced up her arm.

"*A Treatise on the Duties of a Sober Woman*. Chauvinism at its finest."

A distant call of her name told her Armond the Annoying would soon hunt her down. She had to get out of here.

She opened the pages for a quick glance to verify it contained no magic secrets. The book was hollowed out, and the book it concealed was infinitely older. An intricate, mythical picture was tooled into the leather below the title. *The Discoverie of Legerdemain*. Mark's book!

Another sound penetrated. The sound of tires on gravel. She glanced out the window and saw Guy's Jaguar pull in.

Joy's heart raced. Instant fear drew black before her eyes. She couldn't be discovered.

She couldn't leave the book, either; Guy might move it. Joy pulled it from its hiding place, her lips puckering at the metallic zing in her mouth, her skin itching, then shoved the hollow book back into the étagère. Maybe Guy wouldn't discover the magic book was missing.

As she hurried to the door, Joy pulled off her voluminous apron and folded it around the book. Seconds later she was in the hall.

Armond met her at the kitchen door. "Where'd you go?" He was scowling, while behind him Callie rubbed one finger nervously at the base of her neck. Had he known where she was? How could he? And why would he care?

"Nature's call," she said, nodding toward the powder room, unable to meet his eyes. Had it been only five minutes? Or a lifetime? Surreptitiously, her fingers clammy and shaky, she tightened the apron around the book.

The front door opened. Armond and Callie ducked into the kitchen just as Guy entered.

Joy wanted to flee. She'd never stolen anything in her life. She didn't know how to hide. Acid rose in her throat, and she swallowed. She wanted to melt, to run, to leave the fastest way possible, but if she did, Guy would get curious.

A curious Guy she didn't want.

How would Mark do it? Smile, pretend, cover his ass.

She shifted her precious bundle to the crook of her arm, making sure the book wouldn't fall out and lifted her lips. The gesture was a far cry from a smile. "Hi, Guy. Food's all set and the rooms look great."

Guy touched her lightly on the arm. "Are you okay?"

"Sure. Fine. Why wouldn't I be?" Could he smell her sweat? Feel her nerves zap?

"Last night. Your allergy?"

Joy gave a high-pitched laugh. "Yes, my *allergy*. No problem. Got it under control."

"I didn't get a chance to talk to you afterward to make sure there were no lasting effects."

"We were both busy," she agreed.

"The charity was a success, by any measure. You made more for the foundation than any other single event."

"I'm glad." At last the whole truth.

"We make a good team." Guy leaned over and kissed her cheek, his lips lingering longer than was acceptable.

Joy stood still, afraid to move, afraid to open her mouth, Galatea in marble. Guy's gaze was the headlights, and she was the bunny. Her throat burned.

He kissed the other cheek. "Think about it. Think about what I have to offer. How good we'd be together."

She couldn't answer. No social murmur, no lie to save her skin, no evasion or illusion could pass her lips. Only truths, and she couldn't utter a one.

Guy's cold, dry palm cupped her chin. "I'm looking forward to tonight's performance." He kissed her lips.

Joy gripped her burden. Even wrapped in the cloth apron, the book bit into her arm and burned into her flesh. It jump-started her heart and gave her the power she needed. She stepped back. "It's going to be . . . special. Now, I've got to go."

"Think about what I said."

"I will," she promised, knowing that she wouldn't be able to scrub out the sound of his voice and the imprint of his hand. She scrambled into the kitchen and out to her car. Dimly she noticed that Callie and Armond had not yet left. They pulled out behind her.

Mark had been right to suspect Joy would try to get the book, Armond Marceaux thought, remembering her obvious frustration when he'd continued to thwart her attempts to go out on her own.

He'd had her in sight the whole time . . . except for those last minutes when she'd disappeared. His complacency faded. She couldn't have found the book in that short time. Could she? He'd looked in the office earlier, and he didn't think she'd had time to move the chair and the rug.

"One of my staff?" Callie slapped him on the shoulder, interrupting his thoughts. "Not when you don't even know the difference between a shallot and a leek."

"Callie! I'm driving."

"This had better be important."

"It is."

They reached her parked car, and Armond stopped. Callie got out, then leaned her head down. "Don't *ever* ask me to deceive a friend like that again. Consider this my apology . . . for last winter." She slammed the door, then, head high, stalked to her car and peeled out of the lot.

Armond watched her go, and it was a long time before he flipped open his cell phone.

"Hennessy," Mark answered shortly.

Mark would be wrapped in the details of the show, Armond knew, so he kept his message brief. "She tried for it."

"Damn. I knew it!"

"I kept her in the kitchen. She's safe."

"She won't be when I get my hands on her."

Armond smiled. Before, Joy had been only a suspect to him, someone who, in theory, looked guilty as hell. Working with her, he understood why Mark could never believe in her guilt. Even in the brief time they'd been together, Armond found he genuinely liked Joy, and there weren't many people about whom he could say that. He'd spent too much of his life among scum. "I filched a couple of tastes of what she prepared. You've a talented lady there."

"Yeah, I know, and I'm going to lock her up when this is over."

Armond laughed softly. In the background, he heard Mark's crew calling to him.

"Put it center stage," Mark answered, then spoke to Armond again. "Did you find anything?"

"Didn't look. No warrant. Anything I found wouldn't be admissible. I'm doing this one right, Mark."

"Sure." The hubbub in the background continued. "Look, it's a zoo here. I gotta run. Thanks, Armond."

"My pleasure." Armond disconnected, his smile turning bittersweet as he put the phone away. It was more than irritation and affection for Joy he heard in Mark's voice, it was worry and love. Once, he would have sworn Mark would never be tied by either.

The magician and the chef. It was a worthy match.

Joy had never been backstage at a magic show, or any show for that matter, and the workings of it fascinated her.

Mark's crew had come in last night and spent today converting the gazebo-like country stage to a setting worthy of a master magician.

They threw up drapes to create a backstage area invisible to the audience, erected lighting and sound systems, pulled scaffolding into place, arranged props and scenery. Most of the crew was young, but Joy suspected Mark had a knack for assembling up-and-coming talent. All did their jobs with a jovial efficiency, which illustrated how familiar they were with this rapid setup mode and how much they enjoyed being part of the crew.

Mark had greeted her with an absent-minded kiss when she arrived, inviting curious glances from the crew, but was immediately drawn into the backstage hubbub, before she had a chance to tell him about the book.

Joy chewed her lip a moment, trying to decide if she should insist he stop and listen.

Right now, Mark was consumed with the show and preparing himself, his equipment, and his people, she realized. Considering the inherent danger of some of his props, like the fire and the daggers, she understood, and wanted, that focus in him. Anything that interrupted his concentration could be a dangerous distraction.

What about Guy? If he found it missing, what would he do? Probably nothing, yet. Not while the show was going on, not while she was managing his buffet. In fact, he probably wouldn't even know the book was missing.

The book was safely hidden, Joy decided, and she would tell Mark after the show. "Mark will be pleased," she said softly, then laughed and shook her head, "And you'll never convince yourself of that."

Her decision made, she set up a table at the foot of the stairs, arranged the food she'd brought for the crew, then propped herself on a trunk and kept out of the way.

Mark was the eye around which the hurricane of activity rotated. He stood on stage and the lights were adjusted to him. It was his voice over the speakers. He was everywhere: supervising, working through the inevitable snags, infusing everyone with creative energy until the air crackled with excitement. He didn't tolerate less than perfection, but it was clear the crew shared his pride and enthusiasm.

Mark was in his element here. This was where he belonged.

Jax passed by and detoured to greet her. "I don't suppose you've got any cabbage rolls in your pocket."

Joy laughed, glad for his open cheerfulness. "Not in my pocket, but there are some there." She gestured with her head toward the table of food.

"You brought stuff you made? Not just cold cuts and sliced cheese? Let me get some before anyone else discovers it. This crew is like locusts." He bounded down the steps.

In a moment he was back, a fork and plate of the cabbage rolls in hand. "Hey, Joy brought food," he shouted to no one in particular, then hunkered down beside her on the trunk.

It didn't take more than one announcement for the crew to discover the supper she'd brought them.

Jax polished off the cabbage rolls, interspersing bites with explanations of what different crew members were doing. "When we're in Vegas, we have more people and a more elaborate set, but it's too expensive to take on the road."

"I think it's very impressive."

"Oh, don't get me wrong; Mark puts on a damn good show anywhere he plays. That's why we had no trouble getting dates for a European tour." Jax put down his fork. "Too bad Mark can't convince you to come on the road with us. I could get real used to this."

"I don't think you travel with a portable kitchen, and food like that doesn't come freeze-dried."

"Didn't think so. Well, I gotta run."

As show time approached, the food she had brought disappeared, downed by the crew who stopped by to thank her and chat a moment, and the atmosphere behind the stage shifted, from the chaotic boisterousness of assembly to the tension of checking details and preparing to perform. Joy peeked out the curtain once and saw a crowd collecting. Many she recognized: Nicole and Henry sat in front with Hope, Guy took a seat by the aisle, Callie was over to one side, and Earl ushered people in. Soon she would be in front of them, performing. Galatea in the finale was the last illusion, the one that would linger in their minds.

Her stomach roiled and pinpricks of fear set her hands

trembling. She must have been insane to think she could do this!

Warm lips teased the back of her neck and a hand reached around her to close the curtains.

"Don't look out," Mark murmured, his breath warming her cold skin. "The spotlights will hide the crowd so you won't know they're there."

She leaned back against him. "Too late. I already know."

Those drugging kisses slid behind her ear. "Then, while you're out there, think only of this." His lips, his tongue, his soft erotic promises worked magic on her, erasing all thoughts of stage fright. "If tonight is to be our last together, then let's make it one to remember."

"Yes," she breathed, tears gathering in her eyes. Their last night. Only desire kept sadness from overwhelming her.

For a moment, he just held her, no kissing or petting, only the bittersweet pleasure of being in his arms; then Mark drew in a long breath. "I have to change, get ready for the show."

"I know."

"You can use the trailer after I'm through to get into costume and makeup. Just make sure you're ready to come onstage before I finish the card trick sequence."

"I'll come right after you."

She felt him smile against her neck. "I'd prefer you to come with me, but then I'd be in no condition to be onstage."

It took a moment for his double entendre to sink in, but when it did, Joy felt her face turn hot to the roots of her hair.

Apparently Mark felt it, too, for a laugh rumbled in his chest. "After all we've done together, you still blush? That's why you charm the magician."

Then, he was gone, leaving her feeling hot from arousal, cold from missing him, lonely from the losses to come, and totally unconcerned about the audience.

When Mark emerged from the trailer, he wore a cloak that billowed around him like smoke. That cloak had been beneath her that night in the barn when she'd—Joy's blush returned.

Mark stood in the wings, awaiting his cue. He turned, gave her a wink, and then strode onto the stage, at once taking command of the audience with the sheer power of his voice and personality.

She slipped away to don her costume and makeup, then as soon as possible returned to her spot to watch the rest of the show. She'd seen bits and pieces of it, watched him practice routines, heard him discuss lighting and other technical details with Jax. She thought she'd known what the performance would be like, but she realized now she hadn't had a clue.

All the elements came together in one blazing fact.

Mark, on stage, was mesmerizing.

She'd been wrong before. It wasn't backstage where he was in his element. It was there, onstage. He was easy with the audience, sometimes bringing laughter, sometimes making them gasp, always holding them spellbound.

He had shed the cloak to reveal the form-fitting black T-shirt and pants that made up his costume. It didn't look as though he could have anything hidden on his person, but Joy suspected that was just another of his illusions.

She'd bet the female half of the audience was enjoying every flowing move of that streamlined body.

Many magicians worked in silence, but not Mark. She heard the power of his voice, compelling the audience to believe that magic was reality and reality was a fluid concept. Yet he had more than the power of his voice. His technique was flawless, his act fresh.

Mark, on stage, was pure charisma.

This was where his talent and gifts, his very nature, found joyous freedom.

Her heart felt like a lump of lead. If she had entertained any doubts about the difference between their two worlds, tonight removed them all. She could not, would not ever, ask him to give this up.

If they were to be together, it must be because she changed. She must trust in her love.

At last Mark was sitting on the edge of the stage, seemingly relaxed, with one of the children from the audience sitting beside him and assisting with what should have been a simple card trick. In Mark's hands it became a baffling puzzle.

"How—?" Joy began, then silenced.

A crew member standing beside her grinned and whispered, "I've seen that trick a hundred times, I know what's going to happen, and I have yet to figure it out."

"Damn, he's good."

"The best." They watched as Mark finished the card tricks and began the final illusion.

He took clay and it became a woman of plaster. He lifted the diaphanous fabric to swirl around the statue.

"Time to take your place, Galatea," whispered the stage hand.

Joy stood and wiped her sweating hands on her diaphanous gown. She took a deep breath.

This she would do for Mark.

The butterflies did not go to sleep, but they settled.

The fabric rippled and flowed.

Joy slipped into her spot.

She was posed on stage before a live audience, hundreds of friends and strangers. For a moment, she was paralyzed, and glad that this part of the illusion required her to be motionless, for she could not have moved if her life depended upon it.

Gradually, the flow of the story, the demands of the split second changes she needed to make, the sheer power of watching the master magician at work took her over. Butterflies went back to the cocoon.

She couldn't see much. She had to keep her eyes nearly shut and the spotlights blinded her. She didn't need to see, for she experienced each moment with more than sight. Scents, sounds, love, all heightened.

Inside she felt glittery. Listening to the appreciative gasps of the audience as Mark created fire from air or sent a globe filled with mist spinning through the air across the stage, sent champagne bubbles through her veins. An exhilarating freedom, much like the parachute jump, washed across her.

Then, Mark was at her side, kissing her cheek. Pygmalion awakening Galatea to life. Mark awakening Joy to the possibilities in life.

Slowly, she lifted her white arm. The muscles protested, stiff from being held motionless for so long, but Joy kept the action smooth and steady.

Mark stood behind her, slightly to the side so they were both visible, and rested his hands at her waist. "Perfect," he whispered into her ear. "Perfect, my love. Awake for me."

Joy lifted her other arm and started to sway. Slowly her eyes opened to the patchwork of bright light and darkness.

Out there was unreal. The only real thing was the warm grip of Mark's hands, the feel of his lips along the side of her neck.

She didn't remember him doing *that* in practice. For a moment, she faltered, lost under the blaze of sensation.

"Time to turn," Mark reminded her in an undertone. He pressed against her hip, and the shift in his arms came naturally. His fingers stroked her cheek, a tender, loving gesture.

He hadn't done that either in practice.

She gazed up at his eyes and saw the crinkle of humor. "Relax. Go with the flow," he whispered.

And she did. He was her lover, her love. With each awakening touch and motion, she told him so.

At last, he bent her over his arm and kissed her.

And it, too, was so much more than he had done in practice.

Joy's arms surrounded him, held him close to her heart.

When he lifted upright from the kiss, he drew her with him. Joy was draped across him, and Mark lifted one arm.

There was a moment of stunned silence, then applause and cheers filled the night air.

Joy blinked. She'd forgotten the audience was there.

A dramatic pause. A flash of lightning-bright light and a thick curtain of smoke, courtesy of Jax.

Pygmalion and Galatea disappeared from the stage.

The illusion was over.

Chapter Twenty-four

Guy Centurion hid his rage with practiced ease. He moved through the crowd of his guests, and none guessed he thought about anything but their ease and comfort. None guessed he planned to punish the very chef they were exclaiming about.

He was a generous friend, but a merciless enemy, and Joy had crossed over from one to the other.

She had twice betrayed him. First, when he was forced to watch her performance with Marcus. Theirs was no casual affair. Feelings between them ran deep and powerful. Everyone in the audience had felt it, been voyeur to it.

Second, when she had stolen the book. After the performance, suspicions roused, he had looked and found it missing. He had not guessed the source of Joy's nervousness this afternoon; apparently the magician had taught her a few additional tricks.

Centurion tossed back his drink. He could have given her everything she wanted and she was throwing it all away on an itinerant magician.

There had been no time to do anything with his guests arriving, but later the situation would be addressed. That book was supposed to leave in the morning in exchange for a very large sum of money. This matter he would handle personally.

A woman—tall, attractive in an Amazon sort of way, too old for a man of his vigor—joined him. "You have an interesting house, Mr. Centurion. I especially like the replica of the Greek statue of Zeus in your entryway. It shows him in his power."

"Madam—" He paused, searching his memory for her name. She had come with that annoying Zeke Jupiter, who thought he could waltz into Centurion's town and court the people with promises of jobs in his fireworks establishment. "Juneau," he finally remembered, "it's not a replica."

She shrugged in pitying disbelief. "Call me Harriet."

Centurion clicked his teeth together. "The dealer assured me of its authenticity, and I have studied Greek antiquities. I am not easily fooled."

"Neither am I."

"What makes you believe it's a replica?"

"Only the artists who were especially favored by—by the gods were allowed to do full body representations. To each such piece, the artist added a tiny lightning bolt, so small it would escape detection, in order to prove their favor. Any statue without the mark? The artist was severely punished. Didn't take but one or two fiery deaths to discourage the others."

Centurion gave a scoffing laugh. "I've never heard such a thing."

"Well, it wasn't something that got bandied about! If others knew about it, there'd be no way to detect the presumptuous fools who dared challenge an edict of the gods."

Centurion lifted one brow. "So, I have only your word."

She merely smiled. "As I said, it's a beautiful piece. The artist has captured well the power of Zeus. Who that artist is doesn't matter." With that, she wandered away from him.

Gradually, subtly, he worked the crowd until he reached the hallway, where he cast a glance at the statue. He had always been proud of it, but perhaps he would sell it.

Zeus joined his wife. "You look as satisfied as Dionysus when he fermented his first grape. What mischief have you been up to?"

"Nothing. Just admiring the statue in the hallway."

"And?"

"I told Centurion it was a replica."

"What! Even I recognize the work of the great Phidias."

"I don't like Centurion. He is more arrogant, more domineering than most men, though he attempts to hide it." She lifted one shoulder. "He should enjoy the art for its own sake, for its impact on him. Not for its antiquity or worth. So, I made up a story that he should find a small mark of a thunderbolt on it if it were genuine." She glanced to the door. "See, he is trying to look."

Zeus looked and stifled a laugh. Centurion was standing next to the statue, talking to a guest, but his eyes kept darting to the marble. "You are so wicked, my love."

354

He struck a pose similar to the one Phidias had caught in marble. "Think they'll recognize the face?"

Hera laughed. "Not unless you grow a beard and hair to your shoulders, lose thirty pounds and a couple of centuries."

"Humans," he sighed, "are so blind. At least we have opened the eyes of Mark and Joy. Did you feel the sizzle from that last illusion?"

Hera fanned herself. "Impossible to miss. I must admit, I thought your Eros-inspired idea was smoke-brained, but you've done well, my husband. Yet, I cannot shake the feeling all is not settled."

"For tonight, though, shall we simply enjoy the dishes our Joy has prepared?" He speared a greenish meatball with a toothpick and took a bite. "What is this?"

"It's spinach, caviar, and shiitake mushrooms," Joy answered, coming up beside them. She exchanged the filled tray she held for an empty one.

Zeus looked at the meatball. "Caviar? That slimy food Poseidon raved about? Never mind. I just need to know that it's good."

Joy braced the empty tray on her hip and smiled. "Glad you like it."

Zeus studied her. She was dressed in her chef's whites, with her hair drawn tight into a French braid. Her face was flushed, but her eyes, those guileless eyes, those were the key. They spoke of her competence and her excitement, her utter pleasure in her work.

He couldn't have been prouder of her if she were one of his own children. "This spread is impressive. You're getting adventuresome these days."

"I'm experimenting more," she answered, turning back

to the table to determine what was needed next. "I've felt creative."

"It's making you a better chef," Hera said. "I've decided to hire you to cater some special functions for my company. Your bid was a good one, and tonight I've seen you can be innovative as well as reliable. We'll draw up the contracts before I leave."

"Thank you." She shook Hera's hand, then left.

Zeus pounced on one important fact when Joy was gone. "What do you mean, 'before I leave'? You aren't going, are you?"

Hera looked at him. "You didn't think I could stay here? I have a business to run, a life to lead. I have . . . things I need to accomplish."

Zeus ran a hand over his hair, feeling a creeping desperation. Why was it Hera so easily kept him tied in knots? "I thought you might stay. With me. You've enjoyed it, you admitted that, and we've done well with Joy and Mark."

"I have, but . . . I have other plans." Her voice held only sadness and regret.

Joy pulled into her driveway; Mark's truck followed. She turned off the engine and, for a moment, savored the peace.

All was dark. The other members of her family were asleep. The hour was late enough that the crickets had folded up their legs, and silence reigned. The air, marginally cooler with the loss of the sun and the addition of a small breeze, wafted into her car. She closed her eyes and leaned back against the headrest, too tired to move.

No flies, no spoiled meat. A new job from Harriet Juneau. No hints about the missing book from Guy. The evening had been a success.

The evening meant Mark would leave in the morning.

Lips nipped her ear. "My bed's more comfortable than this car," murmured Mark, bending into the window. "Join me in it." The invitation was a silky whisper against her lips.

She opened her eyes and turned to him. The kiss she gave him, the kiss he gave back, was so tender it made her throat ache.

He withdrew, then opened the car door for her to get out.

Joy laid a hand on his arm. "I've got something to show you first. I've got the book."

Mark groaned. "Joy, you didn't? When?"

"This afternoon."

Mark swore, and thoughts of romance vanished. "Why didn't you tell me sooner?"

"I didn't want to disturb your concentration before the show. Then afterward, I had to race to get to the buffet. I didn't have a chance until now. I thought you'd be pleased!"

"Damn it, Joy, didn't I tell you not to do anything? You promised not to snoop. You *promised*." He pulled out his cell phone and punched in numbers.

"I wasn't snooping! I thought I knew where it was. But it wasn't there. So I looked in the bookcase, and then I . . . tasted it."

"You tasted it? Oh, that's rich. I ought to—Armond? Where are you? The causeway?" Mark swore again. "Take the first crossover you can and head back here. Joy's got the book."

He paused, and Joy was glad she couldn't hear Armond's—

Armond! Joy flat-handed Mark on the arm. "Armond was *spying* on me? For you?" She stomped away from him.

Mark covered the receiver with his palm. "Armond is the agent I told you about." He spoke back into the receiver. "Anything on the gems? Nothing? Just get here as fast as you can." He closed the cell phone. "Where's the book, Joy?"

"In the barn. I don't think Guy knows it's gone. It was hidden in another book, and I put that back."

"I'm not going to count on that."

Mark hustled her to the barn. On the way, she thought she heard the exuberant bark of a dog, but when it wasn't repeated, she dismissed it.

Inside the barn, Joy flicked on a flashlight. It looked barren, straw and dust once again the primary occupants. Except for the Elements Escape, Mark's equipment had all been taken for use during the performance.

"Where's the book?" Mark asked.

Joy retrieved it from beneath the broken slab of concrete where she'd hidden it. The dry metal taste drew her mouth in again, and she was glad to hand the book to Mark.

"Do you feel anything when you hold the book? Taste something?" she asked.

"What?" Mark looked up from his careful paging through the book. "Feel anything? No. I keep telling you, it's a book of illusions, nothing supernatural."

She peered over his shoulder as he bent back to the pages. Supernatural or not, the book fascinated Mark.

"Can you read it?" she asked.

"It's in Old English, so it will take some deciphering, but with time, yes." He stopped leafing.

Joy stared at the beautiful illustration on the opened page. The fire must have been drawn with pure gold, and the wind was depicted so she could almost feel it blow across the page. Rich earth and flowing water met at the bottom. The four elements. Her stomach clenched. "Is that what you were looking for?"

"Shhh," he said, distractedly, tracing the illustration and the words. After a moment, he breathed, "No wonder they were thought to be witches. This is so advanced, I'd never have imagined the magicians of old could do it. So that's how they did it. Ingenious!"

"Will you be able to use it?"

"Yes." The flashlight flickered, then dimmed, and he sucked in a breath. He flicked through the other pages. "Maybe. No. I don't know." He sounded angry. Abruptly Mark closed the book and handed it back to her. "We have to hope Centurion hasn't discovered this missing."

He froze, his muscles like rocks against her, and she heard what had left Mark still and tense.

Guy Centurion's dry laugh.

Joy spun around to see Guy lounging against the barn door.

"Too late," he said, stepping inside. Flanking him were two bodyguards and even in the flashlight's dimming beam she could see the guns they held. "I'll take the book."

She hardly recognized Guy's voice. Gone was friendliness and pleasantness. The voice had hardened to ice cubes and when each syllable touched her, her skin tightened in cold fear.

"How did you get here?" Mark asked, crossing his arms. He seemed nonchalant, though she felt the tension in him. "I'm curious; tell me."

She heard that note in his voice, the compelling timbre which persuaded and coaxed out answers.

"We parked on the horse trails."

One hope gone. No one would be riding at night. No one would see the car and wonder.

"The guns are extreme," Mark continued. "You'll never be able to pass it off as an accident."

"I don't intend to use the guns, unless you force me to. They're simply to get your attention. Bring me the book, Joy, and we're gone."

Yeah, right, and she put cinnamon in gumbo. Wisely, Joy kept her mouth shut, content to let Mark's magic work.

"Leave now and we'll forget this ever happened." Mark was so instinctively persuasive, she took a step toward the door. The bodyguards' stance loosened, and Guy backed up, almost as if he was going to leave. But Mark's talents could not overcome the instinct for self-preservation.

"No." Guy shook his head. "Joy, the book. If I have to ask again, or if Mark speaks, then Bruno will start smashing fingers. His fingers." He gestured toward Mark.

He couldn't mean that. Joy stared, unable to believe the man could be so monstrous. Mark's hands destroyed? His magic hands, which brought such joy and pleasure? Not just to her, but to a wealth of audiences. The thought made her want to vomit. She swallowed against the acid etching her throat.

She looked at Mark. His face was impassive, but his eyes were unmasked. Hers for the knowing. In the fading light from the flashlight, his eyes showed no condemnation that she had done this, no pleading, only sympathy and love.

The flashlight gave a final flicker, then died. They were left in murky gloom.

"Joy," warned Guy.

"Why, Guy?" she asked as she stumbled forward with

the book. It was so dark, she could barely make out his tanned face. "You have so much. Restaurants, the respect of the town, two showcase houses. Why steal a book from an old woman? Why smuggle?"

"Because I can," he answered simply, taking the book. "It's excitement that keeps a man young. It's power wielded that fills one with the essence of life."

"So you do this for a thrill? To feel young?" Joy couldn't keep the contempt from her voice. "Hellfire, Guy, why don't you just grow up?"

It was the wrong thing to say. Guy backhanded her, snapping her head back and causing tears from the sudden pain.

Before Guy could hit her again, Mark's voice broke through. "Could we turn on the light?"

She heard a tremor in the question, a *hint* of fear. Mark's claustrophobia, his dislike of the dark, she'd heard it before when they were in here, and tonight they didn't even have the dubious benefit of flashing lightning. It was stygian in the musty barn, although her eyes were starting to adjust.

Guy halted his blow to face Mark. "A light? That's right. You have problems with the dark, don't you? With things like Dumpsters. Of course, we can have a light."

He reached in his pocket for his thin cigar case, pulled one out, lit it, then dropped the flaring match to the straw. For a moment it smoldered, almost catching the straw on fire, until Guy stepped on it, extinguishing it. He puffed on the cigar, the red-glowing tip looking like an evil eye in the darkness. "Is this enough?"

"I don't think so," Mark gasped.

"Too bad. It's all you get." He jerked his head toward the

bodyguards, who shifted close to Mark. "You two have caused me a great deal of trouble."

"You've got what you wanted. Now leave us." Mark was clearly edgy. His foot jiggled up and down.

Joy frowned, then winced as the motion hurt her bruised face. Even at his most tense, she'd never seen Mark *look* perturbed. She knew he had complete control of his body language.

His claustrophobia was real, she knew. The question was, why was he reminding Guy?

"It's not that easy," Guy said, "but I'm sure you realized all along that you knew too much."

"Ah, come on. Give us a break. We won't tell. Who'd believe us?" Mark whined.

Guy laughed, moving away from Joy as he enjoyed Mark's fear. The bodyguards chuckled, relaxing, their guns lowering.

Mark whining? No, he was using their one weapon, his voice and his skills at deception.

She looked at him. He couldn't see her clearly in the darkness, but she hoped he understood that she was waiting for his signal.

He did. Mark moved with lethal swiftness. He cracked his hands down on the arms of the gunmen beside him, then on the back of their necks. He hadn't disabled the gunmen, only gained them some time. "Run, Joy," he shouted, as he headed toward Guy.

Joy took off for the exit.

Guy was faster. He grabbed the back of her shirt and stopped her with a savage tug that bent her backward, seconds before Mark reached him. A gun to her temple brought Mark to a skidding halt. The recovered gunmen surrounded him, and Bruno locked Mark's hands behind his back with a ruthless grip.

"Did you really think I came unarmed?" Guy sneered, jerking her closer and upright. The gun gouged into her temple, sending pinpricks of black across her vision. No, she wouldn't lose consciousness. "I know what your end will be, Joy, I came prepared, but I hadn't quite worked out what to do about Mark. As you say, bullets raise questions and this must look like an accident." He looked at Mark. "Strip to your shorts."

Mark crossed his arms. "Why should I?"

"Because you think every second I spare you gives you a chance. And while he does that, Joy, give me your Benadryl." He took a long puff of his cigar and pressed harder with the gun. The bruise on her cheek throbbed.

Joy handed him the medicine, from her bag, her fingers cold and shaky. What did he have planned for them? He seemed so sure that they wouldn't get away.

Mark was standing nearly nude, still looking calm, straight, and proud. Magnificent. His rising and falling chest was the only sign of his agitation.

Guy tipped a flask to her lips. The spout was warm from being in his pocket. "Drink this," he commanded.

Joy gagged when the first of the liquid hit her lips. It was milk. Cow's milk. She turned her head to the side.

Mark lunged forward, silent and deadly. Bruno hit him on the head with the gun, and Mark collapsed.

"You can either drink this or we'll shoot him right now," Guy said calmly.

"What about the no-bullets stipulation?"

"I can be flexible."

Joy took one look at a motionless Mark, then drank the

milk without protest. Her stomach churned, trying to reject it, but the milk stayed down and was absorbed into her bloodstream.

"Search him for any lock picks, then chain him with those," Guy ordered his bodyguards.

Joy saw at once what Guy planned to do, and her heart froze mid-beat. Her mind and body went numb.

The escape cabinet, still filled with water, loomed behind them. The escape Mark had never mastered, even when he'd had a lock pick hidden. The book had not held all the answers, either. He'd drown in there, and it would look like an accident, a practice gone awry.

She struggled frantically against Guy's punishing hold, her limbs flailing. "No, you can't!"

Cooking, lifting pots, chopping, had made her strong, but Guy had devoted a lifetime to physical fitness. She was no match for the staggering blow that brought her to her knees.

Despite the ringing in her ears, Joy heard the rattling of chains as the guards bound Mark.

Her skin began to itch. Every bit of her began to itch. Arms. Legs. Neck. Face. Stomach. Nothing helped. The itch turned to pain. Joy curled over.

Guy laughed. "I doubt the allergy will kill you, but you won't be much help to your lover." He lit a match and pitched it into the straw. A thin layer of smoke spiraled up. "You could have had everything, Joy, and you threw it away."

Joy ignored him to focus on Mark, willing him to wake up. *Take in air*, she begged. *Take in air. Live, Mark.* Dimly, she saw the guards hoisting him toward the death chamber.

You once told me a good magician should be able to

*work naked on the beach. This isn't the beach, my love, but
I pray you meant that.*

As if he heard her entreaty, he blinked and awareness
took over. They lowered him into the water.

Joy clawed at her throat, trying to relieve the itching
inside, even as she crawled toward Mark. She laid her
hands on the cool glass. She had no breath even to stand.

She saw Mark draw in deep breaths, saw his muscles
tense in the chains, tiny movements imperceptible to anyone who didn't know his body as well as she. His gaze
locked on hers. He mouthed something.

Hold on? I love you? She didn't know. Either worked.

Mark wouldn't give in. Neither would she.

Itch. Pain. Fire. Inside, she was on fire.

The water covered his mouth, his nose, came to his eyes,
but still his gaze did not waver.

Joy fought to maintain consciousness. She tried to
throw up and rid herself of the poison. Her muscles
refused to obey.

The lid was fastened on the cabinet. Snap. Snap. The
latches fastened. The padlocks clicked shut.

Air. She needed air. Mark needed air.

Joy hauled herself up, across the glass, and slipped a pin
out from one hinge.

Guy shoved her away from the glass.

The last thing she saw was Bruno throwing a black cloth
over the cabinet.

The last thing she heard was Guy's laugh fading into
the dark.

The last thing she smelled was burning straw.

Chapter Twenty-five

Darkness.

Chains.

The press of glass. And water.

Unrelenting.

No light. No space. No air.

Mark's chest heaved, seeking air that didn't exist.

You rotten failure. Look at the mess you made. His father's voice. *Maybe this will teach you.* The lash of a belt. Worse, the dark of the closet. This time, would he be left forever?

Not the closet. The cabinet. Mark fought the panic. This was different.

If only they hadn't left him in darkness. If only he could see.

The book contained no answers for this.

Rotten failure. Rotten failure.

He was not!

Mark closed his eyes, made the darkness his own. He didn't need to see; he could do this blindfolded. He could get out—if he could control the claustrophobic panic.

A successful escape depended upon air control. Upon not using oxygen for useless motion. Magicians had died because of panic.

Joy. If he didn't get out of here, Joy could die.

He grabbed onto that thought as his muscles and fingers worked to free him of the metal chains.

Work steadily. Waste no energy.

In the darkness behind his lids, he conjured Joy's face. Not as he had last seen her—white-faced, lips swollen, gasping. To think of her like that was to invite back the panic and the fear that would kill them both.

Instead he thought of her as she had been in his bed, in his arms, in his life. Gentle, calm, clear and honest. The proverbial breath of fresh air and the sparkling stream.

His arm bumped against the unyielding glass panel, and his eyes popped open. The water sucked at them.

Darkness. Confinement. He hated it. Panic surged forward.

Mark fought it back. Closed his eyes. Saw flames. Red hair. Blue eyes. Joy. Sweet. She didn't hesitate to mouth off to him. The lady met him nose-to-nose with a "Hell's bells, Mark."

How could he have thought life on the road was more important?

The panic faded. Joy was stubborn. She'd still be alive.

His lungs burned with the need for air. Was it getting warm in here?

His wrists were almost free. Mark wiggled his shoulders in the slight space, and the chains dropped to the bottom.

Pinpricks of light danced before his eyes. His fingers and toes tingled. He was losing consciousness. If he did, he'd automatically start breathing. And drown.

He inched his hands up, barely able to move them through the tight space. Slow. Joy. Get to Joy. He pushed the glass; the cabinet was designed to give just enough that a layer of air could be created. His mouth and nose broke free of the water.

Mark gasped in air with deep shuddering breaths. Yet he couldn't savor the sweetness. Joy needed help.

He worked by feel in the darkness. Damn, they'd latched the cabinet. Wait, on this side there was give. One hinge had been loosened. He worked his fingers through the slitted opening. Muscles bunching, he pushed on the lid. For a moment, he thought it would not give, then the other hinge broke under the pressure, and it flipped open. He levered himself out.

The barn was filled with smoke. Mark bent over, coughing.

Where was Joy? She had been near the cabinet, but he was disoriented. Mark stumbled around the glass, until his foot brushed against something solid. Joy.

His fingertips felt her neck. A pulse, and he thought he felt her breath stir the fine hairs on his arm. She was alive!

He hoisted her into his arms and staggered toward what he thought was the exit. The water on his body evaporated instantly. A sound, like the howling of a dog, led him forward. In moments, they were outside.

Mark found himself caught in a standoff between Centurion, who crouched behind bales of straw next to the ostrich pens, and Armond. Mark hurtled back into the dubious protection of the barn just as the metal siding zinged with the ricochet of a bullet.

Joy was gasping, and her fiery body singed his arms. She needed help, now.

Flames behind him. Centurion in front of him. Armond was outgunned three to one. Joy was gasping in his arms.

A howling—wild as a banshee, heart-stopping as a fury—rent the night.

Cerberus! Mark peered out around the edge of the barn and gave a piercing whistle. Six, glowing, red, devil eyes came into sight. Then came the body—huge, black, with a thunderous howl.

Bruno and friend ran. Centurion stared, motionless, caught between a monster and a fiery end.

The beast landed on the chicken wire around Hans and Gretna's pen, flattening it. The ostriches tore out of the pen, chased by the hellish apparition.

Six red eyes became two. Three heads one. Howling the bark of a dog.

Two eight-foot, three-hundred-pound ostriches raced toward the light of the fire, toward Joy and Mark, the humans who would protect them. Their clawed feet tore up the dirt.

Centurion was in the way.

The ostriches didn't have enough sense to go around.

Hans lifted one clawed foot and brought it down with all his eight-foot, three-hundred-pound strength.

Centurion shrieked as the claw scraped down his side. The gun flew from his hand. Gretna bounded past him, hitting him with the side of her body. Centurion dropped to the ground.

The ostriches ran to Mark.

The dog raced behind, barking with joyous abandon.

"Heel, Cerberus," said Mark.

The dog pulled up sharply.

Mark pointed to the unconscious Centurion. "Guard."

Cerberus tilted his head, gave one disappointed whine, then trotted over to Centurion. He put his front paws on the man, lifted his head, and howled.

Zeus awoke with a start. Cerberus? The howl of the dog at the underworld gates?

A pounding on his door penetrated the fog of sleep.

"Zeus!" It was Hera.

He threw open the door.

She didn't wait for his greeting. "We need to get to Joy's! I couldn't sleep, worrying that something wasn't quite right, so I used the far-see smoke. I knew I didn't like that Centurion. Get dressed, and bring along another pair of pants."

She touched her ring and disappeared.

Zeus followed seconds later.

Benadryl. Joy needed her Benadryl. Mark laid her on the dewy grass, raced to Centurion and, swallowing his revulsion, rummaged through the man's pockets, while Armond slipped a pair of cuffs on the prisoner. Mark found the Benadryl, then sped back.

He snapped open the capsule and sprinkled the white powder on her tongue. Gently he closed her mouth over the drug, willing it to work with speed, then shouted for Armond to dial 911 for an ambulance.

He gathered her in an embrace, rubbing her arm and

hand gently. "C'mon, darlin', wake up." He kissed her forehead. "Don't leave me."

Joy's breath came easier. Though the moonlight washed away color, Mark thought her skin color returned. "Joy. Joy, darlin'," he called.

Her hands moved restlessly across her chest. She was coming around!

"How is she?" Armond asked, coming over.

"Better. She's got an allergy to cow's milk, and that bastard forced her to drink a whole flask of it. You've got him, Armond, on two counts of attempted murder."

Armond gripped him on the shoulder. "And on smuggling. We found the gems with the meat and the feed source led back to Centurion. I'm just glad we didn't lose you two in the process."

In the distance, Mark heard the ambulance siren. It would be here in a matter of seconds. Mark pushed to his feet, Joy still in his arms. He turned—

—and ran into Zeke Jupiter and Harriet Juneau.

What the hell were they doing here?

Never mind. "I'm taking Joy to the hospital," he barked out, not stopping. He gestured with his head toward an awakening Centurion. "Armond's busy with him. Let Nicole know Joy's okay, and that I'll stay with her. Call the fire department. And . . . see if you can do something about that dog."

For a moment, Zeke just glared at him, brows lowered.

"We'll take care of it all," Harriet answered, nudging Zeke.

"Yes," added Zeke. Then he held out the pants draped over his arm. "Here, you might need these."

Mark glanced down and grinned, able to smile now that he felt Joy stirring in his arms.

He'd forgotten he wore only his briefs.

* * *

Joy had roused sufficiently by the time they reached the ER to protest a night in the hospital, but she was overruled by both Mark and the doctor. Too tired to protest further, she allowed them to wheel her upstairs.

"This bed's uncomfortable," she grumbled, pulling up the stiff sheet. "And I want my own nightgown instead of one of these butt-revealing horrors."

"Stop grousing," said Mark. "The doctor just wants to make sure you don't have a relapse."

They were alone, the nurse unable to dislodge Mark from Joy's side, despite the fact he wore no shirt or shoes. Joy shivered in the cold bed as bits of memory, like an old flickering movie, returned. "Will you hold me, Mark?"

"Ah, darlin', you know I'd never turn down an invitation like that."

He stretched out beside her and gathered her in his arms, and she was once again warm.

"What happened while I was out?"

"Shhh, we can talk about it later. You need sleep."

"I need to know what happened," she said tartly.

Mark sighed and related getting her out of the barn, then giving her the Benadryl.

"So you did it? You did the escape? Good for you! Now you can add it to the act."

He laughed softly as he stroked her hair in a soothing motion. "I came close to drowning, you to asphyxiation in that smoky barn, and both of us to burning to a crisp, and you're thinking about my act?"

"It's better than thinking about other possibilities." Joy yawned, the strength and warmth of him lulling her. Then her eyes popped open. "The barn! Did you call the fire department?"

"I told Zeke to, but you know, it was funny. I glanced back as the ambulance left, and a rainstorm was putting out the fire."

"Did you bring the book?"

Mark gave a tiny laugh. "I think I left it lying in the dirt. What was important was you."

She yawned. "I'm sure it will be there in the morning."

"Whatever possessed you to take it in the first place?"

"Don't scold, Mark. It all worked out."

His arms tightened around her. "But I almost lost you. I don't ever want to see that side of hell again."

"It made me so mad he thought he could just *take* it from you, so I thought I'd steal it back and . . ." Her voice trailed away as she felt Mark shaking behind her.

He gave a bark of laughter. "For someone so honest, you are developing a real streak of subterfuge."

"I keep telling you, you're corrupting me."

They settled down into the quiet of the night. His easy caress on her hair made her drowsy again, but she was determined to know it all before she succumbed to the lull of sleep. "Was Cerberus chasing the ostriches?"

"Yup. Again. After Hans and Gretna leveled Centurion, I put the beast on guard duty for Armond. He's really a good dog."

"He's a scary dog," Joy corrected. Scary, but trustworthy. Her eyes drifted shut. Safe in her magician's arms, she slept.

Mark held Joy throughout the night, savoring the spicy scent of her, burying himself in the sunshine of her hair.

She felt so right in his arms, as though his natural state was holding her.

She'd grown into such a beautiful, independent woman. He ran a hand lightly across her arm. There was strength of muscle in those arms and strength of character in that body.

He loved her.

But Joy needed more. Her roots, her stability. He didn't know if she could trust him and his love and believe he'd keep his promises.

When the darkness of night lightened, when he knew she was past danger, Mark gently disentangled himself.

He stood at the bedside, looking down at her, then leaned over and gave her a tender kiss. "The show is over, darlin'. You asked me to leave, and I'm keeping my promise."

She stirred, but did not waken.

Mark walked out and did not look back.

Early morning heat shimmered over the farm when Mark walked out of the caretaker's cottage for the last time. He traveled light, his only luggage a duffel bag thrown over one shoulder. He walked over to the barn—the fire didn't seem to have done much damage—and poked his toe around the grass until he found the book.

Last night's rain and this morning's dew had wrinkled the pages, but the book was still intact. He thumbed through it again and marveled at the ingenuity of the ancient magicians. There would be much to learn from this, yet, ultimately, the secret to conquering the Elements Escape had come not from a book, but from within him.

He got in his truck and drove off.

The Trickster

When Joy awoke, bright sunlight invaded her hospital room. She stretched, feeling no lingering ill effects beyond a soreness in her stomach. She was ready to leave.

Nicole peeked around the door, then smiled when she saw Joy. "Oh, good, you're up." In a moment, she was at Joy's side and had her in a hug. "When I think how close I came to losing you—" Her voice, muffled against Joy's shoulder, cracked.

Mother and daughter clung to each other.

Henry came in and Nicole sat back, wiping her damp face. "Mark called and told us you were fine. He said he'd stay through the night, and we should bring you home."

"Where is Mark?"

Nicole waved a hand. "I think he had some things to do."

Maybe he had gone to retrieve the book.

At the side of the bed, Henry crossed his arms and looked down at her. "Centurion claims the ostriches attacked him."

"What! That creep. He tried to kill me! And Mark!"

"Centurion?" Henry scoffed. "He's always been good to this town. You must be mistaken."

Joy clutched the bed sheets. It was as she feared. Seth had asked whose side she thought the town would take. Well, she had her answer.

"My daughter doesn't make mistakes." Her arms still about Joy, Nicole rounded on her husband. "Good to this town? How would you know? You haven't been here the last two years!" Her mouth snapped shut, as if she was astonished at what she'd just said.

Joy could feel her mother trembling. "Nicole, it's okay. I don't want to make trouble between you and Henry."

Nicole turned to her, and brushed a strand of hair from Joy's face. Tears seeped down her mother's cheeks. "It's not you; it's me, dear, and it's not okay. Like you said, I should be asking some questions." She turned her face up to Henry.

"I love you, Henry Valcour, I truly do, but I can't let you come back like nothing happened. I tried, but now, well, I just can't. I can't live with you, wondering if you're going to walk out on me again. I need to know where you've been and why you left. I won't be depending upon Joy to take care of me. She's got her own life to live, and if I can't depend upon you . . . I have to know that and do something about it." She took a deep breath. "And I don't want to go off gold prospecting. I'm staying right here."

Under the onslaught, Henry crumpled; there was no other word for it. "Aw, honey lamb, you know you mean more to me than any gold."

"Do I?" Joy had never heard such steel from her mother.

"You do. I just got crazy there for a while, scared, but it won't happen again. I love you too much. If you want to stay here, then we will. Maybe Joy can show me what she did to make those ostriches profitable, and you know that old forge I've got out back? I've been thinking about doing something with that. Jewelry maybe. Or trivets."

"Oh, Henry." Nicole flung herself at him.

Henry's arms wrapped around her mother, and from the gentle way he held her, Joy could see he wasn't lying when he claimed to love Nicole. His hangdog look turned tender.

Feeling out of place, Joy slipped around the embracing couple and headed to find a nurse. She was leaving. The Mushroom Festival had started, and despite what anyone thought of her, she was going to be there, chin held high.

As she exited the room, she heard Henry say, "Nicole, you ever think of designing something like that? Jewelry? Or trivets? You've got a real eye for how things look. You could design it and I could make it."

"Do you think I could?"

"You can do anything you want, honey lamb."

As Joy wandered around in the hot afternoon, admiring the craft booths at the festival, sipping Seth's fresh-squeezed lemonade, three facts were brought home to her.

One, the festival was a huge success.

Two, contrary to her expectations, the town had rallied around her once the news got out. Oh, there was shock at Guy's actions and his double life, but for her there was no condemnation, only sympathy, pride, and relief that she was well.

Joy smiled at dancing mushrooms on stage, and one of the little girls waved to her. At last, she had found a place where she belonged. No longer was she the outsider, looking in with an aching longing.

Yet, it wasn't home. Home was where your heart and soul found peace, and her home was with Mark. She wanted to tell him, but then she ran smack into fact number three.

She didn't know where he was.

She had seen Armond Marceaux. No wonder the man hadn't known his way around a kitchen. He was a cop, not a chef. He'd assured her that Centurion's ravings about the ostrich attack were nothing to worry about. They'd need her testimony, but now that the lid was off, all kinds of dirt on the man was spilling out.

Mark had known Joy would be here, and she'd thought

he would join her. When he hadn't, she'd called his cell phone and the phone in the caretaker's cottage, but got no answer.

Maybe he was packing up the equipment in the barn. She had to see him before he left. There was so much she hadn't told him.

On the way out, she spied Hope talking to—actually it looked more like arguing with—Brody, and she detoured toward her sister. Before she reached them, Hope pivoted and stomped away, almost running into Joy.

Joy steadied her by the arm. "Whoa. Having trouble?"

Hope made a face. "He tried to kiss me. With his *tongue*. Yuuuck. And then, he tried to tell me I was supposed to *like* it. Like, I don't know what I like?" Hope looked at Joy directly. "If I ever decide boys aren't really gross, I'm going to find someone like you did. Someone who *respects* me." Her attention wandered. She waved to her friend. "Hey, Eliza, let's get a grape snowball and make our teeth all purple."

Smiling, Joy watched her sister run off. It appeared the family curse was broken for Nicole and for Hope.

What about for her?

When she got home, the farm was quiet. Joy walked toward the barn. Someone had repaired the chicken wire fence, so Hans, Gretna, and the other ostriches were penned. There had been a lot of smoke in the barn but few flames, and, thanks to the unnatural rain, little damage had been done.

She supposed Zeke Jupiter was behind that, too.

The barn was empty. Mark's equipment was gone. All

that remained was a small puddle of water where he'd drained the cabinet.

Slowly, Joy walked over to the caretaker's cottage.

It was empty, too. Mark traveled with few personal belongings; obviously it had not taken him long to pack and leave.

Mark was gone.

Numb, Joy walked outside. How could he just leave?

Because she'd told him to.

She sank down onto the front step. She had asked for his promise to leave, and he had kept it. She had never asked him to stay. Joy shook her head. She had never asked him to take her with him.

Tears welled in her eyes, but she brushed them away with an impatient hand. She wasn't giving up that easy.

Joy rose to her feet. Time to make a few phone calls.

Chapter Twenty-six

The final moments of the Mushroom Festival were at hand. Joy stood on the hill, wringing her hands. Several hundred feet away, she could see the twinkling lights strung through the trees and the crowds spreading blankets, preparing to watch the grand finale, the fireworks display.

Zeke Jupiter and his crew had spent the day setting up. The hill was a mass of mortars, shells, and cables connecting the computers to the firing mechanisms and to the massive speakers that would play the music.

Had the changes she'd asked of him been possible? He assured her they were. Hell's bells, he'd even expanded her request. Looking at the complexity of wires and guns, though, she had her doubts.

Zeke joined her. "We'll start soon. You can sit over there."

"Do you think he'll see?"

"When you called, didn't Jax say Mark wasn't in Vegas? Isn't his ticket for tomorrow morning?"

"Doesn't mean he'll be here."

"He will. Now, go sit."

Joy settled onto the blanket Zeke had laid out.

The first shell took off with a shriek—a red chrysanthemum Zeke had called it—followed closely by flying squirrels, streaks of whistling white lights.

For a while, she forgot about her plans and worries, caught up in the beauty of Zeke's display. It was colorful, filled with bright explosions and unusual fireworks she'd never seen before. It was choreographed to the music playing, so a rainbow shower of sparks punctuated the drum licks and a sky filled with explosions heralded a crescendo.

The air around her was hazy and scented of sulfur and black powder, yet above was magic.

The music segued into the fifties girl-group tune, "I Will Follow Him." Joy sat up straight. This was it, the last segment before the finale, and the one, she hoped, that Mark would see. Her nails dug into her palms. Would he understand?

A bank of mortars shot off, the explosion deafening as one after the other shot its burden into the night.

Zeke had done it! She didn't know how, but he had.

There, in the sky, for everyone to see, in letters made of intense white lights a hundred feet high, she told them how she felt. I LOVE YOU MARK.

The words hung in the night for precious seconds, until the lights winked into smoke.

The music shifted again, to a hot guitar and maracas. Then Elvis started singing, "Viva Las Vegas."

Joy held her breath during the song, her gaze trying to

pierce the darkness. Haze swirled around her, first concealing, then revealing.

Revealing a man. Walking a straight line toward her. He was dressed in skintight jeans, white T-shirt, and boots. Joy's breath caught as she watched that walk she could never forget and that always sent her thoughts straight to sex.

Mark reached her side. He flashed her that devil grin. "Evenin', darlin'."

"You're here," she breathed, trusting more in her rejoicing nerves, than in her eyes.

"I promised I'd leave. I didn't promise not to come back."

Joy leaped into his embrace. She braced his head between her hands, reached up and kissed him. "I love you, Mark."

After a satisfactory return of her kiss, he glanced up as the fireworks spread across the sky in a deafening roar. "I love you, too. You have a definite style about you, Joy, but right now I'm thinking we should find some place a little more private."

In answer, Joy whistled—off-key, but enthusiastic—the song that Zeke had played. "I Will Follow Him."

"How soon can we get married?"

Mark's unexpected question roused Joy from the drowsy languor that held her in a velvet grip. They had returned to Mark's bed at the caretaker's cottage, and though it was several hours later and deepest night, they hadn't been sleeping.

She traced a line through the sprinkling of hair on his chest, enjoying the play of muscles beneath her finger.

"You don't need to do that, Mark. I know you don't like strings or attachments. I trust you. I know you love me, and you'll always come back to me."

"Damn straight I will." He rolled over, settling her beneath him and kissed the tip of her nose. "But you're wrong about the ties. I want every string, tie, and bond I can get to attach you to me."

"I'm not the roaming type."

"Humor my insecurities."

Joy burst out laughing. "You, insecure?"

"Where you're concerned." His fingers traced her cheek, her nose, the curve of her lip, telling her with touch more than words how much he loved her. "When you told me to leave, and all that talk of family curses, I was so scared that I'd blown it with you."

"Never, Mark. It wasn't you, it was me. I was scared, too. Insecure. I was thinking too much with my head and ignoring what my heart told me."

"I guess we both had to learn what was important." He brushed back her hair. "Does this mean you'll marry me?"

She cupped a hand on his beloved face. "Yes. Just one thing."

"What?"

"I refuse to cook my own wedding reception. I'll ask Callie to do it, which means it's vegetarian all the way."

Relief flooded through Mark. "I would eat ostrich feathers if it meant I got you for dessert again."

Joy laughed again. God, how he loved that sound. He wanted to keep that smile on her face. It probably wasn't fair of him to get her promise before he told her his news, but he wasn't above fighting dirty.

Mark took a deep breath. "I know you're not the roaming type, Joy. So I called my agent yesterday and told him to cancel the European tour. I can't do anything about the dates coming up. I've got contractual obligations I can't back out of, but I swear I'll come back to you every chance I can get."

"You can't do that! You—"

"It'll only be for these months, then I swear—"

"—can't cancel your tour."

"—I'll stop touring."

They both stopped and looked at each other.

"What did you say?" The words came in unison.

Mark gestured. "You first."

"Don't cancel your European tour, Mark. I was wrong to ask that of you. I hope you can still get it back."

"Well, after Clive stopped hyperventilating, he said he'd give me forty-eight hours to get my senses back before he did anything."

"Good," she answered. "One thing I've realized is that while you don't fear ties anymore, I don't need to hold on so tight. Our love will last and my home is with you."

"You want to come on the road with me?"

Joy wrinkled her nose. "Well, not always. I talked to Callie yesterday. She wants to do some traveling, so we're going to work together. This next year, I'll stay here and run the restaurant while she's gone. That picture I've always wanted a place to hang? It's going on the wall of the restaurant. Think of it, Mark. Free rein, my own kitchen! I can go with you sometimes, and you can be home sometimes, and the rest of the time we'll run up massive phone bills. It'll work, if we try."

"But Europe? Once I'm there, it's not so easy to hop a flight home."

"Europe is a chef's mecca. Callie and I agreed I'd go with you then. I can learn so much. Maybe I can stay in one place for a while and study. I don't know. There are just so many possibilities, and as long as I've got you, I'm open to them all."

"You've got it all worked out."

"Not really, but I think we can figure it out together."

"I think so, too. What do you think about after? Vegas or Louisiana?"

She gave him a mischievous grin and her fingers reached low. "What do you say we negotiate?"

"Like this," he purred, catching her wrists with one hand and working magic with his other.

Joy pulsed beneath him. Those choices were for the future, and whether she cooked in Las Vegas, or he headlined in the New Orleans casino, it would be home. In the meantime, she wasn't a woman to pass up an opportunity. "I'm open to suggestion."

Mark drew her into a fiery kiss. "I'm sure we can find mutual satisfaction."

"Promise?"

"Forever, darlin'."

"Welcome home."

Matthew Mark Hennessy had returned, just as he'd promised.

Epilogue

Two months later.

A single spotlight lit the stage. In the halo of light, motion-less, sat the magician's assistant, not his regular one. She wore a midnight-blue gown, and her red hair was a flame atop the darkness.

The magician—in unrelieved black—circled her, like the eagle circles its prey. He fastened the rope about her arms and wrists and waist, then tugged at the knots to show they were secure. A security guard also tested them and nodded. Dark musical chords filled the air.

"I heard that's his wife," whispered the teenage girl sitting behind Zeus in the darkened theater.

"He's *married*?" whispered back her companion. "That bites."

The assistant rose, as if in a trance, drawn by the pull of

386

the magician. She stood as still as marble while the ends of the rope were fastened together with wire, then encased in a large, heavy, black box. She was trapped, immobilized.

"I wouldn't let my boyfriend do that to me," said the first teen.

"Guess she trusts him," replied the second.

Zeus turned around and whispered, "She does. Now, silence."

The first girl's eyes widened as she stared at Zeus. "I know who you are. You're that guy—Sean Connery. My mother loves all your movies." The girl thrust her program at him. "Would you sign this for her? To Karen."

"I'm not—"

"You are so right," gushed her friend.

"I'm not—"

"C'mon, mister. Please."

Zeus scrawled an illegible name on the paper and handed it back, hoping they'd be quiet.

"Thanks!" The teen turned to her companion, waving the program. "Now I bet Mom lets me spend the night. Otherwise she doesn't get this."

"Oooh, you are sly," squealed her friend.

Hera, sitting beside Zeus, leaned over to him and whispered, "How flattering. She needed it for blackmail."

"Quiet," he hissed.

A collective gasp from the audience brought their attention to the stage. A huge blade, so sharp it cut the silk scarf the magician held to it, swung across the stage. With each pass, the deadly pendulum drew closer to the immobile assistant, who seemed to come out of her trance and struggled against her bonds. They held her fast.

The magician touched her chin, drawing her eyes up to his.

She stilled and gazed back at him. The rest had been show-manship and acting, Zeus recognized, but here was honesty. Reflected between them, Zeus saw pure love and trust.

The blade swung, so close the wind of its passing ruffled her hair and gown. Two more passes, then the third would go right through where she stood.

The magician ran his hands down the sides of her arms, then stepped away.

First pass.

The assistant lifted her hands, tugged at the ropes. She was still bound. The magician frowned and cast a worried glance at the blade.

Second pass.

He shook the rope, but it held fast. The frown deepened.

"The trick didn't work," gasped the girl behind Zeus. "She's gonna get sliced."

The magician clasped the assistant's hands in his. He leaned over and kissed her.

The blade descended for a third pass.

An explosion of smoke obscured the deadly scene for a moment.

The blade passed through—

—empty space. Only the ropes remained on the stage floor. Magician and assistant had vanished.

There was stunned silence, then applause as the magician emerged from one side of the stage and his assistant—unsliced—came from the other. He caught her in his arms, twirled her around, and they both took a bow.

Zeus and Hera joined Mark and Joy backstage. "Are you touring together?" Hera asked Joy.

She shook her head. "I'm still here in New Orleans. Greenwood is full every night."

Mark wrapped an arm about her waist and kissed her temple. "I had to do some fancy talking to get her help tonight."

Joy gave him an intimate smile, one that spoke of memories shared. "We've practiced that routine before."

Hera lifted her brows. "With the blade?"

"The blade's only for stage. At home we use the ropes, and Mark ties me up, and—" Joy flushed as she realized how her words might sound. "To practice with the knots . . ."

Hera patted her on the shoulder. "Perhaps you should stop right there."

Mark burst out laughing, and a red-faced Joy elbowed him. "It's not like it sounds, and you're not helping."

"No, but it sure did give me a few ideas for later tonight, darlin'." Mark kissed her again. "I've got to see to the dismantling, but wait for me. I'll drive us home." He said it with a natural ease, and a certain measure of pride.

"Is he home much?" Zeus asked.

"Yes." Joy watched Mark disappear. "He's gotten back more than I expected; I think 'home' isn't such a lonely place for him anymore," she said softly, then turned to them. "So, what are you two doing back in town?"

"I signed the papers with Seth Beaumont to purchase land for a factory this week," Zeus answered. He didn't know why Hera had joined him tonight, only that she had taken the seat beside him as the curtain arose. It was the first he'd seen of her since Centurion's arrest.

"That's right, Nicole mentioned that. I've been so busy

with the restaurant, I've barely come up for air, except when Mark's in town or when I travel to be with him."

"And I'll bet you don't then, either," Hera murmured, for Zeus's ears only.

He choked back a laugh, knowing that Hera saw what he did—happiness radiated from Joy. She was doing exactly what she wanted, and doing it well.

Suddenly she gave them both a hug. "I'm so glad I got the chance to see you two again."

"Hey, Joy," called Jax. "Can you give me a hand with this?"

"Be right there." She gave them one more squeeze, then shifted away, calling over her shoulder, "Don't be such strangers. Come by the restaurant."

"We'll do that," Zeus said.

"One day," added Hera quietly.

Zeus gave her a quizzical glance. After Centurion's arrest and her disappearance, he'd tried to locate her. Unsuccessfully. He was going to have to find out how she did that. Zeus felt like he'd been marking time the past few weeks, and he was tired of it. He had other wrongs to set right.

It would be more fun with Hera at his side.

"Let's go some place quieter," he suggested. "Shall we transport back to my home in Colorado?"

"Not tonight. Tomorrow. Your Denver office. Nine o'clock," she said, then disappeared. Again.

Zeus's teeth ground in frustration.

Zeus sat in his presidential suite at Jupiter Fireworks, tossing lightning bolts at a sooty bull's-eye target and feeling

390

eager and anxious. Both were emotions he thought he had long ago lost.

Where was she?

As if on cue, the intercom on his desk buzzed. "Harriet Juneau here to see you, Mr. Jupiter."

"Send her in, Mrs. Hunsacker."

He smoothed a hand over his hair and straightened himself in the chair. Nope, too eager. He crossed one leg over the other and tilted the chair back slightly. Better.

Hera strolled into the office, looking regal and elegant in a peacock-blue dress. She wore her clouded ring, the source of her powers. Zeus's heartbeat jerked to a faster pace.

"Nice office," she said, settling into the chair opposite him. She gave him an amused look, as if she saw right through the faux-relaxed pose. "I like the view of the mountains. They remind me of Olympus."

"And home. Do you ever think of going back?"

He shrugged. "I don't think the Oracle would let me return. I'm not sure I'd want to. I like it here, and nothing has changed there."

"I know." She looked away and beneath the expert makeup, he thought she paled.

Zeus steepled his fingers together. "What about us, Hera?"

"What do you want, Zeus?"

"I want us to be together again. I still love you."

"And I still—" She shook her head, and her eyes closed, briefly, against an inner pain. "I don't know if that's possible. Some terrible things pulled us apart, and since then . . . we've both changed."

The knot of nerves in his stomach grew tighter, but Zeus refused to accept that there was no future for them. Had she not come to him? Had they not worked together for a common good?

"Are not the changes for the better?" he asked.

"Yours? Mostly. Mine? That remains to be seen."

"I like what I see."

"Yet we're almost strangers."

Without a word, he rose to his feet and stalked around the desk. He leaned over and kissed her, thoroughly and with expert knowledge of her.

"That," he told her, "is not the kiss, nor the response, of strangers. If you aren't interested, why did you come back?"

She stared at him.

Hades, but he'd known getting her back would be tougher than breaking a millennia-old curse. Was she angry at him for challenging her? Disdainful of his blatant attempt to use sex?

Zeus never could predict Hera. A slow smile crept across her face. The smile he knew so well. The one that was full of mischief.

She stood and returned his kiss—with a few embellishments. "That's why I came back; we still have that between us. And because it was so much fun with Mark and Joy. We did a good thing there; I could see it when they were on stage. I may not trust you, yet, my husband, but being with you is always passionate and amusing. Those qualities have been sadly missing in my life of late."

Passionate and amusing. It was something to build on. "So, you'll help me to break the curse for another lineage?" Zeus asked.

"Yes."

"I thought Dia might need a little help—"

Rain, sudden and hard, beat at the glass windows. "Dia is not a good choice," Hera warned, her fingers rubbing her ring. "I saw that kiss."

One little interlude, yet still he must make amends. Zeus sighed and laid a hand over hers.

She glared back at him.

His fingers tightened, for Hera in her power was a sight that stirred his blood. He gave her a heated look, a look that she returned in equal measure.

The rain turned from angry to electrifying.

Passion and amusement. As she'd said, they had that.

"That kiss meant nothing, my love. I think you know that."

"Show me," she demanded. A teasing smile played across her lips.

Zeus pressed the button on his intercom. "Mrs. Hunsacker, see that I'm not disturbed for *anything* for the next half hour." He exchanged a glance with his wife. "Make that the next hour. Or two."

He rose and held out his elbow to Hera. She nestled her hand in the crook of his arm, and he led her to the private elevator, the one that stopped only here and at his private domain on the thirteenth floor.

"Besides, I have someone else in mind," Hera said. "Someone who needs our help more than Dia."

"We'll talk about it later," Zeus murmured.

"Later," she agreed, as the elevator doors opened. "But next time, the woman is my choice."

"As you wish." One small step toward making amends; it was the least he could do. Besides, whoever her choice, the matchmaking would be fun with Hera at his side.

Life was exciting again.

More Than Magic

Kathleen Nance

Darius is as beautiful, as mesmerizing, as dangerous as a man can be. His dark, star-kissed eyes promise exquisite joys, yet it is common knowledge he has no intention of taking a wife. Ever. Sex and sensuality will never ensnare Darius, for he is their master. But magic can. Knowledge of his true name will give a mortal woman power over the arrogant djinni, and an age-old enemy has carefully baited the trap. Alluring yet innocent, Isis Montgomery will snare his attention, and the spell she's been given will bind him to her. But who can control a force that is even more than magic?

___52299-3 $5.99 US/$6.99 CAN

Dorchester Publishing Co., Inc.
P.O. Box 6640
Wayne, PA 19087-8640

Please add $1.75 for shipping and handling for the first book and $.50 for each book thereafter. NY, NYC, and PA residents, please add appropriate sales tax. No cash, stamps, or C.O.D.s. All orders shipped within 6 weeks via postal service book rate. Canadian orders require $2.00 extra postage and must be paid in U.S. dollars through a U.S. banking facility.

Name_____
Address_____
City_____ State_____ Zip_____
I have enclosed $_____ in payment for the checked book(s).
Payment <u>must</u> accompany all orders. ❑ Please send a free catalog.
CHECK OUT OUR WEBSITE! www.dorchesterpub.com

THE MAGIC OF *Christmas*

Emma Craig,
Annie Kimberlin,
Kathleen Nance,
Stobie Piel

"Jack of Hearts" by Emma Craig. With the help of saintly Gentleman Jack Oakes, love warms the hearts of a miner and a laundress.

"The Shepherds and Mr. Weisman" by Annie Kimberlin. A two-thousand-year-old angel must bring together two modern-day soulmates before she can unlock the pearly gates.

"The Yuletide Spirit" by Kathleen Nance. A tall, blonde man fulfills the wish of a beautiful and lonely woman and learns that the spirit of the season is as alive as ever.

"Twelfth Knight" by Stobie Piel. In medieval England, a beautiful thief and a dashing knight have only the twelve days of Christmas to find a secret treasure . . . which just might be buried in each other's arms.

____52283-7 $5.99 US/$6.99 CAN

Dorchester Publishing Co., Inc.
P.O. Box 6640
Wayne, PA 19087-8640

Please add $1.75 for shipping and handling for the first book and $.50 for each book thereafter. NY, NYC, and PA residents, please add appropriate sales tax. No cash, stamps, or C.O.D.s. All orders shipped within 6 weeks via postal service book rate. Canadian orders require $2.00 extra postage and must be paid in U.S. dollars through a U.S. banking facility.

Name_____
Address_____
City_____ State_____ Zip_____
I have enclosed $_____ in payment for the checked book(s).
Payment <u>must</u> accompany all orders. ❑ Please send a free catalog.

BUSHWHACKED BRIDE

EUGENIA RILEY

"JUMPING JEHOSHAPHAT! YOU'VE SHANGHAIED THE NEW SCHOOLMARM!"

Ma Reklaw bellows at her sons and wields her broom with a fierceness that has all five outlaw brothers running for cover; it doesn't take a Ph.D. to realize that in the Reklaw household, Ma is the law. Professor Jessica Garret watches dumbstruck as the members of the feared Reklaw Gang turn tail—one up a tree, another under the hay wagon, and one in a barrel. Having been unceremoniously kidnapped by the rowdy brothers, the green-eyed beauty takes great pleasure in their discomfort until Ma Reklaw finds a new way to sweep clean her sons' disreputable behavior—by offering Jessica's hand in marriage to the best behaved. Jessie has heard of shotgun weddings, but a broomstick betrothal is ridiculous! As the dashing but dangerous desperadoes start the wooing there is no telling what will happen with one bride for five brothers.

___52320-5 $5.99 US/$6.99 CAN

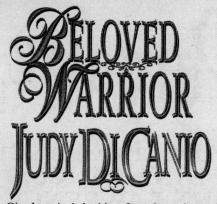

BELOVED WARRIOR
JUDY DICANIO

Jennifer Giordano isn't looking for a hero, just a boarder to help make ends meet. But Dar is larger-than-life in every respect, and as her gaze travels from his broad chest to his muscular arms, time stops, literally. Jennifer knows this hulking hunk with a magic mantle, crystal dagger, and pet dragon will never be the ideal housemate. But as the Norseman with the disarming smile turns her house into a battlefield, Jennifer feels a more fiery struggle begin. Gazing into his twinkling blue eyes, she knows she can surrender to whatever the powerful warrior wishes, for she's already won the greatest prize of all: his love.

___52325-6 $5.50 US/$6.50 CAN

Dorchester Publishing Co., Inc.
P.O. Box 6640
Wayne, PA 19087-8640

Please add $1.75 for shipping and handling for the first book and $.50 for each book thereafter. NY, NYC, and PA residents, please add appropriate sales tax. No cash, stamps, or C.O.D.s. All orders shipped within 6 weeks via postal service book rate. Canadian orders require $2.00 extra postage and must be paid in U.S. dollars through a U.S. banking facility.

Name_____
Address_____
City_____State_____Zip_____
I have enclosed $_____ in payment for the checked book(s).
Payment <u>must</u> accompany all orders. ☐ Please send a free catalog.
    CHECK OUT OUR WEBSITE! www.dorchesterpub.com

Paradise

MADELINE BAKER, NINA BANGS, ANN LAWRENCE, KATHLEEN NANCE

The lush, tropical beauty of Hawaii has inspired plenty of romance. But then, so have the croonings of a certain hip-shaking rock 'n' roll legend. In these tales of love by some of romance's brightest stars, four couples put on their blue suede shoes and learn they don't need a Hawaiian vacation to find paradise. Whether they're in Las Vegas, Nevada, or Paradise, Pennsylvania, passion will blossom where they least expect it —especially with a little helping hand from the King himself.

___4552-4 $5.50 US/$6.50 CAN

THE Last Viking

SANDRA HILL

He is six feet, four inches of pure unadulterated male. He wears nothing but a leather tunic, speaks in an ancient tongue, and he is standing in Professor Meredith Foster's living room. The medieval historian tells herself he is part of a practical joke, but with his wide gold belt, callused hands, and the rabbit roasting in her fireplace, the brawny stranger seems so... authentic. Meredith is mesmerized by his muscular form, and her body surrenders to the fantasy that Geirolf Ericsson really is a Viking from a thousand years ago. As he helps her fulfill her grandfather's dream of re-creating a Viking ship, he awakens her to dreams of her own until she wonders if the hand of fate has thrust her into the arms of the last Viking.

___52255-1 $5.99 US/$6.99 CAN